T0078138

EARLY EARTH
BOOK 1
ELEMENTAL CONNECTIONS

B. A. Norman

Illustrated by Jeffrey Norman

WESTBOW
PRESS®
A DIVISION OF THOMAS NELSON
& ZONDERVAN

Copyright © 2015 B. A. Norman.

All rights reserved. No part of this book may be used or reproduced by any means, graphic, electronic, or mechanical, including photocopying, recording, taping or by any information storage retrieval system without the written permission of the author except in the case of brief quotations embodied in critical articles and reviews.

This is a work of fiction. All of the characters, names, incidents, organizations, and dialogue in this novel are either the products of the author's imagination or are used fictitiously.

WestBow Press books may be ordered through booksellers or by contacting:

WestBow Press
A Division of Thomas Nelson & Zondervan
1663 Liberty Drive
Bloomington, IN 47403
www.westbowpress.com
1 (866) 928-1240

Because of the dynamic nature of the Internet, any web addresses or links contained in this book may have changed since publication and may no longer be valid. The views expressed in this work are solely those of the author and do not necessarily reflect the views of the publisher, and the publisher hereby disclaims any responsibility for them.

Any people depicted in stock imagery provided by Thinkstock are models, and such images are being used for illustrative purposes only.
Certain stock imagery © Thinkstock.

Back cover photo by Virginia Norman

ISBN: 978-1-5127-2046-4 (sc)

Library of Congress Control Number: 2015918980

Print information available on the last page.

WestBow Press rev. date: 11/23/2015

CONTENTS

ACKNOWLEDGEMENTS

My gratitude reaches back to the 5th grade. Thank you, Mrs. Dekam, for being the teacher who commenced, praised and encouraged my story writing. As a solid follower to a strong beginning, thank you Mr. Foster, my 6th grade teacher, for being an amazing instructor in the realm of writing. Things got rusty for a while thereafter but you, Mrs. Van't Hof, for three years of high school English, poured the oil of writing refinement over me – polishing and inspiring me. Good memories abound with you, Chris Vink, Kent Clewley and Garrett Hultink. You were all there to witness Thogwok's birth. Were it not for you three he may not be here today. A tipped hat to you, James Hall. You likely don't even remember it but you were the first to talk with me about publishing a book. That conversation mattered. A mound of gratitude to you, Joe and Evelyn Vissiccio. You were anchors for me during my greatest trial. Both I and this book were rescued from disaster due to your love and sacrifice. May you be richly rewarded and honored. Whereas there are many teachers who inspire their students, you Hope Fischer are a student who inspires her teacher. Thank you for kindly encouraging me to stay on task. My thanks to my publishers for assisting me, green as I was, during my publishing Genesis. This book will be the first of several thanks in part to you. A salute to you, Amber Susek and Scott and Cassie Wakefield of Wakefield Proofreading. You are heroic editors and have endured a lot with this newly enlisted author. Thank you for intelligently pouring over the manuscript and defusing a minefield of errors. Mom and Dad, thank you for providing the solid education all the way through. I see its value now like never before. Virginia, thank you for being my loving, supportive and insightful helpmate. You inspire me and you delight me. Most of all, thank you Lord God of all creation, for planting your Word in me, for sprouting creativity and for bringing this book to full blossom. I pray it bears much fruit.

<>< B.A. Norman, August 2012

DEDICATION

To my firstborn son I dedicate my first-birthed book.
I love you Jacob, and I am very proud of you.

EARLY EARTH
~BOOK 1~
ELEMENTAL CONNECTIONS

Chapter 1

STRANGE ENCOUNTERS

Soda cans teetered on the windowsill. An empty pizza box, sauce-stained plates, and a half-eaten Pop-Tart littered the coffee table. Playing cards and spare change lay scattered across the carpet. A mound of dirty laundry ruled the closet space, rising from the floor to the hangers. Foul odor consumed the room. And music bellowing from the stereo shook the walls. It pumped its way through the door for all in the hallway to hear—whether they wanted to or not.

Sean Zondervan lounged on the couch in the chaos that was his dorm room. Splayed out on his back, his lanky body overhung both ends of the couch. His shaggy blonde hair wildly flapped in and out of his eyes as he bobbed his head to the throbbing music. Not having done laundry in well over a month, he wore the only clean clothes he had left: a neon green shirt that was too loose and blue jeans that were too short.

Sean was a college freshman. It was the end of October. Two months had already passed for Sean to figure out life away from parents and home and he was doing a miserable job at it. He still had no idea that the purpose of college was to pursue an education, prepare for a good career and become a better person. So instead, he zoned out on the couch. It was Tuesday. His Spanish test which he hadn't studied for was

Wednesday. Pointless, aimless, and clueless, Sean didn't realize that in a few minutes something would happen to him that would turn his world upside down.

Outside Sean's third-story window in a small wooded area next to his dormitory, a man stood camouflaged and motionless. Keeping himself out of sight, he spied out every detail of the area—especially Sean's window. He wore a trench coat that was the color of bark, dark pants and a hat. His aim was to blend in perfectly with the trees, and he did. Having a long black beard and costume eyeglasses he didn't need, he hoped that any who were about to see him would think he was a professor, and indeed they would. Yet he was disguised because he felt very out of place. And he most definitely was.

The strange man held something in his palm and stroked it with his thumb as he peered up at Sean's window. Glancing around to see if anyone was near, he buried the item deep in his pocket and uttered in a voice just above a whisper, "Let's get him."

Barreling down the highway, two motorcycles weaved and vied for position on in one hairpin turn after another. Mountainous Spanish terrain loomed on their left and the Mediterranean Sea shimmered on their right as they blasted north toward their goal.

The rippled highway dipped and turned. The screaming cycles bobbed over each hill and the muscular bodies controlling them banked with cool efficiency at every turn. The road was hewn out of jagged rock which was often perilously close to the road. Traveling at intense speeds, the cyclists were in danger at every sharp turn. Yet the brazen rider of the blazing red cycle had no fear. He boldly maintained the lead on this treacherous terrain. This was typical of his life. In everything he did—school, work, sports—he conquered dares, scorned danger and challenged death. His name was Braulio Santos. He was nineteen, arrogant and certain he was bulletproof.

His partner, Juan Crespo, trailed behind. Pushing himself and his engine as far as he could, he maintained sight of Braulio, although just barely. It was important to him to keep up, not so much for ego but mostly for the sake of loyalty. For even though Braulio was a full-fledged jerk he was nonetheless a friend; and friendship mattered to Juan. He also needed to keep up because of curiosity. Juan had recently unveiled a mystery that led the two on this journey, and even if only half of what he read turned out to be true, it would be earth-shattering.

Braulio held a cigarette between his lips as he sped forward. A thin stream of smoke streamed behind him and clumps of ash, snatched by the wind, swirled in his wake and occasionally pelted Juan. As he mocked the sheer rock walls on his left and defied the deadly drops to the sea on his right, Braulio looked back occasionally to check his partner. This was not out of concern for Juan, but rather to congratulate himself on being so far ahead. But more importantly, Juan held both the map and the instructions Braulio needed, so it would be pointless to leave him completely in the dust.

The terrain grew steeper, and the mountain they were headed for loomed in front of them. A dirt road veered off the paved highway. It snaked its way along the base of the mountain and wound slowly up the slope. Braulio banked off the main drag and blasted down the side road, his tires spewing a trail of dust. Juan followed, choking on Braulio's dusty wake.

The mountain road was long and twisting. It curved from switchback to switchback, growing narrower and bumpier, while rapidly gaining elevation. After miles of road and three thousand feet of elevation, the desolate track shrank to an unused, overgrown path which ended unexpectedly at a steep drop. Just in time, Braulio skidded to a quick stop.

Juan pulled up next to Braulio. He inspected the deadly plunge in front of them and noted a slippery rockslide to their right. He turned off his engine, unstrapped his helmet and concluded, "Well, looks like we'll be walking from here."

Braulio, who wasn't wearing a helmet, took a last long draw off his cigarette and flicked it away. "You might be hoofin' it," he said, snapping the throttle back a few times, "because yer a wuss, but I'm takin' my wheels."

And at that, he spun his cycle around to faceoff with the stony incline. With a roar of his engine and a wheelie for show, Braulio tore upwards. Bullying his way up the rockslide, his tires spit out a stream of tumbling stones which rolled down and buried Juan's feet. Then with a final victorious leap over the last granite hurdle, Braulio made a magnificent jump and landed on a lucky spot of flat land at the top of the rockslide. He killed the engine, flicked down the kickstand, and retrieved a beer from his saddlebag. Braulio cracked open the beer and took a long drink. He wiped the back of his hand across his mouth and looked down to taunt Juan who was still standing astride his motorcycle.

"Whatsa matter?" he yelled mockingly down to Juan. "Scared of heights?"

———————————

Alone in the computer lab, surrounded by books and tapping away rapidly on a keyboard, sat a five-foot, Asian dynamo named Fong Chow. She sat erect in her chair, reading, scanning, studying, writing. Noisy college students in the hallway did not distract her. Invitations to parties did not tempt her. And when someone came in to use another terminal she barely said "Hi". A study break by Fong's definition was a moment to reflect, draw a deep breath and take a sip of tea. She was too busy learning all she felt she needed to know and had no time for frivolities. Her family was overseas and she had a very small number of friends—which was all she wanted. Most of her social time was spent with her best friend: knowledge. No, knowledge was more than a friend—it was her greatest love.

Fong was an exchange student from mainland China, studying abroad in California. She had been awarded an academic scholarship and was in her second year at San Martín University. Classes were hard and her schedule was demanding, but Fong was a hard worker. She enjoyed the academic rigor and was almost never distracted from her studies. But right now she was very distracted by one subject in particular. It had dominated her thoughts for the past several weeks and her grades were beginning to suffer because of it—a consequence Fong normally wouldn't tolerate. Nonetheless, she was drawn like a magnet to the subject even though it was a very strange one.

Fong had to keep this obsession a secret from nearly everyone. She was, after all, an educated college student. Others knew her to be well-read and scientific. She was hammering out a double major in history and organic chemistry and was respected by others for her academic achievements. Her professors and peers would laugh her off campus if they heard what she had recently come to believe. But ironically, it was through her rigorous studies that she became convinced, quite to her own surprise, that certain so-called "fantasy beings" were more than just fanciful fiction. Fong had come to believe in elves.

Over her books she poured; not the books that had been sitting on and around her terminal for weeks collecting dust, but books that spoke of the legends and lore of elfin realms long ago. This would seem highly out of character to the few people who knew Fong well, for she was a hard-core, no-nonsense student. And she had been careful to speak to no one about it except one friend alone: Eric.

Eric was also of Chinese descent though he had grown up in California. His parents were first-generation immigrants and he understood both cultures well. Eric and Fong became friends during her first week in college. A year older than her and more proficient in English, Eric helped Fong with the language barrier and showed her the ropes at San Martín. They got along well; Eric serving as a mentor in some ways and a friend in others, but never as anything more than that. Fong certainly had no time for romance.

The two had talked at length in recent weeks about the plausibility of an elfin race having once existed. Eric would listen patiently to Fong's passionate and well-researched explanations for why such a race must have existed. Fong was pleased that he didn't laugh, and after carefully listening, he seemed to agree. He even helped her with research, bringing her books and news clippings that contributed to her findings. Fong was digesting the latest article Eric had given her when a thick history book slammed on the desk inches from her face.

"Ohmyword Fong, I so-o-o don't get this stuff!" proclaimed an overly dramatic blonde beauty just inches from Fong's ear.

"Candice! Don't scare me like dat! Can't you see I try concentrate?" Fong scolded in her broken English.

Candice sighed. "Like, when are you not concentrating, Fong? All you do is look at books and learn stuff all day long." She put a hand on her hip and tossed her hair over her shoulder. "You need a life, girl!"

"I have rife, but you going kill it if you keep scare me!" retorted Fong.

"So-o-orry! But like, if your nose wasn't, like, stuck in that stuff all the time you'd have seen me walk in."

Candice plopped down on the table in front of Fong and put on a sickly-sweet expression. "Anyway, can you show me your notes before we go to history class?"

If Fong had been keeping track, this was close to the fortieth time Candice had asked this question—this semester.

"Yah, in few minutes," responded Fong mechanically, redirecting her eyes and thoughts to her reading.

Candice looked at the wall clock and noted, "But we only have, like, five before class begins."

"Five? Uh ... no, I have seven or eight pages of notes," Fong said, only half listening.

"No-o-o-o, not notes. Minutes! We have five minutes 'til class begins," corrected Candice.

"WHAT!" yelped Fong. "Why you not tell me?" she hollered as she madly scrambled for her backpack and textbook.

"Uhhh, I just did," Candice said.

Fong slung her backpack over her shoulder and bolted for the door. Candice grudgingly peeled herself off the table with a sigh and followed Fong across campus.

The mysterious man left the cover of the trees and sidled up to Sean's dormitory side door. Wrapping long fingers around the handle he pulled hard. The door was locked tight. Just inside was the stairwell. Peering through the window, he saw no one inside. He took a final look to his left and right. All clear.

The stranger waved his hand over the door knob and heard a *thunk*. The steel deadbolt had slid effortlessly at the simple move of his hand.

The next moment he was inside, standing on the stairwell landing. He crinkled his overly long nose as he sniffed the foul dormitory air.

Ascending the stairs swiftly and quietly, he crested the last step and entered the third-floor hallway. Poking his head around the corner he spied no one. This is good, he thought, but the smell was worse. He advanced down the hall. 301, 302, 303 … He was looking for 311. But he only needed to listen. Sean had the music blasting so loud that anyone in that stretch of the hall could hear it.

The stranger now stood at the door of 311 and knocked.

There was no answer. Sean couldn't hear a thing. The man knocked louder. Still nothing. With a wave of his hand the stereo shut off.

The quiet was pierced with a "Dude, what's goin' on?" from inside the room.

The stranger knocked again.

Sean was now entirely preoccupied with his failing stereo and absent-mindedly said, "Uh … like, c'mon in."

Wasting no time, the man stepped inside, snapped the door shut and locked it behind him.

Sean was stooped over his misbehaving music maker, turning knobs and wiggling wires, completely unaware of the shrouded soul now looming behind him.

"This will be even easier than I thought," mused the man under his breath, just loud enough for Sean to hear.

Sean noted some mumbling behind him but couldn't understand a word of it. He stood up. And when he turned to face the strange voice, Sean's jaw dropped. Standing before him was the oddest-looking individual he had ever seen. The man had a full black beard, long pointy nose, pronounced brow, round spectacles, robust, rubbery skin and very wise eyes. And based on the unusual outfit he was wearing, Sean concluded that the man had no clue how to properly dress.

Sean was about to speak but the man's next move stopped him cold. Out of his coat he pulled a short, narrow tube, just a little larger than a drinking straw. Putting it to his lips, and standing just inches in front of the boy, the stranger aimed the tube directly at Sean's nostrils.

Juan slammed his helmet back onto his head and revved his cycle back into commission. He slid and skidded as he clumsily tried to force his bike up the unstable hill.

"This oughta be good," Braulio mused, as he leaned back, beer in hand, and grinned broadly at his struggling companion.

Then it happened, and Braulio erupted into a laughing roar. Less than halfway up the slippery slope Juan lost control. His costly bike skidded down the rough rocks for several grating feet, with Juan leaping off to the side and out of the way in the nick of time.

Braulio cupped his hand to his mouth. "Klutz! Ya should have told me ya needed riding lessons 'cuz my granny could have given ya some!" he yelled in his crass Spanish slang.

With his pride scarred and his bike scraped, Juan whipped a stone at Braulio. It fell far short. Braulio scoffed, kicked a stone of his own down toward Juan and then turned his back on him to scan the mountain.

"Now where's the cave that retarded map said is up here?" Braulio asked himself as he panned his new surroundings. But he didn't search for long; for it was in plain sight. It would be a steep climb, but just a little higher up from where Braulio stood, was the unmistakable entrance of a cave.

"Phss, this'll be easy," he concluded as he siphoned off another swig of beer and looked expectantly at the cave. "Just as long as some idiot hasn't gotten in there and found the thing before me."

Juan left his cycle on a stable slab of rock and trudged up to where Braulio stood.

"'Bout time!" Braulio chided. "Come on, your cave is right up there. Let's find out once and for all if that dumb little necklace you keep talking about is real or not," he said.

Juan, still riled by Braulio's jabs, wasn't keen on absorbing any additional insults.

"Hey, if you're still skeptical go on home. I can do this by myself. Just thought you might want to be a part of it," Juan shot back.

"That'd be stupid after coming this far. I'll leave once I've proven it's a farce," he retorted. And up the mountain he hiked, Braulio aptly handling both the steep terrain and his open beer at the same time.

Juan followed. He knew Braulio wouldn't turn back. Ever since Juan had shown him a the treasure map he found in a mysterious book, both he and Braulio had been obsessed with unlocking clues to finding a priceless necklace described in the book.

Juan loved books, and he stumbled upon this one quite accidentally while looking through some dusty backroom shelves of a used book store. Intrigued by its topic and charmed by its weathered appearance, he bought the odd book and began reading it immediately. It spoke of strange things which at first he didn't believe. But the longer he read the more intrigued he became. Soon he decided to put one of the book's claims to the test.

He told Braulio about necklaces which supposedly could transport people back in time, and according to a hand-drawn map in the book, one of those necklaces was hidden in a cave about one hundred kilometers north of their town.

That bait was too big for the adventurous Braulio not to bite. He didn't believe in all that mystical time-travel nonsense, but a treasure hunt sounded fun. And he relished the idea of ridiculing Juan when it turned out to be a hoax—which he was quite confident it was. Still, a twinge of curiosity was there. And if on the off-chance that necklace really did exist and if it really was priceless, it would buy him all the cars, beer, and adventure he wanted. Either way, for Braulio it was a win.

Upward they scrambled over untamed terrain and soon they were standing in the yawning entrance of the cave. A current of damp air blew from the cavern's mouth, feeling cool on their sweaty skin. Braulio barged straight in, ignoring Juan's warning.

"Better get your gear on because it's going to be dark in there," Juan called after him helpfully, pressing his head back into his helmet and strapping a light to it.

"My flashlight is all I need. Go bang your head on walls all ya want. I'm not gonna." Braulio plunged ahead.

"Even if he does hit his head, it's harder than the rock anyway," muttered Juan. And he followed him into the cave.

The classroom door flung open and Fong scampered in. The lesson had already begun and the professor broke off his sentence and stared sternly as Fong hurried to her seat. The lecture resumed, only to be interrupted again by Candice huffing and puffing as she traipsed in and scanned the room for the best open seat, which for Candice meant one that was in the back and next to a cute guy named Rocky.

Professor Malkin cleared his throat with an "A-hem." Candice took the hint and plunked down in the closest open seat.

The professor resumed his dull lecture. It bored nearly everyone in the class but Fong was immediately enraptured.

"Belief in fanciful creatures such as elves, gnomes, and fairies was common not only in Medieval Europe but throughout Western Civilization's history..." droned the monotone teacher.

Fong's hand shot high in the air as words continued to mechanically dribble out of Malkin's mouth.

"Different names and supposed behaviors of such beings depended on the culture, language and..." The professor noticed Fong's hand, fingers wiggling frantically to grasp his attention. He straightened his glasses and stared hard at Fong as he finished his sentence. "...particular fears and myths that were dominant in a given village or region. Yes, Miss Chow, you had a question?"

"Yes sir. Isn't it unscientific to say creature is fanciful just because we no see them now? We no see dinosaur or Dodo bird now, but we believe they existed. Maybe we should no say elves is fanciful." Fong spoke in the best English she could muster.

Heads turned to face Fong. Stifled chuckles could be heard from the back of the room. Several smirks were visible throughout the class.

Professor Malkin cleared his throat. "Well," he said in a slightly patronizing tone, "I would call dinosaurs and Dodo birds fanciful if there were no evidence that they existed. Clearly, we have no such evidence for the creatures we call fanciful. There is no skeletal evidence like we have from the dinosaurs, nor are there eyewitness accounts like we have of the Dodo bird."

Fong's hand shot up again before the professor could resume his monologue. He raised his bushy eyebrows as if to say, "Yes, what else?"

"But we no have skeleton or eyewitness for transition creature in evolution chain either. We have apes and we have peoples, but we have no living creature in between, not even skeletons," Fong pointed out. "And people say evolution factual, no fanciful."

Professor Malkin breathed deeply through his nose. He was growing perturbed, but coolly responded, "Oh, I wouldn't say that." His opinion of Fong's line of questioning was clear now in his tone. "We *do* have skeletal evidence of evolutionary transition beings." He held his hand out to the side, gesturing to an imaginary example. "Take Ramapithecus, Australopithecus and Nebraska Man, for example."

Fong shot back, this time without bothering to raise her hand. "But no one of those is complete skeleton, professor. No one ever found whole skeleton of any creature between ape and man. Peoples can only guess what missing bones, flesh and hair look like. After study we now know Ramapithecus is just type of orangutan. And Nebraska Man imagined and named by professor after finding just single tooth. Years later we learn tooth belong to pig. Nebraska man never exist. He only pig tooth!"

The rest of the students were now fully mentally engaged. This was in part due to the out-of-bounds subject matter and also because Fong's knowledge and tenacity were clearly agitating the professor. This was shaping up to be the first lively lesson in a very dull semester.

Candice subtly turned to look at Rocky, who was holding up his notebook for his friend to see. He had scribbled a note in large letters that said, "Fong no wight, Fong wong!" Rocky's friend muffled a laugh. Candice lowered her head and buried it in her hands. All she could think about was how embarrassed she was that Rocky knew she was friends with Fong.

"Young lady," said the professor crisply, whipping his glasses off of his face and gripping them tightly as his hand shook, "scientists are allowed to make mistakes, and complete skeletons are not necessary to prove evolution. Around the globe we have numerous skulls on display in museums that are markedly different from those of human skulls today. Some are smaller than ours, a few are bigger than ours, and some are shaped differently than ours, but they are all of the primate family. How much more proof do you need?"

"But, professor," Fong persisted, "some peoples born today have smaller heads, bigger heads and different shape heads. Peoples who is micro cephalic have small skull and peoples who is macro cephalic born today have larger skull. They shaped different from ours—just like those skulls in museum. Just because person has misshapen skull no mean he not human!"

The professor was momentarily silenced. A pre-med student in the class, impressed, raised her eyebrows and nodded in agreement. Professor Malkin's inability to snap back with a quick rebuttal amused some students and the entire class was now watching him and waiting for his answer. The abnormal attention flustered him even more.

Seizing the opening, Fong continued, "Since no hard evidence exist for transition evolution creature, and no eyewitness exist, why we believe in them? But for elves we have many old eyewitness reports from many countries who called them by different names, like you say. We have more reason for believe in elves than believe evolution."

This was too much for most in the class. They were tracking with her on the questionable evidence for evolution, but elves were over the top. Candice buried her head ever deeper in her hands, wishing she could be anywhere else.

Finally Rocky spoke up and blurted out, "I thought this was Medieval History class, not Fantasy Creatures 101!"

Several students chuckled.

The professor snagged the comment as a face-saving escape and agreed with Rocky. "Indeed! We need to get back to what we are here to study," he said. Nodding slightly at Fong he concluded the discussion by saying, "I appreciate your deep thinking, young lady, but history beckons us now. Perhaps you can resume your topic in a philosophy course or a biology class someday," the professor said dismissively. "Oh, and when you find archaeological evidence of elfin remains, do let us know, won't you?"

A burst of laughter from the class followed. Professor Malkin savored it a moment and then resumed his droning lecture where he had left off.

When class ended Candice was the first to exit. Not wanting Rocky to see her leaving with Fong, she made her escape quickly and then loitered around the corner just outside the door as the rest of the class filed out. Rocky and his buddy were debating the outcome of the upcoming football game as they brushed past Candice. Neither one even noticed her. As Fong came out she was moving speedily as usual. She rounded the corner and accidentally rammed into Candice. Then Candice lit into her.

"Fong, you have got to be kidding! Elves? Really?! And ohmyword! In front of Rocky and the whole class! I was so embarrassed I could've died!"

"Who Rocky?" Fong asked, trying to get past Candice who was blocking her way.

"Who's Rocky?" Candice turned quickly to see if he was nearby and then resumed her scolding. "He's the guy who finally shut you up! But more importantly, everyone knows he's the cutest football player on the team! Fong, you have got to get out, meet people and party more!"

"I no party, I study." Fong said, and resumed her rapid pace.

Exasperated, Candice threw up her hands and let out an enormous sigh before trailing after her energetic friend.

The argument continued across campus as Fong rattled off a broken-English-part-Chinese diatribe about biased professors, true evidence, historical documentations and students who don't care about learning. Candice mostly just replied with different ways of saying "lighten up". But when Fong finally ended her sermonette, Candice tried the logical approach.

"All right, Fong, for all your evidence stuff you talk about, where do you see any evidence of little green men running around?"

"Elves not little green men, Candice!" Fong said, getting spirited. "Elves is noble race. They have skin like us only unblemished and much more tougher. They have hair like us only thicker and more healthy. They have body like us human, only they taller, stronger, more handsome and live hundreds of years without dying. And you can see by looking in elf's eyes that he smarter and more pure in heart than human. You think football player cute? Wait 'til you see elf!"

"Oh. My. Word, Fong! These books are making you crazy! Where do you *get* this stuff?"

But Fong did not hear her. For at the very moment she finished her description of elves, she saw him, just ahead in a cluster of trees and shrubs. His clothing was either made of leaves or simply nonexistent. Fong couldn't tell. He was so well camouflaged that only his head was visible, but it was unmistakable what he was—he was an elf!

Chapter 2

DUDE, WHAT A TRIP!

The intruder, mere inches in front of Sean, blew through the straw and a puff of dust engulfed Sean's face and went far up his nose. "Dude, what the—"

Sean had just inhaled a pulverized concoction of herbs that caused immediate paralysis. Sean froze in place. He could see, he could hear and he was completely aware. He just couldn't talk or move at all. Then the man reached into his pocket and pulled out another implement.

It was a small, leathery pouch with a cap—sort of like a tiny wine skin. The man uncapped the pouch and moved even closer to Sean, now standing nose to nose with the boy. He was so close that Sean could feel his breath and practically taste his beard. The man clapped his spindly hand down on Sean's sun-bleached hair. With one firm tug he pulled Sean's head to one side so his ear squashed against his shoulder. Then he poured yellow, syrupy goo out of the pouch directly into Sean's exposed ear.

Wo-o-oah! Dude, whadaya doin'? Ow! That stings! Hey, I've already done the freshman initiation thing!" and a host of other thoughts were banging around in his head ... but Sean was unable to utter any of them.

Within a few seconds the goo oozed its way deeply into Sean's ear canal. Inspecting it, and apparently satisfied with the progress, the man toggled Sean's head to the other side and repeated the process with the other ear. With another matter-of-fact yank, he pulled up the rag-doll head and then tilted it back, leaving Sean staring helplessly at the ceiling. Prying open Sean's mouth, the man of potions decanted yet another concoction down Sean's throat.

By this time, Sean knew he was a goner. As this was happening to his poor immobile body, he had envisioned his funeral, his burial, and a tombstone that read:

R.I.P.

Here lies Sean.

And, dude, beware the long-nosed, bearded weirdo

who offers you a smoke and a drink!

The fluid drained down his throat. It tasted remarkably familiar to him but he couldn't place the taste. Oddly, he felt that he should drink it, that it belonged in his body—under better circumstances, mind you. Then, for the first time in this whole ordeal, Sean heard the man speak intelligible words.

"I imagine you just set a personal record for longest period of silence: a whole 43 seconds," the man chuckled derisively.

Sean realized that the man was speaking a foreign language, one he had never heard before and couldn't identify. Then, in a moment of stupefied wonder, it dawned on Sean that he understood every word of it. This language seemed familiar, right in a sense, much like the liquid that was dumped down his throat. It was as if he should understand it and should speak it. In his wonder, he forgot to be angry at the intruder who had just paralyzed him and treated him like a mannequin.

"Whoa, I've like never had this feeling before, but it feels like I have ... if that makes any sense," Sean sputtered. He realized with a shock that, not only was the paralysis wearing off, but he had just spoken in the new tongue. And the familiar weirdness of it all made goose bumps spread in a wave over his body.

"I suppose it makes more sense than most things you say. I also suppose you're wondering who I am and what this is all about," proposed the bearded assailant pointedly, as he calmly recapped and rewrapped his potion skins.

"Uh, yeah, actually," replied the perplexed Sean. "Who are you?" he said smoothly in his new language, with numbness fading from his tongue.

"My name is Lawth. You could say I work undercover with the Foreign Language Department. We're working on a new …" He paused, looked around, raised one bushy eyebrow, leaned in and continued, "… top-secret, experimental potion. And you were chosen as a test subject. And not to fear, you'll have full feeling back in all your limbs in just a few seconds."

"Wh-o-o-o-a-a … that is sooo cool! You mean just like magic you can drink that goop and then know a language? Dude, I'll never have to study for another stupid Spanish test again!"

It then occurred to Sean he had never actually studied for a Spanish test yet. Not surprisingly, he was failing.

"Hey, Mr. Undercover top-secret dude, you don't happen to have one of those drinks for Spanish do you? One that tastes like salsa or somethin'?"

Lawth bit his lip, thought for a quick moment and said, "Not yet, actually, but that's where you come in. With you as the test subject, we hope to create just such a potion. I'm aware that you're failing Spanish right now. So I take it you'd like to help out then?"

"Yeah, definitely. But … hey, how'd you know about my grades?"

"I'm an undercover agent."

"Oh … yeah."

"So let's get to it then," Lawth said. "No time to waste. We need to get to the library and we'll need that necklace you found the other day also."

"Aw, man, I hate the library. Ev'ry time I go near it I—" Sean paused. "Hey, how'd you know about the necklace?"

"I'm an undercover agent."

"Oh, yeah."

"Plus, you're wearing it."

Sean looked down and touched the polished bright blue sphere suspended from a heavy tarnished chain. He caressed the smooth orb in his fingers and in a dazed voice slowly droned, "Oh ye-e-eah…"

Lawth turned toward the door and with a deep sigh mumbled, "This is going to require more patience than I possess."

⟶≫●≪⟵

Braulio swigged the last of his beer as he walked into the mysterious cave. He crumpled the can with one hand and flung it. The aluminum tinged against the wall and clattered on the rocky floor, echoing in the empty space. Braulio belched as loudly as he could. It echoed profoundly, making him chuckle. Then he swore, just so he could hear the cave repeat the word back to him a few times.

"Don't you care about anything?" Juan scolded. "The book says this cave is sacred! That's why the necklace found a resting place here. We need to be reverent … and pick up your can."

"Pick it up yerself, you recycle-dork! I'm coming here to take somethin' and I'm just leaving somethin' behind. Seems like a fair trade to me. Now where's the book?"

Disgusted, but not prone to argue, Juan unzipped his backpack and cautiously removed the old book. The cover was made of worn leather and the letters on both the spine and cover were mostly illegible. Were it not for the inside cover page they would not even have known the title: *Mysteries of the Ancient World – Volume One*. There was no author, publisher, or print date listed. Juan guessed this copy to be at least two hundred years old, but the knowledge it contained must have been passed down for much longer than that. So ancient and so detailed—and so bizarre—were its claims, that this must have been the hundredth generation of copies, rewritten century after century.

Resting it respectfully in his palm, Juan gingerly paged through, careful not to tear the fragile pages.

"C'mon, what's it say?" demanded Braulio.

Juan delicately opened to a page he had bookmarked. "It says, 'In order to locate the georb, one must recite the incantation within hearing distance of the gem.'"

"Oh, of course. Your magic necklace has ears. I should have known," sneered Braulio. "And if we don't know where it is then how do we know if we're in 'hearing' range?"

"Well, it says it's in the opening of a cave and it's hidden from eyes unless the incantation is chanted. So I suppose we just start chanting right here."

"And if we see nothing?"

"Then we walk deeper in and keep chanting ... I guess ..." Juan trailed off. He knew it sounded idiotic.

"Brilliant plan! Now why didn't I think to get my motorcycle that way? Instead of going to a dealer and spending thousands, I should have just chanted 'til one appeared," Braulio taunted. He forced out another low-rumbling belch.

Ignoring him, Juan began to chant. "Ilgad lo tomarfi. Splinafifla tov andi. Lap blatra lo cipquatri."

He did this several times, scanning around, looking and listening for a response of some kind. Juan moved a little deeper into the cave and repeated. Braulio snorted derisively and went back to using what he knew was tried and true—his own good senses. Using his flashlight and keen eyesight, he inspected every nook and cranny in the right-hand wall, squinting to see anything that might have reflective qualities. Braulio was always observant wherever he went—in part due to curiosity, but mostly because he mistrusted just about everyone.

Confident that he had seen all there was to see on this side of the cave, he was about to move to the other wall when he caught a glimpse of a light other than his. Juan saw it too. But it wasn't reflecting from the wall; it was coming from the ceiling.

The two young men stared upward. Then they stared at each other. Juan beamed from ear to ear and Braulio looked stunned.

"No way! There really is something up there! Here, lift me up!" Braulio ordered.

Braulio extinguished and pocketed his flashlight. In a moment he was standing on Juan's shoulders, his boots pinching his friend's skin every time he shifted his weight. Bracing his hands on the rocky ceiling, he stabilized himself, but the flashing rays of blue light ceased.

"It stopped! Turn off your headlamp and do that chant thing again!" he barked.

"Thought you didn't believe in that nonsense," Juan remarked from below.

"Yeah, whatever! Just do it!"

Juan chanted the melodic lines one more time and quickly flicked off his light. Braulio's face lit up as it reflected a beautiful blue hue cast from a gem just inches from his nose. It was imbedded in a seam in the rock that made it impossible to see when it wasn't glowing. Braulio tugged it from its place of rest and sprang from Juan's shoulders with the necklace secured in his hand.

The two of them marveled at their find, speechless for a few moments while they turned the treasure over and over in their hands.

"So, I guess I was right. What do you say now?" challenged Juan.

Braulio stalled, unwilling to admit the truth.

"For some reason the wavelengths of your voice must cause this type of gem to react. It's gotta be sound waves affecting the molecules," attempted Braulio after some thought.

"You've got to be kidding!" protested Juan.

"Hey, I can see why ancient superstitious folks would think this was magical ... but I'm sure there's an explanation," said Braulio, trying to sound rational.

Irritated, Juan flipped open the book to where he had left off. "It says we now walk deeper into the cave and as the gem begins to pulsate we'll know we're heading toward the hole."

"The hole?" asked Braulio.

"The portal—to transport us to the other world," Juan clarified. "But I'm sure you'll have an explanation for that too."

Intensely curious, and secretly thinking there might be something to all this, Braulio headed deeper into the darkness. Ten, twenty, thirty steps with nothing but their two little lights to spot the way in the black cave. And then, the stone flickered.

"There it is again!" yelled Braulio, overstating the obvious.

"And without me saying even a word to upset the molecules," goaded Juan.

Moving deeper into the cave, the gem continued to blink. With the necklace in his hand, Braulio felt his way carefully across the stony floor with Juan behind him. The gem flickered more. The deeper they went, the faster the stone flashed and the brighter it glowed. It began to vibrate. Soon it was rotating in Braulio's hand. Braulio suddenly gasped when the whirling ball rose into the air, pulling up on the chain that Braulio held. Pulsating vigorously, it illuminated the cave and both of their amazed faces.

Determined to see if this was a hoax, Braulio took action. He snatched Juan's precious book from his hand. *If this crazy time travel thing is true, I'm going to be the first to try it,* he thought.

Juan already had the book opened to the right page. On it were written the phrases that supposedly allowed one to travel from one time to the next. Neither Braulio nor Juan knew what the strange words meant or even what language they were. But Braulio recognized them since they were nearly identical to the mantra Juan repeated over and over to locate the gem. He quickly recited them.

Seconds later the whirling ball transformed into a mini-earth. The blue of the gem was punctuated by white swirls and a green blotch, clouds and a single giant landmass in a massive ocean. It rose higher into the air.

"Wait!" shouted Juan, panicking. "It says we need to hold onto each other for both of us to go! Besides, we're not ready! We still need to—"

But it was too late. Brilliant beams of white light shot from the gem. Gusts of air, sprays of seawater, and pebbles pelted them. Braulio yelled as he condensed and vanished into the tiny earth which closed and disappeared around him.

Dead silence and total darkness were all that remained in the cave. And there, engulfed in both, Juan stood alone.

Fong's jaw dropped as she instinctively grabbed Candice and pulled her close. With both little hands shaking, she cupped them around Candice's cheeks, and steered her head toward the clump of trees.

"L-l-l-look over there … l-l-l-ook at the face … just like I describe," Fong stuttered in an almost inaudible whisper.

Candice stared blankly, her lips puckered up like a goldfish thanks to Fong's intense squeezing. "Wha-a-t?" Candice groaned through a confused and distorted face.

"Right there! In front of us! Green eyes, gold hair, tan skin, strong cheekbones … he staring at us!" Fong emphatically whispered.

Given a description like that, Candice couldn't help but look harder. Then she screamed.

Fong slapped a hand over Candice's mouth, never taking her eyes off the figure. "Shhh! No draw attention. You might scare … no, not scare, scare not possible. I mean no scream because he no want to be seen."

Fong wouldn't have been able to explain how she knew this. Just something in his face … she thought. The expression on the face was one of sober strength—a kind very rare in the human race. One could easily see by looking at him that this being would not be frightened by a girl's scream—or anything else for that matter. It was equally apparent that he wanted to stay concealed. Then, almost imperceptibly, Fong saw him move. The head in the trees beckoned the girls discreetly.

Fong immediately moved toward the head that summoned them. Candice froze in place.

"Come on!" Fong whispered, impassioned. "He not hurt you, he good."

Candice, now recovering from the initial shock of seeing a "man" secretly staring at her, was beginning to believe that Fong was right. Not that she was buying into the whole elves story, but rather the part about this guy being "good." In all her years, from her first puppy-love boyfriend in third grade through Rocky just today, she had never seen a face as enticing as this one. Flicking her hair and straightening her posture, Candice controlled her fear and sauntered toward the good-looking face in the wood.

Fong, with no such pretense, got there in no time. She was within a few feet of the watching face before she could make out the rest of his body. Bedecked in various hues of greens and browns, he was a perfectly camouflaged. His clothing appeared as many form-fitting small leaves sewn together in a single garment. She thought she saw the handle of a knife sticking out of a bulkier, loose-fitting leafy wrap around his waist, but not wanting to stare, she looked quickly back up at the chiseled face which never stopped staring at her.

"Hello?" she ventured.

"Nephil Eskes Hosswee," he responded in a quiet, strong voice.

Shivers ran down Fong's spine. This was the real thing. Here before her was a living creature she could only have ever dreamed of meeting in her wildest imaginings. He was right in front of her. She just talked to him. And he talked back! She had no idea what he said, of course, but she believed it must mean something like "hello."

Before Fong could decide what to say or do next, Candice arrived. She batted her eyes slightly and said, "Hello".

"Nephil Eskes Hosswee," he answered in the same manner as before.

Glancing over and behind the girls to see if anyone was near, the elf-man turned and moved deeper into the trees. He motioned for them to follow. Now mobile, his camouflaged figure became visible to them and the girls marveled at his mannerisms and his frame. Candice quickly concluded that this was the most gorgeous guy she had ever seen. In addition to being over seven feet tall, he had bulging biceps, perfect skin, a chiseled face, and serious eyes. She began to forget someone named Rocky even existed.

Fong focused more on the way he moved. He didn't run but didn't exactly walk either, covering ground with fluid, gliding strides. Even though he was very tall and muscular, he left no traces when he stepped. It was as if a thin, invisible barrier kept him a bit elevated. Gravity just didn't seem to have the same effect on him as it did on them.

With his back to them, the girls were able to take more time observing his clothes. The main garment stretched from his collar to his shoes, covering all skin but his face, hands, and powerful arms. What fabric it was made from the girls could not tell, but it looked like many hundreds of leaves sewn together. They rustled and fluttered as he moved, mimicking the leaves all around them. But most amazingly, the leafy garment changed color as the elf-man walked. In front of a large brown tree trunk the garment turned brown. Passing before dark green leaves the outfit turned dark green. If more than one color was in the backdrop the uniform adjusted accordingly. The leafy dressing seemed to have a chameleon-like mind of its own. Fong concluded whoever designed it was a genius. It was the perfect camouflage.

The elf-man cruised smoothly through the brush and trees, as natural as the surroundings themselves, until he was out of sight of the sidewalk. The girls trailed behind him less smoothly, and stopped where he stopped. Then he turned and faced them. It was impossible to focus on the clothing now—his face was far more captivating.

The elf-man pulled something out of his hip bag and handed it to Fong. It was also leafy but more durable, like a piece of leather, and was rolled up and tied in the middle with a thin vine. Then he nodded to both girls, turned, and scurried up a tree as if this were as natural to him as walking. Soon he was thirty feet up and out of sight, his coverings flawlessly camouflaging his movements. And like the breeze rustling in the trees, the invisible man leapt from limb to limb, crossing from one tree to another until eventually he was gone.

Sean had to move his lanky legs fast to keep up with Lawth. Lawth moved efficiently and stealthily. But he didn't take the shortest distance to the library or stick to the sidewalks. He opted for trees and grass, empty spaces instead of peopled places. This made sense to Sean, being that Lawth was a secret undercover dude and all.

The huge, four-story library loomed ahead, and a broad, green lawn and well-traveled sidewalks were the only avenues for getting there.

Lawth turned to Sean and said, "It's time to cloak that orb with your vestment."

"Huh?" quizzed Sean.

Frustrated, Lawth hissed, "Hide it! Hide the blue part of the necklace under your shirt! And keep it there until I tell you to remove it!"

Sean could see Lawth was getting antsy. "All right, all right, I'll keep it under my shirt, Mr. Super-uptight, everything-is-so-serious, secret agent dude."

"And don't call me that!" Lawth snapped. "Just call me 'professor' if we're in earshot of anybody. Better still, just don't say anything."

As Sean pulled forward his shirt collar to conceal the necklace he noticed something different about it. The perfectly smooth stone which had been a brilliant light blue was now a shade darker. "Aw cool, I didn't know this was a mood ball!" he yelled.

Lawth, who was striding two paces in front of Sean, whipped around and angrily whispered, "Keep your voice down, and hide it in your garment like I told you! I'll explain why it keeps changing once we get there."

"*Keeps* changing?" Sean repeated with curiosity as he dropped it down his collar.

Lawth spun back around and resumed his brisk advance on the library, cautiously scanning the nearby surroundings and observing every detail as he went. Sean trailed carelessly behind, looking down his shirt.

With every step Sean took, the blue ball jiggled against his chest; but not like just any regular necklace would jiggle when its wearer is moving. This one pulsed and vibrated with energy all its own. It began slowly rotating too, and the closer he got to the library the faster it spun. The color continued to shift also, with the former light blue darkening to an ocean blue. Even weirder, there was now a large green splotch consuming about one third of the sphere. And even though Sean's face was buried in his now-elongated collar, all this was easy to see, for the spinning, colorful orb was now glowing, illuminating his chest and shining in his face.

Whump! Suddenly Sean was stopped cold. The top of his downturned head slammed into something solid. It was the chest and crossed arms of Lawth.

Sean stared up into the glaring eyes and started to say, "Dude, this little ball is incredible! It glows, it dances, it changes colors ... we gotta take it to the geology professor 'cause he—"

"NO!" Lawth retorted. "We don't need to take it to anybody here. We have to get it out of *here* and to *there!* Now keep your nose out of your shirt and soon you'll learn everything." Then Lawth thought a second longer about Sean's stupidity, shook his head and said, "Strike that. You'll learn something … *maybe*." And grabbing him by the arm, they hastily moved on.

The two cut across the campus lawn, with Lawth steering them as far away from others as he could. And instead of heading for the main entrance, Lawth escorted Sean around the side of the stately building to a nondescript side door. While blocking the boy's view, Lawth briskly waved his hand over the knob and the door popped open. And with one quick glance behind him, the "professor" scuttled his student inside.

The door opened into a dark stairwell. Lawth slammed the door shut and advanced down the stairwell toward the basement. Sean followed, his shirt pulsing with light and illuminating all the steps before him. Soon, the two of them set foot on the bottom landing. And there stood a door labeled "BASEMENT LEVEL – ARCHIVES & ANCIENT MANUSCRIPTS." Lawth grabbed and tugged the knob but the door was locked. Removing his hand for a moment he wiggled his four fingers and the door unlatched with an echoing thud and then smoothly opened wide.

Sean's jaw dropped. But before a word could exit that gaping hole in his face, Lawth stuck a finger in front of it and commanded, "Don't even ask. Just walk." And pushing the boy in ahead of himself, Lawth and Sean entered into a vast abode for old books.

The archives and ancient manuscripts room was an infrequently used storehouse containing a sizeable number of valuable antique books, a very small number of priceless, ancient manuscripts, and an unbelievable amount of worthless archives. It was always locked; accessible to library guests only by request and by escort of the key-holding head librarian. Consequently, the odds were good no one else would be in there, and that appeared to be the case at the moment. The room was dark and spooky, illumined only by Sean's glowing shirt, lit up compliments of his pulsating necklace which by now was going absolutely crazy.

"We're alone now. Pull out the georb," Lawth ordered.

Sean mused as he pulled out his necklace and nonchalantly scanned the room. "Dude, I never knew this room in the library even existed."

"Did you even know the library existed?" quipped Lawth.

"Yeah, 'course … duh!" Sean said indignantly.

"The question was rhetorical; you weren't supposed to answer. Do you even know what 'rhetorical' means?" sneered Lawth as he grabbed the swirling sphere's chain and yanked both it and the teenager attached to it close to him. Sean now stood face to face with the snippy secret agent as the gem whirled wildly.

"Yeah, 'course I know what 'retordical' means," answered Sean defensively. "It means a retarded question that yer not supposed to ans—" Sean stopped short and stared. Lawth dropped his hand and the georb, as he had called it, hung on its own in the air between their two noses. The little ball had a life of its own—and an energetic one at that! It was rotating and pulsating. Its dominant color of ocean blue and the dark green splotch were now shrouded by a grayish white swirl.

Lawth then petitioned in a deep and reverent voice,

"Lord of light, sky, water, and land,
time and space are in your hand.
Master of the heavenly span,
and of every grain of sand,
transport us to my time and land,
from this place where we now stand."

"Aw'right secret agent Lawth dude, this is getting pretty weird," Sean said a little nervously. "This reminds me of a show I watched about cult members who take people and—"

Lawth, with no words at all, stared Sean into silence.

Suddenly, beams of radiant, white light streamed out from the energetic gem, fully illuminating the dusty room! In this powerful light, Sean saw the blue of the stone turn into ocean water, the green splotch transform into a vegetation-lush continent and the whitish-gray swirls condense into atmosphere.

Before Sean's wide and wondering eyes, this little ball had morphed into a miniature earth. What's more, he could feel gravity pulling him toward it.

"Hey Lawth, man! Dude, help! The thing is pulling me in!"

Lawth only responded with a grin and a cavalier retort of, "Hang on *dude*, for a trip like you've never had in your thus-far wasted life!"

Lawth grasped Sean's forearms. The two of them were blasted by a gust of air, a splash of water and a peppering of dirt. A magnificent explosion of light illuminated their faces. And with a wild laugh from Lawth echoing through the library chambers and a high-pitched scream from Sean, the two of them condensed headlong into the little earth!

In an instant, the air gust, the water droplets, the dirt, the light, the georb and Lawth were all gone; and so was Sean.

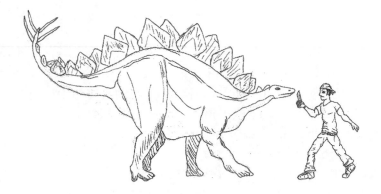

Chapter 3

AN OLD NEW WORLD

Braulio landed on his feet with a thud. The blast of wind stopped as soon as he hit soft grass. Disoriented and bewildered by the wild windstorm, he looked down. The necklace was still in his hand, the blue gem dangling innocently at the end of the chain. "Yes, I still got the necklace," he grunted.

He took a deep breath. It was the best breath he had ever taken. Inhaling deeply a second time, Braulio thought about how different the air was. It was fresher and fuller than any air he had ever breathed before. As an athlete, he sensed this would be an ideal place for a workout.

His eyes having adjusted to the light, Braulio saw he was no longer in the cave. Rather, he was in a small meadow in the middle of a vast forest—a forest bursting with every type of tree, plant, vine and flower imaginable. He was stunned at the immensity of the trees, the abundance of vegetation, the songs of a hundred birds, the chatter of insects, the … Braulio's thoughts were immediately halted by the sound of a hissing growl. It was so low-pitched that it could only have come from a beast that was very large. And it was so close that he felt the creature's breath on his back. Whatever it was, it was directly behind him.

Stunned and speechless, Fong and Candice looked at each other and then down at the scroll. Fong had felt a surprising calm wash over her while she was with the elf-man. Though logic told her she should be terrified by a strange man hiding in the trees staring at her and beckoning her to come hither, she was very much at peace in his presence. Now that he was gone, some fear returned.

Hands trembling, Fong untied the vine-wrapped binding and unfurled the little scroll. The first thing that caught her eye was a small stone embedded in the center of the thick, leathery material. Above and below the stone there was writing—writing of a most unusual style. It was a script that neither girl had ever seen, beautifully written in its form and flare. Best of all, it was in English ... most of it anyway. It read:

> *Seeker of nephilim,*
> *we seek you as well.*
> *We invite you this eve*
> *for a feast and a meeting.*
> *Choose one guest to bring—*
> *one of same faith and heart.*
> *Hold hands in a woodland,*
> *and recite the enchantment.*
> *The nofec will answer,*
> *and open your portal.*
> *We'll be there to greet you*
> *upon your arrival.*

Fong was stunned. She looked at Candice, who was staring back up in the trees, trying to catch a glimpse of her newest boyfriend-to-be.

"Candice, you see this? He asking me to come to his place ... for meeting and feast."

"What?" Candice snapped, tearing her attention from the trees and narrowing in on the little scroll. She snatched the parchment out of Fong's trembling hands and glared—clearly jealous—at the invitation as she read it.

"Why'd he invite you on a date and not me?" she whined.

"I not think it date in that way," Fong said as she reached over to carefully retrieve the precious parchment. "Look what it say. It say 'we seek you as well'. 'We' mean many people. He also want me to bring guest."

Candice thought about that for a few seconds. "Ahhh, he wanted to ask me out but he was just nervous. He's using you to get to me. I get it!" she exclaimed, beaming from ear to ear and thoroughly smitten.

Fong was now indignant. This had just become the most remarkable moment in her life. A man—make that an elf, or nephilim, or whatever he was—just appeared out of nowhere, spoke to them, glided across the ground, handed them an invitation and then shimmied away through the treetops with a smooth fluidity that would make a squirrel drool with envy. Most astounding of all, she held in her hand a little parchment that proved it wasn't all a dream. It even explained how to go to "elf land" for a visit. This was the moment of Fong's dreams, but Candice could think of nothing more than cute guys. And as a final insult, she thought Fong was merely a pawn with no greater purpose than getting her a date!

"You so rude, Candice! I never said I invite you as guest!" Fong fired back.

"What? Of course you're going to invite me." Candice flipped her hair over her shoulder and put her hand on her hip. (Fong hated when she did that.) "Who else would you invite?"

"Lots a people," Fong said, even though she could only think of one. "Like Eric."

Candice realized this was true and didn't want to blow the boyfriend chance of a lifetime; so she played it cool.

"Oh, well, that's not a bad idea," Candice lied. "Eric would probably be a good choice. But...doesn't he keep really busy?" she asked, knowing the answer full well.

"Yes, he hard worker. But who wouldn't make time for thing this big? Only a fool, and Eric no fool!"

"Oh, no! Certainly Eric is no fool. He's really smart I'm sure," Candice agreed, trying to calm Fong down. "In fact, he's so smart ..." Candice paused as she thought quickly. "He's so smart that he studies all the time, like you. And he probably would only stay two or three hours at that elf meeting … four hours at the very most."

"Why you say that?" Fong asked defensively.

"Well, because he'd have to get back to his studies, of course," said Candice.

Fong mulled this over for a moment. If anyone understood the rush to get back to studies it was her. Eric was a serious student too. That was one of the things she admired about him. And whereas she was every bit the rigorous student he was, there was absolutely no way she'd cut short an invitation to a world of elves. She'd fail a class and sacrifice a shelf of her most prized books for an opportunity like this. But would Eric?

Candice guessed what Fong was thinking and finished her thoughts for her. "I just don't know if it's possible for your guest to come back without you. And once you do return home, will you ever be able to visit that place again? If it's a once-in-a-lifetime thing, you might want to stay as long as possible."

Fong looked down at the invitation and read it again.

> *Choose one guest to bring—*
> *one of same faith and heart.*
> *Hold hands in a woodland,*
> *and recite the enchantment.*

Below this were a few lines written in a language Fong had never seen. She glanced over it and recognized only one word—and that was because she had just read it: *nephilim.* She wasn't entirely sure what that word meant, and she was clueless about the rest; but she reasoned that those lines must be the enchantment. According to the parchment, going to the stranger's marvelous land would be as simple as doing what it said.

How could this be any easier? Fong thought. *Here's the woodland, the enchantment and a guest who wants to go. Why wait? Besides, the only other person who would even consider being a guest is Eric. Anyone else would just laugh at me. And Eric is probably busy anyway, and he probably would want to return home long before I would want to return.*

Fong looked at Candice and wondered if she qualified as "one of same faith and heart." Even though Eric cared a lot more about the same things Fong did, she and Candice were at least friends. What's more, Candice was now a believer ... well, at least she had been for the last ten minutes. That should at least count for something, Fong reasoned.

What clinched it for Fong was when she thought about who would be calling the shots. If Eric went, he would be making most of the decisions about what was safe and what was not and what they should and shouldn't do. Fong didn't care much for that. And she outright couldn't stand the thought of having to return before she was ready to. No, if Eric went she wouldn't have total control. However, if Candice went, her dependence on Fong would force her to do whatever Fong directed. And that settled it.

"Let's go!" Fong said.

———⟫◆⟨———

Sean and Lawth were clinging to each other in a radiant whirlwind, Sean screaming all the while. Though it seemed much longer, the trip lasted only a couple seconds. The roaring wind rippled Sean's lanky body, violently flapped his wrinkled shirt, and reshuffled his hair into a blasted fray. When the cyclone ceased, Sean was left standing, just barely, with his mind spinning and his mouth gaping.

"Dude, what a trip! Can we do that again?" he asked Lawth.

Ignoring the question, Lawth let go of Sean's arms with a shove and stepped away from him—glad he no longer had to embrace the boy. As Sean shook the hair out of his eyes he noticed he was in a totally different place with no sign of the library anywhere. Everything looked different. Then, from just behind his ear, came a strange voice.

"Hello Sean."

Sean spun around and was startled as he stood nose to nose with the *now* oddest-looking man he had ever seen—even odder than Lawth, who had just positioned himself next to the new man.

Lawth folded his arms, turned up the corner of his mouth in a sardonic smile, and shook his head. He let out a sigh and said to the new man, "Well that could have gone worse, I suppose."

But Sean didn't even hear Lawth. He was entirely fixated on the new man. His head was aglow with dazzling white hair which was briefly interrupted by a colorful braided headband before blending seamlessly into his bleached mustache and long, tidy beard.

The man's nose captured Sean's attention next. It was long--even longer than Lawth's—yet not too long, thought Sean. In fact it seemed to be appropriate for this man's face. This was true of his ears as well, for the lobes were long and droopy but seemed to perfectly fit the rest of his features.

The new, mysterious man was wearing a bright blue robe with long flowing sleeves that shrouded him from the neck down. The man seemed old, very old in fact, but not in a wrinkled and stooped-over sort of way. For the man stood upright, seemed strong, and had only a reasonable amount of wrinkles.

And as interesting as dazzling white hair, flowing robes, and a long nose all were, it was the pair of eyes that captured Sean's. The man had eyes, oh, did he have eyes! The eyes were deep, oceanic blue, as if all the hues of the sea could be swirled into two irises. Sean gazed deeper and deeper into those pupils which were fixed on his. They were black, like any pupils, but they were more than that. They were wise. This was why the man seemed more ancient than he appeared. His eyes were full of wisdom that only a very long life could acquire.

Sean gazed deep into those eyes, and could have stared, mesmerized, far longer had the man not said, "Again I say, 'Hello Sean,' and welcome."

The voice was calm and controlled. It carried a tone of gentle leadership. It was melodious to the ears and soothing to Sean's recently frayed nerves. "Uhhh … hello," he finally said.

"Bad move, you made it speak. Now the challenge will be getting it to shut up," piped Lawth.

"Lawth! Is that any way to speak of one of our guests?" the older man reprimanded.

Lawth lowered is head in deference, shamed but not exactly sorry.

"Dude … where am I?" asked Sean

A chuckle gurgled out from deep within the wise old man, who replied, "Perhaps I should introduce myself first. My name is Enosh. I am an element wielder. Lawth here, whom you've already met, is my apprentice. As for your question, that would be difficult to answer based on your perspective of the earth. Perhaps we should start with the easier question of *when* are you. But lest I utter much of what you already know ..." He paused and turned to his apprentice. "What exactly have you told him thus far, Lawth?"

Lawth lowered his head again, looked down at his feet and shuffled from side to side as he tried to conjure up an acceptable answer, but Sean jumped in and excitedly responded instead. This was the first time in the whole ordeal that he thought he knew the answer to something, and he was happy to share it.

"Oh, Secret Agent Lawth told me about the way cool top secret experiment you dudes are doing—the one where you pour slimy goop down people's throats and in their ears so they can know another language. He told me I could help out with the Spanish junk yer makin' and I'm all cool with that. Actually, the stuff tastes pretty good as is, but you might want to consider giving people breath mints or somethin' afterward."

Enosh turned and raised his bushy eyebrows at Lawth. "Oooh, I see. A secret agent are you now? And how exactly did you earn that credential in the 37 minutes you were there?" Enosh rhetorically asked as he dealt his apprentice a rebuking glare. Then he added, "La-a-awth, you mean to tell me you misled this little boy?"

Braulio spun around, raised his fists and crouched into a defensive posture. As he did, he found himself nose to nose with what was unmistakably a stegosaurus—a beast twenty times the boy's size!

Braulio yelled, heart racing. This startled the dinosaur and it took a step back. Its curious eyes blinked and stared. Its nostrils flared. Sniffing the airspace which Braulio occupied must have been unpleasant to the sensitive lizard, because, before Braulio could react, the creature sneezed.

Large, moist plugs of dinosaur snot and half-chewed leaves were spewed all over Braulio. Sputtering and cursing, the slime-covered boy wiped his face. Horrified, he looked down at his clothes and became instantly furious.

"U-u-u-ugh! You stupid beast!" Braulio squawked. "You just threw up on my designer shirt, you worthless, overgrown toad!"

Acting on anger instead of common sense, Braulio pulled out his knife and charged the huge reptile, which backed up another few steps and hurriedly turned around. As it turned, it swung its tree-trunk-thick tail toward Braulio. The boy ducked just in time and the massive tail, replete with long, bony spikes, sailed overhead—a near miss. The tail crashed into a clump of underbrush and dislodged two thorny bushes. One was flung wide. The other was snagged on the spikes.

"Wo-o-oah!" yelled Braulio as the tail and bush came swishing back at him. This time it was swinging too low to duck so he jumped, only not high enough. One of the spikes caught his shoe and tripped him, sending him crashing face first to the ground.

The reptile seemed bent on crushing this foul-smelling attacker, and the tail came swinging back again. This time it came fast and it came low—aimed directly at Braulio. And since jumping didn't work the last time and there was no room to duck this time, Braulio got desperate. Scrambling to his feet, he tried to scurry away. But the tail came too soon for a clean escape. With one solid, leathery-skinned whack, the tail pummeled Braulio in the side and sent him sailing several feet in the air before he landed and crumpled into a roll.

Winded, terrified, and pumping with adrenaline, Braulio rose dizzily to his feet and scampered for a cluster of palm trees. Glancing behind as he ran, he saw that he was out of the tail zone and that the beast didn't seem interested in pursuing him. Still, taking no chances, Braulio hid in the cluster of thick trees.

Safe in the cover of foliage, Braulio leaned against a palm trunk and sucked in some deep breaths. He lifted up his shirt and felt his ribcage. Luckily, not a single spike had impaled him. The blow had knocked the wind out of him, but everything else that was inside of him seemed to still be intact. He breathed a sigh of relief. But then he heard a new sound, and it caught his breath in his throat.

Enosh was waiting for an answer from his apprentice.

"Well he wouldn't have come had I told him the truth," protested Lawth.

"And do you truly know that?" queried the older and wiser Enosh.

"Well, no, but it would've taken *so* long to get him to under—"

"Do not say another word," interjected Enosh. "You should know the Element Wielder's Code better than that. You evidently still have much to learn. And think of the example you set for children when you say such things. Apologize to the boy."

"I— I'm sorry for lying to you Sean," Lawth mumbled quietly but probably not sincerely.

"Aw, that's alright man. Yer only human ... uh, I think you are anyway. Just clue me in to what's really going on and we're cool. Oh, and I'm not a child, by the way," he added as he looked at Enosh. "I'm eighteen."

Lawth sputtered. "Phhh! HAA! A whole eighteen years under your robe, eh? I'm in awe. May I be your apprentice and sit under your tutelage when you've become a wise, seasoned eighteen-and-a-half-year-old?" he taunted.

"That'll be enough, Lawth. Change back into your clothes and we'll be on our way," Enosh commanded. Lawth complied and headed toward a clump of thick trees where his normal clothes were awaiting him. He mumbled something as he went about getting out of these baby garments and into adult robes once again.

Enosh smiled understandingly at Sean. "Well, since you know nothing about any of this, I suppose that last comment would be a fair place to begin. You see, Lawth scoffs at your young age because he is 316 years old."

"Yeah, right! I'm sure!" Sean responded with a wide grin. "And I bet you're 500!" continuing what he thought was a joke.

"Close! I celebrated my 505th birthday just last week."

Sean squinted one eye and tilted his head at what he had just heard. Enosh said it so confidently that Sean wanted to believe him even though his common sense screamed against it.

"That makes sense only if you know the answer to the question of *when* you are," the wise, old man continued, "for you are presently in the antediluvian period of world history, known more commonly as the pre-Flood era. We call it 'Early Earth.' The year is 1056 S.C. The 'S.C.'

refers to 'since creation.' And putting it quite simply, things are different here … very different."

As unbelievable as all that would seem to any reasonable human being, Sean sensed what he was hearing was true. And now for the first time since he got here, he took his eyes off this Enosh guy and took in his surroundings. Lush vegetation surrounded them. Exotic birds sang from their perches while others soared overhead. The calls of beasts and insects peppered the air—air which was fresh and alive and enjoyable to breath.

In a moment, Sean's single sense that what he had just heard *might* be true was overwhelmed by his five senses all concurring that indeed it was true!

"So you mean, like, I just traveled back in time thousands of years?"

"Correct."

"Will I ever be able to get back home?"

"Oh, yes indeed my boy! No need to worry there." Enosh paused and examined the lad. "Sean," he continued, his face grown serious. "My apprentice was wrong to mislead you. You must know that you may return home right now if you so choose. You have been summoned here for an important purpose, and we wish you to stay, but know that if you stay you will certainly encounter hardship and danger. The choice is yours."

Sean thought about it as he panned his surroundings, inhaled deeply again, and looked back into Enosh's eyes.

"So, what do you say?" Enosh queried with a hopeful look.

"Yeah, this place is cool. I'll stay," Sean said.

"Delightful!" Enosh replied.

"So how do you dudes live hundreds of years, anyway?"

Smiling genuinely, the wise Enosh replied, "Happy I shall be to explain that and much more to you, my lad, but we have an appointment to make first. You shall come with us, and a bit later Lawth and I will inform you about the vast differences between your world and ours."

"Well, how about just one more question for now?"

"Alright, what is the one question?" smiled Enosh graciously.

"Aren't you B.C. dudes supposed to look like cavemen instead of professors and wizards?"

Enosh radiated a knowing smile, ready to answer. But before his smile could be infused with words, Lawth emerged from the thicket, now clothed in a dark, rusty orange robe. It was faintly metallic and it shimmered as he moved. The robe was trimmed with a matching sash and it complemented a braided cord which was wrapped sweatband-style around his head. Lawth carried a staff in his hand while his satchel, which held the potions and various other bizarre items, was tied to his belt. To Sean, Lawth seemed altogether more natural and comfortable in these clothes than he did in his secret agent/professor disguise.

"Good. You are ready," Enosh noted. "Let's go then."

Still speaking to Lawth, he turned to look at Sean, raised one bushy eyebrow and said, "We indeed have much to explain to this young one, but no sense in doing it more than once. Let's first meet the others."

"The others?" asked Sean.

Chapter 4

BRAULIO BARGES IN

As Braulio crouched in the cover of the palm trees trying to catch his breath he heard the sound of laughter, and Braulio sensed it was at his expense. He scanned the perimeter of the trees. Knife in hand, he was already on the defensive, full of adrenalin and ready for another fight.

"Who's laughing at me? Who dares? Come on, bring it on!" he yelled through heaving gasps of air.

More laughter. It was coming from directly above him. Braulio looked up and spotted the source. In the branches above, a large family of monkeys was enjoying the spectacle of seeing the boy get smacked around by a dinosaur. There were at least a dozen of them; some were sitting up high on palm branches and others were clinging to the tall trunks. They were munching on dates, looking curiously at the newcomer and, at least in Braulio's mind, they were taunting him.

A baby monkey dropped a date down to Braulio, who, viewing it as a hostile attack, deftly deflected the date with his knife.

"Hey! You stupid baboons want a piece of me? Come and get some of this!" Braulio picked up the date and rocketed it back at the little monkey, nailing him squarely on his ear. The baby monkey howled and scampered over to his mother, tattling all the way. What happened next was sheer bedlam.

The baby monkey's mother saw it all, glared down fiercely at Braulio and let out an offended screech. Chattering, threats, and chest-beating then erupted from the father. Several others joined the battle cry of the outraged parents with screeches of their own and suddenly, the grove was in chaos.

Palm branches and many more dates were hurled at Braulio. Howls, screeches, shaking branches, and riled monkeys were scattering everywhere. Braulio had the foolish idea of throwing his knife at one of the attackers. It missed and got lodged high in a trunk. The shiny blade caught the eye of a curious monkey who picked it up, smiled broadly, and calmly carried it off as Braulio roared with rage.

It was at this moment that Enosh, Lawth, and Sean appeared. Screeches from primates mixed with the yells of an irate Spaniard penetrated the thick undergrowth. Palm trees and large, nearby leafy bushes were aflutter with hairy tails, arms and legs. In the midst of the fray was a cursing, red-faced teenager who was running from tree to tree, dodging date bombs and screaming absurd threats.

OOO! OOO! OOO! SCREECH! SCREECH!

"Give me back my knife or I'll have ya for supper, you un-evolved fur ball!" he hollered.

WHACK! A branch walloped Braulio on the head.

"THAT'S IT! YOU'RE FINISHED!"

OOO! OOO! WAAAA!

Enosh chuckled at the chaotic scene and, eyes twinkling said, "Lawth, Sean, meet Braulio."

Lawth just shook his head and folded his arms in disgust. Sean didn't even notice Braulio. He stood motionless and gaped at the stegosaurus that was chewing on some slimy plants while casually observing the monkey mayhem.

Braulio suddenly became aware he was being watched. Out of the corner of his eye he noticed the bizarre trio standing several yards away, and he immediately ceased his monkey battle so he could face them instead. Braulio sized up the three strangers and knew at a glance he could take the skinny guy in a fight. The kid was so distracted by the dinosaur that he probably wouldn't even see Braulio coming. That one would be easy. But as for the two guys in robes—Braulio was not at all sure what to make of them. He couldn't get a read on their builds because of those absurd outfits. That made him suspicious. *What might they be hiding under them? And what kind of men go around outdoors wearing gowns anyway?* He wondered for just a moment. But Braulio knew he had to think fast. His only weapon was up a tree and he was outnumbered three to one. So he puffed out his chest and tried to look menacing as he was deciding whether he should fight or make a fast break for it. Then the one in blue said something in a very soothing, almost musical language. The sound of the language seemed oddly familiar to the boy, but he couldn't place his finger on why it did, nor could he understand a word of it.

"Better get over there with your language potions. He'll need lots of explanations," Enosh directed.

Sighing, and not looking forward to dealing with another child, Lawth approached the fiery Braulio. Braulio stood his ground, assuming that a delegation of one must mean peace. Soon he and Lawth stood within handshake range. Lawth, knowing Braulio's culture, extended his right hand as if to shake. Braulio took his hand and Lawth gripped hard. Then, raising the powder straw he had hidden in his left hand, he blew the paralyzing dust into Braulio's shocked face.

The powder took immediate effect. Braulio had only enough time to realize he had been tricked and he cocked his left arm back for a knockout punch. But as he lunged forward for the attack, the powder halted him in mid-strike, his fist frozen just inches from Lawth's face. Lawth got right down to business and dumped the comprehension potion into Braulio's ears and the communication concoction down his throat.

Enosh moved forward to join his apprentice, lightly tugging on Sean's sleeve to get him to follow. Sean was still mesmerized by the stegosaurus.

"Yes, my boy, seeing a giant plated lizard for the first time is a lot to take in, but believe me, you will see many more. More importantly however, we must greet our new friend," he said with genuine excitement.

Waiting for the paralysis to wear off, Lawth savored the moment. Braulio, who was red-faced, enraged and beaten up by a family of monkeys, was too much for Lawth to resist.

"Awww, is wittle beefcake boy Braulio a wittle bit stuck wight now?" Lawth teased.

Silently inside, Braulio boiled with rage.

"The comprehension potion takes only seconds to work its way through the ears; he can already understand every word you're saying," Enosh reminded Lawth with a wary look.

The stegosaurus was plodding out of sight now, more interested in eating than watching more monkey brawls. And for their part, the monkeys had settled down now that Braulio had been stilled. The three guys stared for a moment at the frozen fighter.

"Okay, I get it," Sean finally concluded. "This dude already speaks Spanish and so he's here to help make the English potion just like I'm here to help make the Spanish potion, right?"

Enosh turned to Lawth, squinted one eye disapprovingly at him and answered, "No … no, you don't quite get it yet, Sean, but you will. Lawth will get it too."

Lawth turned sharply to look at Enosh. He already knew everything that was going on here. Why would Enosh say that he was going to get it? He mused on this for a second too long when … SMACK! Braulio's fist resumed motion and rammed full throttle into the side of Lawth's head. The blow sent Lawth sprawling.

"You should have seen that one coming," Enosh said, with a glint in his eye.

"Yeah, really dude! He's been tryin' to hit you for like over a minute, and you just stood there the whole time! Ha!" chuckled Sean, who for a split second seemed wiser than Lawth.

Braulio jeered, "Come on! Want some more—whoa!" The boy clapped his hands over his mouth with a look of shock on his face.

Seething with anger and red-faced with humiliation, Lawth sprang back to his feet. He raised his staff and lunged toward Braulio. Lawth's face was a mask of vengeful menace. He raised his staff toward Braulio, gripping it tight like a baseball slugger about to hit a home run.

Braulio was too amazed at his own words to even notice. "What in the world!" He clutched his throat in disbelief. "I'm, I'm speaking … I'm speaking a different language…"

"And understanding it when you hear it," Enosh added, as he nonchalantly waved his hand toward Lawth's staff just before he would have landed a crushing blow. The staff shot out of Lawth's hands, flying high in the air. Braulio's eyes went wide as he watched it sail away. Then he heard it come crashing down in some underbrush off in the distance.

"Go cool down as you fetch that, Lawth. And why would you raise your staff at a child? You know better." Enosh scolded.

Fuming, Lawth spun around and stalked off toward the staff.

"I gotta admit, whoever you are, that was cool," said Braulio very quietly, still very unsure about the sounds coming from his throat.

"Aw, dude that's nothing," added Sean. "This dude can teleport too! We just did it to get from wherever we were to wherever we are. It's so-o-o awesome!" Pausing for a moment of dull reflection, Sean looked at Enosh and asked, "Yeah, about that ... where are we anyway?"

Braulio glanced from Sean to Enosh, then to the briskly walking backside of Lawth, and then back to Enosh. He looked over to where the dinosaur had been and then back to Enosh. Then he craned his neck to leer at the monkey arena where he had just been beaten in battle. Some of them were staring back, dates in hands and wary looks on their faces. Braulio turned back and delivered a final penetrating glare at Enosh.

"Alright, enough with the theatrics and special effects. Where am I? Where am I really?"

"*When* are you may be the better question," Enosh suggested. But introductions first: I am Enosh, and I am an element wielder. This is Sean. He hails from your time. Now that you two speak the same language you'll no doubt find much to talk about. And of course, you've already had a close and personal encounter with my apprentice element wielder, Lawth."

There was a pause. Braulio was staring daggers at him. Then he dryly challenged Enosh. "And I'm supposed to believe I am in a different time," he said, in a tone that made it clear he did not.

"Correct. You catch on quickly!" Enosh said, smiling.

"So what's with the powder straw and the goopy stuff in my mouth and ears?" asked Braulio. He folded his arms across his chest, not hiding his defensiveness.

"Ah, yes, Sean was wondering that too," Enosh noted. "You see, boys, deep within all of us we all have knowledge of the mother tongue, the very first language humans and animals ever spoke. It is the language that all speaking creatures used before The Corruption. It's as common to our being as our blood and our very souls. It's native to all intelligent earthly creatures, so we call it 'Earthen'..." Enosh's thoughts appeared to drift; his eyes grew unfocused and his voice carried a touch of sadness as he continued. "Distressingly, many creatures are losing their ability to speak it and are resorting to inarticulate grunts, growls, squeaks, chirps, and the like. Very sad ... very sad, indeed."

Sean was becoming increasingly intrigued with Enosh's every word. His eyes grew a bit wider and his jaw dropped a bit lower. Beside him, Braulio remained expressionless.

"And the serums for the ears and throat," Enosh resumed, looking back up at the boys, "are complex mixtures that unlock such abilities. Oh, you still have knowledge of your other native language, but now you can enjoy your *true* native language as well. I hope that clears some things up for you, Sean." Enosh gave Sean an apologetic look.

"Huh? Oh, yeah, Lawth's secret agent story. No prob." Sean was holding no grudges. This was all far more exciting to him than learning Spanish anyway.

Braulio stood stone-faced with arms still crossed. "I don't believe a word you just said," he retorted.

"Ah, but you understand every word I just said, and you are speaking a language you've never learned or even heard before. How's that possible?" Enosh asked him kindly.

That made Braulio pause. He frowned, considering. Then he said, "I'm dreaming, that's all."

"A mighty vivid dream it must be where you even feel pain," answered Enosh, as he scanned the lad's scratched and muddied body.

Braulio's side, which had been walloped by the stegosaurus tail, was still throbbing. He knew the bearded weirdo was right. Were this a mere dream he wouldn't be feeling pain. There was no need to pinch himself to prove he was awake.

"I'm hallucinating!" he finally said. "You freaks put me on a drug trip with that stuff you forced down my throat. Yeah, that's it! You're all messing with my mind! Juan's part of this, too, isn't he?" Looking at Sean derisively he pointed his finger and continued, "And I bet you guys got the stuff from this junkie right here!"

"Whoa, hold up, dude! I may be relaxed and all but I'm no druggie. And you're not hallucinating. You just need to chill out and trust these guys," corrected Sean.

Braulio whipped a cigarette pack out of his pocket and thudded the bottom of it against his palm. Sticking one in his mouth, he mumbled, "You guys are all drug heads and you think it's all so funny seeing me hallucinate. I'm not buyin' any of it."

"Well, I'm glad to hear you are against inhaling drugs," said Enosh with a wry smile, eyeing the cigarette.

Braulio pulled out his lighter, held it to the cigarette tip, and leaned in to it.

"I wouldn't do that," cautioned Enosh.

Ignoring him, Braulio flicked the flint and a flame three times the height of what was normal blasted out. The tall flame licked his forehead, singeing an eyebrow. Braulio dropped the lighter. "What the—?!"

"Oxygen-rich air," answered Enosh before hearing the question. "Plants and trees grow much bigger and better here than in your time. The earth is full of them and they produce oxygen abundantly. Consequently, things which thrive on oxygen such as people, animals ..." Enosh bent down and scooped up the lighter, "and fires, all do much better here," he finished with a satisfied grin.

"Uh-huh, sure they do," Braulio said coolly as he snatched up his lighter from Enosh's outstretched palm and slid the flame control to low. He held the lighter away from his face and lit the cigarette with a flame now only twice as large as normal. He then took a long drag and glared fiercely at Enosh as he exhaled. "Even with all your tricks, I *know* I didn't travel back in time," he proclaimed, pointing a finger accusingly at Enosh.

"Oh?" said Enosh, raising his bushy eyebrows in amused anticipation.

"Yeah. Because dinosaurs are here and you dorks who say you live in this time period are also here. Well, duh! Men have only lived on earth for the last million years. But the last dinosaurs have been wiped out for over 60 million years! So which is it? Which time did I travel back to anyway? It can't be both, can it? Oops! Didn't think of that, did ya?"

Confident he'd won the argument and would soon be getting a confession, he took another long drag from his rapidly burning cigarette.

Enosh took no offense to this challenge but merely chuckled and said, "Well, I don't suppose there's any sense in trying to convince you. It seems you've made up your mind for now. So, since you're hallucinating anyway, I hope you wouldn't mind imagining that we're about to teleport three thousand miles."

"Cool! I love teleporting! Where we goin' this time?" asked Sean.

"A village named Erflanthina. It is in an area I think you call 'California' in your day," Enosh noted.

At this point Lawth returned; staff in hand, still scowling. He looked at Braulio with a steely glare. The walk had cooled him a bit but he wasn't over the punch. Lawth still had much to learn about the fine art of forgiveness.

"Splendid," Enosh said, seeing Lawth again at his side. "It looks like we're ready to go! Soon we will explain everything to you boys. But first we need to get to the girls."

"Girls?" repeated Braulio, raising his singed eyebrow.

"What girls?" asked Sean.

"Wait, what? Are you serious? You're really taking me?" Candice gushed. "Oh, Fong, let me hug you!"

Fong grabbed Candice's incoming hands and said, "No hug. Just hold hands." And with the parchment awkwardly gripped between her left hand and Candice's right, she began to recite.

"Wait!" Candice interrupted, "Not yet! I need to—I mean we need to go to our rooms and get ready. This is an invitation to dinner with the most gorgeous guy ever! I need," here she did a little nervous dance and looked down at herself, "um, we need to spend a couple hours putting on nicer clothes and makeup."

"You no get it, Candice! This no about you getting date! This about most important discovery of lifetime! Are you ready for this? Because if not, I go get Eric. He understand what this about. You don't!" Fong blasted.

"Alright, alright, calm down, Fong," Candice said, pulling a hand away so she could retrieve a compact from her purse. She did a fast assessment of her looks and, snapping the mirror shut, mumbled, "It'll have to do. Ready when you are, I guess."

Looking studiously at the parchment wedged between their hands, Fong took a deep breath and recited the foreign words. And even though she had never spoken them before, there was a smoothness and rhythm to her speech that impressed even Candice.

"Oh Fong, that's so pretty! Say that again," Candice begged, but before either girl could speak another word, their world upended.

The small stone lit up and pulsed with warm light. A swirl of leaves began spinning around their feet, moved up their legs, whirled around their torsos and then engulfed their bodies. Nearby tree boughs bent and swayed and wove their way toward Candice and Fong. Like enormous suspended serpents they surrounded the girls.

Fong was amazed; Candice wanted only to scream. But the strong gust of air and the inevitability of leaves in her mouth kept her quiet.

The wind gust grew so fierce and the swirling leaves so tumultuous that the girls shut their eyes. But just as quickly as the maelstrom had begun, it suddenly stopped, and all was still. When they opened their eyes they were no longer standing in the copse of trees on campus, but someplace entirely unrecognizable. They didn't have much time to take in their surroundings though, because staring down on them were the faces of more than twenty elf-men—each one of them every bit as handsome, strong and tall as the one they had just met. Huge and incredibly fit, they all were holding weapons, and none of them looked pleased to have company.

Chapter 5

VILLAGE OF NEPHILIM

Enosh lifted his staff and spoke. The air crackled, and with a flash of light the four disappeared. Three seconds later and three thousand miles away, a contented Enosh, an irritated Lawth, an awestruck Sean and a defensive Braulio reappeared. The portal, which was invisible except for the split second in which it was being used, split open and poured out the travelers. They were greeted by a chorus of bowstrings pulled taut, ready to unleash a slew of deadly arrows. Braulio, always on the lookout for a fight, assessed the size and number of his attackers. Quickly noting the odds, he instantly stepped away from the other three.

"Hey, hey! I'm not with these guys! Not even sure how I got here but I'll be leaving right about now," he proclaimed with hands lifted high in a gesture of surrender.

"You'd better be with us or you'd be dead before you took a step," Lawth growled at him.

Enosh raised his hand and in his friendly voice said something in a language that Sean and Braulio did not understand. Fortunately for them, the bow-wielding giants understood, and without discussion the huge archers slung their weapons on their backs and quivered their arrows.

Now that they were no longer staring down the shafts of the arrows, Braulio and Sean could take in the appearance of the archers. There were ten of them: all massive men, most of them over eight feet tall. Their arms were firm and bulging and they wore clothing made of leather and leaves. Long, healthy hair flowed from each of their heads and was tied back with leather thongs. Their faces were stern, but it was a sternness that brought comfort to Sean, though he couldn't have explained why if you asked him. Braulio, however, was terrified. He just couldn't let himself show it.

"Boys, these are some of the nephilim," Enosh said. "They are friends of ours and they mean us no harm. In fact, one reason they are here right now is to protect us from the ones who do seek to harm us."

Braulio determined that was some undeniably solid protection, but he wondered who or what wanted to harm him.

One of the nephilim spoke with Enosh in a language other than Earthen, and the boys couldn't make out a word. But Enosh understood him, and gestured toward the two boys as he answered the giant. The towering archer seemed very pleased with what Enosh said, and motioned two of his fellow warriors to escort the four newcomers safely away. Enosh, Lawth, Sean, and a very reluctant Braulio followed the two giants through a camouflaged gate which swung open and revealed a wooded path.

The boys, completely distracted by their enormous would-be attackers, hadn't yet paid any attention to the surrounding landscape. Looking around, they realized they were on the edge of a staggeringly tall forest. Long branches stretched out overhead, grasping for nearby trunks and swaying in the breeze so that the whole forest seemed on the move. Jewel-bright birds soared above and dove in and out of the canopy, disappearing in the distance with flashes of color against the broad green leaves. And directly ahead of them loomed a thick hedge, tangled with thorns, extending to the left and to the right and disappearing in the distance. Braulio wondered if it surrounded the entire forest.

After walking through a gate made of giant logs and wound with thorn-covered vines, Braulio, Sean, Enosh, Lawth and the two nephilim escorts entered the shadows of the forest. A narrow path wound beneath the vaulted canopy. The sound of the breeze and the chirping of birds were muffled in layers of dense foliage, making the forest floor hushed and still. The two bow-carrying giants moved smoothly, stealthily and very quickly. Braulio noticed that their bodies seemed to glide over the ground in their long-legged strides. The four normal-sized guys had to run in order to not lose sight of the giants.

Braulio was an avid hunter who loved the wilderness, and this vast display of unspoiled nature nearly overwhelmed him. His eyes darted in every direction, trying to take in the grandeur of the forest. Trees so dense with branches that he could not see their tops towered above him. Stalks thicker than his wrist with leaves shaped like arrowheads spilled over the path beside him. Thin beams of sunlight streamed through gaps in the canopy above, making thousands of flowers explode in a riot of color, carpeting the forest floor below. In all his time in the wild— hiking, hunting, camping—he had never seen a forest with such amazing vegetation as this one, but the wonders didn't stop with the plants. He caught glimpses of ground squirrels darting across the path, frilled lizards scurrying up trunks and lime green frogs perching on broad leaves. A herd of gazelle-looking creatures leapt out from hiding and tore across the path just a few feet ahead. A large panther crept into the light and then disappeared into the foliage. Rabbits, deer, anteaters, butterflies, birds, and many animals that Braulio didn't recognize scampered and climbed all around them. A monkey swung on a vine overhead, missing Braulio by just a few inches. Braulio flinched. Then he pinched himself. Nope, he still was not dreaming.

Am I just hallucinating? Braulio wondered. He felt normal. In fact, considering the scuffle with the stegosaurus and then the monkeys, he felt surprisingly good. His soreness was already subsiding and he was invigorated by the atmosphere around him. He filled his lungs deeply with a long inhale … the air was rich and refreshing! He gripped his necklace and looked down hard at it. As much as he hated to admit it, he had to believe Juan was right. He really *did* transport to a different world! But as for where and when he was—he didn't know what to believe. More importantly to Braulio, he didn't know how being here would benefit him nor did he know how he would get back home.

"So, where are we?" Braulio asked.

"We are in a nephilim forest in the region of Erlinthone," Lawth answered. "And we're heading toward the tree village of Erflanthina. But since you're hallucinating, I suppose you can go wherever your little mind takes you," he snapped as he sped up to stay close to the nephilim guides.

"Now Lawth," Enosh chided, "these boys have experienced enormous changes in the last few minutes. We can't expect the young lad to be a believer immediately. He will be soon enough. In fact, he may already be." the wise man said, with a knowing twinkle in his eye.

Sean, now slightly winded, asked, "Hey, elder dudes, this scenery is really cool and stuff, but why are we running instead of teleporting?"

"There are only select places in the world where one is able to teleport. It may only be done from one portal to another, and though there are several portals, they do not exist everywhere," answered Enosh. "The one we just used is the closest to Erflanthina, the nephilim village to which we are heading. We often use portals when we can, but in some cases it is best to avoid them altogether. Sorcerers and other wicked ones are moving through portals with some frequency these days. Some of them would even seek to move an army through a portal for a sneak attack! That is why nephilim are so heavily guarding the one that is close to their village."

Braulio, in much better physical condition than Sean, was still marveling at how strong and fit he felt. For as far and as fast as they were traveling, he wasn't tired. Every breath invigorated him, and the scenery was an amazing distraction.

Time went by quickly as Braulio and Sean jogged behind the speedy nephilim and breathed the healthy air. Moving fast through this unknown forest, the boys had no idea where they were. Then suddenly, the landscape changed.

A very narrow, deep valley stretched across their path with steep, rocky cliffs punctuated with bursts of ferns and flowers up and down the sides. The forest rushed to its very edge and seemed to tumble into its depths. Far below them, a flock of blue and red birds swooped through the chasm. Sean's eyes were drawn downward to where a bubbly blue stream gushed a crystal gash through the gray stone. The scene was at once beautiful and frightening.

The nephilim stopped in their tracks and the other four halted immediately behind them at the trunk of an especially enormous tree growing at the edge of the narrow valley. Some of its roots crept over the valley's lip and several massive branches jutted out over the void.

The lead nephil notched an arrow, pulled back his bow, and loosed the arrow which plowed into the trunk of the huge tree. This triggered the dropping of six thick vines. The lead nephil motioned at the elders, who each grabbed a vine and wrapped it around their waists, while the nephilim quickly tied loops at the bottom of their vines. Once secured, Enosh kindly handed a vine to Braulio as Lawth whipped one at Sean.

"Dude ... you aren't serious," Sean said, with the vine drooped over his head, his wide eyes assessing the long drop.

"Have you ever seen me not serious?" Lawth asked with a raised eyebrow.

Braulio tugged hard on his vine and then hung on it with all his weight. Satisfied, he coiled it a couple of times around his muscular abs and took several steps back from the cliff, ready to get a running start.

"Well, I see your confidence is beginning to return to you," noted Enosh. "It is advisable, however, that you let our leader go first. Archers stand ready on the other side."

Suddenly, the first nephil took a running leap, stepped into the loop in the vine, and glided smoothly across the gulf. Dropping lightly on the other side, he held up one hand and said something to the nearby trees. The trees then moved—or so it appeared. In actuality, other nephilim archers hiding in the trees materialized and lowered their weapons.

Frightened at the thought of how many more giants might be armed and hiding, Braulio gulped.

"You're safe now, lad. No need to fear. Swing on over," Enosh said encouragingly.

Braulio breathed deeply and, with a last wary look at the warriors on the far side, sprinted forward and took a final long jump at the edge, which catapulted him perfectly over to the other side. Landing solidly, he took in his new surroundings, noted the height and structure of the camouflaged warriors around him and tried to act cool.

Lawth, wasting no time, swung across after him while Enosh assisted Sean in tying his vine correctly and encouraged him to take the leap.

"Uh, I think I need to … like … watch you do it first, Mr. Wielder dude," he said nervously.

With far more agility than Sean expected in an old man, Enosh smoothly swung himself across and dropped lightly to his feet on the other side. Sean paused and bit his lip. Taking as many steps back as the vine would allow, Sean breathed hard, closed his eyes, and took a blind run toward the cliff. As he went airborne, Sean screamed his way across. His feet flailing wildly, one of them caught Lawth square in the chin as he spun erratically upon arrival.

But Sean didn't let go. Failing to release the vine, he sailed back to the other side where a helpful nephil caught and stopped him. The agile giant deftly untied Sean's vine and then held him tight against his own chest. With one muscle-bulging arm gripping the vine and the other wrapped around Sean, the giant ran to the edge, stepped into the loop, and the two sailed off the cliff. In seconds, he and the nephil landed securely on the other side.

"Imbecile," muttered Lawth under his breath as he wiped dirt from his chin.

The six of them turned away from the ledge and plunged into the forest. After traipsing a few hundred paces they came to a hut. It was a relatively skinny, yet tall structure made of logs, sticks, and vines, and it was lodged high up in a tree.

"Whoa! That's like the coolest tree house I've ever seen! Can we go up in it?" asked Sean.

"Why, certainly! It is the entry gate for the village of Erflanthina," Enosh said with a smile. "Once we are inside you will think it is quite 'cool' indeed."

The lead nephil motioned with his hand and three vine ladders dropped from the tree house. Up scampered the two nephilim, flying over the rungs in their ascent as if climbing were as easy as walking. Enosh and Lawth followed with little effort, but without the speed or grace of the nephilim. Braulio, who was always proud of his fitness, climbed as quickly as he could—which wasn't quite as quickly and as the 505-year-old Enosh. And Sean swung his vine-woven ladder back and forth erratically as he fumbled for the proper grips all the way to the top.

The ladders led to openings in the floor of the tree house and upon emerging through the hole, Sean was assisted by a helpful nephil who, with one strong arm, pulled him up and set him on the floor as if he weighed no more than a child.

The boys soon realized the treehouse they had entered was merely a guard shack—an entry point to the village and a final defense station against any attacker. And whereas the treehouse room in which they stood wasn't much to look at, what it protected most certainly was. For when Braulio and Sean looked out beyond the room, their jaws dropped.

There was no back wall on this guard shack. Rather, there was a panoramic view of the village of Erflanthina, a village unlike anything the boys had seen before. The entire village was in the trees!

Treehouse dwellings, all of them huge, were embedded in massive trunks, suspended from strong boughs, and sprawled out from limb to limb in a complicated maze of structures. Beginning at the edge of the guard shack was a wooden walkway that weaved, dipped, turned, and stretched for miles, connecting the entire village. Hundreds of heavy vines tied to overhead boughs held the walkway in place, making it a long and sinuous suspension bridge.

Sean and Braulio gazed in awe at the village that sprawled in every direction—literally. Several levels of houses above and below the walkway were reached by ladders. Nephilim went about the business of the day, scaling ladders with graceful ease, while children scampered along the walkway and swung on vines or played games on open platforms that must have served as a nephilim version of the neighborhood playground, complete with swings made of vines. Sean's eyes bugged out as one child leapt from a platform to catch a vine, swinging easily across to a house where his mother waited, smiling. Even their kids seemed superhuman!

The nephilim guides motioned for their visitors to follow, and they resumed their usual fast pace—but this time it was over the wobbly and twisty treetop network of bridges. And even though the nephilim bodies were enormous, the walkways barely swung or dipped as they glided effortlessly over the numerous planks and vines. Every step they took seemed to land on a cushion of air that sped them further ahead.

Enosh and Lawth followed quickly and their comparably heavy footsteps plunking along the planked walkways alerted some nearby giants to their presence. The bridge system began to bob and weave a little as the two elders race-walked to keep up.

Braulio followed the two elders and competitively tried to remain close behind them. But even as athletic as he was, his movements jarred the walkway more than those of the older men ahead of him. Several village giants turned and stared. He felt his face flush.

When Sean stepped on he nearly toppled off. Gripping the vine-like handrails he bobbed and swayed and clumsily trailed the others with all the grace of a hippopotamus.

In less than a minute, Enosh, Lawth, Braulio and Sean were surrounded by the village on all sides—which included both above and below them. And thanks mostly to Sean, the relatively small visitors caught the attention of nearly the entire village. Gardeners tending their lush, fruit-laden vines, stopped their pruning and looked over. Tailors, their large hands nimbly weaving giant swaths of cloth, ceased their sewing and stared. A group of female nephilim who were sitting together on a branch, spotted the four and immediately began leaning in and whispering to each other as they kept glancing over at the new arrivals. Children, some of whom were taller and stronger than Braulio and Sean, ceased their play and curiously watched the guests wobble their way over the network of bridges.

The boys, when not struggling to maintain their footing on the bobbing walkway, noticed how very open the village was. For example, all the dwellings had windows carved into them—large windows without any panes of glass or even screens. Most did not have shutters or curtains either. Doorways were big and tall and almost all of them were wide open.

Strangest of all to the boys was the lack of roofs. All the houses had wooden rafters stretching from wall to wall. Vines bearing colorful flowers and clusters of fruit twisted themselves around the beams. These rafters supported lush hanging gardens, providing an ample supply of fresh fruit and the marvelous aroma of budding flowers. Yet apart from these rafters and several canvases over bathrooms and bedrooms, there were no actual roofs in the village, and the boys could see directly into the giant dwellings below the walkway. Braulio gaped at the size of the homes, estimating the average room height to be about fifteen feet tall.

"Almost there, boys. Just one more stairway," Enosh said helpfully, gesturing upward. Large wooden steps carved into the trunk of a mammoth tree climbed upward, wrapping themselves around the trunk and disappearing in the leafy foliage above. The nephilim guides ascended the curving stairs, the element wielders and Braulio following, while Sean slowly brought up the rear. Spiraling up three very high stories, the party arrived at the highest dwelling in the village.

Once at the top of the trunk-wrapping stairway, Braulio and Sean looked around in awe. They were standing on a terrace outside of an enormous treehouse, ornately carved and impossibly huge. Braulio gaped, wondering how it could stay suspended even in such a giant tree.

An extravagantly jeweled wooden door towered before them, and unlike most other doors in the village, this door was closed. The lead nephil called out something in the nephil language and immediately the door swung open. An especially intimidating giant emerged and glared at the small figures standing before him. Braulio strove to hide his fear but he jumped when something rubbed against his ear; it was Enosh's beard.

Leaning in close, the wise man said, "No fear my boy, this is the palace of the village chief. His porter looks frightening, but you will feel more comfortable once inside." And in they trooped.

As with the other open-roof rooms in this village, this one had many of the same things. A thick-vined, fruity garden hung beautifully from the rafters, shading the large, central room. Earthen pots containing many gallons of water and wine were neatly stacked in a corner. Dozens of quivers stuffed with arrows and over one hundred longbows hung prominently on racks, alert for battle. A dazzling display of crystal vials enclosing colorful potions lined several shelves. Weathered parchments and rolled-up scrolls filled hundreds of canisters which were stacked together sideways. Yet this highest and grandest of the village tree houses contained something the other dwellings did not have. This one had two girls in it, and they were about the same size and age as Braulio and Sean.

Chapter 6

FEASTING HIGH IN A FOREST

S ean and Braulio were shocked to see normal girls. In the wonder of the forest and village, they had forgotten all about the girls they were supposed to meet. Sitting before them at a large round table with bowls of fruit, jugs of steaming liquid and a jumble of sprawled-out scrolls, sat Candice and Fong. The nephil who had met the girls at their college was near them. Several other important looking nephilim were also in the room. One in particular, who held a very stern face, was seated in some elaborate vines which were suspended from the rafters above. Over his leafy garment he wore a dark green robe made of a bizarre fiber unknown to the boys. It was belted with fine leather, and on his head sat a twisted crown of vines embedded with flowers and jewels. Braulio guessed correctly that he was the one in charge.

Braulio tried to act cool and unafraid. He zeroed in on Candice and gave her a macho smile. Candice, who would have normally accepted the attention and returned some attention of her own, ignored him. In fact, seeing regular-sized boys made her smirk to see how diminutive they were compared to the big guys. The dark-haired boy may have been cute, but he was nothing compared to the musclemen all around her.

"Whoa! Awesome! A village full of big tree houses and right-sized girls! Hey, Enosh, dude, can we stay here?" Sean asked.

Fong, for her part, continued to pour over a scroll, her head moving back and forth as she read feverishly. She had not even noticed the arrival of the newcomers.

"Welcome, travelers!" boomed a room-stilling, authoritative voice. It was from the robed giant who had been sitting in the vine chair. He stood up and towered over all others in the room. In just three and a half impressive strides he was standing in front Braulio and Sean. Tearing his attention from Candice, Braulio looked up—way up in order to make eye contact with the nephil. He tried to suppress a gulp as the giant took his massive hand and placed it close to Braulio's face. Braulio shuffled a step away.

Enosh nudged him and quietly said, "He is offering to shake your hand, for he has heard that in your culture that means, 'I come in peace.' It would be wise to accept that offer, don't you think?"

Braulio immediately gripped three fingers of the hulking hand and his internal organs vibrated as the giant gave him a vigorous fifteen-second shake. The nephil shifted to Sean whose wiry body flopped about until the giant decided the handshake was done.

The huge nephil then turned to Enosh, whom he apparently knew, and greeted him differently. Enosh knew the greeting well. Resting his staff against his chest, both he and the giant chief raised their heads toward Heaven, stretched their arms out wide and lifted them over their heads in an A-frame figure. Then, lowering their arms straight down until they were perfectly horizontal, they looked at each other and raised their arms in the same pattern again. The arms then circled back down and came to rest in front of each of their chests with palms up and empty, as if ready to give a part of their hearts.

The chief shared the same greeting with Lawth. Then in a deep, resonating voice, the chief spoke to the boys. "We welcome you to Erflanthina, time travelers. I am Barzuga, chief of Erflanthina; this great village of the nephilim. You will stay with us for a season so as to learn the ways of our day and time. After you have completed your training you will be ready to complete the mission for which you came."

"Awesome!" Sean yelled. "Hey, big chief dude, do we get to pick our own girl and our own tree house?" Formal courtesies and graces were not Sean's forte. Neither was tact.

The chief stared hard at the uncouth boy. He firmly said, "You will make yourselves at home right here and will be spending the nights under my rafters. It is time you met your companions. Come." He strode to the table.

Sean shut his mouth and scurried over to the table, hoping he wouldn't melt under the stern glare of the no-nonsense chief. Braulio headed cautiously toward the table as well, observing everything and everyone in the room. Candice kept eyeing Braulio, smirking at how puny he seemed. Fong's nose was still in a scroll.

"Ladies, meet Braulio and Sean. Gentlemen, meet Candice and Fong."

Candice straightened. For the first time, Fong looked up. Braulio gave a quick nod to Fong and a *hey-there-babe* look to Candice. Sean simply said, "What's up?"

Fong, finally realizing there were other normal people in the room, stood up and grabbed Sean's and Braulio's hands. She briskly shook them as she started speaking.

"Pleased to meet you both. I'm Fong Chow and this is Candice Singletary. Welcome to the Antediluvial Period of Earth's history. The year is 1056 S.C. and I will assume you already know that 'S.C.' stands for 'since creation'. I am still working on the calculation to determine what year that correlates to a year in B.C. chronology, since nobody here seems to know. But anyway, we are in Erflanthina, an elfin tree town as I call it, or an earth-based nephilim village as the element wielders, Enosh and Lawth call it. Elves, or rather nephilim, typically live to be hundreds of years old and hence they have accumulated incredible knowledge. With the re-recognition of our mother tongue, Earthen, we can read many of their writings and apprehend vast amounts of knowledge lost to the modern world. Candice and I arrived just hours ago by invitation from Eskes Hosswee, an elf—I mean, a nephil who belongs to an elite group called the Nephilim Time Teleportation Team. So who are you, who brought you two here and how did you arrive?" Fong said in one unbelievable breath.

Before either boy could answer or even process what Fong had just said, Candice laughed and rudely blurted, "Fong, it's so funny hearing you talk in normal English!"

"I'm not speaking English and neither are you. We are speaking our true native language, Earthen," Fong corrected curtly. "Remember the serum?"

"Oh! Don't remind me of that disgusting goop. And what good is speaking this Earthen thing if these huge, gorgeous guys mostly speak their stupid giant language?" Candice murmured peevishly, not realizing how well nephilim could hear.

"We speak both," corrected Chief Barzuga in perfect Earthen. "We speak Nephilim to communicate amongst ourselves and we speak Earthen to communicate with you humans and certain creatures." he corrected, as he stared coolly at the little girl who had just called his language 'stupid'.

Candice blushed deeply and stared at the floor.

"Who-o-oah! You mean we can talk to animals too?" asked Sean.

"Certain ones, yes. But it is getting more difficult with every passing year since The Fall," answered the chief. At the mention of "The Fall" all became silent and a palpable gloom fell over the room. The four kids could feel it emanating from both the wise men and from the nephilim. Enosh interrupted the saddened silence by clearing his throat and changing subject.

"You young ones undoubtedly have many more questions like these. There will be time to answer them later. But first, if I'm not mistaken, Chief Barzuga, we have a gathering to attend."

"Indeed. We have been eagerly awaiting you, our guests, and festivities are planned for this evening, including food. I'm sure after your journey you are all hungry. Serflina and Azmarpin are here to show you your quarters. Take some time to wash and then adorn yourselves with new vestments. We have taken care to see that your needs are met, but if you find yourselves in want for anything, ask Serflina or Azmarpin, your personal attendants. Also, after a quick measurement, Shomarin will be bringing you your new vestments within the hour."

And with that, the giant named Azmarpin and the female giant named Serflina smoothly glided over to the kids as the other guards dispersed and the room emptied. They introduced themselves using firm handshakes that went on way too long (Nephilim had heard of handshakes, but were not really sure how long or vigorous they were supposed to be, so they did their best). A third attendant, Shomarin, bounded over to them and, after giving each of them yet another brain-rattling handshake, whipped out an odd-looking vine. He efficiently wrapped the pliable vine around Braulio's head, pinched the vine, and then did the same thing around the boy's chest and waist. Whistling as he worked, Shomarin took a final brisk measurement of Braulio's height. Each measurement was recorded with an indent on the vine. Satisfied, the oversized tailor tossed the odd measuring cord over his shoulder. He repeated the process with each kid. He finished in a flash and disappeared from the room, four thin vines draped over his shoulder.

Serflina and Azmarpin told the four kids to follow them as they turned down the hallway deeper into the palace. All four simultaneously looked to Enosh. His face creased in a smile and he reassuringly said, "Go on. Everything is fine. We will see each other soon at the festival."

The four new arrivals followed their giant guides down a long and twisting corridor, away from the watchful eye of Enosh. The corridor, like the rest of the chief's palace, was built on and around the boughs of several ridiculously large trees. Fong had already calculated that, whereas most of the massive trees in this village held two or three dwellings each, the sheer size of the chief's palace meant it had to span at least seven or eight monster trees.

After crossing over several huge boughs and following a few sharp bends in the corridor, Serflina flung open a door and motioned for the girls to enter. Fong, with much anticipation, darted in immediately. Candice cautiously followed her as she critically judged the suitability of her new quarters.

"Take some time to get ready. There are bathing facilities in your room and your nephil attire will arrive shortly. We will escort you to the feast two sun stations from now," Serflina told them.

"Two *whats*?" asked Candice.

"Sun stations," piped Fong before Serflina could answer. "They don't go by hours here; they go by stations of the sun in the sky. It's a different way of telling time but it's the same concept. Two stations are just two hours—which is almost enough time for you to make yourself beautiful," she added mockingly.

"If you girls are in need of anything, let me know," added the hospitable Serflina as she closed the tall and knotty door behind her.

Two doors down, Braulio and Sean were shown their room and told the same thing before the nephilim named Azmarpin went away.

The four kids stood in their new dwellings and looked around. Each abode was furnished with two very long and wide mattresses which were stuffed plump with soft leaves. In the center of each room sat a high table surrounded by U-shaped vines. The vines hung from stout rafters and served as typical nephil chairs. The rafters were hung high and were lush with leaves, fruit and flowers—which when taken altogether created a partial, although incomplete ceiling. Wide windows looked out on bountiful green foliage as it welcomed a soothing breeze to sweep through the room. Several hooks which were twisted into the rafters held short ropes. Braulio, inspecting the ropes, surmised they were there for doing exercises. He was right. Back in her own room, Candice guessed those ropes were used for hanging laundry and decorations. She also was right.

The guests' rooms were ornamented with beautiful woodwork and colorful fruit and flowers. Carved panels ran down the walls and the table was an intricately etched masterpiece. On top of it sat a large earthenware bowl of vibrant and exotic looking fruit—almost all of which the kids had never before seen.

Off to the side of each habitation was a bathroom, of sorts. Sean and Braulio began inspecting the odd room. Above their heads, suspended from the rafters, hung a water trough that ran through the whole palace from room to room. Cords dangled from the trough which opened and sealed small holes in the bottom of it.

"Well, well, these guys even have indoor plumbing," Braulio mused. He pulled a cord and dodged a spray of warm water. He released the cord and the water stopped flowing. A small drain in the floor lapped up the water which then sloshed through some piping until it emptied outside in nearby gardens. Braulio noted that this room had a roof: a canvas canopy draped over the rafters which let in light, but not sight.

And his eyes were drawn to plush towels—made of something very soft and perfect for drying large bodies—hanging on hooks.

"I gotta try this out," Braulio said a little skeptically. He started to undress and barked at Sean, "Hey, skinny boy, how 'bout a little privacy?"

After Sean left, Braulio basked in the warm shower. It was even more refreshing than he thought it would be. When he finally exited the bathroom wrapped in a giant towel, he was greeted by fresh clothing. The garment looked unusually small as it sat there, folded neatly on the massive table. Sean was already wearing his new outfit and was bouncing around the room doing some kind of awkward, gangly exercise.

"Dude, these vestment thingies Azmarpin just gave me are like so totally flexible I can move in ways I never knew were possible," Sean said as he fell over backwards while trying to extend his leg over his head.

Braulio rolled his eyes and critically inspected the strange item on the table. It looked like rubbery leaves which would serve as excellent camouflage. But the material didn't rustle or make any sound at all. Whatever the material was, it was smooth to the touch and exceedingly flexible. It reminded Braulio a little of some of the better gym attire he had seen professional athletes wear. He was curious, yet still suspicious as he cautiously put his on his new attire. Checking himself out in the mirror, he realized he looked a lot like one of the nephilim ... miniaturized. And even though he thought Sean was acting like a fool, Braulio had to admit that the comfort and flexibility of the outfit was unsurpassed. It seemed to give him more mobility and even more energy. Braulio reasoned this must be psychological, but he liked the feeling anyway.

Back in the girls' room, Candice and Fong were trying on their new clothes too. Fong was busy analyzing the material, trying to deduce which plants could produce a fabric so flexible, so soft and yet so strong all at once. Candice, meanwhile, was complaining about how tacky hers looked, and she felt she would just die if any of her friends saw her! Nevertheless, for the moment she was more interested in the hulking men of the village, and as long as she looked better than the giant girls, wearing the dorky garments was worth it.

After several more minutes of fashion questions, weird fruit testing, and incessant chatter about all they had seen today, there came a large-fisted, gentle rap on the door.

"Come in!" Fong called.

Serflina opened the door. Below her stood Braulio, dressed and ready, but with arms defensively crossed and still very suspicious of what this was all about.

Serflina kindly asked the girls if they were ready. Before she could get an answer, Fong peppered her with questions about the purpose of the party, the names of all the strange fruit in their room, why the shower wasn't designed more efficiently and even whether Serflina was satisfied with her current job description.

While Serflina patiently tried to satisfy Fong's bombardment of queries, Azmarpin was back in the boys' room helping Sean, who in one of his flexibility tests somehow got his right leg stuck in one of his sleeves. Once he finally got unstuck, he and Azmarpin joined the others, and off they went.

After several minutes of hazardous walking across wobbly rope bridges and crooked steps, the four visitors arrived at the festival; and it was immediately clear that they had been expected. Singing erupted the moment of their appearance. Nephilim voices are low, and their songs carry a special anointing. Beautiful harmonies wove themselves around the deep, slow melody. Candice caught her breath as she listened to the joyous sound. The song was one that none of the kids had ever heard, nor could they understand a single word. Nevertheless, the words resonated with a gorgeous melody that anyone with ears could appreciate. What's more, the nephilim were singing *to* the visitors. Fong, Braulio, Candice and Sean were beginning to see that they were the very reason for the celebration!

"What is this about? This party can't be for us can it? We only just got here and they don't even know us," Fong said turning to Serflina.

"Indeed. It is precisely because you just arrived here. We welcome you," she answered.

"That's my kind of welcome," said Braulio, strutting forward and soaking in the praise he knew he deserved.

Candice, noticing dozens of gorgeous male faces, tossed her hair and looked coy. Sean just stood there with his mouth hanging open.

The villagers gathered along a wide section of the central walkway and on large platforms and porches above and below the walkway. There were many tables on porches and landings, and in the center of it all was an especially long and lavishly decorated table. Four empty vine swings hung along one side of it, reserved for the four young travelers. And several prominent members of the village were standing behind their own vine swings at this table, welcoming the newcomers with their song.

Braulio, Fong, Candice, and Sean sat on their vine swings. Enosh and Lawth showed up and took vine seats beside them. It comforted the kids to see Enosh. As strange as the element wielders had appeared to them at first, they now seemed downright normal compared to the bizarre surroundings and their gigantic hosts. Even the irritable Lawth was a welcome sight!

The singing soon gave way to dancing and a most amazing scene developed. Candice gasped. "Ohmyword, Lawth, what are they doing!" she exclaimed with some horror.

"This is a traditional dance of the nephilim," replied Lawth with little enthusiasm. "Female nephilim wave long, flowery vines and male nephilim wield swords and whips. And, yes," he said, answering her question before it was asked, "the dance is as dangerous as it looks." He smiled wryly at her wide-eyed look.

"Yet remarkably beautiful in the competent steps of agile performers," continued Enosh. "The idea is for flowery vines, and only flowery vines, to be sliced during the dance, producing clouds of bright petals and wisps of perfumed air."

And that was what happened. Within minutes the air was aflutter with brilliant petal confetti. Air-born bits of fragrant flowers floated and drifted about the guests. Candice was awestruck. Fong was moved by the beauty of the spectacle, but fell to analyzing its anthropological significance. Braulio wanted to get his hands on one of those swords. Watching sword-wielders so skilled while he was so entirely unarmed left him feeling insecure. Sean, captivated by the sweet aroma and controlled by his belly more than his mind, ate some of the delicious-smelling petals that floated close to his face.

With the last colorful flower slices fluttering down and an atmosphere thick with the aroma of a hundred bouquets, the chief gave a cheer. The villagers took up the cry and the thunderous yell of the giants was deafening.

"Let the feasting begin!" Barzuga bellowed.

Teams of servers streamed out of nearby doorways carrying a colorful abundance of food. Basket after basket of fresh bread was deposited on the many tables. There were huge, round loaves smelling of honey; small, sweet twists, sprinkled with spices; dark, hearty rolls; crusty on the outside and soft on the inside. Their freshly-baked aromas penetrated the already pungent air. Bowls of fruits, bigger and more ornate than the ones in the guest rooms, appeared next. Drinks in large earthenware pitchers were sloshed down here and there and huge carved goblets were distributed to all. At last, the meats arrived.

Roasted beasts on spits—some recognizable and some not—were paraded along the walkways to the dozens of tables. Braulio nearly drooled as a roasted pig passed by, followed by some sort of marinated foul that looked like an enormous duck. The four travelers had never seen such an array of varied and delicious cuisine. The smell was captivating and the sight of it was overwhelming. With everything that had happened in the last several hours, none of the four even realized how hungry they had been until now. So with reserved caution on the unidentifiable entrees and reckless abandon on the rest, the four hungry travelers dug in.

Enosh and Lawth sat at the table, flanking the four youths. Several nephilim were at the table with them, but it appeared this was only for the purpose of politely accompanying their guests, for nephilim do not normally sit at tables. The giants were lodged anywhere but at the tables themselves. Some were clung on long, twisty vines, suspended high above the ground. A few perched on rungs of ladders and many several sat on thick branches. Many balanced themselves on precarious, leafy places that could not have supported even Fong's small frame. There seemed to be no limit to where these giants could stand, hang, or comfortably sit. The oddity of seeing beings so large on branches so small amazed all the kids, but none more than Fong. Her scientific mind still had not wrapped itself around the concept of gravity having less effect on these huge nephilim than it had on other creatures.

Enosh, who was sitting next to Fong and interpreting her wondering gaze, asked, "You've studied elves and their nobility for some time now, haven't you, young one?"

"Yes, quite a bit!" she replied.

"And of those books you've read, which theory about the origin of elves do you like best?" he queried.

Fong thought for a moment and was unable to answer. She had read a few theories about elfin origins but had never fully embraced any one of them.

"I guess I don't have one," she finally said.

"Would you like to know from whence they came?" Enosh offered.

Fong's eyes widened. Oh, how she had sought such answers! "Yes, please!"

"Certain non-earthly beings married women of the earth and had children with them. The nephilim, or elves as you call them, are the children that these heavenly beings bore with the daughters of men."

Fong looked puzzled. "Non-earthly beings?"

"They go by many names," Enosh answered, "'cherubim,' 'messengers,' or most commonly, although it is a very misunderstood word, 'angels.'" Enosh shook his head and muttered, "Hmmm, angel, a most misunderstood word indeed! Anyway, the simplest explanation as to how these giants can climb so nimbly and glide so smoothly is because their fathers can fly. Angels are winged beings, hence nephilim are not nearly as ground-bound as you and I. They can't fly like their fathers can, but they are very agile. Also, since angels possess pure and flawless hearts, nephilim are purer than humans, for they are half-angels. Their purity keeps them lighter and less weighed down than humans. They are not laden with sins to the degree we are. So due to both their heritage and their hearts, gravity doesn't hold much weight over them."

Fong pondered the correlation of sin and gravity. That was a new and strange idea, but really, none of this seemed as strange to Fong as it would to most people. She had read so much unbelievable lore that this seemed more than reasonable. In fact, a wave of understanding washed over her. Enosh could almost see the proverbial light bulb click on over her head as she said, "So that's why they can live so long: their fathers are immortal!"

"Precisely," Enosh said. "Nephilim have no natural causes of death. They are immune to diseases and to biological deterioration. Fatal accidents and death at the hands of others are the only ways they can be killed."

Fong surveyed the village surrounding her. Nephilim balanced precariously on thin limbs. Nine-foot-tall, three-hundred-pound giants leapt from branch to branch. Young and old swung from vine to vine. Most of this took place three stories or more above the ground. If ever there were a time and place for fatal accidents, she thought, this was it! But none occurred. Fong marveled.

The party lasted for several hours and the guests of honor lost all track of time. After devouring a wide assortment of unusual foods, Braulio, Sean, Candice, and Fong were included in some odd games which the young nephilim played. They were also taught some songs, and thus some of the nephil language, though they still had no idea what they were saying. They were even included in a dance—a dance which thankfully did not involve swords. Keeping up with dancers that have legs longer, stronger and less affected by gravity than your own is a chore, and by the time the party had ended, the four kids were thoroughly exhausted.

Braulio, Sean, Candice and Fong were escorted back to their hallway, one guide hovering around Sean to prevent disaster on the swaying walkway. Once within sight of their doors the guides left them and said, "good night."

"This is so-o-o awesome!" Sean said. "We get to travel back in time to have a feast with a bunch of giants in a tree house village. How cool is that! Wait until I tell the guys! Hey, how many more days of partyin' do you think we'll get before we have to go back to school?"

"Sean, are you really that simplistic?" rebuffed Fong. "Do you actually think they brought us here just to throw a party? That whole event was for us and because of us. They were expecting us for some reason and they are all excited we are here. Clearly they are planning on our doing something for them; the question is what," she said, looking intently in the direction of the festival, as though she could see through the wall to where the nephilim leaders were in conversation.

"I knew it! I knew there was a catch!" said Braulio, pounding a fist into his palm. "What do these guys want from us? They couldn't want us for our size and strength. So if it isn't to fight an enemy, then what is it?"

"Maybe …" Candice said slowly, "they need a beautiful young girl to sacrifice," she murmured, looking dismayed. She turned on Fong. "How could you? You are the one who got me into this!"

"Me?! Candice, you argued with me until I finally let you come! And besides, what makes you think you are the one they would want to sacrifice? Do you think you are the only beautiful young girl here?" Fong fixed Candice with a steely glare, daring her to answer.

"Well, no," Candice lied, even though secretly, she didn't think there was any real competition between herself and Fong. Backpedaling, she said, "They probably want two sacrifices … they do everything big around here, you know."

Fong wasn't fooled. Her eyes bored a hole through Candice.

"Well, I think you are all making a big deal 'bout nothin'," Sean said, yawning wide. "An' dude, like, I need some major sleep before whatever cool thing we get to do tomorrow. See you babes in the morning." And stretching his long, skinny arms and yawning again, he turned and went to his room.

Watching him yawn, stretch and stagger toward his bedroom without a care in the world, Fong said, "Well, Sean is right about one thing at least—we need rest before whatever we do tomorrow. Come on, Candice, you'd better get your beauty sleep before you get sacrificed. Good night, Braulio. Just be glad you aren't as beautiful as Candice," she said bitterly as she disappeared into the girls' room.

"Fong, I didn't mean anything by it," Candice pleaded as she trailed after her into the room and shut the door.

Braulio stood alone in the knotty-walled hallway. He could still hear the girls bickering in their room as his thoughts drifted down the corridor toward the giants back at the festival. *What do they want with me?* he pondered. *If it's anything like Blondie said, it's better to find out now and fight than die in my sleep later.* Resolved, he walked back toward the festival area to find some answers, somehow.

Within minutes he was escorted back to the room by a pleasant but firm guard. "We require that all guests stay in their quarters during the late night hours," the guard explained.

Braulio tried to escape several more times—each time with the same result. And as the evening waned, each of the kids dropped off to sleep. Sean was out moments after hitting his bed. Lying flat on his back with a full belly and an empty mind, he digested his gigantic feast in peace.

Candice was next. After apologizing enough times to satisfy Fong, she lay down on her leaf-stuffed mattress. Moments later, the chief entered the room with a ring of guards and took her to the edge of the village. Drums were beating and there was wild chanting as the terrifying sacrificial rite began. A knife was pointed at her heart, ready to penetrate her soft flesh when a handsome nephil, overcome with love for her, rescued her and they lived happily ... ever ... yawn ... safe on her mattress, Candice fell asleep.

After her brain was too tired to figure out any more answers or even formulate any more questions, Fong fell dozed off as well.

Finally, after all was quiet in the village, all attempts at escape had failed and a guard was posted permanently at his door, the wary but weary Braulio lost the battle with his eyelids, dropped on his mattress and fell into a deep sleep.

Chapter 7

LESSONS IN A LUSH LAND

A deep voice startled Braulio from his sleep. Sitting up on his large, leaf-stuffed mattress, he briskly rubbed his eyes and tried to determine where he was. Surrounding him were high open ceilings, vine-covered rafters, and bizarre fruit in a bowl on an intricately carved table. Then it hit him; this was not a dream. He was in a strange bedroom high up in a treetop village full of giants, two bearded weirdos who called themselves element wielders, and an annoying roommate, who at the moment was sound asleep on his back with his mouth hanging open.

He heard the deep voice again. It was coming from the other side of the door. It was a familiar voice but he couldn't place it. And it was singing. Braulio slid over to the door, opened it, and found himself staring into the navel of the giant attendant, Azmarpin. Looking kindly down at Braulio, Azmarpin stopped singing.

"Good morning, young one. Your master Enosh has sent me to inform you that the first of your lessons is to begin shortly. He requests that you join him for breakfast on the eighth level patio of the palace. You are both expected to attend."

"My who wants me to do what where?" Braulio asked, half awake and confused.

Azmarpin repeated the message and, seeing Sean lying on his back, recommenced his hearty singing.

"Why are you singing?" asked Braulio in his grumpy morning voice.

"Song is one of the ways we prefer to begin our days. Beginning a day with harmony tends to keep the day harmonious," Azmarpin answered serenely before taking up the song again.

Within a few seconds the melody woke up Sean. After a wide yawn and a long stretch he said, "Dude, that party rocked! Can we have another one tonight?"

"No," said Azmarpin matter-of-factly, "You have other plans for today. Today is to be your first day of lessons and your professor will be expecting you. Prior to that engagement, your master, Enosh, has requested an audience with you over breakfast."

Sean rolled off his oversized, plump mattress at the sound of breakfast and had his super-flexible nephil garments on in moments. Braulio, not thrilled about the words 'your master' being lightly thrown around, grudgingly dressed and trailed Sean out the door.

In the hall, the boys met up with Candice and Fong. The girls had been awakened by Serflina in a similar fashion, and Fong had already bombarded the female nephil with an array of fresh questions before the boys met up with them. Azmarpin, rescuing Serflina from even more questions, led the four visitors through the winding, roofless corridor to an outdoor sitting area that boasted a majestic view of the village. It was situated up in some of the highest branches in the village on one of the upper decks of the chief's palace. The view was stunning. Seven levels of dwellings were below them. An endless expanse of colorful, lush forest canopy stretched out before them. Birds, butterflies, and enormous dragonflies soared in and around the tops of the gigantic trees. The four leaned on the rail, gazing in amazement until they heard a voice behind them.

"Marvelous creation, is it not? Almost too much for the eyes to take in," said Enosh, who was sitting at a table in a corner of the open-air patio. He gestured to the table, which was spread with a substantial breakfast. "These giants have a habit of preparing enormous amounts of food. There seems to be enough for five of us, don't you think?" he said with a twinkle in his radiant blue eyes.

The four joined him at the table and passed around baskets of colorful fruit and warm loaves of sweet bread.

"So, I imagine you'd all like to finally know why you are here and why here is so different from the place you call home. You are presently in the Early Earth period of Earth's history. 'Early Earth' refers to the time before the Great Flood. At this present moment in time, the earth has been around for 1,056 years, meaning you went back in time nearly 4,700 years. Naturally, that explains why—"

"Wait! Hold up," Braulio interrupted. "Did you say 1,056 years? The earth is five billion years old, dinosaurs died off millions of years ago and people have been around for about a million years. You guys don't even know about the Big Bang and evolution yet do you?" Braulio asserted with an arrogant sneer.

Before Enosh could reply, an enormous bird with a high, rounded crest and a menacing beak soared just inches over their heads and clumsily perched on the patio railing. Braulio and Candice both jumped. Fong immediately recognized the bird from books she had read.

"Wow! A real, live pteranodon!" she exclaimed.

The giant creature stretched out her bat-like wings. Each wing was twice the length of Sean's lanky body, and her beak was as long as his arms. Opening her beak wide, she screeched a loud and raspy *CRA-A-A-A-A-W!*

"Who-o-oah, dude!" hollered Sean. Candice screamed and crawled under the table. Fong looked fascinated and yearned to get closer to the menacing creature to get a better look. Braulio wished yet again for his knife.

Enosh addressed the bird. "I'm sorry, but you'll have to wait until we have finished. However, when we are done I'm sure we will have something left over for your young ones. In the meantime you are welcome to stay and listen," he said in a parental tone.

The pteranodon seemed to understand this and answered with a softer, more polite *crauw.* She flapped her wings once more, dug her talons into the railing, and sat quietly, keeping one watchful eye on the horizon and one on the food.

Fong leaned forward, thrilled. She wanted to talk to the bird too, but before she could speak, Enosh answered Braulio's question.

"Actually, some of us here are quite aware of the teachings of your day," the wise elder answered. "And like many other myths of how the earth and life came into being, I am familiar with the ones of which you speak. However, I am going to tell you some *facts* about the world in which you now sit. And I think you will find they are quite different from the things you have been taught."

Braulio folded his arms and leaned back in his chair. He would listen and humor the old man, but in Braulio's judgment, the guy was clearly cracked.

Enosh looked out across the vast expanse of beauty before them and said, "The Creator made all that you see. He did this in a very short period of time, and based on the written record he left us, it appears he completed his work 1,056 years ago. Now, the creation was marvelous and flawless when the Creator finished it. The first man and woman, our initial forefather and foremother, lived in a perfect world. Birds, sea creatures, land animals and humans all lived in harmony. An abundance of vegetation provided plenty of food for all. There were no carnivores, there was no sickness and there was no disease. There was hardly even anything in the world that could cause death! People and creatures were designed to live forever an indeed they would have … had things not changed."

Enosh paused. The young people sat in rapt attention. Sean leaned forward, mouth agape. Even the inveterate skeptic Braulio was captivated by a vision of a perfect world.

"But," Enosh said slowly, "because they chose to disobey the Creator, evil entered the world. This we call 'The Corruption'. Some people call it 'The Fall,' and it has had devastating effects on us all. The harmony in which all creatures lived was replaced with fear, savage survivalism and death."

Suddenly, the pteranodon swung her beak with lightning speed and impaled a plump lizard that had scampered too close to her. The four kids jumped. The huge bird flung the body up in the air and caught it head first in her beak as the lizard frantically thrashed its thick tail. Cocking her head back, she gulped it all down with three swift flicks of her beak. Looking again at the table, the winged carnivore stared at the meat in Candice's hand. Candice noticed the meat, which she thought was sausage, looked much the same size and shape as that lizard tail. Grimacing, and wondering what she might be eating, she set it down.

Enosh glanced over at the pteranodon—witnessing the last tragic seconds of the lizard's life. Then he looked down. His voice grew sad. It sounded thinner, older. "The Corruption has affected every creature and every part of the creation. Before that earth-altering event, the wilderness was free of poisons, diseases, thorns and all other things that harm. Creatures did not attack people or one another and people did not attack one another or creatures. Everything was so idyllic there was no need even for clothing."

Braulio snickered.

"You laugh because of your limited perspective, young man," Enosh said knowingly, "but in a perfect world there is no shame and there is no danger. There is no such thing as embarrassment, violence, hunger or want. Each being is free to live with the Creator and with the rest of creation in absolute harmony. In a perfect world, people are sin free, the wilderness is danger free and the weather is always ideal. There isn't even so much as a light rain—to say nothing of extreme temperatures and storms. Think about it: if there were nothing in the world that caused shame, harm, discomfort or pain, why would there be any need for clothing?"

Fong had to jump in. "I'm sorry, Enosh. Did you say 'no rain'? How would such vegetation exist?" She gestured to the towering trees.

"Ah yes, that is one of the things that thankfully has not changed since The Corruption. It is still the case that we have no rain here in Early Earth, nor do we have need for it," Enosh said, brightening. "Follow me," he instructed as he stood up and walked over to the railing. Everyone followed, but they each kept an eye on the pteranodon and stood on the side of Enosh that was furthest away from the penetrating stare of the bird.

"Take a look over the forest below and notice the mist," Enosh said.

They looked down from their lofty balcony at the vast expanse of forest and observed hundreds of tendrils of mist wafting up from the ground, twining about the trunks of trees and gently watering the lush vegetation. From their high vantage point the young people also spotted five beautiful bubbling streams. As it was still early morning, thick mist was rolling off the streams and dispersing into the dense, green forest.

"Water does not come from the sky in this day and age. It comes only from springs below the ground," Enosh explained. "But there is an abundance of water because there are countless springs bubbling up into streams all across the earth. With so many streams crisscrossing the landscape, mist rises every morning as the warmer air moves over the waters. The mist provides drink for all the wildlife that does not visit the streams, such as crawling insects that live up on high branches. Furthermore, the mist provides a daily washing for the plants and trees. Rain in your world does that on the occasional days it falls, but here, there is a predictable morning misting each and every day. It keeps things clean and green."

Braulio, Fong, Sean and Candice tried to imagine a world without rain. Braulio thought about all the times he could camp, hunt and ride his motorcycle without a worry about getting drenched. Fong had more thoughts than she could process at the moment whereas Sean had no thoughts at all on the matter. Candice only thought about how all that mist would make her hair too frizzy.

"In order for trees, plants and grasses to grow most places in your world, water must evaporate and then return to the ground as rain," Enosh explained. "In our world, there are springs, rivers and streams aplenty. Vegetation grows almost everywhere. And all leaves—even the highest ones—get a misting every morning as the sun rises and warms the rivers. Then the mist drops back to the earth and the cycle repeats itself the next day. Hence, almost every place on earth is well-watered every day."

"No rain ..." Fong mused for a moment. "So that's why there aren't many roofs here," she concluded.

Braulio sighed loudly. He didn't want the speech to go on any longer. He just wanted to finish eating and then figure out how to get the head of that vicious-looking bird mounted on his bedroom wall.

"Correct," said Enosh. "There are a few reasons, actually, why roofs and even hats are unnecessary here."

Candice thought about that for a moment. The missing roofs were obvious at a glance, but she just realized there wasn't a hat to be seen anywhere either.

"Roofs and hats are used in your day to shield people from harmful things that come from above; but such things are minimal here in Early Earth," Enosh continued. "For example, all sunrays are filtered through an atmosphere which is denser than the one you are used to. Therefore light gets through, but most destructive rays from the sun are kept out. No one here gets skin cancer—a malady I have heard is common in your day—and no one gets sunburned. I would say that our weather in general, with no hailstorms, blizzards, or even rain, although not perfect like it used to be, is still quite excellent," he concluded with a satisfied exhale.

No one standing there could disagree. Fresh, oxygen-rich breezes wafted past fragrant flowers and ambled over the balcony. Both the air quality and the temperature were most agreeable.

"Rarely do we have a day that is too cold or too hot," Enosh continued. "Our atmosphere is notably denser than that in your world. And the dense air does more than just shield the earth from ultraviolet sunrays which shorten life; it also keeps the world insulated and warm enough to support abundant life from pole to pole. Most places in Early Earth have a comfortable temperature year round and nearly any place you set your foot is land fit for a multitude of life forms. The lay of the land also plays a major role in the differences between your world and ours. There are no deserts, ice caps, inhospitably high mountains, or uninhabitable swamps. So thanks to both the lay of the land and the atmosphere which keeps the earth at a fairly constant, life-conducive temperature worldwide, creatures that you would consider "tropical" live comfortably almost everywhere here in Early Earth."

Photographs Fong had seen of dinosaur skeletons found in Siberia, Antarctica and other cold places flashed across her mind.

"By the way," Enosh noted, "since the air pressure around you is denser, the air you are breathing is concentrated. Hence you are getting more oxygen with each breath than you get back in your world."

"So I suppose you're saying it's the opposite of being on a mountain where the air is thin," said Braulio, who hadn't forgotten about his cigarette lighter and his singed eyebrow.

"Precisely. But back to those unnecessary roofs," Enosh resumed, "Perhaps you have noticed, or better said, *not* noticed those annoying insects such as mosquitoes, flies, and gnats. Think for a moment; has anything bitten or stung you since you arrived here?"

"No. Nothing," answered Fong.

"Dude, that's awesome!" Sean was mostly out of his depth in this conversation, but he could appreciate not being snacked on by bugs.

"With such an abundance of wildlife, biting insects are just a tiny part of a long and uninterrupted food chain," Enosh explained. "They have far more natural predators here than in your world; so we are seldom annoyed by them and we never suffer from insect plagues or giant swarms. Even when we do see them they are usually busy feasting on something other than human blood—for there is plenty of protein-rich food for them here. So that is another factor in the choice to forgo roofs: biting insects, flying creatures and wall-scaling reptiles rarely enter our roofless houses. It helps that we are on speaking terms with some of them, of course. And since we humans have dominion over all creatures, they normally do as we say and stay away."

"N-n-normally do what you say?" Candice gulped. "Meaning, sometimes they don't?" She looked nervously at the large-beaked pteranodon that was still eerily staring at them and evidently understanding every word.

"Well," Enosh began, "the cruder ones do not always respect our words, but even in those cases there is little need for them to enter our dwellings. After all, why would they want to come indoors? In your world, a creature would invade your territory to get food. But take a look around you." Enosh paused as he pointed his staff toward a fruit tree with branches overhanging the balcony. He blasted it with a gust of wind. Several yellow and orange fruits larger than cantaloupes thudded to the deck. Petals from fresh blossoms on the tree blew off and were scattered in the air. Hundreds of butterflies fluttered away and engulfed the five onlookers in a shower of color. The pteranodon casually snatched six or seven of the colorful insects out of the air. "Food is plentiful here," Enosh finished saying. "Rarely is there a hungry creature who has to seek very long for food. Nourishment grows, swims, and creeps everywhere. So, since no precipitation falls from the sky and since most winged creatures are either respectful toward us, afraid of us or just plain disinterested in our dwellings, harm seldom comes from above."

Braulio shot a glance at the hulking, carnivorous bird and remained unconvinced that no harm could come from such beasts.

"Privacy," Enosh continued, "particularly in a vertical village like this one, is the only reason to have a roof. Hence you will notice cloth coverings draped over some of the beams—particularly over beds and baths. But, all in all, when we are home we enjoy looking up, beholding the gorgeous sky and breathing in the freshest air."

They all sat back down and tried to finish the rest of their breakfast of giant proportions. Fong continued to ask a myriad of questions and the other three continued being distracted every time the pteranodon shifted positions or stretched her ominous wings.

As breakfast drew to a close Enosh said, "Well, that was an appropriate start to a day dedicated to education. It's time for you to go to your next instructor and for me to go to the Council of Wise Men and Noble Giants. The Council meets in a few minutes."

"What is the Council of Wise Men and Noble Giants? And may we go with you?" asked Fong, always eager to meet anyone who was wise.

"Ah, my young lady, you shall meet the Council in good time. But before that you have a class to attend."

"Oh, no," moaned Sean.

"Don't be so sure you won't enjoy it, lad. I have a feeling you have never been in a class quite like this one." Enosh's eyes twinkled with merriment. Sean still looked dubious.

Then Enosh reached into a hidden pocket in his robe and pulled out four vials, each about the size and shape of a test tube, and made of shiny metal. Enosh handed a red one to Braulio, a green one to Fong, a blue one to Candice and a white one to Sean.

"These are your thought vials; 'notebooks' I suppose you would call them, but much easier to use and far more private. A most useful resource to have when it comes to note-taking in classes," Enosh mused.

The students curiously turned the vials over in their fingers, stroking their smooth casings. "Your teacher will show you how to use them today in class. Pocket them and keep them always with you," instructed Enosh.

Then Enosh stood up and sent the leftover tray of meats (most of it Candice's portion) over to the pteranodon by a simple wave of his hand. The tray glided through the air and landed serenely on the floor, its contents undisturbed. The pteranodon croaked a 'thank you' to Enosh before she scooped up all the food, storing it for her young ones in the vast stretches of her beak. Then, with a powerful wing thrust that ruffled everyone's hair, she lifted off from the porch and soared toward her nest.

"How do you and Lawth do that, Mr. Enosh, dude? That is so cool!" Sean hollered.

"We call ourselves element wielders because we have become wise in the ways of the elements. To be a wielder, one must master at least one of the four elements. What you witnessed was a simple mastery of the air which lifted and moved the tray for me, just as if I were to move my body through the air to do the same thing," Enosh said as he strode toward a long rope walkway attached to one end of the lofty patio. The four followed him and wobbled their way down along the hanging sidewalk. In minutes they arrived at a thick vine cable that bore a resemblance to a zip line. Enosh continued, "An element wielder, or elder, as we are also called, is one who has learned how to wield either air, fire, earth, or water. And element wielding is not magic, or sorcery, as some mistakenly think it is. In your world, I believe you would call it 'science'. For element wielding is accumulated knowledge of an element which is gained only after much systematic study—study that takes hundreds of years. Later on, after a wielder becomes proficient in one element and studies for another hundred years or more, he may learn to master two elements. And some, although very few, study long enough, become wise enough, and live long enough to master three," he said.

"Has anyone ever mastered all four?" asked Fong.

"Very few have, and there is much controversy over that subject, my dear. For many people believe that such vast power is far more than any one individual should have. But it is best that we save that discussion for a later time," Enosh said. "Right now you must join your teacher who is waiting for you down on the forest floor. I will see you again in the afternoon when your lessons for the day are done."

And with that, he handed a vine to Braulio, instructed him to place his feet in the stirrups and lean forward when ready. Doing so, Braulio instantly shot down the "zip-vine," descending several levels and disappearing into the forest below.

"Ladies," said Enosh as he offered Fong and then Candice zip-vines of their own. Fong took hers with little reluctance, always eager for another opportunity to learn. Candice had noticed that their group had drawn the eyes of several handsome nephilim standing nearby. So, fearfully, but not to be outdone by Fong, she put on a brave face and quickly followed. Sean descended last, whooping and shrieking all the way down. He drew the stares of residents on each level of the tree village as he swished past.

Down below, the zip-vines came to a smooth stop at the forest floor just beyond the village. All four kids stepped out of their vines and instantly met an unpleasant sight: Lawth.

"You're all late!" he barked. "You need every minute of class time you can get if you children are ever going to learn enough to survive! We've only been allotted a certain amount of days for training, and trust me; you'll need every one of them. So from this day forward I expect punctuality from you juveniles. Is that clear?"

"You are our teacher?" Braulio was glowering at Lawth, his arms crossed.

Sean's thoughts, always wandering, mused that Lawth had made a pretty convincing secret agent, but he was an even better drill sergeant. "Dude, is this like the military or somethin' cuz if so, I think I'd rather go back to college," he said.

Lawth was already annoyed at their ignorance and the day had just begun. "No, thankfully I'm not your teacher," he continued in his usual growl. "I was able to ditch that awful task and pass you on to someone else. I'll introduce you to the *lucky* teacher here shortly. He might be able to keep you hapless babies alive so you can get back to your dear little college and out of my hair—if you don't end up killing him in the process. But there is much you must learn about the world before you can proceed. We live in a land filled with monstrous reptiles, bloodthirsty giants and evil beings who skillfully wield the elements in dark sorcery. There is no way you could survive a single night in this forest as ignorant as you are."

Candice began to cry. Fong ignored her and became more interested in inspecting an enormous beetle that was clumsily climbing over twigs on the ground. She bent down low and watched it closely. And Sean, already bored at the lecture, yawned wide, leaned casually back against a vine-engulfed tree and folded his hands over his stomach. Since Lawth was probably going to keep yelling at them for a while, he decided it was a good time to relax.

Braulio pulled out a cigarette. He subconsciously did that when he was afraid. He'd never admit it, but he was getting a bit unnerved by what he heard. Preoccupied with Lawth's ranting, he forgot what happened the last time he used his lighter and a tall flame shot up his nose.

"OW! OW! OW! Blasted stupid oxygen-rich air!" he yelled as he threw his lighter.

His shriek startled a curious lemur that had been clinging to the back of the tree Sean was leaning against. It had been cautiously watching the odd visitors from above Sean's shoulder. When Braulio yelled it screeched—right in Sean's ear—and scampered up the tree. Sean, startled, blindly fled forward as he looked back over his shoulder for the source of the noise.

"Hey! Watch it!" squawked Fong as Sean tripped over her and the two tumbled to the ground.

Meanwhile Braulio kept mumbling profanities as he rubbed his burned nose and inhaled several times in quick succession, trying to get the most out of his rapidly burning cigarette.

Unsure of even where even to begin in correcting all that was wrong with this lot, Lawth shook his head and said with a sigh, "Just follow me and try not to die on the way." And turning his back on them, he plunged into the thick forest.

As they left the village behind, the wildlife once again sprang up in profusion. Leaves like umbrellas shaded the path. Brilliant scarlet flowers shaped like bells swayed from vines above their heads. Animals roamed everywhere. Two armadillos the size of large sheep crashed through the underbrush as they rooted for grubs which were the size of sausage links. Chattering monkeys swung from limb to limb overhead, some of them curiously eyeing the travelers below. Braulio instinctively felt the empty sheath where his knife used to be and cursed the monkeys under his breath. A flock of enormous emerald butterflies fluttered over their heads. Many hovered about Candice, some landing on her shoulders.

"Look!" she exclaimed. "These adorable butterflies love me!"

"It's not you they love; it's the fragrant aroma you are wearing. You are like a giant moving flower," Lawth retorted.

Happy to hear this, Candice whipped out her perfume and sprayed herself again, congratulating herself on always having a small bottle in her purse, which she had kept with her throughout the journey to Early Earth.

"The honeybees are very large as well, as are their stingers. They are attracted to flowery scents too," Lawth said, quite satisfied with the look of horror on Candice's face.

They crossed a narrow stream and came upon a clearing. There they found a tall hut with a wide open door. It was evidently built by one of the nephilim but had a rustic look that was unlike the elaborately carved tree houses up in the village.

"This is your area of study for all classes related to forest, field, flora, and fauna," Lawth said. "Your instructor awaits you inside, I presume. Either that or he's lost in the forest with his head stuck in a tree. Let's find out."

"Hey, Thogwok! You in there?" Lawth hollered.

As the sound of Lawth's voice echoed in the clearing there came an enormous crash from inside the hut. Then a very deep voice let out an alarming yell. The kids all jumped at the loud noises, but the noises didn't stop. The crash and yell were immediately followed by the sound of something large rolling. Just then, a huge barrel bounded out from the doorway and was heading full bore toward the group.

Lawth and the kids all dove aside as the stout barrel tumbled by, barely missed them, and pummeled into a tree. But the kids were no longer concerned about the barrel, because what was following it was far more frightening. An enormous, bearded giant—twice the bulk of a man and weighing over four hundred pounds—came storming out the door, running directly toward them!

It happened in a matter of seconds. No sooner was the giant visible than he wobbled. Then he tripped. Then he badly stumbled forward. Spastically, he tried to catch himself but it only made matters worse. Yelling wildly, the giant fell face first to the ground—right on top of Sean!

Chapter 8

THOGWOK

Candice was screaming. She and the other kids all stared in horror at the ground where Sean had been standing—ground now covered by a fallen giant with no Sean to be seen.

"That thing just killed him!" Braulio yelled.

Candice continued screaming.

"Would you shut up already?" Lawth snapped at her. "The skinny kid is fine! I put an air block between the two of them as soon as I saw him going down. Now get up, ya big oaf!" Lawth ordered, turning his attention to the giant.

Grabbing fistfuls of earth, the fallen giant lifted himself off the ground, exposing Sean who, incredibly, was still three dimensional. Lawth had indeed cushioned the blow with a thin wedge of air that kept the giant suspended an inch above the boy, who nobody could see because he had been momentarily shrouded by the giant's loose outer garment.

The giant stood upright, staggered, and caught his balance. He was a hefty nephil who towered above them at eleven feet tall. He swayed a little as he attempted to lean forward, extend a hand and help Sean up. Losing his balance again, the giant leaned forward a bit too far. Missing Sean by mere inches this time, he pummeled his fist into the dirt to brace himself. He dropped to one knee and the ground shook. The impact of it would have snapped any of thin Sean's bones. Then the giant thrust his other arm straight at Sean, who scurried backwards in the dirt.

"Oh, sorry 'bout that! I do that sorta thing a lot, I do. Had a bout with a dark warrior sorcerer once and he did a blow to me head that took away a lot o' me sense of balance. That barrel there got away from me and I din't want it to run over yuz. Din't means ta scare yuz or nothin'. Oh, and greetings! Pleased to meet yuz! My name is Thogwok," he said in a booming voice.

Candice, Fong, Braulio and especially Sean, breathed a collective sigh of relief. Thogwok meant no harm. He was just a clumsy giant who was attempting to catch a runaway barrel and was now trying to help Sean get to his feet.

Sean tentatively reached out to him and Thogwok hoisted the gangly boy two feet off the ground and in an upright position with a single flick of the wrist.

Then Thogwok stood up—sort of—and he offered his right hand to shake each of theirs. Sean, Fong, Candice and Braulio each in turn took his enormous hand and got a full body shaking from it.

"Hope I did that right. No offense meant if'n I din't. We nephilim greet a bit diff'rint, yuz know."

Thogwok's handshake was far from correct but no one was about to tell him so and risk enduring several rounds of experiments.

"Well hullo there, Lawth," Thogwok said, turning to the perturbed elder who was standing, hands on his hips, safely behind a tree. "Looks like we got a good class righ' 'ere. I can already see they're gonna be some fine students, they are."

"Ri-i-i-ight," said Lawth with a tone that meant he believed nothing of the sort. "I'm sure they will increase their already vast vats of knowledge under your insightful instruction."

Fong frowned, bristling at the sarcasm thick in the ornery element wielder's voice.

Lawth stared back at her coolly and curtly said to Thogwok, "Be sure to have them back to the ladders before dark—assuming they're still alive." And without as much as a 'goodbye,' Lawth turned and strode back to the village, his robes briskly flapping behind him.

"Will do!" said Thogwok clumsily waving goodbye. He swayed backwards and forwards and eventually stabilized. Looking at the four worried expressions, he tried, unsuccessfully, to alleviate their anxiety.

"Aw, yuz kids don' 'ave to worry abou' him. Lawth is just like that. He means well and all, he jus' don' know how to show it. But stick close to me an' I'll make sure yer treated well. Come on, follow me into me hut."

Thogwok didn't realize that Lawth wasn't their main concern. "Sticking close" to Thogwok, however, had just become a serious concern for every last one of them.

Thogwok took hold of the runaway barrel, which had come to rest at the foot of a tree. Then he bobbed and wobbled toward his front door, the barrel in his arms, almost toppling over twice before he successfully ducked inside. The four followed at a distance and warily stepped in after him.

The hut was disheveled but homey, and the pleasant aroma of something sweet filled the air.

"I made yuz some of the Cerebrum Serum we'ze like to drink around here," Thogwok said, casually tossing the rotund barrel across the room and into a corner with several others. "Helps a person think. Figured it'd be good to swig some before we get started. The stuff don' taste very good by itself so I mixed a little boysenberry juice and honey inter it."

He served up four large mugs with the steamy golden serum—spilling a large portion as he sloppily poured.

"Come grab yerselves a mug and have a seat out the back door there. I know yuz are used ta studying inside in yer day and time, but inside just isn't me style," he said.

"Sweet! Mr. Thogwok, you are the rockiness teacher, ever!" Sean said. "I wish all my teachers let us have class outside. That is too cool!"

"Oh, uh, well if yuz are too cool I gots plenty o' furry skins hangin' right here on me wall." Thogwok said, looking a bit concerned. "I don't wear 'em much seein' as the weather is almost always good. Then again," Thogwok observed, squinting one eye as he looked down at Sean, "you are mighty skinny there, young-un." And he plunked an enormous fur from some unidentifiable creature on top of him. Sean nearly collapsed under the force with which Thogwok dropped the heavy pelt.

"Oh, an' I made yuz some chains, too, just the way ya like 'em!" Thogwok said excitedly. "Come out and take a look at 'em."

As Thogwok turned his back to walk outside, the four kids shot quick glances at each other.

"He made us chains! Why?" Candice mouthed silently to Fong.

Fong could only shrug her shoulders. She had no idea why Thogwok would make them chains, how he would know the way they liked their chains, or why he would even think they liked them at all. Chains were things most people tried to avoid.

Concerned, but mostly curious, the four grabbed their large mugs and traipsed out Thogwok's back door. As soon as they did they came upon four high desks. They were roughly hewn from a rich-looking wood, and they were accompanied by four chairs. They weren't a whole lot to look at, but when it became clear from the look of satisfaction on Thogwok's face that they were made by hand, by him, and specifically for them, Candice and Fong thanked him enthusiastically. Candice elbowed Braulio, who glared at her but thanked Thogwok halfheartedly.

"Aw, yuz is all very welcome. Wouldn't want yuz uncomfortable the whole time we're doin' lesions," Thogwok said warmly.

"Did you say while we're doing lesions?" Fong asked with some concern.

"That's right," said Thogwok.

"But lesions are localized areas of diseased or injured body tissue. Do you mean lessons?" Fong, whose studies had delved into the medical field, asked.

"Oh, right. I mean lessons, o' course. Sometimes me mouth gets the wrong word and me brain misses it. 'T'all goes back to that injury I was talkin' 'bout," Thogwok said.

Fong was beginning to see that this teacher was going to be like none she had ever had before.

"Anyways, back to those chains," Thogwok resumed. "I know what those vine chains can be like. They're not the best sittin' arrangement for me either," he said as he staggered toward a heavily reinforced vine chair hanging from a high branch.

Fong, Braulio, and Candice all then realized that Thogwok was referring to chairs, not chains, and they all felt quite a bit better. Sean didn't make the connection but soon his mind wandered to something else anyway and he forgot all about the chains.

Thogwok let himself sink into the specially designed chair. Unlike the other vine chairs in the village, this one was reinforced with a back. It looked like a vertical hammock, and it seemed impossible for anyone—even for Thogwok—to fall out of it. The giant motioned for the four to take their own chairs and they did so, Fong eagerly leading the way. She was always in the mood for another class, even if it was literally a backwoods one.

Hoisting herself into the high wooden chair Thogwok had made for her, Fong unconsciously reached for her book bag to begin her class ritual: arranging her binder, notebook and pencils on her desk. Of course, she didn't have her bag; it was in her room way up in the chief's palace. *Drat! How could I have come to class unprepared?* She chastised herself for the oversight and looked around for some sort of quill and parchment but found nothing. She was about to point this out when Thogwok began to teach.

"Well, seein' as I'm yer teacher for lessons of the forest, and seein' as this is our first day of class, I'd like to get to know yuz a little before we begin. I'm supposin' yuz might wan' ta ask some questions 'bout me, too. That's on'y normal. Yuz are in a strange place after all, 'specially compared to where yuz come from," he said with a thoughtful look in his eyes, "So, gots any questions for me? Ask away!"

Candice spoke up. "Do you have a wife and kids?"

"Ay, I do, er ... did. Wife died sev'ral years back. Three of me kids died too, they did," he said quietly.

"Oh, I'm so sorry," said Candice, stricken. Fong likewise tried to offer condolences.

"Thank yuz both," he said with two large tears welling up in his eyes. He heaved a sigh and raised his head with a look of pride. "It was fer a noble cause they died—fighting the Dragon Master and his wicked host during the Fire War. We won, o' course, but not without a price—a terrible one. Tragic thing, war is ..." Thogwok trailed off, his mind clearly in a dark part of his past.

The kids felt adrift. None of them could relate to what Thogwok had just said. Losing one child would be terrible enough, but three—plus your spouse—all in one war! Fong and Candice looked distressed, Sean was bewildered, and even Braulio had lost his aloof expression and felt completely at a loss.

"But the other thirteen are doin' quite fine!" Thogwok said abruptly, his customary gleam back in his warm eyes.

"Thirteen!" "You have thirteen kids?" Candice exclaimed.

"Sixteen. 'Member that three have passed on. Eleven of me livin' kids are all grown and are off doin' quite well. The two youngest 'uns are still just boys. They live up in the village with some relatives. Charwok and Shivlok are their names. I miss them boys, I do," Thogwok said, shaking his head slowly.

"Why don't your boys, like, live with you?" Candice asked.

"They visit me a lot they do," Thogwok continued, but did not answer Candice this time. "Wouldin' mind havin' me a few more kids either, considerin' I prob'ly got a few hundred years ahead o' me yet. 'Course, I gotta find me a wife who would'n mind me condition and the place where I have to live," Thogwok said as he swigged down a gulp of his sweetened cerebrum serum.

All but Candice followed Thogwok's lead and took a drink. She merely glanced down at the yellow goop in her mug and turned her attention back to Thogwok.

"So, do a lot of other giants live down here away from the village?" she asked.

"Nope. I'm the only one who's not a tree-dweller," he said. "Reason bein' the blow to me head I received durin' the war. Did somethin' ta me balance. I can't walk straight, as ya mighta noticed."

"No-o-o-o. Really?" Braulio muttered under his breath.

Fong elbowed him.

"So leapin' from limb to limb like I used to just isn't possible no more," he said, sad but resigned, and took another big swallow.

Sean also took a big gulp of his cerebrum serum, very much liking the sensation it was giving his brain. Mental stimulation of such magnitude was unusual for him.

"Almost died in that battle, I did. But they gave me some strong potion that recovered me, for the most part. But I never could walk straight since." Thogwok tipped his mug up high, draining its contents.

Then he set it on the ground, almost teetering off the edge of his hammock chair as he leaned down. "But all the rest o' me is perfectly normal: a regular, good ol' forest-lovin' nephil. I just gotta love the forest from down here on the ground, is all."

Thogwok righted himself in his chair and looked up in the direction of the village. His face was stern and solemn. "And it don't matter what any o' them up there say 'bout me. I know that blow to me head din't affect no other part of me brain. Some 'o them up there in the village don' understand me no more—think I'm somethin' odd because I live down here alone…like I'm not rightly fit to be a warrior no more …" his voice trailed and he lowered his head. "… or rightly fit to be a father," he finished quietly. Then lifting up his head, he resumed in his booming voice, "But I'm just as much nephil as the rest of 'em!" he said loudly, as if daring anyone to contradict him.

Thogwok was most certainly a nephil. At eleven feet tall there was no denying it. But his earthy, garrulous personality was miles apart from any of the stoic giants up in the village. The four kids each privately had their doubts about the head blow's effect on other parts of Thogwok's brain. But they weren't about to argue with him.

"So now," Thogwok said with an introductory 'class begins' tone, "Master Enosh has given yuz some thought vials, 'as he?"

"Yes, sir," said Fong, excitedly pulling hers from her pocket. "He said they were like spiral notebooks only better."

"*Spy rull no t'books*?" Thogwok asked inquisitively. "What are those?"

"You know, like three-ring binders," Fong said.

"Well I don' know 'bout *ring by enders* either, but whatever they are it sounds like yuz need three of 'em to do the job of one thought vial. Those little things work pretty good just by 'emselves I tell yuz," Thogwok said, pointing at Fong's vial.

Fong figured it was pointless to try correcting Thogwok's understanding of binders, and she was dying to know about the thought vials. "Well anyway, tell me how you use them," she said.

Like this," Thogwok instructed. And he fumbled with a clasp on one of his pockets and pulled out his own. Dirt flecked and slightly tarnished, the little thought vial rolled around in Thogwok's massive hand.

"These yuz'll find mighty useful, no doubt," Thogwok said as he flicked open the cap. Immediately a stream of air poured shimmering out of the vial. It expanded before their eyes into a screen of gray mist about two feet square that hung in the air.

"These thought vials contain air screens," Thogwok said. "They're used fer recordin' stuff you want tuh remember." Clearing his throat, Thogwok addressed the square patch of air, "Voice: roll call for day one of class," and immediately his words were scrawled on the screen.

"Who-o-ooh," uttered Sean, as Thogwok's command magically popped onto the screen in the air.

"So much for keeping anything to yourself around here," said Braulio cynically.

"It only gets recorded if'n yuz tell it to record it. Yuz gotta say 'voice' first. These clever things also record writin'. Come here and sign yer names," and taking his finger, he marked "1,2,3,4" below the words "roll call."

Braulio stepped forward and signed his name on the air screen with his finger. The rest followed suit. Thogwok then poked the bottom of the screen and it collapsed and was replaced by a fresh piece of square air.

"Ready to try it fer yerselves are yuz? Open yer vials. Jus' give 'em a flick with yer fingers," Thogwok instructed with an over exaggerated hand motion that nearly made him topple out of his chair.

The four flipped out their air screens with varying measures of success. Candice flicked her screen on top of Fong's. Sean flicked his so hard that it landed on Thogwok's chest where it rippled weirdly with the giant's sporadic movements. But soon, after a little practice, they each had an air screen hovering serenely in front of them. As the kids began writing and speaking things onto their air screens, Braulio was the first to discover you could put things onto someone else's screen. He took advantage of this by dropping a flirtatious comment on Candice's. She responded on his with a cold rebuke.

"These are amazing," said Fong as she folded down screen after screen and flipped out more, labeling each one a different category and filing it away. She had quickly devised an organized system for filing her air screens. "Is there any limit to how much these can hold?!" Her eyes were glowing with excitement.

"Not that I know of," said Thogwok. "Air is pretty lightweight stuff, yuz know. Plus, them air wielders like Master Enosh know how to manipulate the air in ways I can't understand. It was a wielder like him that invented the thing."

"Anyways," Thogwok continued, "now that yuz know how to use 'em we'ze got to personalize and protect 'em so that no one can get intuh yer air screens but yuz alone. So then, repeat after me, and take care to speak only to yer own screens and no one else's when yuz say this." And clearing his throat he said, "Initial voice recognition."

They all repeated the words at their own screens. Then Thogwok said in a very low whisper, "Now each of yuz say yer full names, but quiet-like."

The students whispered to their vials in turn.

"Braulio Santos."

"Fong Chow."

"Candice Singletary."

"Sean Zondervan."

Again in a whisper Thogwok said, "Now say a code word; it is okay if all of us hears it. It has just gotta be somethin' an enemy would'n be able to guess."

Fong piped up first and whispered, "Organic chemistry."

Braulio spoke next. "Beer."

Candice thought for a minute and whispered, "Azmarpin," deciding he was the cutest of all the nephilim she had seen so far.

Sean's mind had already drifted someplace else. When he finally realized they were all staring at him, he quickly said, "Oh, uh, chocolate Pop-Tarts, I guess".

"Good," Thogwok said. "Nobody will guess that. Yuz all now have yer names and secret passwords encoded on yer thought vials, which means even if they fall intuh the wrong hands, yer thoughts are preserved. Someone would have to know yer full name and yer password to get in there."

"I don't think we need to worry about Chocolate Pop-Tart Man's thoughts getting stolen. He'd actually have to have some thoughts first," Braulio gibed scornfully.

Sean's response, "shud up dorc," popped up on Braulio's screen.

Ignoring it, Braulio asked Thogwok, "So who are these enemies you keep talking about?"

Candice's eyes grew wide. She hadn't forgotten Lawth's dire predictions for their lifespan in the forest and the mention of enemies was hardly reassuring.

"Ay, their numbers grow as the world grows more evil. As I mentioned b'fore, there are the dark ones who followed the Dragon Master and fought us during the Fire War. We defeated them, we did. Now o' course we have a new threat. And he seeks to control not only the Fire, but all the elements. His name is Sihsnue Maboa. He's outright evil he is, and his followers keep swellin' in numbers."

"So what is this 'sinews and bones' guy trying to do," asked Braulio.

"Sihsnue Maboa is the name and, like I told yuz, he's tryin' to control all the elements. I know that don't mean much to yuz at this point, seein' as you haven't gone to the Council meetin' yet ...," Thogwok paused and said, "And really that's all I'm supposed to speak—but let's just say yuz four play an important role in winnin' a battle for us."

Fong had been taking notes on Sihsnue Maboa but that bit about the battle brought her up sharp. She frowned and glanced at Candice, who still looked tense, and Sean, whose usual vague expression had been replaced with concern. Apparently the cerebrum serum had at least woken up his instincts for self-preservation.

"So that's what all the hype was about at the feast last night," said Braulio, his eyes gone hard. "You guys want us to go up against a giant who's bigger and tougher than you, don't you? You're trying to trick us into fighting a battle for you—a battle you're afraid to fight!" He accusingly jabbed his finger at the giant before he thought through the stupidity of such a move.

Thogwok's kind eyes closed into a squint and he fixed the boy with a steely glare. His large chiseled head bent forward and he slowly and ominously stood up, staring at Braulio. "Are you accusing the ancient and most noble race of the nephilim with the charge of being disingenuous with our words?

"Uh ..." stammered Braulio.

Thogwok was booming now. "Are you suggesting that the ancient and most noble race of the nephilim is crafty in its intentions?"

"Well no, not at all, I just meant—" said Braulio, who was thinking fast about what other way his words could hopefully be taken.

Thogwok, now at a fevered pitch, stood tall, wobbled, and leaned in close to Braulio, thundering, "Are you alleging, that the ancient and most noble race of the nephilim would set out to misrepresent the facts, cower from fear in the face of battle and harm innocent children?!"

"NO, NO, I'm not! I'm not!" Braulio yelled back, his eyes wide in terror.

Thogwok drew back, caught himself from falling, and sat back down. Satisfied with Braulio's answer, Thogwok's face brightened, like the sun coming out from behind a cloud, and he regained composure.

"It's fine really. I want to fight this Maboa guy," Braulio said with hands lifted in surrender. He struggled to keep his voice from trembling. "So, um, where do we enlist?"

"Ay, that's what this class is all about, ma' lad," said Thogwok, so quickly back to his normal self. "We, the noble race of the nephilim, along with a few of the finest element wielders are going to teach yuz some things. Elemental essences are hard things to get to, but them that are part of the Council will give yuz some clues 'bout how to find one. An' my job is to teach yuz the ways of the forest and how to survive in it."

"Find a what?" Braulio and Fong both asked.

Thogwok sighed and hesitated before he said, "Well see, it's really the Council who's supposed to tell yuz this—the forest has ears they says, but it's not just anyone who can get to those essences. In fact, almost no one can get their hands on an elemental essence. Oh sure, any nephil can go against a dark warrior in battle an' even win, but only the Chosen One can locate an elemental essence and connect it to their georb. An' see, ev'ry hundred years we needs a new Chosen One to connect their georb to the elemental essence. On'y that one person in the whole world can do it durin' that hundred year cycle, yuz seez." Thogwok awkwardly turned in his large hammock contraption to scan the surrounding forest for intruders. Turning back, he said with a sweet smile of satisfaction, "And that's the role yuz are to play in defeating Maboa and his forces. Apparently, one, and on'y one of yuz four is the Chosen One!"

His statement was met by stunned silence. Then …

"Ohmyword, WHAT?!"

"The Chosen One? One of *us*! Are you kidding me?"

"How do you know it's one of us? Which one of us? Chosen to do what, exactly? What …"

Thogwok waved his hands, interrupting Fong's barrage of questions. Candice looked afraid, Braulio was incredulous and Sean's mouth was hanging open … as usual.

"Now hold on!" Thogwok was waving so vigorously his vine chair began swinging wildly. "I shouldn'a even said that much! An' I sure can't say anymore 'bout it right now, so yer questions will have to wait. But I will say this," he paused and looked behind him again to make sure no one was listening, "Whichever of yuz it is, we'ze sure are excited fer the Chosen One to finally be here at last!"

Thogwok reached for his mug and lifted it up to toast them. The four followed his lead but with little enthusiasm. But when Thogwok noticed he had already drained his mug he said, "Ar, would ya looka that! I've talked so much I already needs me a refill." Realizing how much time had elapsed and how much he still needed to teach, he said, "Right then! We'll get to lesson one, which is Introduction to the Forest. Best if we start with a tour of the immediate area. It's a good long walk for those little legs so why don't yuz come inside and fill up a traveling skin full of serum b'fore we go. I'll get the weapons and anti-venom." Wrestling himself out of his seat he staggered back inside his hut.

"Weapons," repeated Braulio under his breath with longing in his voice as he and the others followed Thogwok inside.

"Anti-venom," repeated Sean. "Co-o-o-l." This reminded him of how warm he was getting with that big furry something draped over him. He was hoping he could take it off without offending the giant.

After they were inside and out of sight, a dark man cloaked in camouflaged robes stepped out from behind a thick tree. He had a piece of parchment in his hand and a hearing enhancement cone hooked around his ear. He scrawled down the last information he had learned.

Right after "Oh, uh, chocolate pop tarts, I guess," he wrote, "Apparently one of you four is the Chosen One," and rolled up the parchment. He then slipped it into a thin metal tube and corked it.

"Come down here, Loswossip," the spy whispered curtly.

Descending from an overhead branch, a vulture about the size of a large goat landed next to the cloaked man. The buzzard had graying black feathers and several patches of exposed, sickly-looking skin. Its face was weathered, its eyes dark and intelligent.

The man tied the little tube to one of the bird's ugly, rubbery legs.

"You know who this goes to," he said.

Under his breath Loswossip answered with an eerie *Cra-a-uw.*

The giant buzzard silently flapped his ragged wings, rose through the towering trees and quickly flew off toward his master: Sihsnue Maboa.

Chapter 9

THE MASTER OF DECEIT

The ugly, disease-ridden vulture flew with the metal vial tied to his leg for nearly two hours before the ground below him drastically changed. The innumerable acres of lush forest abruptly ended; and was replaced by a treeless, barren waste. In the middle of the deserted landscape was a small mountain, its gray bleakness glaring in this vibrantly green world.

Loswossip descended to the foot of the mountain through a series of jagged rock outcroppings bursting forth from the ground. Ending his long flight, he perched on a twisted branch of a gnarly, rotting tree.

Cra-a-aw, cra-a-a-aw! he bellowed, waiting for an answer.

A voice came from behind one of the jagged rocks. "You alone?" the voice asked.

The bird croaked again and a man emerged. He was robed in black. There was a knife in his hand and a smirk on his face. Briskly he approached the buzzard and severed the cord tied around his leg. The vial dropped into his hand.

"I'll make sure he gets it," the man in black said in a sinister voice. Turning to walk away he added, "We had an overpopulation problem in the dungeon a few days ago. To solve it, we relocated the least useful prisoners to the other side of the mountain. You might want to see how they're doing." And he vanished behind the jagged rocks.

Knowing what this meant, Loswossip took off from the decaying tree and flapped over to the other side of the mountain. He could smell the former prisoners from far away, and he followed the stench to a mound of dead bodies—all that remained of the excess inmates—and he gorged himself on their flesh.

Hidden from sight behind the sharp rock protrusions, the man in black slid his knife into a rock crevice and wiggled the blade. A gritty sound of stone grinding against stone echoed in the narrow spaces around him and a dark opening appeared. Inside, a narrow stairway hewn from the rock bored its way deep into the mountain. The man in black stepped in, lit a torch, stabbed his knife into a slit in the wall, and the door slid shut behind him.

Descending the dark and uneven stairs, the man arrived at a winding corridor that delved deep into the heart of the mountain. It was almost pitch black, punctuated here and there by an occasional torch bracketed to the wall. There were no sounds but his footsteps and the occasional groan or yell from a prisoner echoing from deeper within. The corridor was deserted at the moment, as he had hoped it would be.

Moving smoothly along the uneven, winding corridor, the man stopped at an iron door and stabbed his blade into the large keyhole. Being a master of the blade and a skilled thief, it took him but a few seconds to negotiate the lock and pop open the bolted door.

Stepping in and quickly shutting the door behind him, he immediately scanned the room for occupants. He had entered a small library, complete with parchments, scrolls, thought vials and writing tablets. Seeing no one else there, he ripped off a piece of blank parchment from a nearby scroll, grabbed a quill, and began to inscribe something. Then a shrill voice from behind jarred him.

"You got orders to be in 'ere, Sabtah?"

The man in black spun around like lightning and had his knifepoint tickling the shrill speaker's throat before another word could exit. Sabtah's eyes adjusted just fast enough to keep up with the speed of his blade and he recognized the face that was attached to the neck he was about to puncture. It was the dungeon curmudgeon Snodflin, a guard past his better days who thought he was much larger and stronger than he actually was.

Sabtah hissed at the man, "And if I do or don't have orders what business is it of yours, you two-bit, sorry excuse for a guard?" Pulling away his knife and sheathing it, Sabtah sneered derisively at Snodflin and spun around to resume his writing.

"You talk tough, do ya?" the withered Snodflin said with the weak voice of someone who needed to drink a skin or two of water. "Well, what you think about me reportin' ya, huh? I report daily to Maboa. I tells him ev'rythin' I sees. What do ya think o' that?"

Whipping around again, irritation radiating from his narrowed eyes, Sabtah said, "With one move of my hand you would be reporting to the vultures along with the other former residents of this dungeon. And if you must know, I myself am reporting to Maboa this very hour. I have information to deliver and I'm writing a note explaining how I got it." He held up the metal tube he had just retrieved from Loswossip.

"Is that good enough for you and your security measures, you withered waste of time?" Sabtah growled as he shoved the tiny tube at the old man's face.

Snodflin stepped back. The metal tube would have gone up his nose had he not. Still trying to be the big man in charge, he retorted, "I'll be tellin' Maboa 'bout this no matter what you says. You'd better hope for yer sakes that yer story matches mine—'cause he listens to me, he does. Maboa listens to me, I tell ya!"

Sabtah rolled his eyes and turned back to his work rather than waste another breath.

"So," Snodflin asked, his tone suddenly ingratiating, "You got news, eh? What's in the vi—?"

"The information I have for Maboa is confidential," Sabtah interrupted, his patience grown immeasurably small. "So if you could find some other room to "guard" right now, I won't have to inform Maboa that you possess confidential information—information that can't leave this dungeon under penalty of death."

Snodflin glared but took the hint and promptly exited. Sabtah kicked the door shut behind him, bolted it. "Fool!" he whispered hatefully under his breath as he resumed his work.

Several minutes later, Sabtah emerged from the dark library and made his way further down the steadily descending corridor. The narrow walkway opened into an echoing, cavernous room, and the sound of babbling water from a stream bounced off the walls, fracturing and magnified in the subterranean vault.

A short distance into the dark cavern, Sabtah approached a bridge lit by a single guttering torch. A gaunt young guard shuffled nervously, blocking access to the bridge; the one access point for crossing over the rushing stream.

"State your business," he said, holding his ground. He was attempting to sound strong.

"My business is in this message tube. Maboa has sent for information and it's mine to deliver. Step aside."

The guard hesitated, unsure. With lightning speed Sabtah spun the guard around, grabbed a pressure point on his skinny neck and rested the knifepoint in the middle of his back. The guard was at his mercy. Sabtah rasped menacingly in his ear, "What's your name, young guard?"

"M-M-Maswin," he said, barely audible over the echoing stream.

"Well, M-M-Maswin," Sabtah mocked, "Let's do a little soul searching. Deep down I bet you'd rather freely let me step over this bridge while you are alive, rather than letting me step over your dead body. Am I right?"

The knife point slightly punctured his skin, drawing blood, and Maswin's eyes rolled in terror.

"Y-y-yes, sir," he stuttered.

Sabtah pinched the pressure point harder. The guard blacked out. Releasing him to crumple on the bridge, Sabtah regained his stride.

"Maboa will send someone to punish you. I'll see to that personally," Sabtah said coolly as he continued across the bridge, passed through the cavernous room, and strode into another corridor.

Unlike the last corridor, this one was wide and well-lit. Torches hung on both walls and the stone floor was smooth and even. Two guards ordered him to halt and justify his presence.

Sabtah ducked his head and wrung his hands. He loved the opportunity to indulge in a little acting. "I'm here to deliver a message for Lord Maboa," he said, his voice convincingly fearful and desperate.

"No one gets through to Lord Maboa unless Maboa orders us to let him through! All messages go through us," bellowed the larger of the two guards.

Sabtah, continuing with the ruse, heaved a great sigh of relief. "Really? I thought I had to deliver it myself. Well, in that case, here. Take it!" And he shoved the parchment-carrying tube into the hands of the smaller guard.

The small guard looked concerned as he tentatively held the vial at arm's length, asking, "What's this got in it?"

"Bad news. The enemy found out some stuff about us. Can't repeat it—but it's a big setback for Lord Maboa. He's gonna be irate," Sabtah said in very depressed tone.

The smaller guard eyed the vial nervously. Sabtah could tell his plan was working.

"I really appreciate you doing this for me," he continued, sounding very relieved. "I'll make sure I'm long gone when you give it to him. Just tell him my name is Magadai, even though it isn't. That way I can stay out of it."

Sabtah looked again at the little metal tube now in the guard's hand, dread plain on his face. "Of course, once he reads what's inside, anyone inside this mountain is going be in his line of fire."

"Why? What's it say?!" demanded the smaller and stupider of the guards.

"I already told you I can't tell you. Just be glad you aren't the one who sent it! Delivering it to him will be bad enough!" Sabtah said, adding a slight tremble to his voice.

"I ain't takin' this—you take it," the more gullible one said, shoving it into the larger guard's hand.

"It's no big deal, Marfol," said the larger guard. "You think this is the first bad news Lord Maboa has ever heard? Just take it to him," he said, pushing the tube back to Marfol.

"If it's no big deal, then you take it to him. I'm not gonna be in the room when he hears it, whatever it is," Marfol said resolutely, stepping back and crossing his arms.

"That's just it," Sabtah interjected before the big guard had a chance to say something that might sway the dumber one. "You know how he gets when he's mad. He focuses all his hatred on whoever is in his path. You who work so close to him know that better than anyone. Glad it's your job and not mine." Sabtah was convincing. He started to back away from them, every inch the shrinking, gutless messenger.

The two guards looked at each other, the big one still holding the vial.

Sabtah sensed the timing was right for wrapping it up. "So, remember I told you my name is Magadai—and that, following orders, you refused to let me go any further. That should keep you out of trouble—at least until he reads the news in that vial." He turned to go, but stopped suddenly to add, "Also, be sure to wait at least an hour before you give it to him. That'll give me time to—"

"Wait an hour! If this news is so serious, it can't wait no hour!" roared the large, loyal guard indignantly.

"Well then … let's just say I have given it to you …" He paused and gave them a conspiratorial wink. "… an hour from now, which will give me just enough time to be in the clear. I'll leave right now. Thanks again! You saved my life!" Sabtah said hastily as he turned and rapidly began walking away.

"I don't think so, you lyin' scum!" said the big guard, lunging after him and taking Sabtah by the collar. "I wasn't born yesterday, ya know!"

Sabtah slid his hand into his cloak. Stealthily gripping his knife, he was ready to slice both guards like butter if necessary. He preferred to reach his goals more subtly when he could—by conniving rather than by knifing. It was a game for him to see how many people he could deceive in a single day. Yet when knifing was needed, Sabtah had no qualms about hacking his adversaries to bits. But in this case it appeared unnecessary; Sabtah had won his little game handily, for the big guard proved to be far dumber than he looked.

"I don't go 'round lyin' to me lord," the big guard said. "An' if you're fool enough to lie to his face, then you take that thing to him!" Stuffing the supposedly toxic tube back into Sabtah's hand, he barked, "I ain't got nothin' to do with any of that news, whatever it is!"

Sabtah looked down at the small vial in his hand—which was once again right where he wanted it. And he had just been ordered to do exactly what he wanted to do. Artfully cloaking his true thoughts, Sabtah looked crestfallen.

"Go on now!" the big guard roared. And he shoved Sabtah toward a long entryway to the underground throne room.

Sabtah reached the end of the corridor which turned sharply and suddenly stopped at a cold, iron door in a small antechamber. Bored into the door was a tiny hole. Sabtah spoke into the hole.

"Master, it is I, Sabtah, your servant, with important news," he said.

There was a long, unnerving pause. There was no verbal acknowledgement of Sabtah's arrival. Instead, there was heavy breathing, a scratching, a pulling at a chain: the restless sounds of some restrained beast. Fierce sniffing ensued and then the chain rattled feverishly. Whatever is was, the smell of Sabtah was driving it mad. The creature's ravenous hunger seemed to spill through the hole. The tension in the air was thick enough to be tasted.

Finally, a shuffling of feet or paws—he couldn't tell which—grew steadily louder behind the door. A low, gurgling growl oozed through the door. The growl was followed by a sudden, heart-stopping shriek. It was high-pitched and devilish.

Sabtah dropped his right hand on to his knife handle more out of habit than fear. He wasn't afraid of such creatures. He was a master butcher with a blade in his hand. He listened closely. Underneath the shrill shrieking and savage growling he heard a soothing, melodious voice.

"Relax my dear one; it is someone we know. I sense he brings important news," said the voice in a fatherly tone.

Sabtah recognized the unnaturally sweet voice: Lord Maboa. Maboa could cloak his voice a thousand different ways to soothe a thousand different ears. Sabtah waited. He knew to speak only after being spoken to. He stood still, removing his hand from his knife hilt so as not to appear antagonistic.

The growling and shrieking came to an abrupt halt as Maboa spoke through the door.

"Sabtah, you have news for me—good news, I suspect," said a new voice of Maboa. This voice was business-like, but Sabtah thought he detected a tone, ever so slightly, of appreciation.

"As always, you are correct, my lord. It is I, Sabtah, and I bear news. But I do not know whether the news is good or—"

A black-gloved hand and cloaked arm passed directly through the solid iron of the door. The hand opened, palm up, before Sabtah's chest.

"Give it to me," said the voice, no longer fatherly or businesslike, but harsh and imperious.

Sabtah dropped the vial into the outstretched palm which immediately closed over it and withdrew again behind the door. This did not shock Sabtah. He knew that Lord Maboa was the most skilled sorcerer in the world. The thickest metal could not contain Maboa or veil anything from his sight. Consequently, Sabtah knew Maboa was watching him with one suspicious eye while the other eye gleaned the news. So he acted patient and blissfully ignorant while the vial's contents were being examined on the other side.

"You have done well, Sabtah." The voice was velvet. It might persuade a foolish man to relax.

"Thank you, my Lord, but it wasn't me. I merely received this from Xurthun. It is he who heard it all and sent it by vulture. I do not even know what it says," Sabtah lied. Xurthun would most likely suffer from Sabtah's treachery, but Sabtah was rarely burdened by feelings of sympathy or pity.

"It is just the information I need. I will give Xurthun his due reward. You may leave."

Bowing low, Sabtah rasped in a most respectful tone, "Thank you, my lord. And if I may be of service in any way, let me know."

"I will."

"One more thing, my lord. The guard at the bridge tried to take the vial from me. Said his name was Maswin. I don't know what he wanted it for. Perhaps he is a spy for the Enemy. Fortunately, I was able to overcome him and deliver this. You may still find him unconscious at the bridge. I thought you should know." Sabtah lied smoothly. He had done it so well for so many years that he was often able to block his mind from the truth and believe his own lie as he told it. He had randomly selected the hapless guard to be the object of Maboa's supposed wrath over the vial's message.

A menacing voice ripped through the hole. "I will deal with him most severely." And then with a change so abrupt it was eerie, a soothing, even alluring voice said in a reassuring tone, "Thank you, Sabtah, for all you do. You mean a lot to me and the Cause."

Bowing low again, Sabtah serenely left the antechamber. After turning the sharp corner into the torch-lit corridor, he scurried quickly past the two guards, trembling as he ran.

"What'd he say?" bellowed the big guard after him.

Sabtah didn't answer but let out a muffled sob, just loud enough for the guards to hear. Once out of their sight he muttered, "Fools!" and kicked the side of the unconscious skinny guard who still lying unconscious beyond the bridge.

Sabtah sprang up the dark and twisty corridor, weaving his way through darkness as a needle through thread. He stopped only to briefly harass the still curious Snodflin, who was hanging around near the entrance.

"Lord Maboa is very pleased with me," Sabtah taunted, getting in Snodflin's face. "And he is very displeased with a guard down there who doubted me. Just be careful what you say."

And with the sneer never leaving his face, Sabtah bounded out the rock door and toward the place where he had just learned that the Chosen One had been spotted.

Chapter 10

THE WISE ONES AND
THE CHOSEN ONE

Thogwok led his four new pupils through breathtaking terrain and showed them bizarre sights. Being a nephil, he had a natural understanding of the forest. What's more, because he couldn't dwell high up in the trees with the other nephilim, he was left to survive down on the forest floor all on his own. Consequently, he had grown to understand the forest intimately, perhaps better than anyone in Early Earth.

Fong, Candice, Braulio and Sean followed their skilled forest ranger through wildly lush vegetation; virtually dripping with fruit of every size, shape and color. Flowers of breathtaking fragrances and tremendous size dazzled their noses and eyes. Insects, reptiles and birds scurried beneath giant leaves, clung to branches and swooped through the forest canopy. Mammals, some of them huge, bleated, brayed and roared. Braulio was stunned by the quantity of wildlife. He decided there had to be ten times the amount one would see when walking through a forest in the modern world.

And though the forest was mesmerizing, and worthy of captivating one's full attention, following Thogwok demanded attention of its own.

The giant's awkward clumsiness frequently sent him a few steps off the path or knocked him a few steps backwards—precariously close to his followers! More than once he went all the way to the ground, but he rebounded quickly every time and, oddly enough, never got hurt. Fong remembered Enosh saying something about nephil immortality and she figured this must have something to do with falls not hurting Thogwok. After one particularly spectacular fall, her curiosity was piqued and she asked him a question she had been pondering.

"Thogwok," she hesitantly asked the giant who was lurching ahead of them and using a walking stick the size of a Christmas tree.

"Ay, what is it young 'un?"

"Enosh said nephilim never die of natural causes. Is that true?"

"That's right," he answered.

"Well, umm … if you don't mind my asking …" Fong was thinking about Thogwok's wife and three children who had died. "What can kill a nephil?"

"On'y a bad accident or the hand of one more powerful. O' course accidents like that hardly never happen since we nephilim are so agile," he said as he tripped over a root, stumbled and clumsily slammed the trunk of his tree-sized walking stick in the ground to right himself. He continued talking as if nothing had happened. "Basically, nephilim would live forever were it not for murders and wars. We'ze got angel blood in us, we'ze do. Pure angels can't die at all, o' course. They are perfect, so they don't have accidents, they are immune to all diseases and they never age. An' so ya see, we nephilim inherited our immunities and the trait of agelessness from them."

None of the kids had thought about that yet, but the adult nephilim they had seen all looked about the same age. There were none who were wrinkled or graying. None were sickly-looking either. Once they reached adulthood they stopped growing—just like humans do. But unlike humans, they stopped aging also. So once fully-grown, a nephil lived the rest of his days in the prime of his maturity.

"But we also got human in us," Thogwok continued, "which means we can be killed," he said as he stumbled again. Accidently dropping his walking tree, he grasped a shiny, low hanging vine to steady himself. The kids blinked in surprise as the vine twisted of its own accord, contorted itself and violently writhed. Then all four stared in horror at the very long, very fat, irate snake which Thogwok had accidentally pulled down off its branch. The startled reptile raised its head and faced Thogwok, who still had a hold on its mid-section. Angered, it snapped at the giant's face and just barely missed. Thogwok blundered to one side, avoiding the snake's second swinging pass—this time close to his side. The serpent muscled up its thick torso again, drew back its head and hissed. It opened its mouth wide, bared razor-sharp fangs, and lunged again toward Thogwok's face.

The girls screamed and Braulio and Sean were speechless. But Thogwok was not alarmed and knew what to do. Still holding the heavy reptile mid-body, he flung it high above his head, caught the creature by the tail on the way down, and snapped its head rapidly several times against the ground as if the reptile were a giant whip. The snake's body soon hung limp and lifeless in his hands.

"Ay, another offspring of the cursed legless serpents; them are the nastiest beasts in the forest, they are," Thogwok said matter-of-factly, as if this kind of thing were a routine activity for him.

"Nice move, Mr. Thogwok, dude! For a second there I thought you were a goner!" said Sean.

Braulio was also impressed by Thogwok's speed and surprising agility in this instance, but was too proud to say so.

"When yer out here in the forest as much as I am, yuz have tuh develop a quick hand and eye. Here, hold this," Thogwok said as he casually draped the limp snake over Braulio's shoulder. Braulio suppressed his instinct to cringe and tried to look brave. A heavy snake around his neck? No big deal. Shudder.

Thogwok fumbled with his wide belt to loosen a large drawstring bag. He held the bag out to Braulio, wobbled a little, steadied himself, and said, "Drop 'er right in 'ere."

Braulio quickly did so, unable to hide his loathing at the scaly bulk sliding through his hands. Thogwok drew the string and handed the bag to Braulio.

"Careful as yuz carry 'er …them fangs'll probably puncture that bag b'fore we get back and yuz wouldn't want 'em stickin' yuz in the leg,"

Thogwok said helpfully as he grabbed a real vine, spun around, and resumed his instructional tour as if nothing unusual had occurred.

The others followed, paying closer attention to the vines than they had before.

"Thogwok," Fong began, as she quickly recorded this latest event on her air screen, "Why do you call it a 'legless serpent?'? What other kinds of serpents are there?"

"Well, there are serpents that have legs—"

"Lizards, you mean," interrupted Fong.

"Sure, if yuz wanna call 'em that," Thogwok answered. "But there are several different types and they go by lots o' different names around here. O' course, there are also the serpents that have both legs and wings. Most folks call those 'uns 'dragons'."

"Dragons!" they all cried at once with varying levels of shock and incredulity.

"As if dinosaurs aren't enough, you want me to believe there are dragons here, too?" Braulio asked.

Thogwok looked quizzically at them all, puzzled by their outburst, and said to Braulio, "Why wouldn't yuz believe in dragons? Yuz believe in all the other lizards, don't yuz? Dragons are just another kind o' lizard—the kind that has legs and wings. They're all in the same big family."

Fong protested, "But, Thogwok, even if we hadn't seen dinosaurs here with our own eyes, we know dinosaurs are real because in our time we have the bones to prove it. Why don't we have bones in our day to prove dragons were real?"

"Hmm," said Thogwok as he thought about that for a moment. "I guess I don't know anythin' about what bones they gots in yur day, but I do know one thing about the bones of winged serpents here: they are always crushed."

"Always crushed? Why?" Fong asked.

"Because of all the creatures here in Early Earth, winged serpents are the most hated," Thogwok said, "Even more than the legless ones. People blame 'em for the trouble we're in today. Makes sense when you consider who their ancestor is."

Thogwok noticed they all looked confused.

"Y'see, over a thousand years ago, it was a dragon, that ancient serpent who goes by a few other names, that tempted our foremother to turn against the Creator. That was what started The Corruption and got us into the mess we're all in today. Pretty sure that dragon was a winged serpent before he got cursed. He certainly lost some legs in that curse, that's fer sure, an' I suspect he lost a set a wings too—jus' my opinion. But anyways, there is quite a lot o' fear among folks that if the bones of a winged serpent are left alone, the creature will rise again," he explained. "So instead of ever allowing a dead 'un to rest in peace, the bones are always crushed. Plus, that bone powder is valuable stuff. Them sorcerers out there—an' evil brood they all are—will pay any bone dealer a handsome sum o' gold fer it. They use that dragon bone powder to make some mighty powerful an' terrible spills!"

"You mean 'spells'," Fong said very quietly, not wanting to be rude.

Not hearing her, Thogwok continued, "That's bad, o' course. And no self-respectin' nephil would ever sell crushed dragon bone to a sorcerer— no matter what the offer. But there are good things 'bout dragons, too: their venom, fer instance."

"How could dragon venom possibly be good," asked Braulio, holding the bulging and occasionally twitching bag as far from his body as he could. He remained unconvinced the foul creature was entirely dead.

Thogwok replied, "In the same way that snake venom is good: it makes a powerful antidote! Dragon hides are useful for all kinds o' things, too," he said as he proudly patted a scaly red and black sheath strapped to his belt. "No stronger skin on any creature anywherz!"

Braulio looked down at his horrible snake bag, wishing he had any kind of sheath at all—so long as it held a knife.

"So, yes, o' course dragons are real," Thogwok finished saying. "They are really dangerous, really feared (even after they are killed), and really valuable for their parts."

Lessons such as these went on for three days. Thogwok always conscientiously returned the kids to the ladders early enough so they'd be safely out of the forest by dark.

As they embarked on the zip vine for their fourth day of forest exploration, Lawth left them with a warning. "Make sure you are back up here before high sun today. This is the day the Council wants to meet with you. Don't be late!" he ordered.

The fourth day of lessons began like the others. Fong took copious notes of everything using her thought vial. Candice jumped whenever there was the slightest movement of a vine. Sean struggled to stay focused. And Braulio awkwardly carried whatever lumpy, squirming bag of creatures Thogwok gave him. Each day it was something new. The bag he was holding at the moment contained several very large luminescent green spiders. They dwarfed the biggest tarantula Braulio had ever seen.

As much as Fong enjoyed learning, and as easily impressed as Sean was by strange plants and animals, no one had as much fun those days as Thogwok; he absolutely loved the forest. And having company to share the wonders of the wild was a thrill for him. So engrossed was he in teaching, that he totally lost track of the time.

"Oi! It's past the time yuz are supposed ta be back!" he suddenly exclaimed way too late in the day. "And yuz have a special Council meetin' too! It's where they're goin' to tell all the stuff I can't tell yuz."

"You mean the meeting where they tell us one of us is some kind of Chosen One and we have a mission to beat Maboa? You mean *that* stuff which you can't tell us?" Braulio asked as a furry green spider leg poked out of the opening in the top of his bag.

"Yeah, exactly," Thogwok replied with all seriousness. "Drat! I was gonna show yuz how to milk a live lime spider without gettin' bit. The venom comes out real easy; ya just gotta know where not tuh put yer fingers. I was even gonna let yuz try it yerselves, but we aren't gonna have time today. Sorry 'bout that."

"Oh, that's fine, Thogwok. I think I know all I need to about lime spiders already, really!" Candice said, looking to the others for support. They all quickly nodded in agreement.

Thogwok, not believing children so young could possibly know much about lime spiders, said, "Oh? I don' think yuz do … yer far too young. But one day we'll get yuz the spider blessin', chest insured! But fer now we need to hurry! You know how grouchy Lawth gets."

Candice looked more confused than usual until Fong whispered, "He means 'spider *lesson*, *rest* assured.'"

The five headed at a quick trot to where the zip vine met the forest floor. Luckily, they hadn't been too far away when Thogwok realized the time. The moment they arrived at the outskirts of the nephil village, a ladder made of twisty vines dropped to meet them. Thogwok firmly grabbed hold of it, steadying it for the climbers (and steadying himself a little at the same time).

"Good luck at the meetin'," Thogwok said as each climbed up past his tall head.

The kids scampered up the rope ladder and were greeted at the top by a scowling, cross-armed Lawth.

"So, I suppose you think your little trip through the forest is something the entire Council of Wise Men and Noble Giants should wait for?" he sneered.

Thogwok was still below, waiting to see that they all made it safely to the top. He hollered up to Lawth in their defense.

"'S'all my fault, Lawth. I kept 'em away fer too long. Tell the Council 'sorry' fer me."

"I'll tell the Council whatever I feel like telling them, you irresponsible oaf! Maybe I should tell them the kids need a new teacher!"

Thogwok made no reply, dropping his head slightly in shame. Fong, who loved Thogwok's teaching, felt sorry for him and rose to his defense.

"I think you're a great teacher, Thogwok!" she yelled to the giant and turned to look up and meet Lawth's glare defiantly. The apprentice element wielder curled his lip in a sneer. Below, Thogwok waved at her cheerfully and weaved off into the forest.

"Now then, since you are finally here, hurry and follow me. There is really no time at all for you to wash up, but since you all need it so badly," Lawth said as he surveyed them with a look of disgust, "do so anyway."

Lawth yanked down on a nearby cord and very thin streams of water dribbled down next to the kids from an overhead trough. The four of them rubbed their faces, arms and hands in the warm water. All were successful in keeping their new uniforms dry except Sean. The top half of his flexible nephilwear was sopping wet and dirt streaks still remained on his face when Lawth insisted they had to leave.

The four then briskly followed their irritated leader down some winding vine-crafted bridges and eventually across some branches of a tree that was large even by Erflanthina standards. They turned a corner and immediately came face-to-thigh with two of the largest nephilim they had yet seen. The giants were twelve feet tall, muscular, armed with spears, and clearly guarding something very important. Behind them was a door twice their height, carved into the trunk of a gargantuan tree.

"Hail, Guardians!" Lawth said formally. "I come to the Council at the invitation of your chief. I am Lawth, apprentice of Enosh, who is also present at this Council. I am also tutor of the four travelers you see here with me. We respectfully request entrance."

This introduction was sufficient for the guards. Lowering their spears at once, they opened the massive door and ushered Lawth and the four kids into the hollowed-out trunk. The tree was exceptionally large—it appeared large enough to fit ten or perhaps twelve people inside of its rotund trunk. Yet upon entering the tree, the kids were shocked to see that they had stepped into a hall the size of a grand ballroom!

The door thudded shut behind them. Light emanating from an unknown source made the walls glow. A lofty ceiling, one of the very few ceilings in the village, soared nearly eighty feet above them. Beautiful wood furnishings and ornate tapestries lined the curving walls. High tables that were ridiculously long, displaying marvelous wood grain, gleamed with polish in the warm glow. Two tables off to the side were spread with delicacies—mostly strange fruits the kids were beginning to recognize now after their days in the forest.

But the center table, the longest and most impressive of them all, is what drew their eyes. Around this massive table sat an array of wise element wielders and nephilim—at least thirty of them. Every eye around that table was focused on the new arrivals, and Candice and Braulio suddenly wished they could run. Braulio turned to do just that, but Lawth grabbed him by the arm, holding him fast, as the eldest wielder of them all, who sat at the head of the long table, spoke.

"Greetings, travelers! We are glad you could make it. We had begun to fear your excellent teacher had lost you. We were about to send out a search party," said the kind, element wielder. The humor in his voice somewhat eased the kids' anxiety at being the subject of general scrutiny.

"Please, have a seat," the elderly element wielder said in a voice so mellow and consoling, yet so confident, unwavering and authoritative, that the four knew there was not another option.

Close by were five very high, empty stools. The bottom of the table was above the kids' heads as they stood straight and tall next to it. But after scaling the ladder-like rungs on the high stools, they were at eye level with everyone else in attendance. Lawth took the first stool, and, comfortingly, the kids instantly saw Enosh, who flanked them in the sixth seat. He winked at them as they sat down.

Now able to see all the way down the long and high table, Fong, Braulio, Candice and Sean noticed that every regular-sized person was sitting on a tall stool, while all the giant nephilim were balancing on vines suspended from high beams. Then from the farthest end of the table, about fifteen giant-widths away, the consoling, authoritative voice spoke again.

"You are now at the Council of Wise Men and Noble Giants. It is a council comprised of some of the wisest element wielders and some of the noblest nephilim in the world. We convene here every one hundred years. Few outside of The Council ever enter this room or even know of this place."

The kids stared at the speaker. He was quite a bit older and wiser looking even than Enosh. He had a longer beard than Enosh, a longer nose, an even more prominent eyebrow ridge, and long, saggy earlobes. What was unusual about the appearance of one so aged was the color of his hair. It was golden yellow—surprising for someone who was clearly quite ancient. And matching it was a golden streak accenting his mostly white beard.

He continued, "But you four are here because it is most likely true that all of you in general—and especially one of you in particular—have been chosen for a special task that only you can do. But before we begin that discussion, I know you have questions. Go ahead. You may ask them," the old man offered.

Sean spoke up first. "Yeah, dude, like how is it possible that—"

"By the skilled wielding of air, young man," the wise man answered before Sean could finish the question. "Air mastery is a skill certain elders seek to achieve. Your master, Enosh, is one of the finest of his craft.

When you know how to wield air, you know how to make an air space temporarily larger than it was—like this room, for instance."

Sean, who was generally a bit slow, grasped this explanation right away.

"Other questions?" asked the venerable elder.

"So how does a guy—" began Braulio.

"Well, that is a skill that one begins to study after they have reached a certain level of maturity," explained the golden-haired grand master. "Elemental mastery is a powerful tool, or a deadly weapon, as you can imagine. It cannot be handled by children. Hence, before lessons begin we set a minimum age requirement of 100 years. Then, once having started their training, an apprentice studies under an accomplished element wielder for well over one hundred years before they end the apprenticeship. Apprentices are novice wielders of one or more elements but masters of none. Most young learners, you know, like those under 300 three hundred years old, can do simple, lightweight tasks in the wielding of one or two of the elements. But to truly have mastery over a single element—this takes many years and much wisdom. Then and only then do we confer the title of 'master' to the element wielder."

Braulio, a little surprised that his specific question was answered without ever being asked, seemed satisfied with the answer nonetheless.

Candice asked the next question—or tried to, at any rate.

"Um ... what—,"

"My name is Yarthuselah. I am 912 years of age and I have the honor of serving as the grand master element wielder of the Council. The others here are all younger—the youngest being our dear, youthful Lawth at the tender age of 316."

Candice, having gotten her answers, didn't say another word. She was shocked that the old man revealed not only his name, but also his age—which is exactly what she wanted to know but wasn't sure how to politely ask.

Fong opened her mouth to speak but then stopped short, concentrated on her questions, and looked directly at the grand master wielder, saying nothing at all to him.

The wrinkled old sage stared back and studied her intently. Then a wide smile erupted on his face and he excitedly answered, "Why, yes, young lady! Very good! Very good, indeed! Your theory is correct. When an element wielder has nearly mastered the four elements of air, water, earth and fire, and when that element wielder is in close proximity to another person and in tune with that person, that wielder can read their mind!" Braulio and Candice's mouths hung open, both of them looking for a few seconds like Sean. Neither one liked the thought of this guy seeing inside their heads.

"And why not?" the wrinkled, old sage continued. "Your mind is made up of air, water, elements from the earth, and heat. Thus if one can wield all four elements, the mind itself can be readable and even … *wieldable.*"

A chill shivered down Fong's spine at that last word, which had sounded grave and ominous. But before she or the others could fixate on that thought, the grand master wielder continued.

"How impressive it is that one as young as yourself theorized that mind reading was possible—and so quickly too! My dear Council members," he said, now addressing the room, "as you look at these four, let it be known that I am even more convinced than before that one of them is indeed the Chosen One!"

Smiles flashed across the faces of most of the wise men. The sober-faced nephilim all gave respectful nods of approval. Murmurs followed as individuals turned to those sitting next to them. The old leader's proclamation evidently was the news they had been waiting for. Yarthuselah was just about to explain to the kids what this meant when a loud crash caused them to jump.

The massive door had slammed open. A wide-eyed and disheveled nephil from a nearby village had burst through and was yelling something unintelligible to the guards who tried to stop him. Running up to the table, the frantic giant caught his breath and said, "Azgazaron has been savagely attacked! Many of our kinsmen are dead!"

Gasps went up from many of the elders, and war-ready nephilim leaped from their vine chairs, ready to go the aid of their kin. Yarthuselah called for silence.

"Azgazaron attacked? They are more fortified than we are! How could invaders have gotten in? Tell us everything you know, Larzuna,"

Yarthuselah instructed the harried messenger whom he personally knew from the neighboring village.

Larzuna gasped for breath and continued. "It must have been the sorcerer, Maboa! We think his dark magic blinded the eyes of the forest guards. Vultures serving Maboa swooped in on the village, attacked some of our little ones and spied out the village. Then, men riding on huge, spiked lizards knocked down trees and pulled down walkways. Rephaim as large as ourselves sliced through hundreds of our brothers with their swords and then torched the village! And the rephaim leader, Calneh, murdered our village leader, Chief Hazuja." He paused for a few seconds, gasping for air.

The momentary silence erupted with laments, threats, vows of revenge and the pounding of massive fists on the table, for nephilim were painfully aware of who the rephaim were. The rephaim were similar to the nephilim in that they were half human and very large, but the similarities ended there. Whereas nephilim were almost entirely noble, rephaim were almost entirely evil. For centuries, the two giant races had lived in constant conflict with another.

Yarthuselah called for silence again and the messenger continued, "They are looking for the Chosen One!"

The room erupted again. "How did they know? There is a spy! Master Yarthuselah, what do we do?" And other cries of shock and disbelief echoed off the curved bark walls of the enchanted room.

Calming down the shocked element wielders and the remorseful giant warriors, who already had swords drawn, ready for revenge, took more work this time. Yarthuselah eventually stood up and, with a flick of his left hand, split the air in the room, causing a booming thunder clap. The room fell silent.

"Larzuna, does Chief Barzuga know this yet?" he asked calmly.

"He will at any moment. Rothelsalu ran to him as I went to you. He and I escaped together."

"And you say this was a united effort by certain forces in Maboa's army: sorcerers, riders of spiked lizards, rephaim and wicked birds?"

"Yes, Grand Master."

"And why do they believe that the Chosen One has arrived?" Yarthuselah asked.

"That we do not know, but their words betray they have information. The rephaim leader, that vile sorcerer Calneh, tortured and eventually strangled Chief Hazuja, demanding he reveal the whereabouts of the Chosen One. Of course, our noble chief never would have told him even if he did know! But if the Chosen One has indeed come to our time, it is news to us. Our village has known nothing of any such arrival." Several of the Council members glanced at Braulio, Sean, Candice and Fong but said nothing.

A buzz and stirring was rising outside the bark walls of the enchanted tree. The news was spreading throughout Erflanthina and the villagers were all thinking the same thing: if Azgazaron could fall so quickly, and the enemy force was so intent on finding the Chosen One, how long before the bloodthirsty horde penetrated the defenses here? The Council members' dark expressions reflected the same thoughts.

"Thank you, Larzuna," the Grand Master said to the ragged messenger with a blood-smeared face. "You have endured a great trial today and your wounds need attending. You are dismissed." Larzuna left and Yarthuselah quickly closed the large door with a wave of a finger.

"He knows. Maboa knows," Yarthuselah said ominously. "We can no longer hide the young ones here. Even with our best cloaking enchantments, a force like that is too large, too dangerous and too empowered by dark magic for us to take such a risk." Yarthuselah stroked his white and gold beard as he spoke and, thinking out loud, he continued, "But who shall take them and where shall they go?"

Enosh stood up. "These four were sent to me for mentoring. I take responsibility for their training and safety. You can entrust them to my care, Grand Master," he said.

"Agreed, Enosh, I believe it should be you. But where will you take them?"

"I'm not entirely sure yet, I just know it is not here. We will go through the portal to a distant and hidden place at once," Enosh replied.

Yarthuselah locked his wise eyes with Enosh's. Stroking the gold of his beard, he read Enosh's thoughts again and nodded. "Yes, take them, you and Lawth. And take their other trainer with you as well," he thoughtfully concluded.

"What? You want us to take Thogwok?!" protested Lawth. "Are you cra—" and he broke off upon seeing the stern glares of both of Yarthuselah and Enosh.

"Yes, Thogwok," Yarthuselah decreed, and he dispatched a nearby giant to alert Thogwok of their immanent departure.

Chapter 11

A HASTY ESCAPE

There was a flurry of activity all around the high tree village of Erflanthina. Women grabbed their children and scurried them inside. Windows that had been open for years were sealed and boarded. Those who were less fit for battle stayed inside the village, guarding valuables and getting war supplies ready. The strongest of the nephilim scattered to all points of the village perimeter to string their bows, take positions high in trees and prepare for the savage assault headed their way.

Yarthuselah ordered some guards to grab survival supplies for the seven that were about to make their escape. Enosh ordered Lawth to go get their satchels and staffs and hurry back. Braulio demanded weapons from one of the guards but was refused. Candice began to cry, saying she just wanted to go home. Fong tried to reason with her to calm her down but had little success. Sean was mesmerized by the uproar around him and remained utterly unaware of the danger they faced.

Yarthuselah and Enosh stood face to face, communicating partially in thought transference and partly in words, for Enosh had not yet mastered mindreading. Yarthuselah, however, read Enosh's mind and responded to him.

"Yes, we must find out how Maboa learned the Chosen One had arrived, and why he mistakenly thought Azgazaron was the location. No nephil in the village has been permitted to utter the words 'Chosen One' for fear that an insect spy or bird spy would hear. And none of our fellow elders would have been foolish enough to speak such words outside the safe confines of a room such as this," Yarthuselah noted.

"And the children couldn't have said anything because they didn't know until you told them here in this room mere moments ago," Enosh added.

Sean, for some inexplicable reason, snapped to attention and tuned in to what the elders were saying about him and the other kids.

"Aw, well … not to burst yer bubbles there, extra-super wise dudes, 'cuz I know yer both like, really smart and everythin', but we kinda already knew," Sean revealed.

"How can that be?" Enosh asked, puzzled and concerned that Sean could know such a thing.

"Well, Thogwok said—*OUCH!* Hey, why'd you kick me?" Sean barked at Fong, utterly unable to take a hint.

Fong, who didn't want poor Thogwok to get in any trouble, gave Sean a shut-your-big-mouth glare, but it was too late.

"Thogwok said *WHAT*, exactly?" asked the two element wielders, in a tone stern enough that Sean knew he must answer honestly and immediately.

"Just that one of us was the Chosen One is all," answered Sean innocently.

Enosh and Yarthuselah exchanged knowing looks, both thinking the same things. There were spies in the forest, and Thogwok, being apart from the rest of the villagers most of the time, had perhaps not heard the stern warning to keep quiet. And even if he had, both elders knew he was not the most prudent person when it came to keeping secrets.

"Word travels fast these days," Enosh lamented as he looked at Yarthuselah.

"Indeed it does," the Grand Master Elder agreed. "Now the only question is why a spy in our part of the forest would send word to Maboa that the Chosen One was in a village half a day's journey from here, instead of right here. I suppose we will learn that soon enough;

but for now," he said, looking at the kids, "we must focus on getting all of you out of here as quickly as possible. You will be safer wherever Enosh takes you than in the village where a spy has seen you. Enosh will guide you in many things. Thogwok will offer much insight on the world you will be traveling through, not to mention being a good bodyguard when trouble arises … and, yes, trouble will likely arise. Lawth will also be at your side as an instructor and indispensable assistant," said the aged element wielder as he looked compassionately at the young people.

Yarthuselah detected the confusion that clouded their minds, and he knew that most of their questions remained unanswered and that there was no time to answer them now. But there was one more thing they needed to hear, so he continued, "And, yes, you will be fine so long as you do as your instructors tell you. They are older and wiser than you so listen to them, for they know the way. Take courage now; learn and complete your mission and do not fear! If you do what they say, you will succeed."

At that moment, Azmarpin burst through the door and bellowed, "Masters Yarthuselah and Enosh, Serflina and I just scouted out the portal, and we must warn you that it is not safe! The children cannot go that way! Warmongers from Maboa's camp have either killed or scattered our portal guards and they are thick in the forest surrounding it, waiting for the Chosen One to slip through. Not having found the Chosen One in Azgazaron, the whole army is on the march, headed this way, and the portal is fully under their control!"

"Indeed, it appears Maboa was ill-informed of the location but quick to make the correction," Yarthuselah conceded. "He naturally assumes that, wherever the Chosen One is, he or she will be using the portals eventually. We must not allow the youths to proceed through them."

"But if they cannot utilize the portals …" Enosh began to ask as he was already figuring out the answer.

"Regrettably, that is right, Enosh. You will need to travel through the forest by foot, beginning here at our very gate," Yarthuselah said with a sigh, finishing Enosh's thought.

"But they are not properly trained yet!" objected an elder with an exceptionally long grey beard which he hadn't shaved in two hundred years. "How can they survive the journey in this increasingly wicked world if they can't fend off the evil that will surely come against them?"

Others nodded in agreement. Enosh looked at Yarthuselah. "Yes, I agree," the Grand Master responded to Enosh's unspoken thoughts. "However, they are safer with you, Lawth and Thogwok—a small band of travelers discreetly on a journey—than they would be barricaded in here with hordes marshaled against them. The enemy suspects they are in a village for training. They will not suspect the Chosen One to be mostly unguarded, outside of village walls, next door to danger."

Just then, Lawth sprang back into the room with staffs and satchels in his hands.

"We need to leave, Lawth. Our journey has grown more difficult. I will explain as we move," Enosh told his apprentice.

"I am ready," he replied.

At that the two wise men said their respectful goodbyes to Yarthuselah and sprang out of the enchanted room with the kids in tow. Now they hurriedly ran along the winding walkway they had calmly walked less than an hour ago. Earlier, it had been a serene, vine-draped bridge system fresh with the scent of flowers and replete with the sounds of singing birds. Now it was a hustle and bustle of giants who zigged and zagged, glided and jumped, swung and ran here and there. Even in her haze of fear and confusion, Fong couldn't help but marvel at how little the planked walkway shook despite the rush of nephilim action moving across it.

"We need to meet up with Thogwok before we can make the escape," Enosh said to Lawth.

"That bumbling fool will hold us up! He can't even walk straight!" Lawth retorted.

"Yarthuselah's orders. Trust him, Lawth, he knows what is needed," Enosh replied as he hurriedly led the group down to a lower level. "But we will need to leave the village in the opposite direction of Thogwok's hut. The spy who overheard him is likely in his area. We need to avoid him, or them, by all means."

"The spy who overheard him? What are you talking about?" Lawth asked.

Enosh did not immediately answer but continued flying along the walkway, just missing an oncoming group of three nephilim who leapt onto the rope railings to avoid the six little humans. The nephilim scurried atop the narrow railings for several yards before dropping back to the planks.

Braulio spoke up after almost getting clobbered by another rapidly passing nephil. "A spy overheard Thogwok telling us that one of us is some kind of Chosen One, whatever that's supposed to mean," the boy said cynically.

"What! You mean it's his big mouth that got us in this mess!" Lawth yelled, almost smacking into the long feet of a nimble giant swinging on a vine in front of him.

"It doesn't matter at this point, Lawth. What matters is getting the Chosen One and the other three off to safety; and they need you, me, and Thogwok to get there. There! Look ahead. He is on his way!" Enosh announced as they approached the top of the ladder and zip vine that entered Thogwok's side of the forest.

Enosh called down to him and said something in the Nephil language. Thogwok understood immediately and headed underneath the village on the ground, moving clumsily but as fast as he could go. Turning to the kids, Enosh said in an undertone, "Whoever the spy is, he probably doesn't speak Nephil. That language is seldom learned by any who serve Maboa. I told him to meet us on the other side of the village and lead us out by the most secretive path he knows."

At that moment, a fireball tore through the air and splintered into shards of flame in the branches of a tall tree. Male nephilim ran, swung and jumped to rescue any women and children under the branches while several other warrior nephilim darted off in the direction from which the projectile came, their swords drawn and ready.

Enosh looked out over the forest horizon with concern etched in his wrinkles. "The enemy is close," he ominously said. "They may even have the village entirely surrounded with spies. Thogwok knows this forest better than anyone; if there is someone who can get us out of here undetected, it is him. Come! We must hurry!"

They scurried as quickly as they could through the twisty, tree branch village, the elders moving surprisingly fast on the wobbly walkways with the kids racing to keep up.

Braulio snagged an abandoned bow and some arrows. He struggled to get the quiver secure on his back—the strap was huge. And actually trying to use the oversized bow was practically impossible for him. He practiced pulling back the taut string. It took nearly all his strength.

Now far behind the rest, Braulio awkwardly thudded down the walkway trying to catch up, dragging the tip of the bow on the wood behind him. After a few clumsy minutes he had almost rejoined the others when a nephil boy called to him from behind.

"Braulio!" the boy called out. He was a young nephil, but as big as Braulio. "Take my bow and arrows!" he said, extending them generously.

Braulio dropped the huge bow and it clattered to the platform. Taking the child's bow, he pulled it back once to test its strength. It was perfect.

"Awesome, kid! That's just what I need." And dropping the oversized quiver he slung the small one—which the boy had freshly filled with arrows—on his back. Without saying 'thanks' Braulio tore forward, light, unencumbered and finally armed.

"And tell my dad I love him!" the little nephil named Shivlok said. If Braulio had bothered to look back, he would have seen the tall boy look suddenly young and frightened as tears filled his eyes.

Braulio barreled ahead, gaining on the rest. He quickly passed Sean, who had momentarily stopped to snag some delicious-looking cake from an abandoned lunch table.

Soon, they arrived at the west side of the village. Enosh descended a ladder that went all the way down and everyone followed. Plunking on the dirt, they ran toward the very last building on the village's ground level. It was camouflaged well with bushes and thorns for its protective outer wall but was dangerously within earshot of any spy who might be lurking outside the village. As they hurried inside the hut, Lawth, who was running very fast ahead of the rest, slammed face first into Thogwok's large belly. The giant was not so much as budged or bothered by it. Rather, he was excited to see they had made it.

"Ah, good, ya found it! Here's the secret ent—" he began.

"You worthless oaf!" Lawth yelled, "Look what you've done now! The village is under attack and we have to run because of your oversized mouth!"

"That is enough, Lawth!" Enosh rebuked, rapidly entering the hut after him.

Thogwok lowered his head, looking ashamed. Lawth was purple with rage.

"Correction," replied Enosh in a quieter tone, "the village is under attack because of the choices made by Maboa and those who follow him. And as for Thogwok's worth, you will soon see a small portion of just how valuable he is; for I believe there is none better than him to rescue us from this."

At this, Thogwok raised his head a little, but still looking down at the six around him, he said, "I owe yuz all an apology. I knows that spies hang out in these parts, they do, and so I never shoulda said out loud that one of yuz is the Cho—"

He stopped short as he caught a withering glare from Lawth.

"Oh! Right! Sorry, yuz know what I'm sorry for, don't yuz?" he concluded.

At that moment another bright orange fireball blazed across the sky and pummeled into the side of a tree house far above their heads. Chunks of wood and flaming particles of tar from the fiery bomb descended very close to them.

"No worries, Mr. Thogwok dude, we all have a big mouth from time to time," Sean said before looking up with his mouth dumbly hanging open, mesmerized by the fire.

"Time for talk later, let's move!" Enosh ordered as shattered wood and showering sparks rained down around them.

"Right," Thogwok agreed as he opened a trap door and stepped onto a ladder that descended into the ground. He disappeared into the darkness and the rest followed him down the ladder and into a tunnel. Lawth, coming last, pulled the trap door shut behind them.

Several miles from the besieged village of Erflanthina, Maboa sat in his camp and fumed. He was enraged at what he had just learned, but he hid it very well. The messenger bird, Loswossip, perched near him. A dark veil hung in the air just off the ground, held in place by magic and surrounding Maboa on all sides; for no one was permitted to gaze directly on Maboa. Loswossip had just arrived with a message penned only minutes earlier at a place in the forest not far from Thogwok's hut. It read:

> *Greetings to our lord and master, the great and powerful Maboa;*
>
> *We here in the front lines, spying for the cause of our lord, could not be more pleased to serve you, nor could our esteemed positions as spies be more desirous. With our allegiance to you unfailing, we look ahead with great anticipation to your rule over all these lands. Loswossip delivered your message to me mere moments ago and it is delightful to hear Azgazaron has fallen to your might. This is great news! So know that it is with gratitude, awe and reverence that some of your servants were wondering the following:*
>
> *Why is it, my lord, that the troops attacked Azgazaron, a village half a day's journey away, when the message I, your servant sent to you, clearly identified the Chosen One as being in Erflanthina? Word of the attack spread quickly and Erflanthina is now prepared for battle. As a result, I sense it will be much harder to take this village than it was to take Azgazaron. Worse still, surely the enemy is now hiding the Chosen One or scurrying the Chosen One out of the village even as you read this. With complete respect I must ask, would it not have been wiser to take this village first, capture the Chosen One, and then take Azgazaron at your leisure?*
>
> *Nevertheless, I am certain you, our wise lord and leader, have a plan of which we, your faithful spies, are*

as of yet unaware. We stand ready to follow your next orders.

Sincerely, your foremost informant,

Xurthun

Maboa hid his true emotions as he read this wretched news. In a voice that was sinisterly sweet he asked, "So tell me, messenger bird, have you delivered any other messages in the last few days?"

Loswossip replied merely with a simple nod of the head.

"Have you delivered any messages to my mountain in the last few days?"

"Ye-e-s," the bird replied as his voice cracked. Speaking was always a strain for Loswossip.

"And who sent it?" Maboa asked, already quite sure of the answer.

"Your-r se-r-rvant, Xurthun," he said, his voice straining

"And who was it that took the message from you to deliver it to me?" Maboa tenderly asked.

"Your-r se-r-rvant, Sabtah," he said in a voice now weakened from such labor. Maboa's gaze pierced through the veil and he concentrated for a few deliberate seconds on the four elements coursing through Loswossip's brain. Reading the bird's shallow memory, he could see the image of Xurthun tying the vial to his leg. Then he saw an aerial view of the village of Erflanthina from Loswossip's perspective as he flew away with the vial in tow. Maboa perceived, and correctly so, that both Loswossip and Xurthun were telling the truth.

"Sabta-a-ah! You accursed liar!" Maboa shrieked. The yell came with no warning and the air around Maboa crackled and a gust of hot, dank air blew Loswossip back. Screeching, the bird fluttered several feet away, trembling. The veil between them fluttered in the gust of hate. Maboa's eyes narrowed into slits. "Sabtah, you will pay for your treachery! You will pay more than you know!" Maboa vowed to the absent traitor, saliva like venom dripping from a corner of his mouth.

"Loswossip, you have a new assignment," Maboa said harshly, eyeing the bird with a look that Loswossip could feel through the veil. It sent chills through his quills. Then out of nowhere, Maboa's voice shifted, becoming calm and steady. "Locate Sabtah. Do not let him or anyone with him see you. And bring back word to me of his whereabouts and which way he is heading."

Loswossip, glad he didn't have to stick around, quickly flew away.

———————>•<———————

The tunnel was dark and dank like most tunnels. With a fluid wave of Enosh's hand, a flame ignited at the end of his staff.

"Thanks, Master Enosh, that helps," said Thogwok, who was in front of Enosh and kept bumping into tree roots.

The four kids followed Enosh through the tunnel. Lawth, who was taking up the rear, tried unsuccessfully to light his staff. After a few failed attempts at wielding a flame with his hands, Enosh, his master, looked back, waved his hand toward Lawth's staff and an orange burst of flame sprouted out the end. Lawth was embarrassed and glared at Fong, who quickly turned away and pretended not to notice his failure.

Thogwok proceeded quickly. He used the earthen walls, which were cluttered with a web of tangled roots, to his advantage. Whenever he started to fall, which was often, he would simply grab a root and use his own momentum to propel himself further forward. Enosh nimbly kept pace behind him, his staff-turned-torch bounding up and down with his fast strides. The kids fumbled and tripped themselves across the uneven tunnel floor, just barely keeping up.

"Tunnels like this are rare here in our day," Enosh said to the kids. "With streams coming up from the ground flowing across the whole surface of the earth, it is usually hard to dig without coming upon water. Thankfully, this land is high enough that it can accommodate a dry tunnel."

"Good thing, too," said Thogwok. "Them Maboa assassins are ruthless. They'd stop at nothin' to kidnap yuz kids and torture the rest of us b'fore killin' us. But no one knows 'bout this tunnel. It will take us beyond the far end of the village and we can take to the forest trails from there."

"But how do you know there aren't Maboa units at the other end, or another spy like the one who overheard you the first time?" Fong asked.

"Th' army of Maboa is behind us," Thogwok explained as he stopped and pointed backwards.

"And that very army is gaining on us the more we talk!" bellowed Lawth from the back of the line. "Keep running!"

"Oh, right!" Thogwok said apologetically as he resumed rapidly pulling and grabbing his way through. "Like I was sayin', Azgazaron is behind us and that's where all the Maboa folks were at. Fer some reason they musta thought yuz was over there. Some stupid spy that must be, huh!" said Thogwok, now a little more satisfied that he hadn't completely blown it when blabbing about the Chosen One. "Anaways, this tunnel takes us far to the opposite side of the village from where they are attackin'," Thogwok continued. "And besides, the other end of the tunnel is well-hidden and no one outside the village knows nothin' 'bout this tunnel anaways," Thogwok confidently declared again.

Little did Thogwok realize that at the end of that very tunnel, Sabtah the spy sat comfortably hidden behind a cluster of thick bushes on the back of his own personal dinosaur; a spike-backed kentrosaurus named Straktor. Monitoring the tunnel exit which he'd learned about from Xurthun, Sabtah took the time to muse about some things. First, he could hear that a ferocious battle had just begun. Even at this distance, the melee could be heard. Shouts from the attackers on the far side of the village faintly drifted through the trees and intermittent fireballs lobbed overhead caused momentary mayhem and screams. Secondly, he reasoned it was likely that the band of humans which contained the Chosen One were headed in his direction through the tunnel—the most secretive way to get out of the village in the direction opposite the attackers.

Sabtah thought about those things briefly, but quickly moved on to a topic he liked much more: himself. He thought about how skilled he was; feeling he was unmatched in sheer cleverness. He knew how to navigate twisting city alleys and trackless jungles. He knew who to befriend and who to avoid. In a tight spot he could always talk his way out with persuasive words. And whenever he got tired of talking he could fight his way out with sharp edges. Sabtah was a knife master; able to defeat anyone at the wrong end of a short blade. But he found it more entertaining to con his way out of trouble—and he could con almost anyone. Frankly, Sabtah thought he was smarter, fitter and just plain better than anyone he could think of. In fact, he was so superior to others that he felt it was time for Lord Maboa to step down. Sabtah had served the powerful warlord for many moons, learned all he needed to know, and now he was done with it. He had critiqued Maboa's errors and determined that he could do a much better job. It was his turn to rule and he need not take orders from his former "lord" Maboa anymore.

So when Sabtah had seen an opportunity to secure his own future, he crafted a plan. Sabtah diverted Maboa and his forces to an entirely wrong village by covertly keeping for himself the message Loswossip delivered and inserting his own message in the vial in place of it. When Maboa and his horde would then cause mayhem in nearby Azgazaron, Sabtah reasoned that those protecting the Chosen One would quickly flee from Erflanthina. So he decided to quietly wait, secretly follow the group, and when the time was right, acquire the georb from the Chosen One. And before Maboa would know what had happened, Sabtah would wholly possess the power of the air, bringing "Lord" Maboa, and the rest of the earth under his rule. This was Sabtah's plan, and thus far it was working without a hiccup.

Silently sitting on the back of his beast in a nephil forest, Sabtah listened with demented delight to a battle he played a part in starting but for which others would be blamed. Satisfied with himself, he patiently awaited the arrival of his soon-to-be victims, who, unbeknownst to them, would deliver to him the final tool he needed to take control of the world.

A nephil scout sprinted from branch to branch not far from where he and his mount crouched in perfect stillness. The scout shot by without seeing him, his mind occupied on what was erupting on the other side of his village and the well-being of his family.

"Nephilim are so observant are they?" Sabtah scoffed. "Soon enough they will all be observing my every command." He grinned wickedly.

There was a rustle at the tunnel exit. A rabbit six times larger than any the kids would have seen back home leapt from a thicket that had overgrown and completely hidden the tunnel exit. The rabbit bounded out of sight, clearly spooked by something.

Sabtah turned his head sideways and placed his hearing cone, one like the kind Xurthun used, up to his ear and aimed it toward the tunnel exit.

"Don' yuz kids worry. I know the end is comin' up real soon," spoke a muffled voice ever so faintly. Sabtah didn't recognize the voice, but it was deep—definitely a nephil.

Sabtah smirked smugly. His plan seemed on the verge of success. *Could it be this easy? Could this be the Chosen One attempting a feeble escape with some nephil body guard?* He held the cone tighter to his ear. He listened several more seconds and heard some very young voices say some absurdly ridiculous things. "Victory," Sabtah said under his breath.

Sabtah held his breath, listening intently. His eyes were fixed on the opening from which the rabbit fled. He watched ever so closely for the slightest rustle of a leaf, the tiniest turning of a branch, the faintest indication of any subtle movement at all … when suddenly, out popped an enormous and very loud nephil!

"AHA! See, I told yuz it led to a secret opening no one knows about!" the giant yelled way too loudly as he rocketed from the tunnel.

Sabtah pulled the hearing cone away from his ear and winced. Not only could he hear fine now without it, but the giant was so loud he had hurt Sabtah's ear. Barreling through the bushy thicket, the loud and clumsy nephil tripped over his feet and tumbled into a roll on the ground. Following him far more serenely, was an observant element wielder trailed by two boys and two girls—all four of them very young by Early Earth standards. Sabtah kept watching closely as the last one emerged—a young and obviously frustrated element wielder who was cursing energetically and barking orders at both the giant and the kids.

Then Sabtah spotted it: a georb hanging around a kid's neck! A wicked, covetous smile spread across Sabtah's face. This was going to be easier than he had thought. A georb was right in front of him, and the only protection these vulnerable kids had were two element wielders and a loud, bumbling nephil. But even in all his arrogance Sabtah knew he couldn't defeat two element wielders and a giant face-to-face in a fight. He would have to be sneaky. It would be risky, but well worth it in the end. The prize was nothing less than elemental domination.

Sabtah watched and listened, intrigued. The young ones were clearly unaware of their surroundings, let alone the presence of Sabtah. But unlike the others who were bickering, blaming, and paying no attention to anything around them, the older of the two wielders stood apart from the group. He calmly scanned the area. As the wise elder steadily moved his eyes around the clearing, Sabtah stayed frozen in the thick cover that shielded him from view.

Then the elder spoke commandingly to the fractured group, saying, "We'd better move on out and find shelter; the attackers could easily arrive on this side of the village. If they get a hold of a georb, what they did to Azgazaron they could do to the world! Thogwok, if you would lead us please …"

The giant led the crew into the forest, swaying back and forth as he clumsily moved through thick foliage with the others close behind him. Once they were out of sight and the sound of swishing branches had faded, Sabtah twitched the reins of his trained kentrosaurus. At just over six hundred pounds, the beast was small compared to most giant lizards, but strong and robust enough to hold Sabtah's weight and take him great distances. More importantly, the creature was stealthy; no one would hear it move. And it could sniff out a scent over a mile away.

"I found them, Straktor. Now you track them," Sabtah said quietly to his beast.

The dinosaur lifted up off its haunches and swished its tail. It had two rows of curved spikes on its back spaced in such a way that Sabtah had room for a comfortable saddle, stirrups and reins. And with reins firmly in hand, Sabtah turned the trained lizard toward the path and halted him where the seven had stood just minutes before.

"Take a good long sniff right here," he said as the lizard flicked its long tongue several times to absorb and memorize the new scents. Sabtah then tossed some morsels of food on the ground and Straktor snatched them up.

"More of that when you find out where they are going," he said as he dug his heels into the dinosaur's scaly side. And they followed the scents of the seven.

Sabtah had a plan; and he thought he knew everything he needed to know in order to succeed. What he did not know, was that he wasn't the only one watching the georb-holding group. Someone else was in the forest spying on the group as they escaped. They were also spying on Sabtah.

Chapter 12

IN THE RING OF CAMPFIRE

The seven travelers scurried through the thick forest, away from both the tunnel and the besieged village. Thogwok stumbled along in the lead. He was moving faster than he was accustomed to and was consequently clumsier than usual. More than once Enosh sent a small blast of air from the direction Thogwok would have fallen, keeping him upright for the time being.

"Much obliged, kind air wielder," Thogwok said each time.

"Don't mention it," replied Enosh, who not only helped Thogwok stay upright but also saved himself from getting squashed.

They journeyed for the better part of three hours, either running or walking steadily the entire time. In this oxygen-rich world their bodies were slow to fatigue.

Enosh sighted a small clearing suitable for rest and refreshment and called the group to a halt. A clear, refreshing stream gurgled past the spot and tall plants with leaves the size of elephant ears blanketed the area, providing concealment from above. Peppered throughout were trees bearing ripe clusters of shiny orange, green, and yellow fruits.

"This should suit us quite well, I think," said the wise elder, his brilliant blue eyes scanning the surroundings.

"Good. I'm starving!" Candice whined.

"Ah yes, that is one reason I chose this location. I think you will find the fruits here quite tantalizing," said Enosh.

"Fruits? You mean there is only fruit here?" asked Candice with a bit of a scowl.

"Well, what else do you expect to see growing on trees?" snapped Lawth as he brushed past her to get the first pick for himself.

"Like … is there anything you brought with you to eat?" she asked, looking hopefully at Enosh.

"Well, no, my dear. We have supplies necessary for survival, but we didn't have time to prepare or pack food," Enosh answered.

"You can thank your buddy, Thoggy for that one," grumbled Lawth as he swung his staff and knocked down a bulbous, green pear-like fruit dangling above him. He deftly caught it and then bit in.

"But food is abundant," Enosh continued. "Fruit is plentiful on the trees and other tasty delicacies are to be found here and there. You just have to know where to look."

At that he tapped the end of a long pod hanging from an overhead branch. It spread apart and revealed glistening red seeds, similar to those of a pomegranate only larger.

"Try these. We call them pod jewels," Enosh said, politely handing the pod to Candice. She tested one with the tip of her tongue. Then she put a whole seed in her mouth and cautiously bit in. And despite Candice's instinct to complain about almost everything, she had to admit the fruit was quite good.

Thogwok groped through some extremely thick vines which swarmed around a large tree trunk and entirely obscured the ground underneath. Promptly, he pulled out an enormous, dark purple orb three times the size of a large watermelon.

"Here yuz go kiddos! Violet honeydew! Guaranteed to fill yuz up, repel monster bees an' even eradicate the effects if'n yuz gets stung. It'll be good to have some of this in yer blood b'fore we go any further. Likely we'll hit a swarm of several thousand of 'em buggers on this path," he said calmly.

"M-m-monster bees?" stuttered Candice.

"Yeah, they can be quite nasty," answered Thogwok, who raised his eyes upward and motioned the rest to do the same.

The kids all looked up at the tallest flower they had ever seen in their lives. At fifteen feet high, the bloom towered over Thogwok. Jiggling around inside its overgrown yellow blossom was an enormous honeybee. Striped in yellow and black, it brandished a ten-inch-long stinger and had an abdomen the size of a large rat. The kids stared in silence as the bee wrestled the flower for nectar—its buzzing sounding like the whir of a small engine.

"Things are able to grow quite a bit bigger here," noted Enosh as he looked way up at some three-story-high stalks of sugarcane. He sliced through one of the sweet stalks with repetitious sharp blasts of air, slicing it into several pieces as the remainder of the stalk crashed to the ground like a skinny tree.

Thogwok proceeded to tear the enormous purple fruit apart into seven jagged pieces and distributed them as he continued talking to Fong. "Just one sting from a monster bee will make that thin little arm o' yerz puff up bigger than a good-sized nephil arm! But get a good dose of violet honeydew in yuz and it's a perfect antidote."

Sean, Candice, and Fong all quickly started eating.

Enosh brought over the sugarcane stalks and handed a thick slab to each of them. "Thought you may want this for desert instead of attempting to gather honey," he said with a wink.

Enosh then looked around for Braulio and spotted him sitting on a log a ways off, his back to the rest, tenderly taking long drags off his cigarette. While all the others began making themselves comfortable on a spongy spot of grass and peppering Thogwok with questions about large and dangerous insects, Enosh strode over to the lone boy.

Taking a seat next to him on his log, Enosh asked, "So, how many more of those do you have left?"

"This is it," Braulio answered curtly, as he took another drag, never taking his eyes off the rapidly burning tip. The empty packet was crinkled tightly in his other hand.

"I see," said Enosh. "Do you ever look forward to the day when you will be free?"

"What are you talking about? I already am free," Braulio said defensively. And he took another long drag. As the boy blew out the smoke and observed the cigarette now at less than half its length, Enosh saw the anxiety lurking in his eyes.

"Oh, I know you are free in many ways, my young man. But won't it be nice to someday not need a plant or a beverage or … *any* substance to make you happy?"

Braulio glared at Enosh. He was already in a foul mood and didn't need a lecture about smoking. He was about to let loose a massive verbal assault when he made eye contact with Enosh. In Enosh's burning blue eyes Braulio could see not only wisdom, but also genuine concern. This old man truly cared about his well-being. He was like a wise, helpful grandfather, something Braulio had never had.

Braulio looked back down at his cigarette. It was nearly gone. There were three good puffs left, maybe four. His chest tightened with anxiety. His mind raced.

What am I doing? he thought. *I'm being hunted by a brutal army and all I can think about is that this is my last cigarette. That's messed up.* And as frightening as it was to realize this was his last one for however long, deep down he knew Enosh was right. It would be great to be free—to never need or even desire this addictive thing again. But he wasn't about to admit that to Enosh.

"You may want to talk to Thogwok sometime," Enosh said. "He is highly knowledgeable in the realm of botany. He may just have something that will help you get through the withdrawal you are about to endure. I imagine he can find something that would be a non-addictive, temporary substitute. If you hand him a sample of what you have left there, he might be able to give you something better."

Enosh got up to return to the others and said, "Do come join us for a refreshing snack when you are finished, won't you?"

A few minutes later, Braulio rejoined the group and wolfed down some tantalizing fruit. By now, everyone had bellies full of overgrown pears, pomegranate-red pod jewels, sweet grapes, plenty of clean, crystal-clear water from the stream, sugarcane for dessert, and just for good measure, a double dose of violet honeydew bee sting antidote. As they were about to go, Sean stuffed more sugarcane in his pockets like a squirrel storing away nuts for winter.

"What yuz doin' that fer?" Thogwok asked. "There's plenty more o' that stuff on the way. But if you wanna be weighed down on the journey, that's up to you I s'pose."

The sounds of their departure were fading as Straktor entered the clearing with Sabtah on his back. Sabtah dismounted and scanned the ground for clues. His kentrosaurus repeatedly flicked out its long tongue, absorbing the scents of the seven travelers, while Sabtah examined the ground and noted the fruit peels and an empty cigarette packet.

"Forward, Straktor," Sabtah said to the kentrosaurus, remounting on his back.

Straktor sauntered onward, his forked tongue following the fresh trail.

<hr />

As evening approached, Thogwok found a perfect clearing for the group to make camp for the night.

Braulio scanned their surroundings. "So where's the tent?" he asked.

"A tent? What's that?" asked Thogwok.

Braulio was incredulous. "You don't know what a tent is? It's a canvas used for shelter when you're camping, of course!"

Thogwok was mildly curious at the concept but still confused. "A canvas … for shelter… hmmm. Sounds int'restin' enough. But why?"

Braulio's last dose of nicotine had nearly worn off and he was low on patience. This was about to be the first night they'd be sleeping away from the protection of the nephil village and no one seemed to care about proper gear but him.

"Oh, I don't know!" he hollered sarcastically, throwing his arms in the air. "Maybe bloodthirsty mosquitoes, rain forest-caliber downpours, dinosaurs that will trample us—just stuff like that, is all!"

The look of bewilderment on Thogwok's face goaded Braulio into continuing.

"Of course, if those things don't bother you we could talk about huge, flesh-eating pteranodons. Or if those are no big deal, how about bees that have stingers the length of swords! Maybe those are some reasons why! But hey, what do I know? I'm just a guy with the crazy idea that maybe a little protection wouldn't hurt!"

Enosh, Thogwok, and Lawth exchanged glances.

"Pathetic," murmured Lawth as he shook his head and walked away. He grabbed Sean by the collar and pulled him along as he began lecturing him on the precise kind of wood he needed to gather for the fire.

Thogwok tried to politely hide his smile and answer as empathetically as he could. "Well … um … y'see, Braulio—" Thogwok began.

"Allow me to explain," Enosh interjected. "You go prepare the campsite with the others."

Thogwok staggered a few paces away and began gathering some soft silky leaves that would make fine bedding for the girls. Candice and Fong followed his lead.

"To address your concerns one by one, my anxious young man, I will go in reverse order for ease of understanding," said Enosh. "First of all, the matter of monster bees has already been addressed and remedied by your healthy dose of violet honeydew. Besides, unless you look and smell very much like a flower, there is no reason for one ever to sting you anyway. Second, pteranodons do eat flesh, but they prefer the flesh to be both smaller than you and also deader than you. Third, dinosaurs, as you call them, will not approach us if we are inside a ring of fire. No beast who has succumbed to the eating of flesh will pass the fire circle for they fear fire. I'm not so sure a piece of canvas would have the same effect on creatures intent on doing us harm."

A roar from something deep in the thick foliage far off to their left rumbled through the air. It sent chills down Braulio's spine and a squeal from Candice who clung to Thogwok's leg. After assessing that roar, Braulio agreed that surrounding themselves with fire would be a much better defense than a flimsy tent.

Enosh continued as if he hadn't heard the roar, "Remember also, my boy, that we are not in a rainforest. This land has never seen a drop of rain. We are in Early Earth and the land is watered by streams. There is seldom anything falling from the sky from which one would need protection."

"Finally," Enosh continued, "you mentioned mosquitoes. Whereas it is true that over the past several hundred years we have seen a disturbing trend of more insects choosing to be blood-drinkers, they still do not exist in overbearing numbers. For one thing, many of that kind still draw protein-rich nourishment from a wide range of plants just as their ancestors did. Secondly, our world here is still mostly in ecological balance. No single species has become dominant while others have become extinct. There is no place on this earth where a horde of insects overwhelms the environment. On the contrary, many, many creatures exist together in quite large numbers. Surely you have noticed that on our journey today."

Admittedly this was true. Since Braulio first arrived in Early Earth, he had been smacked around by a stegosaurus, attacked by monkeys and been surrounded by more wildlife than he ever imagined possible.

"As you lie in the open darkness tonight and hear the howls, cackles, chirps, cries, growls, and roars," Enosh said with a raised eyebrow, "this will become even more obvious to you."

Braulio looked toward his left for whatever had made that sound but saw nothing. He looked back at Enosh and tried to appear unafraid.

"But back to the blood-drinkers of which you speak: In your world mosquitoes are prolific in areas where there are swamps, ponds, and other stagnant waters; but look around you," Enosh instructed with his outstretched staff.

Braulio scanned the horizon. They were on high ground and a nearby stream gurgled and babbled over small stones as it tumbled down a gentle incline into a valley below them. The sun was setting over the valley and its rays danced and frolicked over the ripples of many narrow streams below. It was breathtaking. Braulio had been too worked-up to even take in the spectacular panorama all around him.

"You will notice," Enosh continued, "all the waters here in Early Earth are moving. We call them, 'living waters.' There is little room for stagnation, decay, or many of the diseases in your world that fester in such places, to say nothing of mosquito breeding."

Enosh paused for a moment, allowing this bath of information to wash over Braulio before he said, "Now, I hope that answers all your concerns about not having a tent. If so, why not help Lawth and Sean gather some wood?"

Braulio knew he had been beat. He had nothing else to say, and agreeing that fire would be very nice to have at night, he joined Lawth and Sean. This gave Lawth one more person to ridicule and berate about his inability to recognize slow-burning magentawood.

When the three returned to the campsite with armfuls of slow-burning wood, Lawth arranged the sticks in a large ring. Once finished, he had made a nearly perfect circle with one break in it just wide enough for a person to pass through.

Lawth then pointed his fingers at a stick and nothing happened. He did it a second time and significant smoke, but no flame, bellowed out of the stick. Frustrated, he threw down his staff and with both hands outstretched he forcefully shook his fingers. Two small flames finally shot out, missing the ring of wood entirely and lighting Sean's pant cuffs on fire.

"Who-o-o-a! Dude! Watch where yer throwin' that fire around!" Sean yelled as he jumped around, frantically slapping his pant cuffs. He ran away and splashed into the stream.

"Lawth," Enosh said softly clearing his throat, "how about if I tend to the fire while you take our water skins and fill them? That way if we need water during the night none of us will have to leave the fire ring." He handed Lawth two very thin, expandable skins which rolled up compactly to fit in any sack. "While you are in the stream, see to it also that the boy's ankles have proper ointment on them."

"Why sure, that's all I'm really good for as an apprentice element wielder, isn't it? I get to be water boy and nanny," Lawth griped as he snatched the skins and stomped over toward the stream Sean was now standing in.

Enosh flicked his fingers at the ring of magentawood and instantly all the sticks kindled. Magentawood was useful because of how long it took to burn. It was a slow, cool burn; which meant it would go all night long while they slept, the flames never getting too high or too hot.

Meanwhile, Thogwok and the girls laid down some leafy, soft bedding—one spot for Candice and Fong and a separate, much larger one for the five guys to spread out on. The leaves they picked were velvety soft to the touch. When several were laid on top of each other they made a cozy mattress. The leaves were also large enough that just two of them together made a good blanket for most folks; though Thogwok needed four. Once in place, the bedding looked very inviting when surrounded by the ring of low-burning fire. And the kids, frightened and frazzled most of the day due to the sudden attack and their flight from the village, finally felt calmer, safer.

Taking turns in the nearest stream, each one washed themselves and their stretchy nephilwear in the privacy of dense vegetation. Hanging their new garments up on nearby branches to dry, the kids put on their regular clothes and flopped down on their freshly plucked, leafy beds.

"I realize your regular garments are not what you are accustomed to sleeping in, but after a day of running in your nephilwear I think you will be pleased to don clean clothes in the morning," Enosh said with a smile.

Candice agreed. After a day of sweating, the supple material was beginning to get a little funky.

Thogwok stabbed some unknown fruit and cooked it over the fire ring. He handed a piece to each of the kids. It tasted a little like fried banana, only more robust in flavor. Sean squished a piece of it onto his stick of sugarcane and pretended he was eating s'mores. Some of the squishy fruit dribbled down Sean's front and landed on his georb, which was dangling prominently on his chest.

"Way to go, smooth one," Braulio taunted. "It's not like we're gonna need these for anything important," he said sarcastically as he dangled his perfectly clean georb in Sean's face. Fong agreed with Braulio's sentiment but didn't say anything. Even before they left the village, she had hidden her precious stone under her nephil uniform where it couldn't be seen by anyone. And that is where it remained.

"You might as well just eat it now, you slob," Braulio quipped to Sean.

"Braulio, may I see your georb please?" Enosh asked.

A little reluctantly, Braulio handed over the prized gem to the element wielder.

"It is time you children heard the rest of the story about the georbs," said Enosh.

Surrounded by the crackling of the fire ring, the gentle gurgling of the closest stream, and the warm breeze that blew through the camp, the four young people listened carefully to Enosh. They had known the georbs were important ever since the small gems had dragged them through space and time, but they did not understand them—how they worked, why they existed or what one was supposed to do with them. "You see kids," Enosh began, "these delightful little gems contain a particle of elemental essence from each of the four elements."

"They do what?" asked Sean as he held up his georb in his sticky hand and looked at it in the firelight.

"It means they are comprised of earth, water, air, and fire, Sean," Fong said impatiently, eager to hear Enosh reveal more about the georbs.

"Correct," Enosh said, "But more than just being *comprised* of the four elements, each of the four georbs—and there are only four known to exist—contains within it a trace of elemental *essence* from all four elements. All four georbs are identical in that *sense*, but each one is also unique; for each georb has an extra strong connection to just one of the four elements."

"Now you lost me," said Braulio.

"Well, as you already know, the four elements currently exist distinct from one another, but at one time they were all mixed together as one," Enosh replied.

"Wait a minute ... air, water, fire, and dirt all mixed in one clump?" Braulio asked with one eye squinted. "That doesn't make sense. What would that even look like?"

"I'm not sure either, but everything we see around us, and all the matter out there which we *don't* see was at one time united. Later on it became separated. So if it were a 'clump' as you say, it was a massive clump indeed. But whatever it may have looked like, the Creator separated it all into the four elements as we know them today. Fire became the lights in the sky that keep us warm and give us illumination. Those lights tell us what season, day and year it is. Air became the delightful, oxygen-rich, fragrant thing which we and all other creatures breathe. Water became the fluid that gives nourishment and life to all that lives. And land, or earth, became that solid backbone which provides room and board for all living things."

Enosh paused, stroked his beard and concentrated on the georb he held in his hand. His listeners looked closely at it too.

"Now, the current separation of, and different functions of the four elements is quite clear. Just by looking around us we can observe the differences. What we are not so sure about is what it all looked like when the four were together in one giant mass," Enosh continued, "but when the one giant mass was separated into four distinct elements, evidently a pure essence of each element was also formed."

"A pure essence of each element?" Fong repeated.

"Indeed," Enosh continued. "There is a pure elemental essence for air, a pure elemental essence for water, another for fire, and one for land. Each of the four exists in pure form somewhere on earth and each must be reunited with its own georb every four hundred years. They are on a cycle so that every century one of the four georbs must be reunited with its unique essence. And this is the four hundredth year since the last reuniting of the air elemental essence with its georb."

"So all we gotta do is get that air essence, attach it to whichever georb is the air one, and we're done. Doesn't sound so bad. No big deal," Braulio concluded with a shrug.

"It may not be so very simple, but you are right—that is what we know and that is what one of you needs to do," Enosh said.

"Why does it have to be one of us?" asked Fong. "Aren't there people here who can do that better than we can?"

"Apparently not, seeing as the georb chose one of you," Enosh answered.

"But why would the little rock choose some dude from thousands of years in the future? The whole time travel thing is way awesome and all, but it seems like a lot of trouble," Sean said through a mouthful of sugarcane.

"Trouble? Not for the georb. It chooses whom it wishes and trifling details like time shall not stand in its way. Time is way too fickle of a thing for a georb to take seriously as a limitation. Just think—it changes every second! " Enosh said with a chuckle.

"So, what's the holdup? Let's do it!" Braulio demanded with candid impatience.

"The holdup is in what we *don't* know," Enosh said with a mysterious glint in his eyes. "What we don't know is which of the four georbs is the one connected to air; all four georbs are identical in appearance and there is no way of telling which is which just by looking. Furthermore, you will note that not all four georbs are represented here. Beyond that, even if we do have the actual air georb, we don't know where to go to find the air essence. It moves you see, and no one is able to track it.

"Wait a second," Braulio interjected. "If even *you*, Mr. Smartypants don't know where this essence thingy is, how in the world do you expect one of us to find it? We don't know this place!" he said indignantly.

"The essence goes where it wishes. We do not know where to find it, but…the essence can find the Chosen One," Enosh answered confidently.

Braulio didn't like that answer. "So what are we supposed to do? Just run around the jungle and wait until we bump into this essence thing? No plan, no map, no time frame … is that all you got for us?"

Enosh gave no answer. He gazed calmly at Braulio, waiting for him to finish his rant.

Braulio threw up his hands. "This is stupid!" he said. "Why are we even doing this? Forget it. With no plan and no information, it's never going to happen. I guess they just won't get united then."

"Oh, but they will unite. It is only a matter of who unites them; either the Chosen One, as it should be, or an evil one who will try to control the element," Enosh corrected. "And that is the most distressing thing of all. We are not the only ones who are on this quest. As you so vividly witnessed back at the village today, there is a horde of murderous mercenaries who are pursuing us even as we speak. They are hunting us down in order to get a georb. They are sent by and controlled by the most deceptive, bloodthirsty and power-hungry soul that presently walks the earth. If he were to get the air georb and reunite it with its essence, he would then have great power over the movement of the air for the next four hundred years. Doubtless, he would use it to gain as much control over the inhabitants of earth as he could, depriving air to villages and even entire regions unless they pay tribute and submit to him. The havoc he would wreak would be disastrous for humans, nephilim and all other air-breathing creatures. It would certainly be the death of millions of people and billions of creatures."

Braulio fell silent. Candice's face dropped into her palms. Sean's mouth simply fell open.

"So let me see if I understand this," Fong summarized. "We need to find the elemental air essence. We need one of the georbs to connect to it, but we don't know which one it is or even if we have it. Also, we don't know where to look for this elemental essence; we only know that it's someplace on this earth that is so foreign to us. Am I right so far?"

"Quite right!" Enosh said, clearly pleased that she understood.

"And as we are searching for this elusive essence thing, we will have a horde of murderous thugs trying to kill us so they can get a georb and control all the world's air, " Braulio added dryly.

"Quite right again!" Enosh said with a proud fatherly smile. "You are indeed a ripe bunch for being so green in this world!"

Candice, Fong, Braulio, and Sean stared at him in bewilderment. None knew what to say. Thogwok yawned and stretched and flumped down on his several large leaves, not in the least bit phased by any of this. And Lawth was already asleep.

"Well then," Enosh said, looking very satisfied that all understood the task at hand so well, "it looks like that wraps it up for the night!"

Enosh handed the georb back to Braulio, who hesitantly took it and held it dangling at arm's length. The brazen boy had suddenly become much less eager to hang a stone around his neck that people would kill for. Enosh then rapidly wiggled his fingers, thereby creating and fluffing-up an invisible air pillow upon which he laid his head.

The four just stared at him, not sure what to think about all this.

Enosh sank into his verdant mattress with his head suspended a foot off the ground on what appeared to be nothing. Turning his head to the four he said, "Remind me in the morning to deflate my pillow. People have been known to trip over such things." And he peacefully closed his eyes. In seconds, his magnificent blue eyes popped open again, making Candice jump!

"Oh, and another thing: be sure to have those georbs at all times around your necks and at most times on your minds. Those who seek to use them for evil may be closer than we think. Good night!"

And with a contented look on his face that showed not a worry in the world, the venerable Enosh closed his eyes again and went immediately to sleep.

The four kids didn't move. They just sat in the flickering firelight, glancing furtively at one another. The strain of the day—the attack on the village, the narrow escape, the flight through the forest—it all began to weigh on them. All they could do was sit there a bit stunned, thinking about what Enosh had just said, what they already experienced and what on earth could possibly lie ahead. Who could sleep after such a revelation and such a day? Nevertheless, just a minute later, Sean conked out—the first of the four to doze off.

Candice was lightly sobbing as she lay on her bed. She was scared and wished she hadn't insisted on coming here with Fong. She had gotten herself into all this and now she wanted out. She wondered how or even if she'd ever get home. Fong and Braulio heard her gentle sobs but said nothing to console her; they were too wrapped up in their own worries. But after several minutes, her sniffling noises ceased as she whimpered herself to sleep.

Fong had pondered plenty today and her brain was already at its max when Enosh dropped that bombshell. Most of what he said was stuff she already knew or had a hunch about anyway. But the parts that she hadn't yet known were all very bad and frankly too much for her to process. So, like an overloaded computer hard drive, Fong crashed. Her mind defaulted into unconscious sleep mode.

That left only Braulio awake. He was still holding the georb in his hand. As it hung off his fingers it reflected the firelight and glistened a dazzling blue. Braulio wondered how a stupid little stone could have such power and cause so much trouble.

Paranoid, he scanned the woods around him. Unlike the forests of Spain that he was used to hunting in, this forest was not quiet or still. A continuous chorus of chirping, cooing, calling, and grunting streamed from the dark perimeter outside the fire's light. This was nature to the hilt. The sounds blended nicely together to a make a soothing, melodious chorus that was beautiful and conducive for good sleep. But with all that noise from nature, mixed with the crackling of the fire, Braulio concluded he wouldn't hear an assailant coming. So he set the georb on the ground next to him in plain sight. He thought it better that they take the stone and leave him alone.

Then he looked over at Sean who was slumbering away in perfect peace, his georb hanging haphazardly outside his giant leaf blanket for the entire world to see. Braulio looked over at Fong. Her right hand was clenched to her chest, probably clutching her georb through her shirt.

"If those wimps can wear one, then I can too," he mumbled before he slung it back around his neck with a heavy sigh. Besides that, he figured that in some way the georb, which got him here, would also be his ticket home. So he positioned himself in the dead center of the fire ring, manipulated several giant leaves and made a thick blanket roll out of them. Then he lay back with his head elevated so he could get maximum vision of anyone breaking the perimeter. Ready for battle, Braulio stuffed the georb tightly between his shirt and his chest, pointed his face toward the one opening in the fire ring, and vigilantly scanned the perimeter. He set the bow which the nephil boy gave him by his side, one arrow notched and ready for an assault. After an hour of diligently listening to and watching everything, Braulio finally gave up his night vigil and fell asleep.

Chapter 13

VANISHED DURING THE NIGHT

Fong awoke the next morning to a crash, an *"Ouch!"* and a curse. Braulio had tripped over Enosh's invisible air pillow. He toppled into some charred logs from the extinguished fire and was now brushing ashes off his clothes with soot-blackened hands while trash-talking Enosh. The calamity made Sean stir to consciousness as well.

"Dude, it's early. What's up with all the noise?" Sean groaned as he sat up from his leaf mattress.

"That crazy element wielder and his invisible air balls! That's what!" Braulio barked.

"You tripped over air? Dude, *all* air is invisible. Like, how stupid do you have to be to trip over air?" Sean said laughing.

Braulio kicked the air pillow at Sean and it pummeled him in the face, muffling his laughter.

Sean grabbed for the air pillow to whip it back, but he had to fumble around on the ground to find it. Before he could get his hands on it, another huge hand grabbed him and hoisted him off his bed of leaves.

"Good morning!" boomed the very un-morning-like voice of Thogwok. And with a brain-jarring shake, Thogwok vigorously shook

Sean's hand in what he thought was the customary way of greeting their kind.

"G-g-g-g-g-o-o-d m-m-orning, Thogwok," Sean stammered back, his whole body feeling like a human jackhammer. Thogwok let go and Sean fell limp back on his leaves. Thogwok then gave Braulio the same greeting—which only worsened the boy's foul mood.

Fong sat up and gave a quick yawn. She seemed very small in the midst of such enormous leaves, her whole body mostly enveloped by just one. Her bright eyes looked very alert for having just awakened. And without so much as a pause after her brisk yawn, she began teaching.

"That was an especially efficient night of sleep. I noticed before I dozed off that no one was snoring. That must be due to the purity of the air flowing through our nasal passages thanks to the lack of allergens and other contaminants normally found in the air of our day. Furthermore, the uncontaminated, super-oxygenated air ventilating through our lungs and coursing through our bloodstreams while we sleep makes our bodies physically regenerate faster. Analysis of amber samples—amber being fossilized tree sap, of course—reveal that at one time, earth's atmosphere had thirty-two percent oxygen content. If that is what we are breathing here now, versus twenty-one percent back home, not to mention all the pollutants absent here that we are accustomed to breathing back in our world, I calculate we could survive here on five hours of sleep and still have more energy and feel better than we could in our world on eight hours of sleep. Furthermore, smell that fragrant air," and taking an unusual pause, she inhaled deeply and then continued. "That is the combined aroma of hundreds of different flowers. Such fresh smells wafting around a person may do nothing for their physical well-being, per se, but studies show that the psychological impact aromatherapy has on improving people's moods causes increased productivity. Furthermore, we cannot overlook the stimulations given to our other senses. There must be fifty birds singing around us—many of them within sight. Their array of vibrant colors mixed with the music they make also lift an individual's spirit. Hence, I conclude a person's brain function, workload capacity and overall attitude are all significantly elevated in an environment such as this."

Sean had to pull a leaf over his head—too much instruction too early in the morning.

Braulio stared at her incredulously and sneered, "You don't *really* wake up talking like that every morning, do you?"

Thogwok took three giant steps from the boy's side over to where the girls had slept and extended his hand for a hearty, good-morning greeting to Fong.

Before he could reach her, however, Fong interjected, "Thogwok, do you realize that in our culture handshake greetings aren't done every morning?"

"They're not? When, then?"

"Usually just when we meet each other. After that, a simple 'good morning' or 'good afternoon' will do."

"Oh. Seems sort'er impersonal ... but alrigh' then, uh ... good morning," he said and awkwardly dropped his hand, not knowing what to do next.

"Teach me the nephil greeting," Fong said, folding back her giant leaf blanket and standing up to face his navel.

"Why sure! That's easy," Thogwok said. "First of all, yuz extend out yer arms like this." And throwing his arms out to either side, he stumbled and almost crushed Sean, who had emerged from his leaf cover once Fong had stopped talking long enough to take a breath. Catching himself, Thogwok straightened up and, as if nothing had happened, said, "Then yuz raise yer arms over yer head and point up to the sky."

Fong followed his lead. Sean got into it too, after taking a few steps back for safety. "Then yuz take yer arms down and do it a second time," Thogwok continued. "But the second time yuz bring yer arms down, put 'em in front of yer heart and cup yer hands."

Fong finished duplicating the greeting and asked, "So what does all that mean?"

"It's all about who we are, where we come from an' where weze are goin'. We nephilim are half earthly human an' half heavenly warrior. O' course, we live here on earth, but half our ancestry is heavenly. We greet each other by first honoring our mothers, who are daughters of humans," he said with his hands extended out. "Then we lift our arms up to honor our fathers, who are sons of God," he said as he lifted his arms high above his head. "Then we bring our arms back down to show we are to dwell fer this life here on earth with the other humans. But we lift 'em back up toward heaven a second time to point to the place we will eventually go. Finally, we bring our hands down in front of our hearts and cup them as a pledge of loyalty, honesty and integrity toward the individual we are greeting."

Sean said, "A simple 'what's up?' seems simpler to me, but that arm-moving thing beats your version of a handshake any day."

Fong was impressed at the symbolism and re-greeted him one more time just to make sure she got it right. Thogwok returned the greeting and smiled warmly at her.

Braulio was exceptionally disinterested. He would have much rather been alone smoking a cigarette, but he was all out. The withdrawal Enosh predicted was setting in and he was getting edgy.

"Hey, Thogwok," Braulio said, "what do they smoke around here? Like, are there any super-sized tobacco leaves?"

"Smoke? Oh, y'mean like them incense straws you've been inhalin'?" Thogwok asked.

Braulio thought the term 'incense straw' was a ridiculous way to describe a cigarette, but, not wanting to offend his source, he went with it.

"Yeah. That. Where do we find more incense straws?" Braulio asked again as he handed Thogwok the butt of his last one.

Thogwok fumbled around with it in his enormous hands, awkwardly unwrapping the tiny paper cylinder. He gave a quick sniff of the remaining tobacco shreds and crinkled his nose.

"No, m'boy, I can't quite identify that 'un for yuz. Sorry to tell ya this, but I never even heard of 'su pursized two back o'leaves.'"

Braulio's heart sank. Thogwok knew everything about the forest. If he hadn't heard of tobacco leaves, no one here would have.

"However," Thogwok continued, "I do know of an incense plant some good folks inhale. Non-addictive and good for making peace with enemies. Come t' think of it, I remember seein' a small patch of it on the path jus' before we made camp las' night. I'll go take a look for yuz," Thogwok said helpfully as he staggered away.

Braulio said nothing. He just stood there, shook his head and rolled his eyes after Thogwok had turned away.

Fong glared at Braulio, indignant at his rudeness.

"It may not be exactly what you had hoped for, but at least he's trying to help you," Fong whispered, scolding him under her breath. "You could at least say 'thank you' and appear grateful!"

"Inhaling some peace incense? Are you kidding me?" Braulio said, sneering at her. "There's obviously no nicotine here. Why don't *you* go inhale some incense? Or better yet, tell me where to get some smokes since you seem to know everything!"

Braulio turned and stormed away. Between the invisible pillow, that stupid nephil greeting and now the incense, he had endured enough nonsense for one day—and the day had only just begun! Fuming, he stomped several paces away from the campsite and toward a small clearing overlooking a valley. As the cool of the night was being chased away by the morning warmth, a dense mist hung over the valley. The mist was so thick that he couldn't see either the land or the streams in the valley below.

Poking its head above the thick layer of mist was a long-necked sauropod. It weighed several tons, and if its skeleton were displayed in a modern museum, it would have the name 'Brachiosaurus' attached to it.

That dinosaur head suspended above the mist and a multitude of birds flying overhead were the only creatures Braulio could see. He could only imagine what else was roaming below that mist deep in the valley. Then he noticed Enosh. The element wielder was several yards away from the campsite with his arms raised high and his palms upward. He seemed to be looking out over the valley. But as Braulio approached, he noticed Enosh's eyes were closed. He also noticed that Enosh's mouth was moving, but no one else was around.

As Braulio got closer he could hear Enosh speaking but couldn't understand what he was saying. Braulio figured it was that weird nephil language and concluded that Enosh must be praying. Having no time, tolerance, or patience for such time-wasting activities as prayer, Braulio simply broke in and said, "I still can't believe there are dinosaurs here."

Enosh stopped speaking. Slowly he lowered his arms and opened his eyes. He looked at Braulio and, after a pause just long enough to make

Braulio uncomfortable, he said, "Perhaps you can't believe what you see because what you see is inconsistent with what you believe."

While Braulio was thinking about what that meant, Enosh continued, "But I don't believe we've properly greeted each other today. So, good morning, Braulio," Enosh said with only just the slightest rebuke in his voice.

"Oh, so I suppose we need to do the whole routine of arms up in the air and all that junk before I can talk to you?" Braulio retorted.

"No, you and I do not need to do that. But a simple 'good morning' would be a considerate way to start your day with almost anyone, don't you think?"

"Sure, whatever. Good morning." Braulio quickly said. He didn't have the patience for any of these freaks today.

"Now, if your comment of disbelief is really the question I take it to be, consider this," Enosh continued. "With such an abundance of food and drink, and so much space in which to live, coupled with the fact that predators are far outnumbered by prey, creatures generally live much longer here than they could in your world. With so many nutrients and with richer air, some creatures not only live longer, but grow significantly larger here than in your world. And some creatures never stop growing until the day they die. Lizards, for example, never stop growing. They are limited only by their environment and the years they are given. That is why you see 'dinosaurs', as you call them, here in Early Earth. They are merely lizards who live hundreds of years, like many of us do in this environment; but unlike us, they continue growing all the days of their lives.

Braulio was taken aback. What he just heard didn't fit well with anything else he had ever been told about dinosaurs. But he did remember learning in a biology class once before that most lizards never stop growing. He began to think about the possibility of lizards living hundreds of years like Enosh and other people here apparently were doing. And if lizards continued growing and growing for hundreds of years ...

So, how did you sleep?" Enosh asked, interrupting Braulio's musings.

"Alright, I guess, seeing how I'm not dead," Braulio answered.

"Being alive is always a good beginning to a day. It seems to have been a peaceful and uneventful night then, doesn't it? All persons are safe and all georbs are present and accounted for, I presume," Enosh both declared and asked at the same time.

Braulio patted his chest to feel the georb. Though it was heavy on his mind when he went to sleep, this was the first time all morning he had thought about it. But as he felt his chest, there was no stone there.

Braulio quickly grabbed the back of his neck to confirm that the necklace was still hanging there. But it wasn't. Feeling suddenly sick, he snapped his head back to look at the spot where he slept. *Did it fall off during the night? Did I lay it beside me before I dozed off and then forget to put it back on?* Braulio wondered for a moment. But no, he remembered looking at Sean's georb and determining if that dork could wear his, he would be brave enough to wear his too. He was certain he secured it around his neck before all went black. Where was it, though?

"You do have the georb then?" Enosh asked with some concern in his voice.

"Uh, yeah ... someplace," Braulio said unconvincingly. Then he remembered falling over the air pillow. "It must have fallen off when I fell on the burned logs," he said, and then ran over to comb the area. Braulio began searching and became more hurried and stressed with every second that passed. It was not among the remnants of the fire ring. He went over to the place where he lay for the night, shuffling large leaves aside and looking hard.

Fong was the first to notice Braulio's somewhat frantic search. "Let me guess: you just remembered you have an extra pack of cigarettes somewhere, right?"

"Hey, if you want to show everyone how smart you are, tell me where my chain is," Braulio quipped.

"You lost your georb!" Fong announced way too loudly.

"No! I didn't lose the stupid necklace—it's around here somewhere! I know I had it around my neck when I went to sleep," he said grabbing his neck and chest again as if it would have suddenly reappeared there.

Enosh approached the campsite. "Fong," he asked her, "where is your georb?"

"Right here," she said, pulling it out of her shirt collar.

Enosh looked at Sean and there was no need to ask. Sean was munching on his morning sugarcane, dripping sweet juice down his shirt and also on the georb that hung prominently around his neck, oblivious to the mounting crisis. At that point Lawth and Candice, who had just awakened, got involved in the search as they began flipping over leaves and asking Braulio questions that made him more and more tense.

Thogwok reappeared with something in his hand. With his booming voice and a pleased look on his face he said, "I think I found what yer lookin' fur here, Braulio."

That got Braulio's attention like nothing else would have at the moment. And for the first time ever, Braulio was really pleased with what Thogwok had to say. But he looked up only to be dismayed. Thogwok did not have a georb in his hands, just a clump of weeds.

"This here is the incense plant I was talkin' about. The wayz you get it ready for inhalin' is by—"

"Thogwok, we seem to have an urgent matter at hand," Enosh said, gently interrupting. "It seems Braulio no longer has his georb. Search the surrounding area for signs of enemies."

Thogwok immediately delved into the nearby thick bushes, the spot where his forest sense told him a spy might be lurking.

"It couldn't have been Maboa's forces, Master Enosh," Lawth said as he kicked large leaves aside looking for the stone. "There'd have been a swarm of them and we either would have heard them and fought, or not heard them and been murdered in our sleep. Clearly, the boy has misplaced it."

"Likely it would have been one of those scenarios if it were Maboa's forces. But what if it were a quiet, lone thief?" Enosh asked.

"If it were a thief he would have taken all three georbs—especially one hanging in plain sight," Fong said pointing at Sean, who was still paying no attention to anything but his sugarcane.

"Not necessarily," said Enosh cryptically, walking over to the spot where Sean had slept. He stooped over and smelled a leaf that had been Sean's blanket. "Curious," Enosh mused as his large nose detected something on the leaf.

"Listen, you guys, no one stole it from me, okay; it's here somewhere! Just everyone shut up and help me look!" Braulio barked.

Lawth grabbed the disrespectful boy by the back of the collar, shoved him in the direction of the stream, and ordered him to retrace his every step.

Enosh walked over to where the girls had been sleeping during the night. "Candice, you didn't wear the necklace at all last night, did you?" he asked her.

"Me? No! Only Fong has worn it," she said adamantly.

Enosh bent over and looked closely at the ground near Fong's spot. He picked up a couple of leaves and sniffed at them. Then he moved back over to stoop down and again investigate the area where Sean had been laying.

"Curious," he mumbled as he inspected the ground around Sean's area a second time. He picked up Sean's leaf blanket again, smelled it, and tasted it with the tip of his tongue.

"This one is burned. Interesting … how very interesting, indeed," Enosh said as he stood up, still holding the large leaf. He went over to where Braulio had slept. He bent down and smelled the leaves. He tasted one also, but found nothing of interest.

Just then, Thogwok burst out of the thick bushes and yelled, "Tracks, Master Enosh! There's tracks leading tuh here and away again! Two sets: one looks tuh be a medium-sized horned dragon and the other is a man!"

"Then it is a single thief, as I suspected," Enosh muttered, dropping Sean's leaf and standing up straight. He solemnly commanded the group, "Take heed, everyone. We have been followed and a georb has been stolen. We must move quickly to try and recover it. Up and ready! Pack whatever is yours and get into your nephilwear. We will be moving in five minutes."

Everyone, even Sean, kicked into high gear. It was freaky to think they had been followed, perhaps spied upon during the night and then robbed in their sleep. But far worse than all that was the sickening reality that Braulio's georb was gone!

Chapter 14

THE CHASE

West of Erflanthina, the grotesque vulture, Loswossip, let out a loud craw of frustration as he scoured the forest. He looked for any sign of that treacherous Sabtah. The search had so far yielded nothing—not good news for the vulture. Maboa was seldom patient and never merciful. Loswossip had only two choices: find the traitor and live, or fail to find the traitor and fly far away forever, hoping Maboa's forces would never find him.

Then he faintly heard something. Rising above the hum of the birds and wildlife below him were human voices—strange accents speaking loudly in the Earthen tongue. He could see nothing through all the tree cover so he swooped down below the canopy. Then he saw what the noise was: five, no, six humans and one spastic giant—all in a hurry. Loswossip drifted lower and silently perched on a branch. The vulture was a skilled eavesdropper and his silent wings had served Maboa well. Perhaps this discovery would avert Maboa's wrath.

"Moron!" bellowed a man's voice so loudly that it startled Loswossip and made him flutter and nearly fall. The one who yelled was running directly below his perch. Judging by his headband and his robe, Loswossip knew he was an element wielder.

"I said, 'I *thought* about laying it on the ground'—I didn't actually do it! I had the thing around my neck all night!" shouted the voice of one much younger who was running in front of him.

"Why would you even think of such a thing?" yelled the element wielder. "You may be a child, but you're not a total idiot! Enosh plainly told you there were savage hordes trying to steal the georb! And let me guess, instead of tucked under your shirt, you probably had it in plain sight all night long where any thief could see it, right?"

"Well, that's what Sean did!" retorted the young one defensively.

"Oh, I see! Since you have found such a brilliant role model to follow, no wonder you lost it!" yelled the element wielder.

"At least I didn't lose my clothes last night!" the young one replied, referencing Sean, (for at some point during the night Sean's nephilwear, which had been hanging out to dry, came up missing; which meant Sean was once again wearing his too-short jeans and too-baggy neon green shirt.)

"Hey, don't you dudes drag me into this! The thief who stole yer georb must have stolen my way cool clothes too—that's not my fault! But I still got my little stone. See?" said Sean, turning around and running backwards as he dangled his georb up high for Lawth and Braulio to behold. In doing so he lost his balance and fell backwards. Fong, who was running directly behind him, tripped over Sean and also took a plunge.

"Sean! Pay attention to what you are doing!" she reprimanded as she quickly picked herself up. "And haven't you heard a word Lawth just said? You need to wear the georb, yes, but you also need to hide it the best you can, like I am. You're just lucky you didn't get yours stolen last night too! Keep it under your shirt at all times. And don't even talk about the georbs unless you know we are alone."

Loswossip watched with intrigue as the skinny kid dropped the necklace inside his odd-looking garment, righted his lanky body and resumed the run through the forest. He and the others continued following the wobbly giant and another element wielder, who both seemed to know where they were going.

Loswossip salivated at what he heard. Drool oozed from his beak. He could hardly believe what a goldmine of information he had just flown into. He recognized everyone in the group except the two element wielders. He had seen that giant before: he was the one with the wobble who lived outside of Erflanthina. Loswossip had seen all the kids before, too. They were the ones with the georbs that he and Xurthun had been spying on. Loswossip guessed that the traitor, Sabtah, was the thief who stole their missing georb. That a georb was stolen was good to know; better still was the knowledge that there were even more georbs available—two it seemed—and they were right below his beak!

Loswossip was highly tempted to swoop in, distract one of the georb holders with two blinding pecks to the eyeballs and then fatally stab the jugular while simultaneously snagging the necklace. But such a mission would be suicide. A buzzard is no match for two element wielders and a nephil. His only chance at getting a georb would be to isolate the kids. But surely the wielders and the nephil were there to protect the Chosen One and they would never neglect such a solemn duty. Loswossip knew it would take an army to pull noble men from their charges—and an army is exactly what he had!

He slapped the branch on which he perched as he took wing to report everything he had learned to Lord Maboa.

―――――――――

Only two or three hours' journey up ahead, on the same path that Thogwok, the elders and the four kids were on, the sly Sabtah sat with Braulio's georb dangling before him. He was hidden in the overgrowth several yards off the path, leaning against a tree next to a gurgling stream. Straktor, his kentrosaurus, was grazing a few feet away.

Sabtah spoke to the georb. "Talk to me, magical sphere. Where do you want to go? Where is your essence? Tell me and I will take you there."

But the georb said nothing. It did not even so much as twitch.

Sabtah continued his monologue. "Why won't you talk to me? I tried to get your friend, the other stone, but he wouldn't allow me ... he burned me. But you were friendly. You slipped right off the boy's neck when I pulled you," Sabtah reminisced in a weird, almost babyish voice to the inarticulate stone.

"Now tell me, your new owner, where you want to go and I will take you there," Sabtah said, continuing his disingenuous sweet speech to the rock. But the rock did not talk.

<hr />

Back at Maboa's encampment, the vulture Loswossip talked as much as he was able. In strained croaks that were painful to hear, the vulture reported what he knew to Maboa.

"I have found the georb, Lord Maboa," Loswossip croaked. "It hangs around the neck of a young boy who is protected by two powerful element wielders and a nephil. There are three other youths in the group as well. As I spied, I learned that there are two other georbs also. One was lost to a thief the night prior. Another hangs around the neck of a short female. The last carrier is the thinner and taller one of the two males. He has a golden crest."

A sinister smile slithered across Maboa's face. Loswossip couldn't see it for Maboa was behind a veil as usual. He sat comfortably enthroned on his sedan chair with four chair carriers and four bloodthirsty guards standing in attendance. Around the chair on all sides hung thin black veils which Maboa could see through while he himself remained shrouded in darkness. A scarred and gnarled hand stretched out from a veil and landed menacingly on Loswossip's almost featherless crest.

Then a sweet voice—a voice which did not match the hideous hand—adoringly asked, "Is this all true, my faithful messenger?"

Loswossip swallowed hard. With one flex of Maboa's murderous hand, he could wring the bird's neck if he detected a lie while reading his mind. It was imperative he tell the truth.

"Yes, my lord. I saw one orb with my own eyes and I heard the small female with a dark crest speak of one she carries as well," Loswossip wheezed. Then he described in detail the location of the group and the direction they were headed. "They are the same children I saw when I delivered the message to that traitor Sabtah."

"Was there any sign of Sabtah on your journey, my loyal messenger bird?" Maboa asked sweetly.

"I did not see him my lord, but I think he is the thief who robbed them of a georb last night," Loswossip answered.

Maboa finally spoke after an uncomfortable pause. He did not bother to hide his anger with Sabtah, and in a harsh, almost metallic voice he said, "Go and immediately organize the vulture ranks. Tell them my orders are to follow you and that you are to lead us to the georbs. Have them ready to fly when I give the signal. I will gather the ground forces. If you are correct in what you have reported, I shall greatly reward you."

Loswossip bowed respectfully as Maboa lifted his hand from the bird's fleshy scalp and flew quickly to where he knew the rest of the vultures were—on a mound of rotting flesh now available since the recent victory at Azgazaron. As he flew, Loswossip felt exhilarated as he thought about what his reward would be. Once Lord Maboa controlled the air, he would likely designate Loswossip as King of the Winged Ones. In celebration of his certain victory, he croaked orders to the horde of feasting vultures, telling them they'd be leaving any moment. Then he plunged into the mound for a mouthful of flesh.

The battle at Erflanthina was fierce. With the first fireballs streaking across the sky and shattering against homes and tree trunks, the nephilim took positions throughout the perimeter, armed with huge bows, long arrows and thick shields. Swift scouts periodically returned to the village with reports about Maboa's army.

The enemy forces continue to pour from the portal.
Bands of mercenary wild men are massing
in the forest east of the gorge.
Our outpost at the gorge prevents their crossing.

Chief Barzuga had sent reinforcements to the gorge. They could not prevent the fireballs, but they could hold the army back long enough to complete their preparations for battle. The natural barrier created by the gorge would slow the massive army, but it was only a matter of time before they overwhelmed the force of nephilim guarding the crossing.

Rephaim have toppled trees to cross the gorge.
The enemy crosses the gorge but with great losses.

At this report, Barzuga ordered the nephilim at the gorge to fall back to the village but leave behind a select group of archers to target the enemy forces crossing the bridges.

Another report was sent to the chief:

The archers are hidden among the trees,
but they cannot staunch the flow
of rephaim crossing the gorge.

Barzuga offered up a prayer to the Creator and then sped through the village encouraging his warriors in the face of the coming onslaught.

The sound of the approaching army was raucous and rapidly growing—like a tidal wave roaring toward the village. Small children hiding high in the trees clutched their mothers' hands. Nephil kids too young for battle raced around the village with barrels of water, dousing the flames created by the fireballs. Warriors poised for position counted their arrows. Erflanthina braced for the evil and destructive wave about to descend on it as scouts continued to return with reports:

They mass beside the gorge.
Large rephaim warriors,
men who are hired mercenaries,
wolves, hyenas, large plated lizards
and vultures awaiting the carnage.
They number in the thousands.
They seem to await orders.

But the attack never came. The sound of the army rose to a fevered pitch, but then died down and became eerily silent. Then, from out of the dense forest emerged a single rephaite giant. He was larger, stronger and even more vicious than the rest. His body was painted with jagged stripes and pointed crude teeth dominated his wicked smile. Barzuga recognized the rephaite: Calneh, evil leader of the rephaim.

"Hear me, village of the nephilim! My lord Maboa is merciful!" called out the hulking captain of the rephaim. "He will hold back his army on one condition: send him the Chosen One. If you do, your village will be spared. But woe to you if you oppose my lord, for you will be crushed by his mighty hand. The men will be killed, the women and children enslaved ... if they are lucky!"

Barzuga's noble face was drawn. He could not tell this savage that the Chosen One had left the village or the kids and their protectors would not survive to see nightfall. But he did not doubt that the fate of his village was exactly as the rephaim captain stated.

"The One we serve is mightier than your lord!" Barzuga called in response. "Tell your lord we shall not surrender anyone whom we are sworn to protect."

Howls erupted in the forest. Provoked by the nephilim leader's response, the bloodthirsty army was salivating for an attack.

"Silence!" Calneh roared. The howls subsided. "Bring the boy."

A nephil boy stumbled forward, shoved out of the dense foliage by unseen hands. The boy's hands were bound, his face bloody, but his eyes brave. Barzuga went pale. It was Charwok, one of the young sons of Thogwok. The boy must have left the protection of the village and gone to his father's hut to warn him of the coming army, not knowing Thogwok had been sent to protect the Chosen One. Barzuga felt sick.

Calneh grabbed Charwok roughly by the collar.

"I will give you until dawn to make your decision! This boy and the lives of everyone in your village in exchange for the Chosen One is the offer! If at dawn you still refuse, your village and all in it will be utterly destroyed!" roared Calneh loud enough for a hundred nephilim to hear. Then he disappeared into the forest, dragging Charwok roughly behind him.

Barzuga gathered the Council as well as the captains of his warriors. A few wanted to tell Calneh the truth immediately: the Chosen One was no longer in the village. But the majority argued that the mission of the Chosen One was paramount. They would stall until dawn to give the kids time to get away and then they would have to admit the Chosen One was gone if they were to save Charwok.

"But what is our guarantee they will release Charwok when we tell them we cannot deliver what they want?" Barzuga asked. "How can I face Thogwok, who has already mourned the loss of wife and kids in battle, and tell him we let his son cruelly die?"

The aged Yarthuselah laid a surprisingly strong hand on the chief's arm and in a hushed tone spoke something into the nephilim leader's ear. Barzuga nodded in agreement and stood to face the Council.

"It is decided then," he said. "We wait for dawn."

An hour before dawn, a small band of stealthy nephilim warriors descended silently from the village—each one carrying an element wielder on their back. The nephilim nimbly leapt from limb to limb high above Calneh's camp, while each element wielder created gusts of air to mask any rustling sounds in the branches above. Hearing nothing but branches swaying in strong winds, the rephaim sentries on the ground suspected nothing.

Soon they spotted Charwok. The boy was tied to a tree and surrounded by half a dozen dozing giants. While element wielders continued pushing warm, soothing breezes over the relaxed guards, the fleetest nephil warrior cut the binding vines and threw the boy on his back. Within minutes, all were back in the village and Charwok was gratefully reunited with his brother Shivlok.

At dawn, Calneh woke to find Charwok gone. In a rage, he fiercely interrogated the guards whom he found asleep on their watch—their swords all missing. With no prisoner and no good excuse he slayed them on the spot. Fear iced through his veins as he considered his fate were he to fail to deliver the Chosen One to Maboa. He shoved the thought away and roused the camp. Quickly, the army assembled and marched to the village perimeter. Calneh was belligerent once again while standing before the village chief.

"Dawn has arrived and the deadline has passed!" Calneh roared. He was hoping that the boy had run away in the opposite direction of the village, where the guards were fewer, and that Barzuga did not yet know he was safe. Calneh spoke with a deceptive confidence. "Do you doom this child as well as your entire village to death? Choose now!"

"I doom no one, Calneh. If there are any deaths today they shall be on your head!" Barzuga called in response. "But I think you will find that at any rate the life of the boy is not yours to take!"

At those words, Charwok appeared at Barzuga's side with the sword of one of his captors in his hand. Calneh cursed and drew his own sword high. Waving it defiantly in the air he threatened Charwok, Chief Barzuga and all of Erflanthina.

"You have bought the boy a few hours, but he is as good as dead! You all are!" Calneh raged as he whirled and raced into the foliage.

In minutes, the forest was ringing with the screams of the approaching army. Calneh had mobilized his forces and they were moving to surround the village. A new barrage of fireballs roared overhead and arrows began to thud into wood and flesh. Erflanthina once again prepared for battle, likely for the last time.

A terrifying assortment of fierce rephaim and a regiment of Maboa's most aggressive horned lizards were rapidly advancing through the thick foliage, tearing a path for the smaller warriors. They carried torches and tar-tipped arrows, intending to burn the villagers alive. But before they lit the arrows or lobbed the torches, grotesque messenger vultures landed on the shoulders of the lead monsters. In rasping, gurgling voices they whispered something in the giant ears, and it was just the news they wanted! The rephaim in front turned around and barked orders at everyone advancing behind them. Abruptly, the army halted their advance on Erflanthina and surged around the village, racing westward and leaving the village of the nephilim untouched.

The village erupted in cheers, but Barzuga groaned. He knew there was only one thing that would cause the bloodthirsty army to change course.

"The children," Barzuga uttered just above a whisper. "They are following the children. May the One we serve protect those who carry the priceless gems, those who are guarding them, and most of all, may he protect the Chosen One."

<hr />

Maboa's forces were now following the vultures. With Loswossip in the lead, the birds took to wing and assembled in the sky in the shape of a serpentine, curved sword.

Giants on the backs of huge horned lizards were the first to assemble behind Maboa. These were the bloodthirsty rephaim, and they led the ground army. Making a wide arc around Erflanthina's village border, the brute beasts cleared a violent path through the thick vegetation.

Following immediately behind the mounted rephaim were forest wolves and hyenas, sniffing for their prey and patrolling the outskirts of the army's march. Behind them came hundreds of men loyal to Maboa. They loudly traveled in disorderly gangs rather than in disciplined military units. At the tail were the rest of the rephaim ground troops—hundreds of them.

Westward the evil army rushed. Loswossip knew the path the kids had taken, and so following the lead of the vultures overhead, the savage army found the path and raced along it. Inhaling the oxygen-rich air deeply, the battle-ready rephaim and their trained beasts could run for hours without stopping. And Loswossip, with the dark cloud of buzzards behind him, kept an eye on the army below and flew slowly enough so the ground troops could keep up with him at a steady run.

From the first of the giants to the last, the line of warriors stretched for over two miles, crashing through vegetation and leaving a trail of devastation in their wake. Like a violent death march, everything in their path was sliced, snapped, trampled, or driven away. No bud, branch, or beast in their way was sacred. By the time the last of the beasts had passed, this same path the kids had taken earlier was barely recognizable.

Maboa and Calneh gave orders to move quickly. There would be no breaks until they reached their goal. And if one were found lagging behind, he would be dealt with the same as any branch that was in the way. These were Maboa's methods of travel toward battle. He himself road swiftly in the sedan chair carried by eight running slaves, that number likely dropping to six or five—by Maboa's own sword—before the battle would even begin. Such incentives drove Maboa's army.

The kids and their protectors were not moving nearly as fast. After two wrong turns made by Thogwok, three or four arguments between Lawth and Braulio, and a few bathroom breaks, the distance between them and the rapidly approaching army was shrinking at an alarming rate. Worse yet, none in the group, not even the wise Enosh, knew of Loswossip's spying or that Maboa was so close on their trail. Their focus was instead on the fact that a georb was stolen, and they were following the path Thogwok determined the thief had taken.

Thogwok had to stop several times during their pursuit (which also slowed them down) in order to look for clues on the trail and re-find the kentrosaurus tracks whenever he lost them, particularly at junctures where the trail forked. But for as slow as they went, Sabtah moved even slower. In fact, he had hardly moved at all from his position which was only a few hours west of the campsite. He felt no urgency to go far since he didn't suspect the bumbling giant to be the good tracker that he was. Furthermore, he was in no rush to go anywhere until the georb he stole led him somewhere—namely, to the elemental essence.

Back and forth Sabtah paced, talking to, bargaining with and even threatening the georb in his hand. He was feeling foolish talking to a stone, especially since, with hardened resistance, the stone refused to acknowledge him. Frustrated, he shoved the georb into his pocket—warning it menacingly that it would tell him the location of the elemental essence one way or the other.

"Your friend," Sabtah mumbled half to himself and half to the georb in his pocket. "Maybe I need your friend in order for it to work. But why couldn't I get that one? You, I had no trouble with. But the other—why couldn't I …?" His thoughts drifted off, recalling what had happened when he tried to get Sean's georb. Not liking that memory, he shook his head and tried to think about something else.

Then Sabtah heard the faint sound of someone yelling. It came from the east. Straktor heard it also. He raised his head from his motionless slumber and stuck out his tongue and sniffed the air. Sabtah immediately mounted and ordered the lizard back on the path. Cautiously, Sabtah and his beast emerged from the thick tree cover and looked toward the east. He saw nothing, but then he heard a voice again. It was a low rumble of a voice.

"That dumb giant," Sabtah muttered to himself. He thought maybe he heard the higher pitched voice of someone else talking loudly with him.

"Those fools are probably too stupid to even know I robbed them last night," he said to himself. "And since they are so kind as to come to me, maybe I'll just take the other one when they stop by," he smirked. But as he thought about last night he didn't know how he would manage that. Fingering the hilt of his knife, he thought about how easy it would be to slit that skinny kid's throat.

His thoughts were interrupted by a crack and a crash. It sounded like the felling of a tree. He heard the squawks of several birds flying overhead—evidently disturbed by something. And then he saw it—a dark cloud in the sky comprised of large birds migrating his way. Two rabbits crashed through the undergrowth and bolted past him, fleeing toward the west. Sabtah immediately knew what was coming. Then he heard another crash.

The kids heard it too. Coming from the east were the crackling sounds of another tree meeting its doom. A flutter of birds rose in the air not far behind them and soon passed overhead, rapidly heading west.

Enosh, Lawth, and Thogwok all looked at each other with knowing eyes. Not wanting the kids to panic, Enosh spoke to Lawth and Thogwok in the Nephil language.

"Maboa's forces are led by rephaim who don't walk but rather run toward their battles. Their strides are three times ours. There is no way we can outrun them."

"I can head them off and distract them," said Thogwok nobly.

"That's suicide, you idiot," Lawth said. "What good would it do, anyway, if ten minutes after they kill you they still catch up with us? Besides, it isn't you they are after; they want the kids and their georbs!"

"Lawth is right. We will stay together," Enosh said.

The kids didn't have to speak Nephil to know they were in trouble. It wasn't hard to guess that the same army that had attacked Erflanthina and wreaked havoc on Azgazaron was now closing in on them. Candice began to cry.

Another flurry of birds whooshed overhead. Animals sped past them, heedless of the seven noisy humans as they fled the army in panic.

Enosh knew Maboa's tactics well enough to know that diverting off the trail would do no good. Sensitive wolf and hyena noses would pick up the scents and descend on them eventually anyway.

"I have an idea," he said. "Everyone keep following the trail, quickly as you can, but with absolute silence." And putting his finger to his mouth he continued quickly forward, the rest silently following.

Candice did the best she could to stifle her sobs and Braulio and Lawth used a lot of self-control to not bicker or blame. With no one arguing and a huge incentive to move fast, they moved more efficiently than ever.

They had just crested a small hill and come silently over the other side when a beast in their path startled them and stopped them in their tracks. It was a spiked dinosaur with a rider atop who looked just as shocked to see them as they were to come upon him. They had been so quiet coming over the hill he had not heard their approach. And though they had never seen the rider before, Thogwok knew immediately who he was by looking at his boots and the feet of the beast.

"Thief!" he yelled so loudly that the spiked dinosaur bolted. "Enosh, it's him, the one I've been tracking! Stop! Thief!"

But Sabtah's dinosaur galloped all the faster. It looked as though there would be no catching it until a fire burst out in front of him—compliments of Enosh. The beast turned to the right and another flame redirected it back to the left. A third flame blasted over the lizard and then doubled back toward it, forcing the beast to turn back and face the group.

Lawth shot a flame of his own, attempting to wall their quarry in completely, but he missed and only managed to ignite a small cluster of leaves well above Sabtah's head.

Sabtah sneered and drew a long curved sword from his sheath. He twirled it in the air and its brilliantly polished metal reflected the flame pillars behind him.

"Toss us the necklace and you may go," Enosh commanded with calm control.

"Ha!" Sabtah scoffed. "I have a better idea. Why don't one of you cowards come over here and take it from me!" he sneered with the long blade twirling in the air.

"No need for that," yelled Braulio as he unslung his bow and loaded it with a long nephil arrow. "I've been lookin' for an excuse to pull this."

And pull it he did, releasing the shaft straight at Sabtah's chest. Yet as fast as that arrow sailed, Sabtah moved faster and knocked it away with his blade.

"Better try that again, young one! I see you need a lot a practice!" Sabtah taunted.

Braulio immediately did. And the second arrow was as deftly deflected as the first.

Thogwok lunged forward and predictably tripped—this time going face first all the way to ground.

Sabtah howled with laughter. "Is that the best you can do with your giant you brought along for protection?" he chided Enosh and Lawth. "Good luck with that when Maboa's forces get here!"

This was followed by another crash—this one disturbingly close. The growls and howls and yells of foul beasts were rising behind them, and growing louder by the minute.

"And it sounds like that will be in less than five minutes," Sabtah continued with an eerie calm.

Thogwok rose to make a second lunge, but Enosh forbade him, realizing that whoever this thief was, if he was fast enough to deflect arrows, then he could hack away at a clumsy giant with both eyes closed.

Both sides stood fixed to the spot. Sabtah couldn't flee without the threat of a fireball or an arrow in his back and the kids and their protectors clearly couldn't remain there with an army bearing down on them. Nevertheless, they also had to regain possession of the georb and Sabtah wasn't about to hand it over.

Just then, the opportunity Enosh had been hoping for arose. Bounding over the hill and coming up from behind them, a small herd of garudimimuses tore past the group. Fleeing from the coming danger, the two-legged, ostrich-like dinosaurs ran and hopped and artfully darted around the human interruptions in their path.

At once, Enosh ordered Lawth to constrain two with air ropes. He did so. Enosh likewise constrained three more, taking each to the ground with an air tie around their ankles. In seconds, five garudimimuses were on the dirt, flailing, stammering and complaining loudly—unable to get up.

"Boys! Quickly! Each one of you take one!" Enosh ordered.

Braulio and Lawth each leapt astride two beasts. Thogwok climbed atop the largest animal while Enosh grabbed Candice and told Fong to run over and help Sean control his. Enosh and Lawth snapped the invisible air bonds around the creatures' ankles and in a flash the beasts sprang to their feet with riders on their backs. Everyone was now sitting on the back of and clutching the long neck of a wild-eyed, two-legged dinosaur! If they could just stay on their speedy mounts without being bucked off, they might be able to outrun the army.

"Follow me!" ordered Enosh as if they were going into battle rather than fleeing from it. Enosh tore ahead with Candice holding tight and screaming as they bolted off. Lawth pranced behind them on his mount. Fong and Sean awkwardly clung together on one, fighting over the invisible air reigns Enosh had hastily conjured somewhere around the creature's neck. Braulio handled his beast quite well, and passed Sean and Fong as he tried to outdo Lawth. Thogwok lumbered behind the rest, nearly crushing his poor dinosaur.

Away they scurried, faster and faster as they got used to the feel of these strange and speedy bird-like land runners. The army was in hot pursuit, sensing their prey was at hand. But the screeches, howls and sounds of crashing trees grew fainter as the kids, Thogwok and the elders continued fleeing. As long as they could hold on to the air-conjured reins and stay on the backs of the swift creatures, they would be safe ... for now.

But Sabtah and the georb he stole were gone.

Chapter 15

LAND BATTLE FOR AIR

Braulio gripped the invisible air reins looped around the neck of his garudimimus. He banked hard to the left to avoid a tree, ducked below a low-hanging vine, and raced his swift-footed dinosaur just as he would his motorcycle. He followed behind Enosh, who took the lead with Candice clinging to his back. The others followed behind, Lawth going slow enough to keep an eye on Sean and Fong who had already almost fallen more than once.

Suddenly, the scenery changed as the seven riders burst out from under of the cover of trees and into a clearing. Seeing a clearing in this thick forest was unusual; even more unusual was seeing civilization. But just ahead of them they noticed a village—a village that was on the ground instead of up in the trees.

Loswossip, who had been diligently searching from above, spotted the group as soon as they had escaped the cloaking of the trees. The vulture wasn't expecting them to be on the backs of swift runners, but that didn't matter. He could rein them in one way or the other. He gave the command to those flying behind him.

"Bank sharp left and descend!" he rasped.

The vultures followed his lead, and as one dark, predatory swarm the one hundred and fifty or so carcass-eating birds dove downward toward the group.

Farmers were working in the fields all around the small settlement called Porfiznin. As they looked up and discerned the dark cloud of vultures rapidly descending, they ran full-bore into the village, yelling an alarm.

A dark shadow, like a quickly moving cloud, engulfed Enosh, Thogwok, Lawth and all the kids. They looked up and were horrified to see an ominous formation of large, flapping flesh eaters plunging toward them faster than they could run.

"Head for the trees!" Enosh ordered.

Banking sharply to the left on their skittish mounts, they all followed Enosh who was attempting to hide them under tree cover south of the clearing.

"Why not the village?" Braulio yelled at him. "We can gang up with them! Plus they must have weapons!"

"That would only ensure their deaths when the rest of the army comes!" Enosh yelled back over his shoulder as he raced forward. "Besides, with no roofs there is no protection or concealment from vultures, anyway! Follow me!"

Digging his heels into his mount, Enosh raced toward the nearby thicket of trees. The rest followed as quickly as they could as the lead vultures loomed frighteningly closer each second. Fong was sitting behind Sean and wrestled him for the invisible reigns, trying to take control of their shared dinosaur. In the shuffle and confusion she slipped and fell. Sean reached back and tried to grab her as she went, but he lost his balance also, and the two tumbled onto the ground as their freshly liberated garudimimus pranced wildly away.

Braulio crashed through the underbrush as he followed Enosh and Candice under tree cover. Lawth followed close behind, about to join them when he heard Thogwok bellow, "They've fallen! Sean and Fong are down!"

When Enosh heard this he turned his beast so sharp and fast that Candice nearly slipped off. Thogwok had also turned back toward the two who were picking themselves up off the ground, but when he did he saw a horrible sight. All of Maboa's vultures, with Loswossip in the lead, were directly behind Fong and Sean. They were flying fast and low—just inches above the ground intent on attack! Vulture talons would be slicing and puncturing Fong and Sean in less than five seconds!

"Sean! Fong! Duck! Dit the hirt!" Thogwok yelled in alarm.

Fong looked back to see why and Sean instinctively shoved her to the ground and covered her with his own body. Loswossip zoned in on them, unclenched his talons, and went in for the assault with a bird battalion behind him. But in the next instant he and the first fifteen birds behind him were blasted backwards in a violent gust of wind. Upside down and sideways they awkwardly tumbled—flipping and flapping as they did uncontrolled somersaults in the air, smacking into each other and squawking in shock and pain.

Enosh charged forward out of the trees with his staff extended before him, ordering the air to obey. Lawth followed his master's lead and blasted a second wave of vultures. Enosh swished his staff to the right, then to the left, and vultures here and there spontaneously burst into flames and dropped to the ground. The air was aflutter with angry, dazed and wind-blasted birds. In the mayhem and the smoke now rising from their fallen comrades, the birds tried to make sense of the flying pattern, where their leader was and where their prey was. They began to chaotically encircle the humans, dodging and barely missing each other in the air. More air blasts followed by more fireballs set birds aflame and careening to the ground. One flew too close to Thogwok and got its head smashed between two giant fists. Several birds flew high and dive-bombed the group.

The sound of a crashing tree somewhere in the forest and a distant giant voice roaring, "Cha-a-a-rge!" reminded them that they had to get out of there soon. The rapid descent of the vultures had been a sign to the army that they had found their prey.

Braulio wanted to join the fight. He knew he could take down several of these foul creatures if he could only get his bow off his back— but he was using both hands and all his effort trying to stay on top of his hysterical garudimimus. So at the moment, he could do nothing.

The battle looked like it would come down to whether or not Enosh and Lawth could fend off one hundred fifty vultures and safely get the kids out of there before the rest of the army came. Then it happened.

One vulture got close enough to Fong to reach her and clutch onto her shoulders with its strong talons. Enosh and Lawth were engaged in other battles and Thogwok was too far away to rescue her when he noticed it and yelled, "They frabbed Gong!"

Sean wasn't sure what "frabbed Gong" meant, but he could both hear and see that Fong, who had been right next to him, was screaming and frantically flailing her legs—which were already two feet off the ground and rising. Instinctively, he grabbed the vulture's leg and pulled the two of them back down. Squawking loudly, the vulture violently lunged toward Sean's face to take out his eyes. But Sean deftly deflected the large beak, and with a swift slap, knocked the buzzard so hard that it released Fong and fell upside down and unconscious, dangling limply from the leg that Sean was still holding.

"Nice hit!" yelled Thogwok, who had galloped over to the two kids. "I couldn'a done any better myself!" he said with a giant-sized pat on Sean's head that nearly pushed him to his knees.

Sean was equally surprised. He had never hit anything that hard before. And strangely, it took almost no effort to do it.

More vultures swooped in.

"Let's see some more of that!" the impressed Thogwok said as he forcefully smacked away another predator bird that had targeted Fong.

Sean had his chance. Within seconds, four more talons grabbed shoulders. But now they were Sean's own shoulders. Two giant birds were on him, one on each shoulder, and the boy felt himself starting to lift off the ground. But even before he got much air, Sean grabbed both sets of legs, one pair in one hand and one pair in the other, effortlessly flung the shocked birds in circles around his head, and clubbed them into each other before casting them to the ground with a solid thud. Another flew too close to Sean. He clasped his fists together and swung his long arms like a baseball bat, smacking the bird like a major league player. The buzzard sailed toward Thogwok, hit his thick chest and slumped to the ground.

The bird battle with Thogwok and Sean caught Enosh's eye and he noted Fong on the ground ducking for cover.

"Lawth!" he ordered. "Get Fong and get to the trees!"

Lawth blasted a pathetic fire pellet at an incoming vulture which lit only half a wing on fire before he galloped over to Fong. The incensed bird swooped down, talons at the ready, to attack Lawth. Enosh spotted him and sent a stream of fire from the end of his staff that finished it off the buzzard in a spectacular burst of flames. But Enosh didn't see the rock coming from above. A sly vulture had picked up a stone and dropped it on Enosh's head. All before him went black, and in seconds, the venerable Enosh was off his mount and unconscious on the ground.

This left Candice alone atop her wild garudimimus—for about three seconds. She was immediately thrown off and the beast gratefully escaped.

Braulio watched this happen but chose to take a swipe at a nearby attacker before going over to help. He missed. And he nearly fell off his mount in doing so. Thogwok also witnessed Enosh and Candice fall and he tore over as fast as he could on his overburdened beast to get to them. But the vultures flew faster, and within seconds the vile gang of birds had swarmed all around Candice.

"NOOOO!" Thogwok yelled as he galloped toward her.

But there was nothing Thogwok could do; Candice was airborne! Six vultures had her—two on each leg and one gripping each arm, carrying her face down higher and higher above Thogwok's reach. The vultures rose in the air and then banked to the right, flying over the heads of those battling below. When the others looked up, they saw Candice being lifted helplessly away, screaming for help.

Braulio couldn't take it anymore. He grabbed his bow off his back, loaded an arrow, and was promptly bucked from his mount. Picking himself off the ground, he strung his bow again, took aim, and was knocked to the ground by Lawth, still atop his ride, who intentionally smacked into him.

"Idiot! You really think you will hit only the vultures? And even if you did, what would happen to her? Use your head!"

As they watched her being carried away, they had the sickening realization that there was nothing they could do.

Something in the forest howled. Whatever it was, it was very close. More hostile yells reverberated through the forest.

"We need to get Enosh and get out of here now!" Lawth commanded.

"But Candice!" Thogwok protested.

"We can't help her! We have to save ourselves now so we can get her later. Thogwok, you go get Enosh and carry him to safety! Braulio, you protect Fong and get both of you immediately to the trees with Thogwok! Sean, you—" Lawth began to order.

But as he turned to look at Sean, he noticed a mound of dead vultures on the ground next to the boy with a smattering of loose feathers fluttering in the air above him. Shocked, Lawth scanned the surrounding area. There had to be at least another fifty of the nasty buzzards—all dead, littering the ground around Sean.

But most stunning of all was Sean himself. He was leaping and dancing, swinging and kicking. He was charged with an energy like none of them had ever seen before. Gripping two large birds by the legs like giant feathery clubs—one in each hand—the skinny boy might as well have been a bulky barbarian warrior. Forcefully and swiftly swinging his manic, squawking clubs as if he were a Samurai Swordsman, Sean took down one vulture after another until the two he was gripping and all others around him were dead. Soon none were left save three—and they began to flee.

Loswossip had ordered his entire host to attack the tall, golden crested male and the little female—for they both had the prized stones. When this plan was beginning to fail, he ordered the kidnapping of Candice as ransom if needed. Now it looked as if it would be needed. With their flock decimated and their leader, Loswossip, badly injured and crumpled on the ground amidst the carnage, the three remaining vultures retreated, croaking in fear and anger.

"Don't let 'em get away," yelled Thogwok. "They'll tell Maboa which hay we are wedding!"

The three survivors flew away fast, but not fast enough to miss an arrow from Braulio and a halfway decent fireball from Lawth. The two struck birds tumbled to the ground.

"Good shots! One more to go," whooped Thogwok, who had just dismounted his grateful lizard and powerfully whipped a rock just over the last vulture's head. He threw a second one and nearly toppled over after the release.

Braulio shot an arrow and missed. Lawth sent another fire spurt—quite pathetic. The bird became a smaller and smaller target. After two more arrows and one more rock sailed past with near misses, Lawth conjured up his best fire blast yet which pummeled into the bird's backside and sent him smoking to the ground. Lawth had successfully struck the fatal blow and the smirk on his face made it clear to Braulio and Thogwok that he was quite pleased. But the gloating only lasted a second. To his and Thogwok's horror, the flaming vulture landed at the edge of the clearing and at the feet of a snarling wolf.

"Forest wolves!" Thogwok exclaimed in a hushed but urgent voice as another one crept out of the forest and began sniffing at the vulture mess.

"Maboa must be using them to track our scent!" Lawth said as a third one emerged from the forest.

"Those foul beasts are practically blind, but they can sniff out anything. No way we can escape if they are on our trail," Thogwok assessed with uncharacteristic pessimism.

"What are we going to do?" asked Fong.

"You three are going to stay with Thogwok and take yourselves and Enosh to safety," answered Lawth.

At that moment Sean bounded over to the rest of them, the two mangled and bloodied vulture clubs still in hand, and said, "Dude! Like, I've never felt that kind of energy before! That was so-o-o-o awes—"

Thogwok slapped a hand over Sean's mouth and pointed to the wolves—now four of them—circling the first remains of vulture carnage and sniffing out suspicious scents. One of them howled.

"We need to be as quiet and fast as we can, kids," whispered Thogwok solemnly as he turned to head south through the forest with the unconscious Enosh on his back.

"Yes, you do," ordered Lawth. "I will meet up with you later."

"Later? But where—" Thogwok began.

"Just go!" ordered Lawth as he bolted straight toward the wolves on his frantic garudimimus.

The ostrich-like dinosaur began to squeal as it saw and smelled the small pack of canines ahead. The nearsighted wolves heard the squeal, caught the scent, and began howling to alert the rest of the horde which was now just a few feet away in the forest interior.

Lawth banked sharply to the left, heading west, straight down the road that led toward the little village and away from the kids, Enosh, and Thogwok. The wolves followed their sensitive snouts and charged the rider and his mount. Madly barking as they ran, the pack pursued Lawth and his squealing dinosaur all the way to the village while entirely missing the scent of the others in their frenzy.

Thogwok grimly watched as Lawth sped off to what was likely going to be his death. Braulio, Fong, and even Sean realized the sacrifice Lawth was making. They watched speechlessly as he disappeared down the path and into the village, wolves in hot pursuit and steadily gaining.

When they could see him no longer, a tree on the edge of the forest crashed into the clearing and a barbaric roar followed it to the ground. Thogwok quickly ushered the kids into the tree cover on the south side of the clearing and they hid and watched as a giant the size of Thogwok emerged on a gigantic beast.

"Dude, he's ridin' a triceratops!" yelled Sean.

Thogwok once again covered Sean's mouth—which meant that he covered most of his face.

"No wonder they can knock down trees," Braulio said under his breath.

Another beast split through the underbrush and emerged in the clearing. This one had very long horns protruding forward and several horns extending from its neck frill. Modern museums would probably call it a *Styracosaurus*. The overgrown lizard shook and spit as its enormous rider—another giant the size of Thogwok—hauled on the reigns and positioned it next to the first dinosaur. Both riders—scouts for Maboa's army—immediately scanned their surroundings as they stood still for a moment at the edge of the clearing. After quickly assessing the mass of dead vultures around the meadow, they looked up toward the village. Excited howls were emanating from that direction, and from atop their high mounts they could just barely make out a rider being chased by wolves.

The giants scanned to the north and to the south. They looked straight into the thicket where Thogwok and the young ones were hiding and terror struck the kids as they peered into the faces of these vicious beings. Except for their size, the kids could see they were nothing at all like Thogwok. Their eyes were ablaze with bloodlust and their faces showed no warmth, compassion or concern for others. Like ravenous beasts, they were intent only on savage brutality!

Only after the fierce giants looked away did anyone dare speak.

"Rephaim," Thogwok whispered in answer to the unspoken question on all their minds. Part human they'z are but definitely not sons of God. Evil they'z are, and nearly all of 'em follow Maboa. Bitter enemies of ours and feared by yuz humans. Pray they decide to follow the wolves and that their keen forest sense doesn't lead 'em directly to us."

Although no one prayed in those few seconds except Thogwok, prayer must have been heard. The giants roared orders to their obedient horned lizards, and now with the first taste of freedom from the encumbering trees, the massive beasts galloped toward the village. The thunder of their pounding feet shook the ground.

No sooner did the danger of the rephaim and their huge beasts fade away than several more of them emerged. Out of the clearing they poured one after the other. Some were on mounts like the lead two. Others were on smaller beasts of various types. Many more simply ran with long, earth-shaking strides. Fong immediately noticed that although rephaim were large like the nephilim, they didn't move like them. Whereas the good giants effortlessly sprinted and climbed and almost floated when they walked (Thogwok being the exception), the rephaim walked hard—almost slamming the ground with their feet as they went, paying no attention to vultures or anything else they might squash.

Behind the rephaim emerged the most horrible creature they had seen yet. Fong gasped and quickly slapped her hand over her mouth. Thogwok gently covered her shoulder with his massive hand to comfort her. The boys just stared in shock as a wormy, slithering reptile of some sort snaked out of the forest. It had four salamander-like legs that kept its body low enough that its belly still slithered along the ground. It had a long, whipping tail which snapped branches and flattened saplings. A snake-like head with rows of sharp, ugly teeth rose from the serpentine neck. A wisp of steam rose from its flared nostrils.

The beast emerged violently out of the forest, slapping tree trunks and scattering boulders with its tail, leaving a narrow trail of destruction wherever it slithered. Glad to finally be in the clearing, it let out a shrill screech. The thing sniffed the air and detected a scent it had been following. Slipping out its obscene forked tongue repeatedly, it aggressively sniffed the ground, squashing dead and injured vultures as it slinked along. Weaving its elongated neck back and forth, up and down, and in circles, it spied everything intently and intelligently. Its yellow, reptilian eyes peered over to where the kids were hiding. Fong felt a sharp pinch on her shoulder as a chill went down her spine.

"Ouch!" she said a little too loudly.

The monster had not heard her, thankfully, and it went back to inspecting the perimeter, prowling along with its long and twisting body, tongue flicking.

"Oh, sorry Fong," whispered Thogwok, who had gripped her shoulder a little too tightly, "but that's Maboa's dragon. He travels with it. So yuz can be sure he's not far behind. He's a sorcerer of incredible power and he can see through anythin'—includin' these trees. We need to go right now!"

They turned from the clearing and sped through the thick southern forest, hoping beyond hope that none of the walking horrors they had just seen were following them.

Chapter 16

CLOSE TO ENEMY CAMP

He was awakened by a scream. It sounded like it came from the dumb girl who was traveling with the element wielders and the clumsy giant. After the scream came a growl from what sounded like a very large creature. It was followed by a smack and then a yelp from some canine. The injured animal scurried past him, stepping on his face with its hairy paw. That hurt. But it didn't hurt nearly as much as the gash on his leg. It felt like he was missing a swath of skin. His wing was awkwardly bent and it hurt too.

Loswossip shifted his body to adjust his wing. A pain he hadn't noticed before shot like a dart through his side. Opening one eye slowly he peered around. He could see the one who screamed and as he thought, it was the dumb girl. She was sitting in a corner, bound with chains. The thing that growled was near her. He was a hairy, rephaite giant and he was guarding her—not from escape—but from the other beasts in the room.

"Anyone else tries to take a bite and I'll have more than just yer fur, ya mangy mutts," yelled the rephaite giant, releasing a fistful of wolf hair from his massive palm.

Somewhere behind him Loswossip could hear the rumblings and shufflings of the wolf pack. Evidently one of them had gotten too close to the valuable prisoner who could lead Maboa to a georb. Then Loswossip heard a voice far worse than that of the rephaite.

"The bird is conscious. Bring it to me," the voice rasped.

A huge sandaled foot hoisted Loswossip off the ground. Briefly airborne against its will, the large bird landed with a thud and slid to the edge of Maboa's veil.

"Why do I not have a georb in my hand, foul bird?" rasped Maboa. Loswossip sensed there was no good answer. He also knew that a lie wouldn't suffice. He didn't have the mental wherewithal to deceive the mind-reading Maboa, nor should he even be thinking about attempting it. That traitorous thought alone could get him killed and needed to stop immediately! He quickly gave the truth.

"That boy," Loswossip strained to say, "the golden-crested one I told you was a carrier of a georb—he destroyed most of my forces. The rest were mowed down by blasts from the element wielders."

Maboa hissed. That was never a good sign.

"You told me there were two georbs, four wretched children, two wielders, and one nephil," Maboa said through clenched teeth. His voice was harsh, like metal scraping against metal. The sound made Loswossip tremble. "Why did my army find only one child, one wielder, and no georb? Where are the rest?"

"Yes, that is how many there are," Loswossip quickly answered. "I saw them all before I was struck. I didn't see where they fled but they must be near," he desperately croaked, hoping to sooth his irate lord.

Another hiss. This one was slower, more drawn out, and more sinister. "And how do two wielders, one fumbling giant, and four imbecilic children defeat a flock of one hundred fifty battle-trained birds of prey? Answer me!" Maboa spat with a rage that made Candice quiver in her chains and sob.

"I ... guess ... the wielders and the giant must have trained them how to fight," Loswossip offered, almost as a question more than an answer.

He may have imagined it, but the vulture was quite sure he could feel the spit on his feathers from the next hiss. How it got through the veil he wasn't sure, but the anger wasn't just audible, it was tangible. If he had hands instead of wings he could have taken hold of the tension. Even the nearby guards, large and intimidating as they were, took a few steps backwards. And then, in an instant, dizzyingly, the mood shifted.

"You are a wise bird," said the now soft voice of Maboa. "Your story matches that of your pathetic warriors who were injured and strewn about on the field. It also matches that of the only birds worthy of being called true warriors—the six who brought me my prisoner. One of them will surely be exalted to a position of authority over you."

Loswossip fought for control. He didn't dare let his true feelings surface. He knew he was still being scrutinized and that his life was on the line.

"And I am sure one of them will hunt down the remaining prey. Better yet, the prey may be foolish enough to come to us-s-s," Maboa said with another hiss as his voice trailed over toward Candice.

Candice felt a chill wave crash over her. She knew exactly what this meant. But would anyone actually try to rescue her? She was being held in a small village near the clearing where they fought the vultures. She was wrapped tightly in chains and propped up in a corner of a hut. Maboa's army had speedily taken over the entire village, killing all who hadn't fled. Through the roofless building she could see a few of the remaining vultures that encircled her, guarding her from above. Inside the hut she was surrounded by nightmare creatures; the worst one hidden behind that veil.

Candice shuddered to think about what would happen to her. She was terrified even to look at the beasts in the room, let alone try to fight them and escape. Whether or not anyone would attempt to rescue her she didn't know. But even if they did, she couldn't imagine how they'd ever get past her horrible captors. Candice broke down in tears; crying in despair.

***

Thogwok led Braulio, Fong and Sean into a wide stream, walking (and stumbling) a good distance in the water in order to throw off their pursuers from their strong scents. Eventually they crossed over to land, waded into another stream and repeated the process, with Enosh draped helplessly over Thogwok's shoulders the entire time. The three frightened kids followed close behind their savvy forest ranger and away from danger. Gradually, the yells and howls of Maboa's army receded off in the distance.

Thogwok noticed a peculiar plant and quickly plucked five of its massive, bowl-shaped leaves. "Here, everybody take one," he said. "Now each of yuz lay down in yer leaf and roll around in it. Then spit in it and get yer scents all over the thing."

The kids did as they were told. After laying Enosh down gently in a leaf of his own, the enormous Thogwok rubbed his own leaf all around his body as if it were a bath towel. Then he licked it a few times. He snatched up all the other leaves and flung all five of them in the middle of the nearest stream. The leaves floated like floppy canoes downstream toward the clamor of Maboa's creatures.

"*Wafters* is what we call 'em. Those leaves will hold onto a scent only as short a time as they can. They expel whatever odor gets on 'em and keen-sensed critters will smell 'em a mile away. Should do the trick," Thogwok said as the leaves floated quickly away down the stream.

They hurried on and then, just for good measure, decided to splash a short distance up just one more stream. That stream marked the end of Thogwok's balancing luck. He fell face first into the water, Enosh sinking in after him.

"Enosh!" Fong yelled. "Someone grab him before he drowns!"

Braulio and Sean both dove in after the elder. In a second, Enosh emerged in Sean's arms very wet but also very much awake.

"Ah! Well, that was quite a strange set of dreams," Enosh mused. "Did I miss anything while I slept?"

Thogwok and the kids quickly filled him in as they helped him out of the stream and stressed the urgency of moving on.

"Well, if being tracked is your concern, there are relatively simple ways to deal with that," Enosh said as he bunched up fistfuls of his robe and rung them out.

"But before we know which way to send our followers, we need to know with certainty which way we are not going. First off, not forgetting our mission, we need to make sure the remaining georbs are secure,"

Enosh said as he inspected Sean's, which hung conspicuously over his chest. Fong patted her shirt briefly—indicating hers was underneath.

"Second, we need to make sure we ourselves are secure—relatively speaking, considering the circumstances, of course. Third, we must locate Candice and Lawth and find a way to rescue them."

<hr />

West of the village of Porfiznin, Lawth was just barely escaping the claws and fangs of the wolf pack behind him. The clearing he was racing through stretched a good distance west of the village. With his ostrich-like dinosaur growing steadily more tired and the wolves steadily gaining on him, he knew he would need to do something different. As soon as he could, he entered into a patch of forest and then splashed into a surprisingly deep and wide river. A few brave wolves dogpaddled in after him and others following the current along the banks as Lawth wrestled for control of his uncooperative garudimimus. The beast stumbled and Lawth went tumbling over its head and into the fast-moving water, drifting out of reach of the terrified creature, which scampered out of the river and got away.

Now Lawth was on his own, moving quickly downstream in the power of the water with wolves hot on his tail. He was exhausted, scared and out of ideas. He lifted a hand out of the water and attempted a fireball. Mere sparks fizzled from his fingers. He tried again. A thin line of fire missed the wolves and pummeled into the dirt behind them.

Growling and ferocious, the wolves were unrelenting. They would have their prey. The ones on land followed along the bank, daring Lawth to get close to shore, while the ones in the water were catching up to him. Lawth faced downstream to paddle with the current and perhaps outswim them to reach the other shore when, in horror, he realized something in the water was eyeing him.

"Le-Le-Leviatha-a-a-an!" Lawth yelled to no one but himself.

Just ahead, a monstrous, slippery mass of flesh with a serpent-like head and extremely long neck rose from the water—facing him. Lawth knew he had to move fast if he was to survive. No time to swim ashore.

The current was too strong and would carry him within reach of the mouth of the beast in moments.

Lawth had no other choice. He had to somehow get out of this, get back to the kids, and make sure the georbs were safe. He lifted both hands out of the water, remembered instinctively what Enosh had tried to teach him all these years and, knowing what was at stake, blasted for all he was worth.

Two fireballs, good ones at last, tore from his palms. The first one struck the monster solidly on the left cheek. The second bronzed a small section of his long neck.

The creature let out an ear-piercing shriek. Its entire massive body surged upward and Lawth could see the immensity of the water lizard as he drifted steadily toward it. It had the bulk to crush him in an instant, and Lawth was helplessly floating ever closer. Then the monster lunged forward toward Lawth—its enormous body causing a huge splash and displacing a wave which washed Lawth several yards backwards.

Seizing the opportunity, Lawth grabbed hold of a low-hanging branch. He pulled hard and hoisted himself with his dripping, soggy robes upward and clambered onto the precarious branch as the water monster rose up out of the river again, craned his neck high, snorted water out of its nostrils and glared down ominously at the little man who had just burned him. With squinty eyes full of malice and another ear-piercing shriek, the leviathan arched its neck, readied like a cobra to strike his prey before swallowing it whole.

Whipping out his staff, which had been strapped firmly to his back, Lawth pointed it at the beast and concentrated harder than he ever had before.

And it worked.

Blasts of flame shot like a rapid-fire cannon and pummeled the neck and torso of the river monster. With a roar and a violent lunge, the beast spun around flailing. It heaved its mass into the river, causing a surge that sent the swimming wolves yelping backwards in the roiling water as the leviathan escaped downstream.

But Lawth didn't stop firing. He thought about Enosh, the kids, the georbs, and what Maboa was close to doing. He even thought a moment about Thogwok, though that didn't help much. And with a rapid series of blasts with meaning behind them like never before, Lawth pelted the wolves on the shore, one wolf after another, setting fur ablaze. The wolves leapt into the water to put out their flames. Then one by one they all fled. Those already in the water paddled as fast as they could to shore, still terrified by the beast and now the fire blasts. Lawth gave each one a well-aimed shot in the rear as it emerged from the water and sped yelping away.

The deep river returned to its normal, strong flow. The leviathan was gone. The wolves and their yelping were gone. Lawth heard nothing except the rush of the river and then faintly, ever so slightly, he heard the sound of an ocean wave crashing on a beach.

A brilliantly green, gold, and purple parrot fluttered over to a branch not far above Thogwok's head. It sat and waited patiently for Enosh to finish speaking.

"So then, we are quite certain that Lawth headed west toward the sea with the pack of wolves after him," Enosh was saying. "And what is the word on the location of Candice and Maboa's army, dear friend," he said, turning his head up to face the radiantly feathered, intelligent parrot.

"The captive is inside one of the buildings in the village of Porfiznin," the parrot squawked. "She is in the same room as Maboa and his fiercest guards. The army has decimated the town population and has transformed Porfiznin into their temporary base. Six vultures are encircling her building. They would have seen me and attacked had I flown any lower."

"Your superb vision is only your second greatest asset, you know," said Enosh to Dufritter.

The parrot cocked her head quizzically.

"Your courage and loyalty to the Cause is greater still," Enosh said.

Dufritter ducked her head in thanks

Enosh stroked his beard and thought for a few seconds. "Will you do us another favor, Dufritter?" he asked the parrot. "It is a risky one."

"My kind is always loyal to the Cause regardless of the risk," Dufritter replied.

Enosh removed two vials from a hidden pocket in his damp robes. He uncapped them and spit into them. Passing the vials around to the others he had all of them spit also.

"Thogwok, do you think there are any enhancer plants around here?" Enosh asked.

"Sure thing. We'ze just passed a patch of 'em over by the nearest stream," Thogwok said.

He left and returned a few minutes later with a clump of very average-looking leaves.

"Ah, perfect, Thogwok! Only a true master of the forest would know what these are," Enosh said, taking the leaves and grinding them into bits between his fingers before stuffing them into the two small vials.

"Now hold these for me a moment," he said, handing the vials to the giant who awkwardly pinched them between his massive fingers.

Enosh conjured up a wild windstorm in each of his fists. With hands outstretched, two tiny tornados tore around in violent funnels on his palms.

"Condense until you are released!" Enosh commanded the two tempests. Each one imploded into a tiny sphere of tightly packed, rapidly spinning wind just a little larger than a georb. Enosh plopped each of the windstorms into its own vial, firmly pushed stoppers in their tops, and gave them to the parrot.

"North of the wolves," he said. And without any other explanation needed, the parrot sped away, a vial in each claw.

Braulio was feeling incredibly edgy about this time. Withdrawal was setting in. He needed a nicotine buzz like never before and was willing to try anything. "Hey, Thogwok, what were you going to tell me about those leaves you had for me back at the camp site? You know, the incense ones. What kinda buzz can I get from those?" he asked.

"Oh, right! The peace incense! I almos' forgot," Thogwok said, taking a lump of crumpled leaves from his pocket. "These are great little leaves. Ya light 'em afire and they bring peace to all who smell 'em. Good tool for makin' friends when yer mad at each other," he said, dumping the crumpled mass of leaves into Braulio's hands.

Braulio looked down at the leaves. "You've got to be kidding," he said peevishly, shaking his head. "I need a pack and a half of the real stuff along with a good stiff drink and you give me this?"

Thogwok seemed puzzled at his reaction, which irritated the volatile Braulio even more.

"We're in the middle of a war and here you are, this great know-it-all about the rain forest, and the best you can get me are some HIPPIE PEACE LEAVES!"

"Actually, it's a mist forest," Fong corrected.

"Oh, whatever! You're just as pathetic as he is! If you're so smart get us out of this mess!" Braulio was spitting out the words. He threw the peace leaves on the ground and in anger kicked a log—which nearly broke one of his toes. He swore and hopped up and down holding his foot while the others just stared at him.

Enosh sat down on a different log and motioned for Sean and Fong to join him. "It will be getting dark soon," Enosh said to them. "We have run all day and need rest before we can make a wise plan."

"Do you really think we are safe here?" Fong asked.

"Dufritter will see to it that we are for the time being," Enosh said calmly. Thogwok, gather wood for a fire ring, if you would please"

As Thogwok lumbered off to the nearest magentawood tree, Enosh turned to Sean, "So, I hear you had quite a successful battle back there, my young warrior."

"Dude, it was incredible!" Sean exclaimed. "The first bird attacked and I smacked him to the ground. Then another zoomed in and I grabbed him and swung 'um like a stick. Then another ..."

Sean went on recounting the battle. He stood up, flung his arms, and used almost every part of his body as he animatedly told the story. Fong looked on and listened with intrigue, trying to figure out how he did it. Braulio simply paced around with his arms crossed, refraining from kicking anything else, though he very much wanted to.

"Very interesting," Enosh said, interrupting Sean after five minutes of nonstop chatter. "I am a little curious to know why the others didn't have such a successful counter-attack. Why do you think that is?" he asked, looking at Braulio and Fong.

Braulio was feeling especially defeated now since not only had he lost his georb the night before, but was outdone in battle by a scrawny goofball. He sat down, put his elbows on his knees, and slumped his face into his hands

Fong offered an idea. "Perhaps it's the georb. Braulio and Candice weren't wearing one; only Sean and I were. But if so, why couldn't I fight them off like Sean did?

"A reasonable assessment and a fine question," Enosh said. "Before I answer, I have another question for you: it's about Candice. Did she ever eagerly desire to acquire a georb?"

"No," Fong answered. "Neither of us ever knew what a georb even was before we got here."

"I see. And did Candice ever express to you an eager desire to come here?" Enosh now asked with a bit of sternness in his gaze.

"No, not really. She only got excited about coming here when she thought it meant she could meet cute guys."

"And isn't it true that the instructions the nephil gave you said to bring someone of same faith and heart?"

Fong was feeling a little guilty. "Yes," she said sheepishly.

"And do you know of anyone who might have wanted to come here who is of same faith and heart?" Enosh asked her.

Fong couldn't hide the truth. It seemed as if Enosh already knew the answer anyway, even though Fong couldn't see how he possibly could.

"Eric," she softly said.

"Eric?" Enosh queried. "Well then, if you know that this one called 'Eric' is of same faith and heart, why isn't he here with you?"

Fong had no answer.

Enosh went on. "Knowing Eric as you do—the decisions he makes, the way he thinks, the things he does—do you imagine if Eric were here he would be captured and in enemy hands right now?"

Fong was about to give a rational explanation as to why bringing Eric just wasn't as practical. But the moment she looked into Enosh's penetrating eyes she stopped and looked to the ground. In her heart she knew the answer. Eric was wise. He was also cautious. He would not have gotten himself captured and would have probably prevented the rest of them from getting in as much trouble as they were in.

Guilt began to flood her and she looked up at Enosh and asked, "Do you think it's ... my fault ... Candice is captured?"

Enosh did not answer. He simply continued gazing at her.

Then Fong had a horrible thought. Tears even began to well up in her eyes—something highly unusual for her general cold rationality.

"Do you think that she might ... do you really think she might ..."

"Die?" Enosh offered. "Let's pray not. I am hopeful Maboa will hold her for ransom—the price on her head being a georb, naturally. As for determining your responsibility in the matter, you will have plenty of time uncovering that answer later. At this point we must put past mistakes behind us and do what is right from this moment on. And the mission is now threefold: securing the air, rescuing Candice, and finding out what became of Lawth."

Thogwok returned with an armful of magentawood and plunked it down. "Looks like we'ze got just enough for a single night 'ere," he said.

"Dude, that sounds like a plan," said Sean. He had already gathered some big leaves and was yawning widely as he made a cozy sleeping area. "I am, like, totally tired. Here, you dudes can have these extra leaves I picked," he said, offering them to the others.

Braulio ignored Sean and, still highly agitated, blurted, "How in the world are we gonna rescue anybody? Just look at us!" he motioned at Sean, Thogwok, and Fong. "There are only five of us: one is an idiot, one is a little girl and one is a giant who can't even walk straight! And there's an entire bloodthirsty army out there trying to kill us! I didn't ask for this! This isn't my war!" Braulio yelled.

Enosh made eye contact with the other three and shook his head, indicating they should say nothing, and they each went back to what they were doing.

Thogwok began arranging the wood in the shape of a ring—a ring noticeably smaller than the one from the night before. This stirred up a memory that knotted Braulio's stomach. He vividly recalled how he lost a georb—the thing that for whatever reason was central to why they were here. Gnawing at him was the reality that he had lost this immeasurably valuable item to some lousy thief. He began to dread what this might mean when it came to ever getting back home. And he didn't like to think about what he might have to endure in order to survive whatever was coming next. Seeing the wood laid out in a ring ready for fire, Braulio had the sinking feeling that he had lost the battle for all of them.

"Well, we need a few things in order to win the battle, Braulio," Enosh said, interrupting the boy's dark thoughts. "And one thing we need is the right people—namely those who are chosen to do the task. As you pointed out, we are short on human resources. So let me ask you, how exactly did you stumble upon the georb that brought you here?"

"Juan found a—," he stopped short. That sinking feeling in his stomach grew into a sledgehammer blow in his gut when he thought of Juan.

"Juan, you say? You have never mentioned him before. He is a friend of yours, I presume?" Enosh inquired.

Braulio didn't like where this was headed one bit.

"Yes," Braulio said quietly. "He is my friend."

After some prying and pulling from Enosh, Braulio told how it was really because of Juan that he knew anything at all about any of this and that he would never have been here had it not been for Juan. He also finally had to admit that, if only one of them should have the privilege of being here, it would be Juan and not him.

"I see," said Enosh after Braulio had reluctantly spilled all. "It now makes sense why a georb was taken away from you," Enosh concluded matter-of-factly.

Braulio looked puzzled.

"Oh, yes, you took it when you were excited about what you thought it could do for you. But you never really truly believed in its power. Furthermore, you did not seek the well-being of others for the short time it was in your care. You never cared about Juan and you haven't cared about those around you here either. Whenever there was trouble, you looked inward to self-satisfaction instead of outward to others. The georb could not remain with such a soul as that. You had no power to keep it—hence it could easily be taken from you."

The words hit hard. But Enosh wasn't done.

"And as for this not being your war, as you say, perhaps it *shouldn't* have been. Yet you chose to come here, Braulio. When you took the georb from your friend, you chose this path," Enosh solemnly concluded.

Braulio looked down. He didn't want to hear anymore. He wanted to yell, accuse and deny it all. But another part of him was relieved. It was as if Enosh's words were cleaning out a stinging wound. And as painful as it was to hear, he knew it was true, and a wave of clarity washed him.

"Why do you think over one hundred vicious birds of prey were defeated by a solitary boy?" Enosh asked nodding in Sean's direction.

That question cut deep, too. Braulio didn't want to admit that Sean could do anything better than him. But the facts were undeniable. "Because his georb belongs to him," he quietly admitted.

"And ...?" Enosh pressed, not letting up.

"And he wouldn't give it up," Braulio answered just above a whisper.

Enosh nodded affirmingly at Sean, who was listening carefully and rolling the georb over and over in his long, skinny fingers. Turning back to Braulio, Enosh said, "So you now see, don't you, that the georb is a thing which, when it is rightfully yours, no one else can take from you. If indeed it is truly yours, the only way you could ever lose it is by freely choosing to give it away. On the other hand, if it is not actually yours, anyone can take it out of your hands. That is why one of you was victorious against a hundred in battle, yet the other was defeated in his sleep ... by one."

Struck to the core, Braulio had nothing to say. He stared at the ground morosely.

Enosh then broadened his speech to include Fong. "It seems we have two similar stories here. For each of you chose to push ahead with your own plans and not wait on the one who could help you," Enosh said in summary.

"If only I had brought Eric ..." Fong said with deep regret.

"And I am sure you remember what I said mere moments ago. 'We must put past mistakes—'" began Enosh.

"Behind us and do what is right from this moment on," Fong finished. "But the right thing is to have Eric here with us. How can I get him here?"

"What is common sense saying to you right now?" he asked her with one eyebrow raised high.

"The same way I got here," she answered.

"Sounds reasonable to me," Enosh said with a grin. "Do you still have the instructions?"

Fong did. She pulled the leathery, leafy package out of her pocket and unfolded it. She realized for the first time that they were written in three languages, two of which she could now understand. She read the rhyming instructions aloud, tearing up again when she read the words, *Choose one guest to bring—one of same faith and heart.*

"Does this mean I need another person with me in order to get Eric?" she asked.

"Indeed. So, given the choices available to you, whom do you choose that you think is one of same faith and heart?" Enosh asked.

"You," she said.

"Well then, I am honored to be in such good company," Enosh said with a gracious smile as he stepped over to her and took hold of her hands with a comforting grip.

"Thogwok, mind the camp while we are gone and keep these two close to your side. Being divided is not good. We will hopefully return soon, and with backup."

"Yuz can descend on me," Thogwok assured him solemnly.

Fong looked at Enosh and grinned. The twinkle in his eyes confirmed to her that they both knew Thogwok meant *depend*.

Holding hands with the elder, Fong recited the enchantment. In a moment, with a whirlwind of glorious air mixed with spectacular flowers, a salad buffet of leaves and a whirling aroma of fragrances that saturated the campsite, Enosh and Fong disappeared into another time.

Thogwok lit the magentawood and soon the ring of fire had the look and feel of a safe place to lodge for the night.

Sean was overtaken by sleep a minute after the wood was lit. He had fought a valiant and victorious battle after a long day's chase and he needed lots of sleep.

Thogwok made a cushy bed of the extra elephant-ear-sized leaves Sean had plucked for him and, due to the intensity of the day, dozed off just a few minutes after Sean did. Thogwok's deep breathing blended in with the rustlings of the forest, and everyone in the fire ring was calm and still—except for one.

It wasn't dark yet and Braulio could not have slept even if it had been. He sat in deep thought. Then, in an instant, he was up on his feet. He knew what to do. He silently left the campfire ring and, despite Enosh's warning to stick together, in a few short strides he was gone from the campsite. Moving quickly, Braulio navigated his way through the dense forest, ever closer to Maboa and his horde—and all alone.

Chapter 17

PRISONERS

The wild winds frayed Fong's hair and lashed against her cheeks. Had she not been holding onto Enosh, her small body would have been blown over. Suddenly, the winds dropped. When Fong opened her eyes, she realized she and Enosh were standing in the same wooded area where she and Candice had met their first nephil.

"Those winds are insane! I suppose they are made for eleven-foot giants instead of little Asians like me. And ..." She paused to wrinkle her nose, inhale deeply, and cough. "E-e-e-e-w ... this air! It is thin, hard to breathe, and it stinks!"

Enosh gave her a look of understanding and spoke something to her in Nephil.

"What does that mean?" she asked.

Enosh said it again with more emphasis.

"What? I don't understand you. Speak English—I mean Earthen," she said.

Then it dawned on her. "Oh, right. I need to speak English here, don't I?"

Enosh nodded and resumed speaking Earthen, saying, "Otherwise Eric won't understand you. Practice with me once before you go."

It was a struggle at first. It already seemed more natural for Fong to speak Earthen than Mandarin and it was definitely more natural for her than English. Fong tried it once and failed. The second time she achieved an Earthen/English mix. By the third attempt she had it.

"Those wind made fo' giant and no little Asian like me," she finally said.

Enosh had a pleasantly confused look on his face and said, "Since I understood little of what you just said, I think you have it." He winked. "Now go find Eric quickly. If he truly is a believer, he will come with you."

Fong rushed out of the wooded area and sprinted down the sidewalk toward Eric's dorm. She had no idea where he was so she began at the most logical place Eric would be: in his room studying. Running as fast as she could across the quad, she ignored the onlookers and flew into his dorm lobby. Not allowed into the boys' wing, she picked up the lobby phone to call Eric's room.

Eric's roommate answered; Eric had just gone to dinner.

Fong slammed down the receiver and bolted toward the nearest dining hall. The dinner rush had just begun and there was a line stretching out the door. She scanned person after person and saw no Eric. Time was rushing by and she knew that every minute wasted was another minute Candice could be tortured or murdered. The thought almost paralyzed her but she determinedly raced to the head of the line.

"Hey, where you think you're going?" some guy in line challenged.

Fong reached the front of the line where the bored-looking girl who checked ID cards stood.

"Who do you think you are, a V.I.P. or somethin'?" said another disgruntled student.

"The back of the line is over there," mumbled the card monitor dully.

"I sorry, it emergency!" she said as she sped past her without stopping.

"Emergency? Yeah, right!" another student called out. "Where'd you get those cool clothes at?" he added sarcastically.

Chuckles rippled down the line.

Fong ignored them and zipped around the corner into the dining hall. She realized how silly she must look wearing her leafy jumpsuit, but she didn't care. She filed past the first two buffets, scanning the crowd.

He wasn't by the salads, the soups, or the—there! She spotted him pouring a coffee for himself and some girl standing next to him.

Quickly, Fong made her way toward them. She was elated to see Eric, but the closer she got to him and the girl, another emotion surged within her. The girl was laughing at something Eric had just said. He was smiling when he set a cup of coffee on her tray and then offered to carry hers as well as his. Eric turned toward the main dining area with the girl by his side and hands full when immediately before him, just above tray level, stood Fong.

"Fong! Hey, how are—what is that thing you're wearing?" asked Eric.

"I tell you. Come with me," Fong said motioning toward the door.

"Uh, well we are about to have dinner. Can it wait?" he asked. The girl beside him looked a little impatient and jealous.

"No, it no wait. It urgent!" Fong insisted.

"Who's your friend, Eric?" the girl asked curtly with a tight smile of cold civility.

"Jenna, this is Fong. She is a friend of mine. Fong, Jenna," he said.

"Nice to meet you," Fong said coolly and quickly. "Eric, we need go now. Candice in trouble."

"Trouble? It's her grades again, isn't it?"

"No! I mean, yes, Candice always in trouble with grades. But I talk life! Candice life in danger!" she said, grabbing his trays and sliding them on a nearby table full of students. They stopped their conversation and were staring at her now. She didn't care.

"Who's Candice?" Jenna asked Eric.

Eric started to answer but Fong grabbed his hands and yanked him close to her. Whispering in his ear, Fong said, "Eric, they real! Elves is real! I seen them. They gave me this clothes. Come with me to meet them now. We must go fast or Candice die! You must believe!"

Eric stood speechless, staring at Fong. He looked into her eyes with admiration and said, "Fong, you are serious aren't you? You found them. You really proved it, haven't you?"

Jenna was getting noticeably ticked. "Well, if I'm interrupting something, I guess I can leave," she said with a zinging, steely glare.

Eric ignored Jenna and with a beaming smile said, "Fong, you did it! How did you—"

"Eric!" Fong interrupted desperately. "No! I no do it! I mess up bad! I no can do 'dis myself! I need help or my friend die! And it my fault!"

Tears welled up in Fong's eyes—something Eric had never seen in her before. He didn't understand, but he knew she needed help.

"Okay, let's go."

Fong gave him a swift hug and grabbed his hands and pulled him toward the door, ordering, "Follow me!"

Eric followed and ran behind her, ignoring the stares and Jenna's exasperated yelling of "Eri-i-i-ic!"

Minutes later they arrived at the wooded plot. Fong wheezed as she slowed down. Hours of nonstop running had become normal for her in these last few days, but not in such oxygen-poor air.

Slipping into the woods, they quickly came to the place. Fong began to prep Eric, saying, "No be afraid. Element wielder named Enosh here in woods. He good. He help us get back."

"Element wielder? Back? Back where? Fong, what are you talking about? Where is Candice anyway?"

A firm hand grabbed Eric's shoulder from behind. Eric spun around startled. Staring at him was not an element wielder, but a highly suspicious campus police officer.

Candice was being held by some beast with strong, hairy arms. He was dangling her in front of Maboa's black, concealing curtain. Vile words were emanating from the other side. Maboa. She could hear him, smell him, and if she had reached out her hand she could have pushed through the cloth and felt him, (not that she would want to) and she wished she were anyplace but here.

"Don't be a fool again. I will ask you one more time, young pretty one. Where are they hiding—the ones who have the georb? Answer me or no one will ever call you 'pretty' again!" Maboa hissed hatefully through his curtain as the hairy arms began to tighten harder and harder around her.

Dufritter the parrot stayed hidden in a tree on the south side of Porfiznin. There was a disconcerting amount of activity there. She heard a rephaim commander barking out orders as he was organizing a search and capture mission that would head south—right in the direction of Enosh, Thogwok and the kids. Dufritter knew the quicker she could create a diversion on the other side of the village the better.

It was nearly dark but still dangerously bright enough for her to be spotted and picked off by a sorcerer or a vulture. She heard the rephaim commander growling at his troops to hurry up and follow him south. Not wanting to waste a second, she took the risk.

Dufritter tore from her hidden perch and flew high over the besieged village and dared to look down. The sight was horrifying. She knew that village dwellers who managed to escape before the army arrived were scattered here and there in the surrounding forest, for she had already seen several of them. Most were still cowering together and sobbing, waiting with desperate hope to be reunited with missing loved ones. Dufritter discovered the fate of most of those still missing as she flew over the village. Bodies lay in the streets and draped over walls—many half-eaten and mangled beyond recognition. Smoke billowed from some of the buildings. Ugly rephaim guards patrolled the streets. Wolves and hyenas paced the village outskirts, sniffing for survivors and intruders.

Dufritter flew as fast as she could over the carnage, hoping not to be detected as she sped onward toward a millstone just north of the village. She figured that would be a good spot to incite the first ruckus. At just the right moment, she dropped one of Enosh's vials. A perfect hit. It shattered on the large millstone.

A nearby guard heard the faint sound of breaking glass but didn't see anything. In fact, no one saw anything, but those with the best noses smelled something. The enchanted contents emerged in a burst and a gust. Strong scents of Enosh, Sean, Braulio, Fong and Thogwok blew across the clearing and wafted through the village streets. They were magnified one hundredfold by the enhancer leaves and then pushed along by a nice gust of wind—compliments of Enosh's miniature cyclone.

The nearest wolves went wild. They tore toward the north end of town, their yelping setting off a chain reaction. Several more wolves began howling and following. The rephaim guards followed the wolves, plodding toward the source of the commotion and ready for a fight. In moments the entire occupying force turned its attention to the north side of Porfiznin.

Dufritter continued her flight northward over the village's surrounding fields. And just as the clearing was ending and the northern forest beginning, Dufritter spotted a large pile of stones built up over time by farmers clearing fields. She also saw patrol wolves not far away, ears perked and noses pointed toward the commotion.

"Perfect," Dufritter said to herself, and she dropped the second vial.

The faint clatter of broken glass was followed by a swish of wind that whisked past the wolves' fur. The aroma that it carried incited a five-alarm-furor. Patrol wolves howled and barked madly, feverishly sniffing around for the source of the scent. Determining it to be hidden behind trees, they tore into the dense northern forest.

Forces at the northern edge of the village heard the howl of patrol wolves in the outlying fields and watched them disappear in the trees. All the other wolves followed, howling wildly. The rephaim commander bawled out an order of 'Charge!' and a slew of giants thumped loudly toward the northern forest, pursuing prey that wasn't there.

Of the several rephaim who stayed behind to guard the village, one of them went and reported the latest events to Maboa.

———>◈<———

The dropping of the decoy vials was good timing for Candice. She was still being dangled in front of Maboa's black curtain when it happened. Maboa learned practically nothing after reading her mind, for there was so very little information in her brain that mattered to him. But he was nonetheless enjoying terrorizing her when a rephaite ran into the room and reported the wolves' detection of something in the northern forest.

"Ackhhhh!" emerged from somewhere deep in his throat. It sounded like a horrifying cross between a viper ready to strike and someone very sick clearing their throat. But for Maboa, this meant he was ecstatic.

"It looks like your heroic rescuers have arrived, dear one," he said in a voice that suddenly sounded so sweet almost anyone would think it sincere. "Put her down and set her by the window. Light torches and make her very visible." Switching voices again, he maniacally laughed and said, "Those fools are making this too easy for me!"

⟶⟫●⟪⟵

Braulio was hiding in a thick clump of bushes just south of the village when he observed the mass movement northward. Whatever it was that got everyone's attention, it was the break he needed. He sprinted from the bushes and slid up against the wall of the southernmost house of the village. He drew his bow and crept around the corner. A creature he couldn't identify, something like a hyena, spotted Braulio, growled, and charged him. Braulio shot an arrow and the beast crumpled to the ground. He crept along up the side of the house and ducked inside the doorway. He bolted back out—spooked after stepping on a dead body.

Slamming himself up against the wall and panting hard, Braulio edged his way deeper into the village, peeked around a corner and spied one of the main streets. There was movement, but it all seemed to be headed north.

"Once I rescue Candice," he said to himself, "then they will see."

Braulio knew he had a limited supply of arrows, but he believed he had great instincts he could trust. He scampered from one wall to another, edging deeper and deeper into the village. Peaking furtively from around a corner, he glimpsed the building in the center of Porfiznin that the parrot had mentioned. Several huge guards were outside of it. Clearly that was headquarters.

The boy crouched and considered how he'd get in, get Candice, and then get the two of them out alive. He was thinking about the best plan to lure the guards away when he sensed something behind him. Whipping his head around, he met a set of amber eyes and bared, stained teeth inches away. A hyena, sneaky and rabid, snarled in his face. Braulio jumped and then stumbled backwards, landing on his back. He scrambled to draw his bow and shoot the creature. But the hyena let out a cry like an eerie laugh—an alert signaling others. Hiding right around the corner, another howled in response.

Braulio panicked. He shot an arrow and it grazed the fur. The hyena backed away as Braulio drew a second arrow. He knew he had to shut the beast up immediately. Just then, the second hyena appeared, baring sharp teeth and an eerie smile. The first one growled, gained boldness, and lunged toward the boy. Braulio sprang to his feet and sent a solid arrow into its chest. The first hyena dropped.

The second one laughed a wicked laugh and bared its teeth more fiercely. Braulio drew a third time and took aim at the hyena but didn't release before he heard the sound of a horrible roar a ways behind him. He spun around to see a bear, towering on its hind legs and ready for attack. Other creatures were now emerging from the darkness as well as a few rephaim giants who had been alerted to the commotion.

Braulio flung the bow on his back, grabbed the batch of peace incense leaves that Thogwok had given him, and lit them on fire. (Before leaving the ring of fire earlier that evening, he had stuffed them in his pockets as a last resort.) Holding the smoldering leaves like Roman candles, he wildly waved them around, having no idea how quickly, or even if, they'd have an effect.

But it appeared Thogwok was right again: the incense began working immediately. Several of the closer beasts became passive; the nearest hyena even slumped to the ground with a giggle and dropped its head on its paws like a friendly (but ugly) house pet.

It seemed the smaller the creature the more impacted it was by the smoke. But the peace-producing incense had by far the greatest effect on Braulio. Being in the center of all his frantic waving, he was inundated by the fumes. Soon, he dropped the burning incense and smiled genially at his attackers. That was just before the bear knocked him over with a paw to the head—the incense not yet controlling a creature so large.

Luckily for Braulio, the rephaim were explicitly ordered only to capture, and not kill the prey. The first one there, a hulking and relatively stupid rephaite named Org, slugged the bear in the gut, sending the creature into a roll. The other beasts scurried off or simply laid down— passively intoxicated by the wafting smoke. The giant stood over Braulio, salivating and grinning.

By now Braulio was so controlled by the peace incense that he set down his bow and arrows, stood up, and with a big smile, extended his right hand to the giant—fully expecting a friendly greeting.

Org scooped him up with one hand, lifted him victoriously over his head, and hollered, "I got me one!"

Sneers and cackles reverberated among other rephaim now arriving on the scene.

"Snuff out those weeds!" Org ordered, and giant feet stomped out the smoldering intoxicants before anyone else got a whiff.

"Hey, guys … let's talk this thing out," Braulio said passively as he dangled high above the giant's head.

Org guffawed in derision and proudly paraded his peaceful captive all the way down the street toward his lord. He burst victoriously into Maboa's room—the same room where Candice was now chained by a window.

"NO! Not Braulio too!" she cried out when she saw the new prisoner.

"Hey there, Candice … no worries, babe! I bet it's all just a misunderstanding," he said from thirteen feet in the air—clueless that he was a war trophy and that his life was in grave danger.

"Aagghhhh! Delicious!" rasped an ecstatic Maboa as Braulio was brought in. "Set him before the veil."

Org dropped Braulio on the floor beside the black curtain suspended in front of Maboa. Braulio could hear raspy breathing on the other side and reached out his hand to move the veil aside and extend some peace. A cold hand shot through the curtain without ripping or parting it and clamped onto Braulio's wrist with a lightning-fast grasp. Braulio yelled and tried to pull his hand back but the grip was like iron.

"Don't touch!" hissed the menacing voice on the other side.

After a few terrifying seconds, the death-like grip released the boy with a shove, and Braulio fell backwards on the hard floor. The guards in the room scoffed. Org knocked him back toward the veil with a swift kick. This was not going in the way of peace that Braulio had been hoping for. But then things changed; the voice on the other side of the black cloth suddenly became pleasant, even kind.

"So nice of you to stop by, young man," it said very warmly. "What is your name and where have you come from?"

"Braulio Santos. I come from Alicante, Spain."

"Ah yes, yes, I have heard it is a marvelous place," the voice said ever so sweetly, like a considerate host acquainting himself with a guest. "But, I mean where did you come from just now?"

"Don't tell him, Braulio! He wants the ge—" Candice cried before a huge hand enveloped her face.

Maboa softly hissed and Candice was carried gagged and squirming out of the room.

"Look, I've only come for peace," Braulio said. "Just let her go and we won't bother you and we can all be friends."

"Mood alterin' leaves was found with the intruder, m'lord. He got 'imself a healthy dose it seems," Org said to Maboa.

"Ahhh, so that is why this young one wields a weapon and yet is bent on peace," Maboa realized, referencing the bow and arrows confiscated from Braulio.

Continuing with the ruse, Maboa added with a diplomatic voice, "Well, we want peace also. In fact, we would like to meet in your camp for a peace treaty. Where is your camp? We will go right now."

But before Braulio could answer, a ruckus erupted outside the headquarters. Cheers and jeers roaring outside Maboa's lair grew louder and louder as yet another captive was brought in. Carried between two strong rephaim, a man wearing black was plopped on the floor next to Braulio. Braulio recognized him. He was the same thief that had taken his georb! It was Sabtah.

"We found this 'un lurking about in the forest to the north. Wolves caught 'is scent. An' he was tryin' to hide this," one giant said as he held up a georb necklace.

"Hey! That's the one I had!" Braulio exclaimed candidly, and he reached out to take it. The back of a large fist knocked him to the floor. Maboa's hand simultaneously flashed through the curtain and snatched the georb.

"Agh-gha-gha-ghaaaa!" blasted the eerie laugh. "So it is! Surprise, surprise! The fool who betrayed me also stole from you, did he?" The sound of Maboa's glee was like nails on a chalkboard. Even his commanders winced.

"Lord Maboa, I can explain—" Sabtah began.

"SILENCE!" boomed the voice so fierce and loud that it was heard on the outskirts of town. "Put their heads next to my veil," it commanded, and big hands landed on the back of each of their collars and shoved Sabtah and Braulio toward the curtain, the tops of their heads nearly touching it. Two sharp, bony hands reached out and grabbed a hold of each head. There was an eerie silence, followed by raspy breathing and an ominous, foul air which emanated from behind the veil and engulfed the room.

Braulio held his nose and meekly asked, "Wud aboud peace?"

The answer came as a violent shove. Once Maboa had learned all he needed to know by reading their minds, he released the two—hurling them both on the hard floor. Laughter bellowed from behind the curtain. It was so vicious, so intensely wicked, it chilled even the most hardened rephaite. In a devastating setback for the side of good, Maboa had just determined who the Chosen One was and also figured out exactly what he needed to do to control all of the world's air!

"So, there is a ring of fire nearby where the golden-headed one sleeps," Maboa said with intense excitement. "He is holding another georb, and he has tapped into its power! That is why he could destroy my horde of vultures. You, Sabtah, tried to steal that one also, as you foolishly attempted to dethrone me! But as you reached for that georb, it resisted you and burned you." Then, referring back to something Braulio had recently learned, Maboa salivated, hissed and continued. "The fool boy's thoughts reveal the only way to get a georb from the Chosen One is for him to freely give it away; it cannot be stolen from the Chosen One." Maboa shrieked with delight as he put the pieces together and concluded, "The golden-headed one must be the Chosen One—therefore he is the holder of the air georb—and I KNOW HOW TO MAKE HIM GIVE IT TO ME!"

Maboa laughed savagely. Candice heard it from the building next door and it made her skin crawl. Certain of his imminent victory, Maboa gave orders for the final showdown.

"Loswossip, you might be leadership material after all. Lead your few remaining pathetic vultures on an immediate search. Locate the ring of fire. This fool boy is too stupid to know where in the forest it is, but he walked here this very night so it can't be far. I will be on the edge of town ready to lead my army in the charge when you report back."

Loswossip, all this time quiet in a corner of the room, lifted up his head and thought to himself how lucky he was. He flew up and through the open ceiling, scrambling to rally the half dozen remaining vultures that were lazily patrolling the village from above.

Maboa ordered that the prisoners all be chained in separate houses. He assigned two guards to each prisoner and ordered Calneh, the rephaim commander to mobilize his troops but to stay in the village. Maboa would need no troops for a mission such as this—only his dragon Gomorzinz. He commanded the ones who tended to the dragon to bring him to the southern edge of town—the direction from which Braulio had come. He then veiled his face and shrouded himself with a black robe and emerged through the curtain. Maboa stood shrouded in the darkness of his hooded robe and emanated a darkness of his own. Instinctively, the giants—all twice his size—took several steps back as Maboa tore through the room in the direction of Enosh, Thogwok, and the other kids.

Once at the edge of town, Maboa covetously gripped the georb in his fist and extended it out in front of his cloaked face. As a master of all four elements, Maboa knew he could use one georb to summon another georb. And now with the knowledge that the Chosen One was nearby holding one, all Maboa would need to do is summon the georb; and the Chosen One would come right to him! Once in his presence, Maboa would simply need to wield some of the water, minerals, air, and electrical firings inside Sean's brain.

"It will take almost nothing to persuade the simple mind of the fool boy that he should give the georb to me!" Maboa spewed with hateful delight.

Holding the necklace high in the air, he called on the names of fire, wind, water, and land—commanding those contained in the georb which he held to call out to the ones in the georb nearby. As he did, a wind gust whipped by, the earth rumbled beneath him, the stream that flowed past the village surged and splashed, and a lightning bolt split the sky.

Just a few short miles away, lying peacefully in a protective ring of fire, Sean woke up.

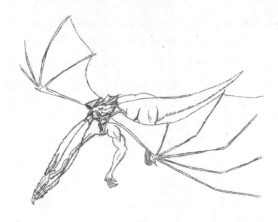

Chapter 18

SUMMONED TO THE SEA

S ean lay awake for only a few seconds before he got up. He was drawn by some peculiar pull. He wasn't sure what it was and had never felt anything like it before. He stood up and looked toward the west. For some reason he felt he should walk that way. He looked around the ring of fire and noticed it was strangely empty. Enosh and Fong had not yet come back. Thogwok, whom nobody could miss, was there. But where was Braulio? Sean felt strange about leaving Thogwok all alone, and he figured wandering about on his own would not have been a popular idea had it been put to a vote. But he couldn't suppress the urge to go for a walk westward. And so leaving the camp, he began to walk. Soon he was out of sight of the campfire, all alone, moving westward.

Loswossip was also heading west. Since that was the direction that the group had been heading the whole time they were being chased, and since that was the direction Lawth was heading when the wolves chased him, it was the logical direction to search first. So with six tired, war-torn vultures at his tail feathers, Loswossip scanned the ground for any sight of a campfire or any movement of humans and a lone nephil.

Loswossip was about to adjust their course when he spotted a fire below. He swooped down and sped toward it. The others followed and soon saw that it was not one fire but a ring of fire—just as Maboa had ordered him to find.

"Too easy," Loswossip cawed to himself. "I must be sure."

He ordered his cronies to be silent, and in a stealth formation they dropped lower and silently whizzed over the fire ring, high enough to not be seen in the dark, but low enough to see what was lit by the fire below. Ascending again, he called back to those behind him, "Six mats—one giant-sized and five human. Only one of the humans was visible but he was certainly one we fought in the field! This is their site!" Loswossip cawed triumphantly. Within minutes they would have the report to Maboa.

Fong quickly spun around to see what had made Eric yell. She had expected to see Enosh with his long nose, strange robes, and penetrating blue eyes—a sight strange enough to make any person yell. Instead, she saw a campus police officer holding Eric firmly by the arm.

"What are you kids doin' out here in these trees?" the officer asked accusingly.

"We not do anything wong, officer," Fong responded.

"I didn't ask if you were doing anything wrong, did I?" retorted the officer. "I asked, 'What are you doing out here in these trees?'"

"I ... I showing something to my friend," Fong replied ambiguously.

"Showing something, huh? Well, I'm sure you want to show me the something also, right?" the officer asked, his voice thick with sarcasm.

"Not really, no?" answered Fong.

"Didn't think so," said the officer, with a know-it-all smirk.

"And how 'bout you mister?" The officer looked at Eric, still holding him by the arm. "I saw the both of you run across campus. You two were in an awful hurry to get to something. Must be important," he said, baiting them to answer.

"Well, it is important," Eric responded. "Fong says we have to hurry to rescue Candice. That's the only reason we were running."

"RESCUE?! Who's in trouble?" the officer said in alarm.

"Our friend, Candice Singletary; she's a student here and Fong says she needs us to rescue her," Eric replied.

The officer reached for his radio to call for help.

"NO! No call other police," Fong said, almost yelling at the officer. "She no need police help—just us!"

"Oh-h-h … I see," the officer said, nodding his head and smirking with disbelief. "So the only ones who can help her are you two, huh? Rather not have the police involved, I see."

Fong rolled her eyes. The last thing she wanted was someone from this world interfering who wouldn't believe them and couldn't help even if he did. *This was wasting time. And where is Enosh?* she kept thinking as she stole glances at the trees around them. He was nowhere to be found.

The policeman observed them closely. Each time Fong snatched a glance to look for Enosh, his eyes followed too; he was becoming increasingly suspicious. The officer took out a pad of paper and jotted some notes. This gave Fong the opportunity to give a zip-your-mouth sign to Eric. He just shrugged.

"C-a-n-d-i-, is Candice spelled with an 's'?" the officer asked as he pressed his pen forcefully against his pad.

"C," said Eric helpfully.

The officer methodically copied down both of their names, causing Fong to roll her eyes again. She had little patience for time-wasting—but even less for stupidity. When he asked for their dorm room numbers and contact information so they could be reached for further questioning, she nearly exploded.

"We not do anything wong! It a crime to run on campus now?! It a crime to walk in woods?!"

Eric shot her a warning glance but she was fed up.

"Ordinarily, without any evidence of drug use, I would have sent you on your way. But you insisted a fellow student was in danger, so it's my duty to pursue the issue, isn't it?" The officer stared Fong down. He turned to Eric. "So where is Miss Singletary and what kind of trouble is she in?" the officer asked, deciding to only half believe whatever they were about to say.

"We no can tell you," Fong said.

The officer took this as a challenge. "Oh, I think I can find ways to get you to tell me, miss. We've had a lot of problems with students doing drugs and drinking out here lately. I can detain you both for suspicious activity until I find out what you're really up to. The sooner you talk, the less time that will take," he said matter-of-factly.

Fong was about to argue when Eric stepped up and silenced her. "Officer, I will tell you the truth of why we are out here," he said. "I just don't think you will believe me."

"I'm listening," the officer said as he resumed writing on his notepad.

"We are trying to find the elves," Eric said without hesitation.

Fong slapped herself on her forehead and hung her head low.

The officer looked up, eyes darting between the two of them, and remained expressionless. He scrawled something else on his notepad.

"I don't know all the details," Eric went on, "I just know that Candice is in trouble. Elves have something to do with it, and there is someone we need to meet here who can help us get to her. He is named 'Enaws,'" Eric said, only having heard the strange name once.

"How do you spell 'Enaws,'" the officer asked, still writing.

"I don't know. Like it sounds, I suppose."

"And who is this 'Enaws,'" the officer inquired.

"I don't know that either. I just know Fong said he is here and can help us, so because she said it I know it has to be true."

Fong's head snapped up and she looked at Eric. Normally, with most people, she would have corrected the mispronunciation; but what Eric said completely caught her off guard, in a good way. *He really believes me doesn't he?* And as stuck as they were and as frustrated as she was, comfort began surging through her. She smiled appreciatively at Eric. He warmly smiled back.

"O-o-o-o-k-a-a-y!" the officer said incredulously, punishing his notepad with a firm period blast at the end of his last sentence as he read aloud for both to hear. "I have a Fong Chow and an Eric Ng, pronounced 'Ing', seen running into the woods reportedly to rescue a friend and fellow student named Candice Singletary. According to Mr. Ng, Miss Singletary is missing and in danger. After being offered assistance, the two claimed the only one who can help them rescue Miss Singletary is a man named Enaws about whom no further details were revealed.

Mr. Ng reported that he and Miss Chow were in the woods for another purpose as well: to find elves."

The officer scanned the two of them with amused suspicion, and with a crooked smile asked, "Did I miss anything?"

"No, I think that's it," Eric said with confidence.

Fong hung her head again, embarrassed.

"Turn your pockets inside out and empty their contents for me, please," the officer directed, putting his pad and pen away and unclipping his flashlight.

Eric did so. He had nothing but his wallet, some loose change, and a pen. Fong had only the necklace and the leather pouch. It was just beginning to get dark, particularly in the wooded area, and the officer shined his flashlight carefully on each of their modest belongings. He then clicked his radio and reported his findings in police-speak jargon to dispatch. Fong and Eric noted him saying he'd file a missing persons report within twenty-four hours if Miss Singletary was not located. As he was winding down his lengthy radio report, he strolled around the immediate area, shining his flashlight back and forth.

Fong looked at Eric and sighed.

"If it's the truth, what stops us from telling it," he simply asked. She nodded her head, as if for the first time realizing something. Then she smiled at Eric again.

The officer finished his inspection. He clicked off his and flashlight and hooked it on his belt. Returning to Eric and Fong he said, "Alright, we're through. You two can go now."

Eric and Fong didn't leave.

"Go on, take off now," the officer said.

"But we need stay here in dis woods," Fong said. "Dis is place we must leave from to rescue Candice,"

The officer folded his arms and looked stern.

Eric backed her. "With all due respect officer, isn't this public campus space? Aren't we allowed to be here?"

Puffing out his chest and pointing his finger, the officer said, "Listen you two loons, you're either crazy or stupid. But I'm neither one and you're not foolin' me. I'll be keepin' an eye on this place, and if I see any signs of drugs, booze," the officer's eyes dropped to Fong's weird, leafy attire, "or nutty cultic activity, I'll be comin' after both of ya! Are we clear?"

Eric and Fong just stood there, looking resolute but polite. Eric nodded respectfully. The officer finally turned in a huff and mumbled, "Crazy college punks," under his breath as he walked away.

There was a long pause, partly to make sure he was out of earshot but also for Fong to conjure up enough humility to say, "Thank you, Eric."

"For what?"

"For believe me," she said. "Story is crazy—too crazy—and still you believe me, without any proof." Switching unconsciously into fluent Earthen, Fong reflected quietly, "You have more faith than I do."

"I agree," said a soothing voice also in Earthen. And even though neither was expecting to hear a voice, its tone did not startle them.

Then Eric, for the first time, saw someone from Early Earth.

"Enosh, where have you been?" Fong asked, still in Earthen.

"Nearby listening, and I am delighted with what I heard."

Eric's mouth hung agape. Silenced by Enosh's unique appearance and calming voice, he simply stood there as Enosh spoke a strange language that was captivating to Eric's ears.

"And might I add to what you said, Fong, about Eric's strong faith," Enosh continued. "You, Fong, recognized that faith. And hence you originally chose him to be your partner in this quest. A wise choice, as we can see already. And Eric, for his part, not only has shown faith in what he hasn't seen, but he discerningly chose to trust not just anyone, but someone whose words are trustworthy. My congratulations to both of you. You are both showing yourselves worthy of the Calling. Now, let's go rescue Candice and the rest of Early Earth!"

Maboa was avidly trying to summon Sean's georb when the battered wolves scurried into the village, hoping to go unnoticed. They had been defeated by a lone element wielder and did not want to face their lord, Maboa. But Maboa knew they were back and summoned the lead wolf.

"Where have you been and who did you find?" Maboa demanded of the pack leader, as he deferentially approached Maboa with his tail between its legs.

The wolf inarticulately growled something so guttural that few Earthen-speakers would comprehend it. Maboa understood though, and smiled menacingly.

The wolf began to relax, relieved that Maboa was not angry. But like a sudden storm, Maboa's mood shifted and he snarled at the wolf commander.

"Oh, you and your pathetic pack aren't off the hook," Maboa threatened, voice low and harsh. "You will be punished severely for your failure to deliver. Just hope for your sake the vultures are able to get me to them since you were too inept. I will deal with you later. Out of my sight!"

Cowering, the wolf fled.

Moments later, Loswossip and his six remaining vultures swooped down to the ground at Maboa's side to report the exact location of the campsite they had found.

"Pe-r-r-rfect," Maboa said, salivating. "I will fly with Gomorzinz."

Mounting his slithery dragon, Maboa soared into the air toward the west, his dark hooded cloak flapping violently in the wind but ever obediently concealing him. Holding the reins in his right hand and the georb in the left, Maboa summoned the other georb as he flew through the sky. He let out a wild laugh as he thought about holding both georbs in his hands this very night and controlling the air for centuries to come. And he felt the power of his summoning was working.

Not far below Maboa and his soaring dragon, underneath the cover of trees, Sean's georb was acting up. The light blue hue was beginning to swirl. And a slight jiggling was coming from within. It reminded him of the trip to the library the day he met Lawth. Still not sure what was going on, Sean kept walking, feeling for some reason like he should. Muscling his way through thick underbrush where visibility was nil, the boy veered around a very large tree, and was caught off guard. Sean only had time to yell "Whoa, du—" when hands grabbed him, covered his mouth, and flipped him head over heels, pinning him to the ground!

Now that Maboa was gone, tensions in the occupied village had eased considerably. The soldiers had been ordered to keep a constant eye on the three prisoners, but aside from that there was little to do besides eat, drink, complain, and fight. Candice, Braulio, and Sabtah were all in their own isolated houses, each under close surveillance. For Braulio, the peace overdose was wearing off and he was realizing what had actually happened and where he was. Fear began to grip him. And Candice, exhausted by the ordeal, was close to despair. Neither of them could see a way of escape.

A blast of wind swirling in a small funnel mixed with vines, leaves, and an aromatic gust of floral fragrances awakened the sleeping giant.

"Huh? What? Nate yur stame and business!" Thogwok said gruffly as he grabbed his walking stick and hoisted himself clumsily to his feet.

"Name is Enosh, Thogwok; no need for alarm," said the soothing voice of the elder as the last leaves and flower petals fluttered through the air. "Fong is with me, of course, and we must introduce you to Eric.

"O-o-oh-ho! A new one, I seez. Well, let me intrude duce myself!" Thogwok said excitedly now that he was awake and aware. He lumbered one large step toward the already frightened boy. Eric yelped and ran, snagging his foot on a vine and falling to the ground.

"No run, Eric! He Thogwok. He no hurt you. He friendly," Fong said in broken English (which, except for the word Thogwok, meant nothing to the others).

Enosh stopped Thogwok's forward advance, explaining to him that Eric didn't have any language potion in him yet and wasn't really sure whether his greeting was friendly or hostile.

"In fact, I will get that potion ready right now so we can all—" Enosh stopped and looked around. Inside the fire ring every single one of the sleeping mats was abandoned. "Where are Braulio and Sean?" he asked as a lightning bolt lit up the sky.

———————⟫●⟪———————

Maboa's dragon slid through the air with silent speed. From high above, the cloaked warlord saw a fire ring. He detected six sleeping mats, one of them very large, inside the ring. "There they are!" he shrieked. Focusing all of his considerable powers, he summoned the other georb again. A lightning bolt rent the sky. He felt power like he had never felt before. Ecstatic, he dove for the middle of the burning ring.

Lawth looked up when he heard the whoosh of large wings. All he could see was a dragon claw descending rapidly down upon him. Before Lawth could react, the claw slammed into him and pinned him tightly to the ground.

"Hold him, but do not kill him yet," ordered a menacing voice that sent icy fear shivering down Lawth's nearly crushed spine.

Maboa dropped from his mount and landed next to Lawth, his veil and hooded cloak shrouding him. He scanned around the fire ring, seeing no one but Lawth. Then he looked down at the apprentice element wielder and viciously stared. Lawth, gasping for breath under the dragon's claw, could feel hatred radiating from behind the black veil now looming over him. When the figure finally spoke, the hairs on Lawth's neck stood on end.

"Where are the others?!" insisted the freakish voice from behind the veil.

An hour or two earlier, after having defeated both the pack of wolves and the leviathan, Lawth had followed the river just a short distance further to its wide mouth where it met the ocean. On both sides of the river rose steep and rocky cliffs overlooking the surf.

Now, Lawth knew that the surviving wolves would report to Maboa. And he knew it was only a matter of time—and not much time—before Maboa sent reinforcements in his direction. But Lawth thought this was for the best; he was brave, and he preferred to have the attention aimed where he was at rather than wherever the Chosen One, Enosh, and the rest of the kids were. Perhaps they could escape, Lawth reasoned, if he drew Maboa's focus long enough. So he had constructed a fire ring encircling six leafy beds. He deliberately chose to put the campsite right near the cliff's edge where the land was free of trees and all would be in plain sight of any bird that could report to Maboa. Then he waited. He did not see or hear Loswossip and his gang when they flew overhead. In fact, when he devised the plan, he had no idea how well his decoy would work or how quickly he would be getting company.

Now he knew.

"They ran," Lawth lied. "I tried to convince them to stay here and they wouldn't listen."

"Which direction did they run? Tell me and I will let you go," Maboa lied in reply.

"Along the coast. When they took off they ran that way," he fibbed again, motioning to the north with a jerk of his head.

"LIAR!" roared Maboa just inches from Lawth's face, his veil roughly brushing Lawth's cheeks. "I have just read your thoughts, you fool. You don't know where they are. You left them so you could go another way and mislead my troops!"

A chill shot through Lawth's bones. Maboa's ability to read minds was like nothing he had ever experienced before. Lawth had the sinking realization that Maboa could read his every thought—including the one which he was thinking right now! He tried frantically to control his mind and make himself think something different, but he knew that his thought about doing this would also be known by Maboa. There was no thought that could escape being known with one so powerful so close by.

Lawth closed his eyes to avoid the horrifying sight of the dragon who was hissing in his face and dripping long streams of saliva on him. Maboa was right in his face too, so close Lawth could feel the roughness of the black robe draped on him and hear each of Maboa's hissing breaths. For a moment, Lawth just wished he could die so this horror would be over. As soon as he thought it, he caught himself and tried to un-think it.

"Too late!" responded the grating, villainous voice again. "Wish granted! You shall die! Dash him on the rocks and let him drown in the sea, Gomorzinz!"

The dragon hoisted Lawth off the ground, clutching him in one huge claw. And with a swift flick of its leg, the beast let go. Lawth was flying headlong in the air, above the fire ring and over the cliff. For the brief seconds he was airborne he felt the heat of the fire, the wind in his face, and droplets of sea surf. His life—all 316 years—flashed before his eyes as he hurtled a hundred feet downward toward the last thing it seemed he would feel: jagged, bone-breaking rocks!

———◦———

"Thogwok, surely you must have some idea where the boys are!" Enosh asserted. "We weren't gone but an hour."

Thogwok was dumbfounded. "I don't know, Master Enosh. I really don't," he said with deep concern as he kicked around the leafy bedding, hoping maybe a skinny kid was somewhere beneath.

"Bra-a-aulio-o-o! Se-e-a-an!" Fong began yelling into the woods.

"Do not yell my dear," Enosh directed. "We need to find them, but we don't want to be found. We will head toward the village immediately. I think that is where at least one of them might be and that is definitely where Candice is held."

Meanwhile, none of this was making any sense to poor Eric, who was thoroughly and entirely confused. Fong gave him a quick briefing in English about the language serum and Enosh promptly dumped some goo in Eric's ears. Once he could understand what was being said, Eric willingly drank the other serum offered to him. In seconds, his tongue was freed to speak its rightful native language.

"We have kids to rescue. Follow me," Enosh directed. And the four of them trekked briskly toward Maboa's hostile forces.

———◦———

Just far enough away from the fire ring that a scream would not suffice for help, Sean lay on his back with a hand over his mouth, a knife to his throat, and a beard dangling over his face.

As soon as they got a close look at each other, the man with the beard was surprised to see just a boy. "Who are you," he said, uncovering Sean's mouth and drawing his knife back.

"Dude, I'm just Sean. And what's up with the pro-wrestling moves? Next time give me, like, a warning at least," he said as he got up and indignantly brushed himself off. Sean's georb had been growing more and more excited with every step he had taken. It was pulsating, it was glowing, and by now it had suspended both itself and the chain it was hanging on a good inch away from his chest and up in the air.

"Just Sean," the man repeated, mesmerized by the pulsating gem. He stepped back from Sean and looked stunned. "But you look far too young to be one of the just and noble element wielders—or even a wielder's apprentice!"

"Oh no, I'm not one of those dudes," Sean tried to clarify. "I mean, it'd be cool to like, move stuff through the air and all, but a hundred years of study?! Are you kiddin' me? I just do what the wielder dudes tell me to do."

"So then, you *are* an element wielder's apprentice," the man said, still fixated on the brilliant blue gem all aglow. The man sheathed his knife, bowed, and apologized. "Do forgive me, Just Sean. My name is Lamech and I was merely trying to protect my family. With all that happened at the village today, one cannot be too careful. I thought you were one of the intruders," he explained as he humbly apologized again.

"No worries, dude, I forgive you. We all make mistakes and like, believe me, I understand; we had to fight our way through a bunch of those smelly vultures and then hide out here just like you."

"I appreciate your gracious understanding, Just Sean. My wife and I and our baby boy barely escaped as Maboa's forces were entering our village," Lamech said as he motioned to a woman crouched by a tree holding a swaddled newborn in her arms. The woman bowed her head slightly to Sean and held her baby close. Sean had totally missed them sitting there.

"Hey, what's up?" Sean said to the woman holding the child.

"You saw it, too, did you? That was Maboa's dragon that soared overhead!" Lamech said, answering what he thought was a literal question. "Since I saw Maboa fly off on his dragon westward, I imagine his army must be following him. That is why we are headed back to our village now. Porfiznin is our home."

"Back to the village! Don't do that, dude! I don't think those creepy monsters are outa there yet," Sean warned.

Lamech looked at the dazzling georb, clearly the gem of a wise element wielder—or at least a wielder's apprentice. He reasoned that only someone with much wisdom would have a device such as that. Lamech looked over at his wife, still mostly in hiding, who nodded fervently in agreement with Sean.

"But I know a place you can go where there are no creepy monsters," Sean continued, pointing back to the direction from which he came. "It's safe that way. And if you see a nephil named Thogwok, you can hang with him; he's cool. You just don't wanna stand too close to him is all."

Concluding that Sean must be an element wielder's apprentice who was both wise beyond his years, and in fellowship with the noble nephilim, Lamech quickly changed course. "In that case, that is what we will do," said Lamech, motioning to his wife to follow him. "If the noble nephil of whom you speak doesn't mind, we will stay on the ground rather than climb up and hang in the trees with him—awkward with a baby in arms, you know. But, if he is still cool when we arrive, I am sure we can find some large and comfortable leaves with which to wrap him and warm him—it is the least we can do to say 'thanks' for the strong protection of a nephil!" the man said resolutely.

"Oh, uh, what I meant was …" Sean began, but was cut off before he could finish.

"We are most appreciative of your wise insight, Just Sean. You just saved the lives of me, my wife and our newborn baby," Lamech said as he made haste toward Sean's campsite with his wife close behind him.

"Yeah, man, don't mention it. And by the way, my name is actually just Sean, not *Just* Sean, er, I mean …."

"Yes, I will remember your name, Just Sean. And once again, you have my gratitude."

Sean was not quite sure how to correct the misunderstandings about his name and about Thogwok hanging and being cool, but he decided it really didn't matter much anyway. Then he caught a glimpse of the baby boy as Lamech's wife swished passed him. Sean and the baby made quick eye contact, and the baby gave him an adorable smile. Sean seldom thought about babies and rarely noticed them, but for some reason this one caught his attention and made him smile.

"Hey, what's yer baby's name?" he casually asked.

"Noah," they both said.

As the two disappeared into the thick undergrowth, Sean turned to continue westward. The steady pulsing of the georb grew stronger. He didn't know it, of course, but it was leading him directly to the spot where Maboa stood. Sean walked quickly forward. He wasn't sure why; he just felt he should.

Back at the village, things were not going well for the captives. Braulio had completely come to, recognizing with searing clarity just how foolish his rescue attempt was and how his pride had gotten him into this mess. He was feeling terrible, and vowed that if he somehow survived, he would do better with his life. As he looked at his captors— huge rephaim who were sneering at him and taunting him about what great pleasure they would get in tearing him limb from limb—Braulio doubted he would ever get that chance.

Candice, who was bound in chains in another building, was in no better shape. The foul creatures around her were getting impatient during Maboa's absence and wanted terribly to devour her soft flesh. They were ordered not to, and hadn't dared make a move while the merciless Maboa had been there, but the longer their leader was away the more restless they became. Candice simply buried her head in her hands and tried to ignore the salivating and howling around her. Feeling this was the end of her life, she did something she hadn't done in years— she prayed.

Maboa ordered his dragon to return to the village and inspect things; he knew better than to trust his unsavory warriors. Staying behind, Maboa climbed over the edge of the cliff and down a level so he was hidden from view. With his back against the granite and his face toward the sea, Maboa held up the georb again, summoning the one held by Sean. Meanwhile, Sean's georb kept pulsating more and more wildly and Sean kept heading westerly.

Enosh, Thogwok, Fong, and Eric scampered through the woods right up to the edge of the forest on the southern side of the village. Before them lay some of the horror wrought by Maboa and his forces. Carnage littered the outskirts of Porfiznin. The villagers who hadn't fled lay dead. Fires still smoldered in several houses and the smell of filth and burning flesh permeated the air. The four of them tried to suppress thoughts about what might have happened to Candice, Braulio and Lawth.

"How are we going to get in there to get her?" Fong asked.

Enosh was silent and thinking as he and the rest sat crouched behind a large and leafy bush, poking their faces through it as they spied on the devastated village.

Thogwok answered Fong, saying, "I don't know how any of yuz can match up against those rephaim warriors. I'd take on two, maybe three at a time at most. But there must be a hundred of 'em. And look a' how big they are," Thogwok said, pointing at one nearby.

"Well, if we can't beat them in numbers and force, we will need to play to our strengths," Eric said, speaking up for the first time.

This got Enosh's attention. "And what do you gather our strengths are in this scenario, my boy?" he asked him.

"We have the advantage of location, for one. We know exactly where they are while they are still searching for us. And we can turn that into the advantage of surprise," Eric said.

"Aye, he's right there, Master Enosh," said Thogwok. "Wha's more, yuz have element-wielding abilities that none of those brute creatures can even fathom. Some of 'em are downright terrified of elements doin' things 'parently on their own."

"That element-wielding part sounds good," Eric continued, knowing only very little about it. "Now if we can find something else they fear— something we can all wield that won't hurt us but will repel them ..."

"I have an idea!" Fong exclaimed too loudly.

A nearby wolf heard her and began growling and racing toward the clump of bushes where they were hiding. Seconds before the beast got to them, a large stick emerged from the thicket and walloped him soundly on the head. The wolf was out cold. The stick hovered in the air for a moment and then dropped with a padded thud on the wolf's fur.

Eric looked at Enosh with awe. "That was amazing!" he cautiously whispered.

"All part of the air wielder job description," Enosh said whimsically as he lowered his hands. "Now Fong, what was it you wanted to say?"

She whispered it very quietly and the rest agreed. "I know where jus' such a one is. I'll be ri' back," Thogwok said as he clumsily crept away.

"And let's not forget about our winged friends," Enosh said, referencing the parrot Dufritter who fluttered down to them and landed on Enosh's shoulder.

"Maboa and his dragon have left the village. The vultures have informed him of a campsite where they believe he will find you," the parrot reported.

"I see. Good that we left when we did," Enosh said.

"But they did not head south. They are west by the ocean. I overheard the vultures talking about it. And, what's more, they aren't guarding the village. They are just lazily hanging around on a perch, not doing anything since Maboa isn't watching. I was able to fly over the entire village undetected and I saw the two captives from your group."

"Two captives! So they do have another one of ours! Who is it?" Enosh asked.

"They are holding the golden-crested female and the dark-crested male," cawed the parrot.

"Candice and Braulio," Fong sighed. "Well, at least we know they are alive. Where is Sean then? Are you sure there wasn't one with blonde ha—I mean, a male with a gold crest?" Fong asked Dufritter.

Eric crouched there stunned, not at all sure what to think of this fluid conversation Fong was having with a bird.

"I perched atop each and every structure," Dufritter assured them. "The lazy vultures took no notice of me. And every house is burned, abandoned, or full of foul creatures. There is only one other prisoner in the whole place and he isn't one of yours. Appears to be some thief the wolves caught."

"A thief you say?" Enosh asked. Musing over this for a moment he said, "As near as Maboa's army was when we nearly caught our thief, there is a fair chance it is the same one—the scoundrel who stole Braulio's georb."

"If it's him, then Braulio's georb is now in the hands of Maboa!" Fong whispered in alarm.

"It's possible," Enosh said. "But for now, let's focus on getting Candice and Braulio out of there before it is too late. Maboa's forces tend to do whatever they want when he isn't around. The sooner we get to them, the better, and with Maboa gone we stand a better chance."

<hr/>

Meanwhile, Sean walked ever closer toward the ocean and the very cliff where Maboa hid. His georb was spinning excitedly on the end of its chain as it danced on air in front of his chest. Sean felt a pull to keep walking. He wasn't sure why; he just knew he should.

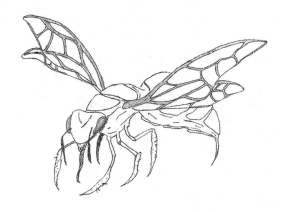

Chapter 19

GIANT BATTLES & SMALL HEROES

The occupied village was growing more and more restless by the minute. Wolves prowled around the outskirts of the buildings that imprisoned Braulio, Candice, and Sabtah. Giant rephaim warriors stomped over corpses that lay in the village streets, picked fights with each other, and kicked wolves whenever one got too close. The giants who were charged with guarding the captives taunted them; taking pleasure in sharing all the horrible things they would do to their small bodies as soon as Maboa granted permission. Grunts and cries emanated from huge, hungry horned lizards, tied to trees with thick chains. They had already overgrazed the small area where they were bound, and needing to feed their massive frames, they wailed for their riders to untie them so they could move on. But the riders had not yet been permitted to move, and tensions were on the rise. As for the others in Maboa's army, mostly men who were hirelings, few cared to do much of anything when Maboa wasn't there. Hence, with no Maboa around and no enemy in sight, drinking, arguing, and fighting amongst themselves prevailed. Nerves were getting frayed and all the army grew increasingly agitated. That is, all the army but one.

The shamelessly arrogant and stunningly ignorant rephaite named Org, the same one who captured Braulio, was feeling especially jubilant about something Maboa told him just before soaring off on his dragon. And though it was good news to Org, it was horrid news for Braulio.

Candice, still chained up in the house where she had most recently been moved, didn't know where Braulio was, but she learned of the boy's impending fate as soon as Org burst through her door. The haughty rephaite who had captured Braulio came in to deliver a message to the rephaim that were assigned to the other prisoners. Maboa had commanded Org to protect Sabtah and to pass on strict orders to the rest of the guards not to touch him. In exchange, Org was allowed to have Braulio. This delighted Org, and the loud-mouthed rephaite took Maboa's absence as an opportunity to brag about his good fortune to the other guards. Bullying his way through the tiny opening, Org burst into the room, boasting obnoxiously to the two rephaim warriors who were guarding Candice.

"Maboa don't need the boy for nothin' so I gets him all to meself ... all meself! Maboa already read the boy's mind and he don't have no georb, he don't. Says he had 'un, but was dumb enough to lose it to that two-bit traitor, Slobber, er Slobtuh ... whate'r 'is name is. An' since we got Slahbtuh now too, Maboa gots the georb and I gets the boy! I gets 'im all to meself!" Then, almost as if he had forgotten why he came, "Oh, and Maboa says you can't touch Slahbtuh—wants 'im all to 'imself. Says he's all his to torture and kill...no one else's to touch. I s'pose Slahbtuh did somethin' really bad ... I s'pose," the dumb giant mused, his thoughts drifting, however few in number they might have been. "But anaways, I gets the boy!" he repeated, emphasizing what he thought was clearly the more important news.

The larger of the two guards was a robust giant named Onquin. He was sitting in a corner tearing the last bit of flesh from a bone. He burped and hurled the bone at Org. The picked-clean bone smacked Org square on his chest and clattered to the floor.

"An' there's yur dessert," Onquin said as he grabbed another bone to gnaw on. He was unimpressed by both Org and his annoying announcement.

Org growled at him.

A smelly guard named Squal who had been hovering uncomfortably close to Candice grumbled, mostly to himself, in response to the news, "He says we can't do nothin' ta this one neither—not yet anaways." Then getting even closer, with the stench of his breath wafting over her face, "But just you wait little lady 'til he gives the word." His thick tongue licked his lips grotesquely.

Candice closed her eyes and shuddered as she turned her head from his horrid breath.

"Whud you say 'bout the fool boy who lost his georb?" Squal asked Org, pulling his attention away from his dinner fantasy. "Yuh says Maboa don't need him, yuh says?" he asked hungrily.

"He's mine!" Org hollered. "I found him and I caught him!" the stingy rephaite growled, grabbing the hilt of his huge sword.

"Jus' bring me an arm, is all. If yuh do, I'll give ya a whole leg o' this one when we get permission. Look at 'er! She's so pretty and tender ..."

Org looked covetously at Candice, considering the offer.

"Come on, jus' an arm is all I wan'," Squal said as diplomatically as a despicable rephaite could.

Candice was horrified. She put her head between her knees and began to cry again.

Seeing Candice cry, Org burst out in laughter. "Ha! The fool came to rescue you! Looka you now—some hero, that boy, eh! Some hero!" More guffaws.

Candice popped her head up. "What? Braulio? Braulio came here to rescue me?" she asked through her tears.

"Yeah, and now he's my dinner! I gets him all to meself!" Org boasted.

"An' yer gonna be mine," Squal said with a ravenous growl.

An unusual feeling began welling up in Candice. It was very different than what she had been feeling since being captured—or, for that matter, most of her life. Instead of worrying about being dinner, or worrying about herself at all, a fiery desire to save Braulio surged up within in her.

Org and Squal resumed haggling over limbs. Candice knew it wouldn't be long before Org would begin his meal—whether he shared it or not. She was shocked and overwhelmed to think Braulio actually risked his life to save her. And she couldn't bear the thought of him dying for her. Then she had an idea.

"Well, you won't find all the others," she said rather meekly.

Org and Squal stopped arguing for a moment. "What others?" demanded Org.

"The others. You might eat Braulio and me, but all the others are safe. And I know where they are hiding and they are close by. Braulio is one of many."

"She's lying," sniffed Squal.

Over in the corner Onquin burped again as he gnawed on his next bone—still unimpressed by any of this.

"Fine, don't believe me. Braulio is one of several. More and more will come to rescue us the longer you hold us captives," she said matter-of-factly. "I'm sure the next one will be here soon. Of course, if we are dead they have no reason to come."

Org thought about that logic and tried to figure out if it made sense. He couldn't. But catching another tasty human made him think. He licked his lips greedily.

"She's lying. It's a trick," sneered Squal.

"And dead or alive, you will never find where they are all hiding because I will never tell you my password!" Candice was speaking boldly now. Had it not been for those chains she would have been in Squal's face.

"Password for what?" Squal growled back.

"My thought vial! It's tucked in my sleeve and you were too stupid of a guard to even notice it!" she taunted.

Org chuckled, proud that his own guarding abilities were better than Squal's. He would have never missed a thought vial, he told himself ... that is, if he had any idea what a thought vial was.

"Rawwrrr!" hollered the shamed Squal, ripping into her sleeve and barely stopping himself from putting a fist through her. The thought vial bounced to the floor and Squal grabbed it.

Onquin, for the first time, took an interest.

"Tell me the password!" Squal ordered.

"I'll never tell you! Whether you eat me or not, I'll never betray my friends to you, you filthy beast!" she roared.

Squal's savage backhand swooshed over her head, missing her by an inch. It would have broken her cheekbone had she not ducked. The fierce giant was ready to lay a hold of her and shake her until she talked, had Onquin not gotten up. He strode over to Squal and plucked the thought vial out of his hand.

"That's evidence for Maboa and none of yer business to look at, fool!" he scolded.

In actuality, there was nothing on the vial either they or Maboa would be interested in. The notes Candice had taken on her forest journeys with Thogwok were of little substance. The only embarrassing things she wouldn't want them to see were a few love letters to Azmarpin that she wrote but never sent. There was certainly nothing in there about anyone's whereabouts. But her plan was working; the focus in the room had shifted away from eating Braulio.

"Who got crushed and made you ruler? Outa my space!" Squal bawled and, snatching the thought vial back, he shoved Onquin into a table. The beefy giant toppled backwards over it, smashing the little table to bits.

This was, of course, much more excuse than a rephaite needed for a fight, and the room explosively came alive with the yells, cracks, smashes, and thuds that accompanied a giant brawl. But small quarters aren't accommodating to rephaim mayhem, and soon a new door was made as the three went smashing through a wall—Org jumping in just for fun. Other rephaim outside followed suit, joining in the melee now escalating in the street.

Candice's solitude only lasted a moment. The distraction outdoors gave an opening to wily, opportunistic predators. With the giant guards gone and occupied, three hungry wolves crept in through the door, making their way toward Candice. She screamed. The wolves bared their fangs, crouching and coming closer. As the lead wolf closed in on her legs she kicked it in the face. He yelped and leapt back.

A second wolf tried his luck and struck. He succeeded in taking out a piece of her pant leg, drawing some blood. He would have gotten more had Candice not brought her heel solidly down on his head.

With bared fangs, the third wolf crouched to spring at the girl. The giant guards would return eventually. The beasts knew now was their chance.

Candice knew it too. She also knew she had come to her end. Her screams, as far as she could tell, were going unheard because of the tumult outside. She closed her eyes and for the second and maybe last time ever, she prayed.

At that moment the mood of the room changed. Something had entered from above and landed in the middle of the floor. It happened so fast that Candice couldn't figure out what it was at first. It was large and loud and constantly moving. A wolf yelped in pain and Candice recognized what had arrived: bees—lots and lots of bees! A hive had plopped in the center of the room and angry bees, some as large as rats, began overtaking the place.

Candice screamed again and balled herself up where she was chained. The wolves bolted for the door—several bees following as they ran. The wolves' yelping got the attention of more than one giant too. Onquin, Org, Squal, and the all others halted their fight and, alarmed, beheld a cloud of huge bees swarming toward them. Instantly engulfed in bees, the rephaim wildly swatted, hollered in confusion, and ran.

Bees poured out the door, the windows, and the open ceiling, filling the air around Candice's jail cell with angry buzzing mayhem. Outside her room she heard the yelling and swearing from rephaim getting punctured by large stingers. Candice wasn't sure which was worse: hungry wolves or enraged bees. She envisioned getting impaled by those dagger-sized stingers and figured she'd be dead anyway. If they stung her, she'd puff up like … fruit! She remembered that Thogwok had given them bee-repellent fruit!

Candice heaved a sigh of relief. She swelled with gratitude for Thogwok and all the rest in her group. She thought about him, Enosh, Braulio, Sean, even Lawth a little bit, and especially Fong. She finally began to appreciate how good they all were to her, and now it hit her that she'd probably seen them all for the very last time. She started crying all over again.

Candice at first figured it must have been her imagination—actively stirred by her emotions as she thought about those who loved her—because just outside her wall she heard the sound of Thogwok's voice. More voices followed it, and they were yelling. She could not see much through either the door or the giant hole in the wall, but she heard the heavy footsteps of what must have been one of the giants running past her building. This seemed to spark a whole new commotion, as it was followed by shrieking and howling. The few creatures still near Candice's quarters who had not been chased away by the bees were suddenly running away, presumably chasing something else. Whatever was happening, it caused everyone to quickly leave. Even all the bees had flown off.

Then the most welcome sight Candice could have ever hoped to see popped her head in the doorway: her loyal friend, Fong.

"Candice?" she called out cautiously.

"Fong!" Candice cried. She couldn't believe her eyes. Amidst all this fear, ugliness, and violence, her small package of loyal friendship arrived in the middle of it all to save her. "It's really you! I can't believe it!"

Eric popped into the room. He took one look at Candice—chained to the wall, her leg bloodied—and he and Fong ran over to her and embraced her. She dissolved in tears.

"Eric! How—" she began. "How did—" Candice tried to ask through her sobs of gratitude.

"Enosh and I went back and got him," Fong answered. "But never mind that now," she said as she took out a vial of some potent-looking neon green liquid. She poured some on the chain that was binding Candice.

"This is venom from those giant lime spiders Thogwok caught with us," Fong instructed. "If you recall, we never got a chance to milk the spiders and learn about their venom to know what it does."

"What does it do?" Candice asked in revulsion as the slimy green venom began bubbling and foaming on the chain.

"Eats through almost any metal," Fong answered. "Probably not good for skin either. Best not to get any on you."

Candice made sure not to, and in a minute she was free of her bonds and scurrying toward the door with Eric and Fong. They were just about to slip through when they heard the distinct sound of a skull getting thwacked. It was followed by a rephaite falling headlong through the door into the room. The kids dodged and the rephaite crashed face first before them.

"Enosh's torch hard at work," said Eric with satisfaction.

The three stepped over the body and outside. Sure enough, a solid stick of wood, lit like a torch so Enosh could see it from afar, hung innocently in the air, waiting for the next foe to come near.

"Enosh is over in one of those trees keeping an eye on this place. He's wielding the air around it to control it," Fong quickly explained to Candice.

"But how did you know where I was?" Candice asked.

"The parrot scoped it out," Eric answered. "We also know where Braulio is. Thogwok is off to rescue him. Once we knew which building you were in, Enosh climbed a tree and kept close watch on it. Thogwok slathered himself and the rest of us with some kind of bee repellent. Then he found a beehive and brought it over to us. When Enosh saw you were in danger he sent the hive over to you by airmail."

"Air-wielding," corrected Fong.

"Whatever. Now follow us," Eric said.

Dodging obstacles and scurrying past giants that were unconscious on the ground from the effects of the bee stings, the three escaped to the south edge of the village where Enosh was perched. His torch followed behind them, knocking out two guards and one nosey hyena.

The three concealed themselves in the bushes below Enosh's tree. Candice looked up. It was dark there at the forest's edge, but she could still see the warm and radiant smile of Enosh.

"It is so nice to see you again, Candice," he said.

Candice smiled at him in relief. She looked around. Letting her eyes adjust to the darkness she asked, "Where are Sean and Lawth?"

After Maboa had blown Lawth off the cliff and sent his dragon away to monitor Porfiznin, he hovered out of sight. Cloaked in darkness, he wielded the air enough to suspend himself high above the jagged rocks and just below the ledge of the cliff. Holding the georb necklace high, he continued summoning Sean's georb. Waves in the ocean surged.

Lightning split the sky. Land rumbled all along the coast and whirling winds swept past. Then, in a moment of darkness between lighting flashes, Maboa caught a glimpse of a faint blue light pulsing from the east. Peering through both his thin veil and several yards of thick rock, he saw the other georb and the boy who was wearing it. And the boy was dutifully walking straight toward him.

The plan to rescue Candice was combined with the plan to rescue Braulio. When Candice thought she had heard Thogwok yelling and running past her building, it hadn't been mere wishful thinking. Knowing the bees would attack whoever they saw first, Thogwok reasoned they would chase the wolves while ignoring the human whose pores, thanks to the violet honeydew, emitted bee repellent. Then, as soon as the beehive distraction cleared her building, Thogwok ran past it, yelling insults at the rephaim and the wolves, intending to draw them away from Candice.

The plan was working fairly well at first. The rephaim and wolves immediately chased after Thogwok. So did the bees, which swarmed the nephil and stung all who got near him. Seeing his enemies laid low by the stings, Thogwok was grateful for the extra doses of bee repellent he had both consumed and rubbed all over him.

It was a sacrificial and gutsy move, nonetheless, because even with the help from the bees, Thogwok was still badly outnumbered. He had been in numerous frays over the centuries and he could hold his own, but in this place there were far too many enemies for a lone nephil to handle. Had the enraged bees not been viciously attacking and distracting the rephaim, wolves, and hired men, Thogwok would have been a goner. But in no time at all, most of the enemy forces were either on the ground writhing in pain from the stings or fleeing altogether.

Nevertheless, three especially tenacious rephaim were undeterred by the bees and relentlessly pursued the nephil. Soon, Thogwok was backed against a wall, fighting fiercely against three foes all as large as him, while still desperately trying to get to the building where Dufritter had spied Braulio chained up.

Surrounded, outnumbered, and with no place to run, Thogwok would have likely died in less than a minute had he not been saved by a most unlikely rescuer. He couldn't see his rescuer—and quite frankly he was glad he couldn't—but he could hear it. The air shook with a hideous screech. Thogwok knew that sound. Maboa's dragon was soaring overhead. With a shuddering thud, it landed in the middle of the street.

The dragon spun around, knocking over hired men and giants alike with its solid tail. Craning its whip-like neck in every direction, it peered over the top of Braulio's cell. He was still there. With a single leap the dragon lunged toward Candice's place of bondage. Landing, it crushed a hyena that was scurrying for cover. The dragon didn't notice or care. But it noticed immediately that Candice was missing and the slithering lizard erupted in a deafening, freakish screech. In its rage, the dragon whipped its tail around the village streets, pummeling any who were in the way.

Men, wolves, hyenas, and rephaim all scattered. Bees were buzzing frantically. One stung the dragon's tail. It was promptly swallowed. The dragon snapped its elastic neck high in the air and belched a stream of fire. Several cooked bees fell to the ground. Most of the others got the message and buzzed away.

The dragon leapt again, landing with front claws on top of another building. Sabtah was still inside. Not satisfied, the dragon flew low over the rest of the village, scanning for Candice. In moments, it had seen through the roofs of all the buildings, burning to ash the few cloth awnings that covered bed and bath chambers and spying all the rooms. But it did not see the missing girl, and its rage increased.

Thogwok's attackers had fled for cover with the rest of the giants. This was his chance to get to Braulio's hut while the coast was clear. It was close—the one right across the street. Thogwok stood still with his back to the wall until the dragon had made a second pass. As soon as it did, Thogwok lunged clumsily for the door and tumbled inside.

"Thogwok!" yelled Braulio in total surprise, as Thogwok scrambled to get to his feet.

"Nephil!" yelled a rephaite guard as he rushed toward Thogwok with a spiked club.

"How yuz doin', kiddo?" said Thogwok as he reflexively dodged the club and punched the oncoming guard in the gut. Thogwok swiftly twisted the club out of the rephaite's huge hand and walloped him over the head with it. The attacker fell to the floor and Thogwok staggered over to Braulio as if nothing unusual had happened.

"Okay, I gotta admit, you're good," Braulio said as Thogwok grabbed Braulio's chain and snapped it like a twig.

"After living hundreds of years, I guess yuz learn a thing or two," Thogwok said with a wink of a bloody eyelid. "And one thing I learned is to get while the gittinz good—and it won't be for long—so c'mon!"

Holding onto each other for support (Braulio had acquired a sprained ankle when Org flung him down in front of Maboa and Thogwok, of course, could always use a little steadying), they hobbled out of the hut and headed together toward the southern forest. The coast was clear to the dragon and it was looking like they'd make it. But then they heard a blood-chilling roar and a cracking of wood beams directly behind them which stopped them dead in their tracks. Braulio and Thogwok turned around to see the dragon, now perched angrily on top of the very building they had just left. Their eyes met. Evil red-black eyes seething with hate and rage cut through Braulio's skin and sent fingers of ice down his spine. The boy had to look away.

But Thogwok stared right back at him, never backing down. "You can't win, dragon. Not you, not Maboa, and not any of yuz who do evil. Good will always be more powerful and will always win!" Thogwok shouted defiantly as he pointed his finger at the beast several times his size and strength.

Ripping out another chilling roar and blasting the house next to them with a stream of fire, the dragon spoke. "Se-e-eize them!"

Rephaim, who had been hiding in buildings, emerged and charged toward Thogwok and Braulio. An attempt at running or, rather, limping toward safety was met by another dragon blast of fire blocking their path.

Thogwok and Braulio stopped and stood back to back. "Awright kid, this might be it," Thogwok said hefting the club he had just acquired, gripping it like a baseball bat. "Stand for what is right, ne'er give up, fight like a nephil, and you'll enter your next life unashamed!"

Braulio put up his fists. Three rephaim with clubs immediately surrounded them and more were on the way. One lunged forward swinging a thorny club. Thogwok dodged the weapon and smashed the attacker's face with a damaging swing of his own. Braulio got in a few good punches to the giant's gut before the stunned monster toppled over.

Two more attacked. Thogwok dodged the first incoming club and slugged the giant on the chin with a brutal uppercut. He blocked the next blow and got into a wrestling hold that separated him from Braulio. The other rephaite grabbed the boy. Braulio fought as best he could, but in seconds he was subdued. Ten more had arrived on the scene and Thogwok couldn't hold them off.

Calneh, the rephaite captain who had kidnapped Thogwok's son, strode in to the center of it all and scoffed at the futile defense attempt the young Braulio and the klutzy giant had made. "You fool nephil! Were you so proud to think you alone could rescue this piece of filth?"

"Not proud—noble. And that boy is of greater value than anything you or your host could ever understand!" Thogwok declared with unyielding resolve.

Calneh spit in Thogwok's face and a slimy glob of goo dripped from his chin.

"Take the scum kid back to the hut. Double the chains and double the guards," the captain ordered. "The rest of you scour the forest for the other prisoner. She can't be far! And as for you ..." Calneh said with cold eyes as he drew a sword and approached Thogwok, who was held tightly by three others. "I can't see any good reason to keep you alive."

The fierce rephaite captain raised his sword over Thogwok's head and grinned wickedly. He was close enough and strong enough to slice Thogwok in half.

"You can't win, Dragon," Thogwok said confidently, looking up and over the head of the rephaite about to do him in.

Calneh sneered. Then instantly, his expression transformed to shock. As his sword came down, the captain came down with it, falling on top of the guard holding Thogwok's left side.

Shock rippled through the gang of giants as they noticed a long sleek arrow sticking out of their captain's bloody back. They all looked up.

Three buildings away, standing resolutely on top of a wall, was a nephil warrior.

"My brothers," breathed Thogwok with a sigh of relief.

"Azmarpin!" cried Candice from where she sat with Enosh, Fong, and Eric up in one of the nearby trees. They had stealthily positioned themselves there to get closer to Thogwok and Braulio.

"NEPHILI-I-I-IM!" hollered several of the wicked giants at once.

The dragon spewed fire at Azmarpin, who nimbly sprang off the wall and ran away before the house he stood on was engulfed in flames.

Suddenly the air was alive with hissing. A volley of arrows whizzed past the tree that Enosh and the kids were hiding in. Arrows lodged in walls. Others punctured leather armor, dropping one rephaite after another. A dozen arrows plinked off the dragon's scales and a few made pinpricks, momentarily distracting him.

Then a rush of rustling surrounded Enosh, Eric, Candice, and Fong. Nephil warriors swarmed out of the forest and descended on the village. Some came from behind bushes on the ground. Many sprang from tree limb to tree limb. Another batch came splashing out of the nearby stream, having used reeds to breath while they had been silently swimming ever closer. In all, hundreds of nephilim swarmed into, around, and on top of the buildings, overwhelming the village.

The kids watched in wonder.

"Where did they all come from?" Fong asked. "Have they been here all along?"

"Amazing, aren't they?" Enosh said. "I think they crept in little by little over the past several hours. Then they patiently waited for all the rest to arrive and for the signal to be given. They always work together."

Swarming the streets and scampering along the tops of walls, the strapping nephilim giants sang a battle song as they descended on Porfiznin.

Thogwok became emboldened. "My brother nephilim!" he yelled as he flipped his captors over his shoulders and onto the ground. He then charged the giant holding Braulio, making as straight a beeline as he'd ever made—bellowing a war cry that would scare anyone twice his size.

Braulio's captor dropped him and ran. Thogwok scooped up the boy in his arms. "Ha-h-a-a-a-a! They're here! My brothers are here! Now run thataway to the south side, ma'boy. There yuz'll find Enosh and the other kids. Yuz'll be safe there!" Thogwok set him down, shoving him toward the forest and away from the fray.

But Braulio immediately turned around, staggered, and limped back toward Thogwok and the battle, the wave of agile nephilim warriors swerving around him, flooding the village.

"Thogwok, wait!" Braulio said, grabbing the giant's shirt and being dragged a few feet before Thogwok noticed.

"Ay, what is it, ma'boy?"

"Thogwok, you said, 'Do what is right, never give up, and fight like a nephil,' right?"

"Actually, it was 'Stand for what is right, ne'er give up, fight like a—'"

A huge rephaite with an arrow through his chest toppled over next to them, nearly crushing Braulio and shaking the ground beneath them.

"Oh, whatever! It's time to fight like a nephil, isn't it? These nephilim, your brothers as you call them, just rescued me. The right thing to do is stand with them! I'm fighting!" Braulio said with a steely resolve.

Thogwok gave a wry smile and said, "I like yer attitude; sounds like a warrior more than a boy."

Thogwok pulled something out of a sheath and handed it to Braulio.

"I hear ya lost yer knife to a buncha monkeys. See if me pocket knife fits yer grip," Thogwok said, handing Braulio his huge knife. In Braulio's hands, it had the feel of a magnificent short sword. The grip was perfect.

"Two are stronger than one. Stick by me side!" Thogwok ordered.

"I wouldn't have it any other way!" Braulio replied.

Thogwok snagged a huge sword from the nearby fallen giant. Doubly armed with a spiked club in one hand and a thick sword in the other, Thogwok wielded the dual weapons like a master, balance being his only problem. Lunging forward, he sliced a gash into the closest enemy warrior. The rephaite swung back, barely missing Thogwok, who in turn lost his balance and fell forward. Braulio charged the wounded rephaite, nimbly ducking and dodging while the armored giant struggled to get a good hit on his small foe. This gave Thogwok time to regain his feet. When he did, he joined Braulio and gave the rephaite thug a fatal blow. In this manner the two warriors continued to battle side by side, Braulio not even noticing his injured ankle in the heat of the conflict.

The enraged dragon, occupied by the assault of nephil arrows, had not forgotten about his prey. He plucked out the last arrow that pricked him like a thorn and screeched a threatening roar. Blasting volleys of fireballs and thrashing with his tail, the dragon held his ground, but lost sight of Braulio. Lurching from his haunches, he toppled the wall on which he was perched and soared over the village, scanning the pandemonium below him for the missing prisoners. Blazing buildings and burning corpses lit up the darkness. The dragon spied the wounded rephaim, many now fighting with one or two arrows lodged in them. They were dropping one by one under the onslaught of bow-wielding nephilim, who bounced from wall to ground to roof, shooting arrows effortlessly as they ran.

Furious, the dragon flew low, skimming over the tops of buildings and belching fireballs at all nephilim he saw. Some caught fire and rolled to the ground. Many others on the roofs who ducked the fire missiles were slapped off by the snap of the dragon's tail. Finally, the dragon spotted his prey: the boy.

Braulio was engaged in fierce swordfight with a big, ugly human hireling while Thogwok stood by his side, battling a bigger and even uglier rephaite. Enosh's air torch was at Braulio's back, clubbing and setting aflame any who approached him from behind. Suddenly, a loud crash behind them got even the torch's attention.

As Braulio turned around, he found himself staring into the mouth of the horrifying dragon. Braulio couldn't move. Terror paralyzed him. The hireling, now behind him, went for the kill, but Enosh was faster, and knocked him off his feet with a swift torch punch to the throat.

"Be gone, boul feast!" Thogwok commanded, defiantly pointing his sword toward the dragon's burning eyes.

The dragon lifted its right claw and smacked Thogwok, along with a few the nearest rephaim, across the street. Nephilim stung the beast with a volley of arrows from behind. Annoyed more than injured, the dragon swept the street with its monstrous tail, indiscriminately plowing over all in its path. Then the mammoth winged serpent snatched up Braulio and held him in front of his mouth.

With breath smelling of death, the foul beast hissed, "Where is-s-s-s the girl?"

Braulio turned his head away and covered his face with his free hand, partly due to the breath but mostly because he was too frightened to look into the devilish eyes.

Nephilim warriors loosed a barrage of arrows at the robust lizard, most of which bounced off the scaly hide with nothing more than a dull plink. Azmarpin and another brave nephil leapt onto the dragon's neck and tried to slit its throat. But the dragon merely craned its serpentine neck high, shook once, and the brave nephilim were flung off.

"I will as-s-sk one more time. Then I will take your right hand, then your left, then your feet, your arms until I get my ans-s-swer! WHERE is-s-s the girl?" the irate dragon hissed.

Braulio knew where Candice was. Thogwok told him that she and the rest were hidden in the trees at the south end of the village. Confirming their close proximity, Enosh's air-wielded torch spun around from behind the dragon's head and dove for its right eye. But the beast saw the torch coming and blinked.

The flaming stick pelted the monster's eyelid but did no damage. Annoyed, the dragon snatched the torch in its mouth and crunched it to bits, ejecting it with globules of spit that pelted the fighters on the ground.

Candice and the rest with her could hear the dragon's threat. It was becoming clear that Braulio wasn't going to reveal Candice's location, even if he lost his limbs and his life to protect her.

"No, Braulio, you can't do that for me," she said aloud. "Not again!"

Serflina, who came with the army of nephilim, had climbed up the tree to protect Candice and Fong. She said, "The boy has become a noble warrior in a very short time."

"But, no, he can't let himself die for me. It's my fault he's even been caught. Braulio-o-o!" she yelled.

Serflina quickly put her hand over the girl's mouth, silencing her and whispering, "NO. You must not endanger those who are here with you. Trust that the noble warrior who does what is right will always be protected. It is the nephil way."

But it was too late to stay hidden now. The attentive dragon's long pointed ears perked up to the shrill cry of Candice's voice. It twisted its long neck toward the tree where Candice and the rest sat.

The winged serpent peered toward the trees where it heard the voice. "So," the dragon hissed, "the girl sit-s-s-s in the tree!"

Braulio was terrified, more so now than even before. He couldn't let the dragon get to Candice or the others but he had no idea what he could do to stop it.

"Brauli-o-o-o! Go fer the eye! Go fer the eye!" Thogwok hollered desperately from the ground.

The dragon sprang from its haunches toward the edge of the forest. It landed hard on two legs, still holding Braulio with the third and readying to grab Candice with the fourth.

Serflina snatched Candice and Fong in her arms and sprang from the tree toward safety. Enosh leapt from the tree, too, and cushioned his fall with a large air mattress.

The dragon lit the tops of the nearby trees with a belch of fire. Then it plunged its lanky neck into the thick foliage and caught a glimpse of Serflina whisking the girls away.

The beast lunged after them, colliding with trees and vines as it plummeted into the forest, Braulio still firmly in its right claw.

"Leave them alone!" yelled Braulio, trying to sound tough while terrified. He still wasn't able to look the beast in the eyes. He looked down and saw Enosh standing boldly in plain sight of the dragon waving his arms.

"Hey there, ugly lizard! Look over here!" Enosh called to the dragon.

The dragon looked and was pelted in the left eye by a barrage of pointy sticks. Enosh wielded them with air and sent them at full speed toward the dragon's weak spot.

The beast automatically responded as anyone would: shutting the injured eye and raising his front claw up to it—in this case the claw that held Braulio.

"Braulio!" yelled Enosh from below. "Attack what you fear!"

Frozen in horror as the dragon's open eye glared menacingly at him, Braulio remembered that Thogwok had said, "Go for the eye." For a few endless seconds, Braulio stared straight into that one horrible, red-black eye. Darkness, evil, and searing hatred shot straight through the boy's bones. Waves of terror flooded him. But he knew he couldn't wait another second. Gripping the knife Thogwok gave him, Braulio thrust through the center of that huge, evil pupil of abject darkness. A perfect strike.

A horrified screech of defeat ripped through the forest, the town, and as far as the cliff where Maboa hung waiting for Sean. All watched in suspense as the vile serpent flung Braulio from its grip and bolted up through the canopy of burning trees, flying madly and blindly away.

Enosh was quick to conjure an air mattress just before Braulio would have hit land. The young warrior bounced twice on an invisible cushion and tumbled softly to the ground as the blinded dragon flew off and was once for all, out of sight.

There were a few seconds of shock, silence and disbelief which were soon replaced by the whoops and cheers of the nephilim all throughout the village. Those cheers were immediately followed by growls and war cries from the rephaim who, even though they lost their dragon, would much rather fight than run. So the battle raged on.

Several nephilim, led by Azmarpin, bounded into the forest to see if Enosh and the kids were alright. Serflina, Candice and Fong all ran over and joined in congratulating Braulio, Thogwok, Enosh and the rest of the nephilim warriors for their heroic bravery. Thogwok stumbled behind the rest. When he got to them, he grabbed hold of Braulio and gave him the most wobbly and precarious hug the boy had ever received. Of course, after being held in the clutches of a dragon, Thogwok's unstable hug felt surprisingly safe and comforting.

"That's jus' what a noble nephil warrior does, eh, Braulio?" Thogwok said, smacking Braulio hard enough on the back to almost knock him on his face. "I'm so proud of yuz, I am!" Thogwok quickly scanned the area. "But wait, we never found Sean!"

"Or Lawth," said Fong.

"And my georb is missing and so is Maboa," lamented Braulio.

"And I have a feeling all those elements are connected," Enosh concluded.

Chapter 20

CONNECTIONS

"The spell is taking effect. I can see the fool boy," Maboa said with raspy avarice in his true voice—a voice so cold, so menacing, so hate-filled he seldom ever let it be heard.

Sean kept walking toward the ocean. He was mostly unaware of where he was going; he was just flowing with the feeling that he had to go that way. By now he was so close to the ocean that, with his mouth slackly hanging open, he could taste sea salt. The strong ocean breeze disheveled his hair and spray from the high waves pelted his face. Not knowing where he was or why he was there, when he could walk no further, Sean stopped and stood on the very edge of the cliff.

Maboa hung suspended just below him beside the sheer cliff wall. Smoothly wielding the air below and elevating himself as close as he could to Sean while still remaining hidden, Maboa moved in for the kill. Levitating just below the rocky ledge, he called on the elements of air, water, earth, and fire inside Sean's head to willingly let go of the georb and fling it over the cliff.

Maboa peered through the layers of rock that separated him from the boy. He licked his dark lips as he ogled the glowing, spinning, pulsating georb. It danced dramatically and beautifully in the air before him. Maboa watched Sean as closely as he eyed the georb, longing for him to remove the necklace. For a while, Sean didn't move a muscle. He simply stood at the edge of the cliff, looking beyond the water at the sky.

"S-s-simply drop it into my hands," Maboa hissed, holding out a gnarled hand just below the cliff edge and mustering all the sorcery of mind wielding he could.

The georb spun radiantly in front of Sean's chest. It excitedly danced and spun in the air, pulling further away from Sean as if it wanted to go somewhere. Sean cupped his hand under the georb and marveled at how beautiful it was. Then he unfastened the necklace, removed it from his neck, and held it in front of him.

Maboa's skin crawled with excitement. "Yes-s-s that's it! You don't need that rock anymore. You have had it long enough. It is time to let it go," Maboa spoke into Sean's mind, wily wielding more of his enticing sorcery.

Sean cocked his head and looked admiringly at the georb reverberating in front of him. "It feels like you want to go away," he said to the stone.

Maboa was ecstatic. "Yes, yes! I must go away. I want to go home!" Maboa said, feverishly beckoning Sean to willingly choose to release the gem.

"I get the feeling you want to finally go home," Sean said, looking affectionately at the georb.

Maboa raised himself higher and spoke directly to Sean's mind. "It would not be right for you to keep me any longer. My time has come to leave you and be united with the air essence. Just hurl me over the cliff and I will find my way," Maboa said, pleased by how smoothly the lie spun in his mind on the spur of the moment.

"Well, alright then, Mr. Georb," Sean said. "Ya know, for being just a rock, you've been real cool. I'll miss ya, but I understand what it's like to want to go home. So, here ya go-o-o-o!" And with a huge heave Sean flung the georb over the cliff and high in the air.

The air and the georb met in midflight. The tiny gem joined the oncoming breeze in a magnificent explosion of wind and light. Maboa grasped for the georb, missed, and raced after it. But the swirling wind transformed into a cyclone which sucked Maboa in and spit him back out. Maboa hurtled directly over Sean's head, screaming and hissing as he tumbled to the ground in a crumpled heap, tangled up in his robe.

"Whoa, dude!" Sean cried as he covered his face and dropped to the ground.

But the powerful wind didn't pull him in or blow him away. It just increased in size and strength, pulling up water from the ocean and spinning wildly—a beautiful water spout lit from within. Sean looked up and could see clearly and vividly inside the storm. Lightning and water harmoniously intermingled, swirling inside the funnel. The cyclonic energy continued intensifying—picking up sand, stones, and shells from the ocean floor, swirling them in a magnificent light show. It was the most beautiful sight Sean had ever seen.

Back at the edge of the village, burning embers dropped from treetops which the dragon had set aflame. Enosh and the kids scooted away from under the trees and crouched down in a hidden spot where they could watch the battle in the village. Thogwok and Braulio, now both proven warriors, decided to stay there to protect the others. Serflina and Azmarpin stuck close by also, keeping a watchful eye for any rephaite who might head their way. Rephaim were fierce and vengeful warriors. Few things would cause them to back down in the heat of battle, and losing their dragon only enraged them all the more. It also made Braulio a more hated foe and a prized trophy for any rephaite to capture and kill.

While the battle raged on, Enosh was just starting to say where he thought Sean might be when a bright flash and thunder boom interrupted him. They all looked toward the west. A massive swirling funnel towered over the trees. The nephilim and rephaim saw it too, and one by one, those engaged in battle stopped fighting and stared. Suddenly, in unison, all the nephilim gave a shout of praise. Whether on the ground, on a roof, or clinging to a wall, they danced and sang and shouted victory cries.

Every wolf and hyena made a beeline for the forest. The few surviving vultures took to the air, flapping over the kids' heads as fast as they could fly, away from the swirling funnel cloud. Some of the older and wiser rephaim also took advantage of the momentary distraction and quickly escaped to the forest. But most of the rephaim, along with Maboa's hired men, resumed their attack, and in seconds the battle was in full force again.

"He did it!" Thogwok hollered with a leap and an awkward landing. "The boy did it! I knew one of yuz would! I just knew it!"

"Did what? What is that thing in the sky and what is going on?" Fong asked.

"Well now, that answers a lot of troubling questions," Enosh said, breathing a sigh of relief.

"Answers what questions? What's happening?" demanded Braulio.

Thogwok was jumping around and whooping too much to answer. Azmarpin and Serflina joined in the excitement (and made sure Thogwok didn't land on one of the kids).

"Enosh, please, what is going on?" Candice asked.

"It looks like marvelous things are going on, young ones. For that funnel cloud is the combination of the air georb with the air essence. That means nothing less than ..." Enosh paused for emphasis, "... mission accomplished!" He beamed at Braulio, Candice, and Fong.

"But Maboa has Braulio's georb, Enosh! How do we know it wasn't Maboa that connected them?" Fong asked with alarm.

"Because of the reaction of the nephilim. Being part angelic, and therefore of purer character, they are in tune with these things more than humans are. They can immediately sense if a thing is good or evil. It will be obvious to us quite soon too, I suspect," Enosh said.

"You mean *Sean* found the place to connect the georb?" Braulio asked with shock. "*He* is the Chosen One?"

"You seem surprised that it would be Sean," Enosh said, raising an eyebrow. "Why is that?"

"Well, because Sean is ..." Braulio hesitated as Enosh peered deeply into him with those radiant blue eyes. "... not all that smart," he finished weakly.

"Not all that smart, eh?" Enosh repeated. "And let's suppose that is true. Do you think the georb would prefer to choose someone intelligent and stubborn, or someone willing to learn and then obedient to what they are taught?"

Braulio didn't need to answer for the answer was obvious. He and the rest looked over at the tornado-like storm in the western sky—swirling bigger and faster second by second, and heading right toward them!

———— >●< ————

Back at the cliff, Sean stood awestruck at the immensity and strength of the cyclone. He was mesmerized; not even concerned that it started moving toward him. Then a dark-cloaked figure grabbed him, threw him over his shoulder, and jumped off the edge of the cliff. They plummeted. Below them was nothing but the rugged and unforgiving wave-smashed terrain. Yelling for help would have done nothing. Instinctively, Sean shut his eyes and prayed.

Suddenly, a gust of air whipped up from below them, vigorously flapping the dark cloak and Sean's clothes and hair. The air gust slowed their speed to a crawl and they landed with a soft thud on a large rock. The cloaked figure dumped Sean off his back and grabbed him by the shirt collar.

"Dude, what on earth!" Sean said before he recognized the man. "Lawth! It's you! Dude, we wondered where you were! Looks like you chose to go the beach, huh?" Sean said before Lawth pulled him down and held him tightly against the rock.

"Dude, what gives?" Sean hollered with his body squashed between Lawth and the rock.

"What are you trying to do, get yourself killed?" Lawth yelled. "Stay down or this thing will tear you apart!"

The wild and wonderfully beautiful cyclone passed over them. Looking up they could see a vivid array of light, water, rock formations, and, more than anything, astounding swirls of wind. It moved inland, gaining speed.

Bruised and battered, Maboa got to his feet and frantically tried to reach out to the tornado and somehow still get the georb. He screamed and hissed at the storm, shouting orders at it from behind his torn and disheveled robe. But the funnel merely picked him up again, spun him around wildly, and flung him. Maboa could barely catch his breath as he gathered himself off the ground the second time and then ran away as fast as he could.

"No-o-o-o-o-o!" he screamed as he ran—the wild, swirling, air storm chasing him away from the cliff that sheltered Sean and Lawth.

"So, Mr. Lawth dude, what was all that?" Sean asked as they stood up.

"It seems as though you just connected the air georb to the air essence," Lawth said dryly.

Sean stared with his mouth open. "I did?" he asked with disbelief. "But all I did was throw the georb in the air when it said it was time to go."

"Trust me, kid, it shocks me more than it does you! When you tossed that georb to Maboa I thought he had you, your georb, and the rest of the world in the palm of his hand. But irony of ironies, you somehow pulled it off!" Lawth mused, shaking his head in disbelief as he turned and began to climb up the cliff.

"Maboa? I didn't toss the georb to Maboa. I didn't even know he was there. I just threw it to the wind like it asked me to," Sean corrected as he followed him up the rocky slope.

"I watched you with my own two eyes!" Lawth said emphatically. "Maboa's dragon flung me over the cliff. I broke my fall with an air cushion like I just did a minute ago with you on my back. I laid there and didn't move a muscle. Thinking I was dead, Maboa sent his dragon away and waited here for you, beckoning you with his georb. He was hiding right under this cliff, coaching you the whole way!"

Sean clambered up the cliff behind him while Lawth broke into a long rant. Sean couldn't make out much of it, Lawth's back being toward him and the windstorm howling as it was, but Sean caught the words "ridiculous," "gullible boy," "most improbable," "unbelievable," and "ironic," all in Lawth's rant.

Arriving at the top of the cliff, Sean noticed the ring of fire Lawth had set up earlier in the night.

"Dude, this isn't where we camped. Who made this?" Sean asked.

"I did. I used it for a decoy to draw Maboa's forces away from the rest of you," Lawth said simply.

"Hey, that was real thoughtful of you, Mr. Lawth dude," Sean said.

"Don't expect it to happen again," Lawth quipped. "Now where is everyone else? Did Enosh regain consciousness? Has anyone rescued Candice? Tell me all you know," he demanded.

"Uh, well we ran through the forest until Thogwok fell in a river and that woke up Enosh. Then we sent some smelly leaves down the river and made a campsite. Last I knew, Enosh took Fong back to my world to get some dude named Eric. That left Thogwok, Braulio, and me in the camp. I fell asleep and when the georb woke me up only Thogwok was left. Braulio was gone. I think it was because Mr. Enosh kinda laid into him for being selfish and losing his georb and stuff like that," Sean paused and thought before he continued. "If I had to guess, I'd say he went to the village to try and rescue Candice so he could be all macho and junk."

"You say Enosh went back to your world? How long ago was that?" Lawth demanded.

"Uh ... like a few hours ago." Sean guessed.

"Then he's definitely back, and the moment he noticed you and Braulio missing he would search for you," Lawth deduced. "You say they are holding Candice captive in the village?" he asked urgently.

"Yeah, that's where all those giants, the dragon, and the last few ugly birds went to," Sean said.

"And that's also where the air storm is headed! Let's go!"

And as fast as they could run, Sean and Lawth followed the wind.

Meanwhile, the village of Porfiznin was in disarray with nephilim and rephaim locked in fierce battle. Arrows thudded into walls, plinked off of armor, and buried themselves in flesh. Spiked clubs, swung with intense power, bent shields in half and bludgeoned bodies. Smoke billowed from burning buildings, still ablaze from the dragon's fury. The clamor of yells, hits, clashes and cries echoed off the walls and reverberated across the forest.

The nighttime battle was brightly lit by flames dotting the village and lightning flashes whizzing about inside the approaching storm. The kids looked on with awe at the sheer strength and brutality of the rephaim compared with the accuracy and agility of the nephilim. It seemed an even match.

"Let's go, Thogwok!" Braulio said. "We can't let your brothers fight alone!" And wielding his sword, he headed toward the village.

"Looka that boy! He's done become a noble warrior he has; beatin' a dragon and everythin'!" Thogwok said, beaming with pride.

"Indeed," Enosh agreed. "And he may have his chance again someday, but I think this battle is already over. It seems some of the rephaim just haven't gotten that message quite yet."

Sure enough, just then, a gust of spinning wind—rather like a lightening-lit skinny tornado—spun off from the georb storm. It rapidly sped inland and blew through the village. As it did, the nephilim gained more strength and fought harder, while the rephaim and Maboa's hired men covered their noses as if smelling the stench of something dead.

Then the main georb storm grew larger and larger until it became a huge and imposing tornado that filled the western sky. It was lit on the inside with flashes of swirling lightning and roared with power as it intensified in speed and twisted itself toward the village—moments away from impact!

"Enosh, that thing is headed right for us! Where can we hide?" Candice cried urgently.

"We won't have any need to hide, young one. In fact, I think you will quite like for it to head right through you," Enosh said as he comfortingly put his arm around her.

Splatters of water droplets pelted the westernmost walls of Porfiznin, flung outward by the strengthening winds. Rephaim on that side of the village groaned in pain as the drops hit them. But the nephilim became more energized.

Lightning flashes from within the storm, now just seconds away from impact, lit the village bright as day. The rephaim shut their eyes. The nephilim had no need to, and several blinded rephaim were stung by arrows and fell to the ground.

Intensifying in speed and roaring like nothing they had heard before, the georb air storm—towering from ground to sky—began sweeping through the village.

The kids fought every instinct in them to run as Thogwok, Azmarpin, and Serflina held them tight, assuring them that all was alright. Braulio, though well-intentioned, never made it back into battle. He dropped low and clung to a tree trunk when the tornado blew through town. Then they all watched as one foe after another was swept up and hurled away by the storm. From the smallest hireling to the hugest rephaite, all were blinded by lightning, scorched by water, pelted by pebbles, and then sucked up in the storm.

The tornado grew with ferocity as it encompassed the village, but not a single nephilim was hurt. The noble giants were dancing, jumping, and doing flips in the streets and on the tops of walls. One by one, rephaite after rephaite and man after man were plucked up in the storm. As the air storm raged through the village it exterminated fires but did no damage to the structures still standing. Intelligently, it selected who and what to save ... and who to consume.

The engulfing tornado swirled around the kids, Enosh, and all their protective nephilim. Cowering in fear, Candice and Fong clutched onto their strong giants and Braulio clung tight to a tree. But the storm did not harm any of them. Instead, the raging winds refreshed them with comfort, and renewed their energy.

Like being resuscitated from the dead and placed in a fresh, new body, energy and vitality surged through Enosh, making him feel like centuries of aging had just been replaced by perfect health and fresh vigor. The blasts of air infused Braulio with the strength of a mighty warrior and the decisiveness of a military leader; and the ankle he had been limping on was suddenly healed. The winds refreshed Fong's mind. She instantly solved the latest dilemmas she was thinking through and, for a few precious minutes, could comprehend everything more clearly than she had ever dreamed of doing before. Comfort and peace flooded Candice and drew her into an ecstatic state of contentment as she saw her potential to be a kinder, less self-absorbed, generous person. Her fairy tale imaginings of life with the perfect guy paled in comparison to what she was feeling as the wind warmly embraced her. Thogwok, Azmarpin, and Serflina were also renewed and energized, and they fluidly danced, practically floating over the surface of the ground. Even

Thogwok, for a few perfect minutes, was moving unencumbered, his brain injury temporarily healed.

(Incidentally, it was a shame that Lawth didn't realize the refreshing, healing power of the wind. As a master element wielder's apprentice, he really should have. It is still unknown what changes for the good would have occurred in Lawth had he allowed himself to experience it.)

Caught as they were in the rapture of the storm's beauty and the terror of its power, nobody noticed that off to the north a dark figure leapt onto a horned dinosaur and galloped out of town. Successfully convincing one of the more apathetic hirelings to release him just moments before the storm hit, Sabtah escaped with his life, the georb he took from Braulio now in the hands of Maboa.

The winds moved inland accompanied by exquisite arrays of lightning and a kaleidoscope of precious gems and water swirling within. The group stood in silence, each one at total peace within themselves and with those around them, watching the storm pass into the distance. The next place it would surround would be the village of Erflanthina, and then eventually to the mostly devastated Azgazaron. Knowing this, all the nephilim were excited about what would soon be happening for their kinsmen there.

Braulio thought about the nephilim of Erflanthina, most of whom were now here, and he broke the calm silence when he said, "Azmarpin, Serflina, thank you. You saved us. We would have died without you."

"You are more than welcome," they said together.

"How did you know where we were?" Braulio asked.

"A man by the name of Xurthun," Azmarpin said. "He used to work for Maboa. He was in the forest near Erflanthina spying on you when he witnessed the destruction taking place in our village, the loss of innocent lives, and you kids as you were desperately escaping. He also witnessed Sabtah following you. But ultimately, it was Calneh's base treachery that infuriated Xurthun. He—"

"Calneh's treachery will require a longer, gentler explanation," Serflina interrupted, glancing significantly at Thogwok. "Suffice it to say, Xurthun had a change of heart. He came to the village and reported the direction of your flight and of Maboa's plans. We took a longer route through the forest to avoid Maboa's army. Then we hid and waited for the right time to strike."

"Look, the winds have healed the fallen!" Thogwok said, not noticing Serflina's compassionate glance in his direction. The group turned their attention toward the village. Nephilim who had been pummeled with clubs or run through with swords were rising to their feet. Healing energy was flowing through their bodies and wounds were rapidly closing.

The seven of them ran over to the village to join the recovering nephilim. Thogwok's fellow warriors embraced him and congratulated him on his bravery and loyalty to the Chosen One and his companions.

"How could I forget?" Thogwok said, slapping his forehead in alarm. "Sean! He's the real hero here! And Lawth! Whatever happened to the both of them?"

Two nephilim with especially keen eyesight quickly scampered up to the tops of nearby trees and peered over the vast horizon toward the sea. A few more dazzling lightning bolts illuminated the sky.

"I see one of them!" a watchman called out.

Sean was racing over the open plain at cheetah speed. Lawth was further back, still not visible from the village, panting hard hundreds of yards behind him and falling further and further back behind the unstoppable Sean.

"C'mon, Mr. Lawth dude, this is fun! Woopeee!" yelled Sean as he tore through the tall grass five times faster than he'd ever run before. He blasted into the village and came skidding to a halt in the center.

"You dudes doin' alright? That was some amazing wind, huh?" Sean said as he stared at the rapidly healing giants rising to their feet.

All the nephilim cheered. They lifted Sean above their heads, flinging him high in the air and softly catching him over and over again. He loved it. He even managed to do a double somersault once. Enosh and Thogwok ran over to Sean and congratulated him as soon as he was finally set down. Thogwok gave him the biggest hug that Sean had ever had ... surprisingly it didn't hurt.

"Sean, I'm so glad to see you are alright," Candice said, tears welling up in her eyes.

"Congratulations, Sean," Fong said. "I can't wait to hear how you did it."

"Gotta hand it to you, buddy, you are a better man than me when it comes to handling one of those georb things," Braulio conceded with a firm handshake and a slap on Sean's back. "And how in the world did you run that fast?"

"Aw, well, when that awesome tornado was headin' your way, Mr. Lawth and I were running after it, hoping you guys were alright. And I said, 'Dude, I wish I could run like the wind,' and right after I said that a tiny tornado spun off the big one and wound itself all around me and went right through me! It was radical, dude! And then I was running like the wind, just like I asked for! Where's Lawth, by the way?"

Lawth finally came within sight, winded (in the normal meaning of the word), and carried on the back of a helpful and speedy nephil. He was brought to Enosh and set gently on the ground next to him. Enosh and Lawth greeted each other in typical element wielder fashion and then embraced.

"You did a valiant thing, young apprentice," Enosh acknowledged. "I was unconscious and useless when you lured Maboa's wolves and then the rest of his army away from us. You saved each of our lives in doing that. Most importantly, you protected the Chosen One and the georb he held so that he could make the elemental connection!" Enosh said, beaming with appreciation.

Lawth looked down, blushing. He wasn't one to give compliments, nor did he know how to receive them. All the nephilim loudly cheering for him didn't help either. Doing his best to change the subject, at least a little, Lawth belted out what had been troubling him.

"But I don't see why it even worked! The kid just stood there at the edge of the cliff and did everything Maboa told him to do!"

"But Mr. Lawth dude, like I started to tell ya before, I didn't listen to Maboa. I didn't even know he was there. I listened to the georb only," Sean corrected.

"No you didn't! I watched and heard it all! Maboa beckoned you with his georb all the way to the spot where he was hovering. You even threw your georb at him when he told you to! How could you be so lucky to have it caught up in a tornado at the moment you threw it? I don't get it!" Lawth said in sheer frustration.

"You say Maboa beckoned Sean with his, that is to say, Maboa's georb?" Enosh asked with a gleam in his eye.

Braulio looked down, ashamed that his georb, which he knew he never should have had in the first place, ended up in the enemy's hands.

"Remember what we discussed back at camp?" Enosh said, speaking to those who had been there at the time. "The georb belongs to the one it seeks, not the other way around. Maboa never owned that georb anymore than the thief who stole it from Braulio."

Braulio appreciated that Enosh left it there and did not call him out in front of the crowd. The point was made.

"You say you heard Maboa beckoning to Sean and trying to get him to listen, and I have no doubt that is what Maboa was doing," Enosh continued. "But it wasn't Maboa that Sean and his georb were listening to. It was the air essence which beckoned them. Maboa sought control and thought he was in control; but he was wrong. The georb is not his to own and hence he has no control over it. The Chosen One, on the other hand, did *not* seek control and was obedient to the orders he was given. He did not know where he was going or why. But he was willing to listen and obey anyway. And that is what really matters."

The nephilim were smiling and nodding. Enosh's explanation was clear to them and they immediately understood why Sean turned out to be the Chosen One out of the four. Fong was beginning to understand also.

"How appropriate," Enosh concluded, "that the one selected to be the bearer of the air georb is as free-flowing and flexible as the air itself. Anyone looking on, as you were Lawth, would conclude that Sean was marching toward his death. But one who is in tune with the wind will follow obediently, even though he doesn't know from where the wind comes or where it ultimately goes. A trusting follower like that is who the air georb seeks, and in obediently following, Sean ended up right where he needed to be."

Cheers went up for Sean again, and for several more giant heaves, Sean went up in the air.

Chapter 21

GOING HOME

The victorious army of nephilim warriors escorted Sean, Braulio, Candice, Fong, Eric, Enosh and Lawth all the way back to the village of Erflanthina. Just before the hidden village came into view, the forest rang with the singing and cheering of village women and children. Young nephilim swung down from vines and sprang out from hiding places among the trees. They bounded toward their fathers and brothers and threw themselves in their arms.

The exuberant children were immediately followed by nephil wives, mothers, and sisters who came out of the woodwork to welcome their loved ones back home. Some of the females stood high in the trees and dropped a cascade of flower petals on the parade of returning champions. Others greeted the heroes by draping fragrant garlands around their necks. Nephil girls, all of them significantly larger than Braulio, dropped flowery garlands around the necks of the returning warriors. Mounds of huge flowers covered their necks and rose as high as their noses.

The very youngest of the nephilim, most of them bigger than Fong, swarmed around Enosh, Lawth and the five young travelers, grabbing them and hugging them excitedly.

"Children, be careful! Our guests are only human," said one helpful nephil mother.

"Yes, they are fragile and easily breakable. Handle them gently," another mother sternly reminded her overly enthusiastic and very strong children.

Azmarpin, Serflina and three other warriors broke Sean, Fong, Eric, Braulio and Candice free of the arms grabbing at them and flung them upon their backs.

"Hold on tight!" Azmarpin warned.

Each of the kids gripped on to their giant, and the five nephilim nimbly scampered up branches until landing on the lowest vine bridge of the village. Two other nephil warriors did the same for Enosh and Lawth. Then all the other nephilim warriors sprang from the ground and adroitly climbed up the trees. There were shouts of praise and cheers every time another landed in the arms of a loved one above.

Thogwok looked upward with a mixture of joy and sadness as all the tree dwellers bounded effortlessly up to their families and homes. He sighed as he watched one kinsman after another vanish into the foliage of the festive village. Cheers and greetings between family members drifted down from high in the trees. He stood on the ground and watched until the last returning hero was enveloped in huge leaves. Soon, all was quiet around him, and he felt very alone.

Earlier that day, on the trek back from Porfiznin, Serflina had gently broken the news to Thogwok of Charwok's kidnapping and subsequent rescue. Thogwok had bawled. He also praised the One who had protected his son and then he bawled some more. Now he just wanted to be with his children. He was sure they would come down to him to visit when they had the chance, one of these days.

Trying to hold back his sadness, Thogwok told himself it would be nice to see his hut again. He slowly turned around to stagger toward it. Suddenly, four stout arms grabbed him, nearly knocking him to the ground.

Thogwok yelled in shock. Instinctively he grabbed for his knife. But the strong arms held his own arms tight to his side so he could barely move. They also steadied him so he did not fall. Then Thogwok got the biggest hug he had ever received. Wrapped around him were the young sons he had so wanted to see, Charwok and Shivlok.

Seeing their faces, Thogwok lit up, smiled large and greeted them heartily. "Ahoy there, m'boys! It's so good to see the both of yuz! So good it is! How yuz both been?"

They simply embraced him tightly for a whole minute—not saying anything.

"We thought you were going to die," Shivlok finally said with tears running down his cheeks.

"Whoa! Die? Me? Yuz must be thinking of someone else! I've no plans to be doin' that any time soon."

Talking through sobs of relief, mixed with a great deal of admiration for his dad, Charwok said, "We heard from the scouts who came back early that you guarded the humans and kept them safe ... and that you even broke into Maboa's camp ... and you rescued a human that got captured and you took on a whole host of rephaim all by yourself ... and you won!"

"Er, well, yeah that's sorta true, I guess, but—" Thogwok blustered modestly.

"They even say you helped fight a dragon—Maboa's dragon!" yelped Shivlok with Christmas-morning excitement.

"Oh! That. Well I suppo—" he began.

"We are proud of you, Dad," Charwok beamed through tears welling up in his big green eyes.

Thogwok couldn't say anything. He just held his boys. Finally he choked out, "I heard all about what happened here and how brave yuz both were. You, Charwok when yuz wuz captured, and you, Shivlok—Braulio told me yuz gave him yur bow. Likely that bow saved me life when Braulio shot yur arrows at a blade-wielding thief who deflected 'em. When we saw how good the thief was with a blade, Enosh forbade me to attack. And had I attacked him, I'd likely be dead. I'm thinkin' yuz saved me life. I'm so proud of both of yuz! Proud to be yer dad! I'm so sorry I wasn't here to protect yuz." He hugged them both even tighter.

"You were where you were supposed to be," Charwok said, still sniffling. "You taught me to trust the One who loves us and protects us the best."

"Thogwok!" came a booming voice from high in the branches above. Thogwok knew the voice: Barzuga, the village chief.

"What are you doing down there, valiant warrior? The feast is up here!" Chief Barzuga said as he tossed down a rope ladder.

Two especially large nephilim gracefully shimmied down the ladder and stood ready at the bottom of it, holding it tight as Charwok and Shivlok led their dad toward the ladder. The two of them steadied Thogwok while he climbed. After he reached the top, his two sons walked by his side, kindly lending support whenever he leaned a little too much. For the first time in years, Thogwok traversed the bridges of his home village.

Charwok and Shivlok led their father toward the central platform where the celebration was in full-swing. Thogwok planted himself on a vine chair. Immediately, two nephil women began tying reinforcement vines onto the chair, giving it a back. Sitting in his improved chair, Thogwok received a hero's honor along with the other warriors at the feast.

The celebration was of giant proportions, naturally. The tables groaned beneath the weight of an aromatic explosion of freshly-baked breads, huge juicy fruits, and an exquisite array of desserts. This party was grander and more high-spirited than even the one on the night of the kids' arrival.

Thogwok was a magnet for attention, but he was not the only one. Sean, Braulio, Eric, and Candice were all equally showered with it. Enosh's blazing blues eyes fondly watched his students. He observed how Braulio was not as arrogant and on-guard as he had been at the first feast. This time he was actually enjoying himself and those around him. He even tried his hand at the vine-slashing dance but soon bowed out after drawing significant blood from his shin.

Enosh watched Candice playing a game with some of the nephil kids. She was lost in the joy of the moment and made no attempt to draw attention to herself. She seemed to have forgotten all about the handsome nephilim who had once claimed her attention.

Enosh also noticed that Sean was more in tune with what was going on around him. He wasn't focused exclusively on the delicious food (although it was certainly on his mind,) rather he was both watching and apparently learning from what was going on around him.

"Hmmm," Enosh mused out loud, mostly to himself. "There is just something about being on a battlefield that makes one more aware of their surroundings."

As for Eric, Enosh could see that he was wholly overwhelmed by this first experience in a tree village. He delicately balanced on a vine chair, eyes darting from the dancers, to the food, to the soaring levels of the village as he tried to take it all in.

Out of the corner of his eye, Enosh barely noticed a small figure seated alone. She was staring down at something in her hand. Enosh sauntered over to her. As he got closer it became clear she was fixated on the necklace she received from the nephil named Eskes Hosswee.

"A party of this magnitude and you choose to stare at a necklace. Interesting …" Enosh said gently as he sat down next to her. "And the celebration is even being held in *your* honor."

"It's not being held in my honor," Fong said sadly. "Sean is the real hero here. What did I do besides endanger people's lives?" she asked solemnly, still staring down at the necklace.

"Well, I suppose you have a point," Enosh said after a pause. "After all, Candice saved herself from danger and imminent death all alone, didn't she?"

Fong didn't reply. She just kept staring at the necklace, sniffing back a tear.

"It's not as if you had anything to do with her rescue," Enosh prodded, refusing to take her silence as an answer.

"I realize what Eric and I did was sort of brave, but it was entirely my fault Candice got in trouble in the first place," Fong admitted as tears beaded in her eyes.

"Oh, yes, Eric. He seems a bit stunned right now. Not knowing anyone here, I imagine he would appreciate your company right about now. He is very new here, you know," Enosh said.

"Of course I know," Fong said as her voice cracked. "Once again, my fault. I should have asked Eric to come along in the first place and we could have avoided all that." Her voice faltered. "I failed him," she barely managed to utter as tears streamed down her cheeks.

After a long pause and many tears spilling onto the wooden platform, Fong was able to continue. "I failed Eric—the only one who believed me and the only one who had the right to come here with me. I almost got my friend Candice killed," she continued, her bottom lip trembling with remorse, "and I failed you. I'm so sorry!"

"Which is precisely why you are forgiven," said Enosh confidently.

Fong looked up at him through watery eyes.

"No one expects perfection from you, child," Enosh said to her comfortingly. "Oh, you might expect it from yourself, but no one who genuinely loves you does. Perhaps you have forgotten that you are loved and appreciated, not for what you know or what you do, but for who you are. A mistake is simply another opportunity to see how much you are truly loved," he said with warmth that made her melt.

Fong grabbed Enosh and hugged him tightly. He held her for as long as she needed, and when she released him she wiped her face and said, "Thanks. I needed that."

"You are most welcome, my dear. The person who admits their past mistakes and then does what they can to fix them is a hero in my book. Apparently there are many here who agree. They'd like to congratulate you. So, what do you say?"

Enosh took her by the hand and lifted her to her feet. She was about to pocket the necklace when she glanced at it one last time and said, "Enosh, there is something I still don't understand. It's about my georb. Sean's georb gave him extra power to fight when he needed it. And I suppose his connection to the air georb is what allowed him to run like the wind. But for me, mine doesn't seem to give me extra powers or harness an element like Sean's. Is there something wrong with ...with ...'

"With *you*?" Enosh offered with raised eyebrows.

"Yes ... me. Because it couldn't be the georb, could it?" Suddenly the questions she had been struggling with came out in a torrent. "Is there something wrong with me? Am I just not good enough? Why didn't my georb respond like his?"

"Because yours is not a georb," Enosh replied, eyes twinkling.

"Not a georb? What? But it looks just like the others!" Fong said with alarm.

"Oh yes, it looks like the others. But your calling is different from the others. What you are holding in your hand is what you diligently sought: not a georb, but a nephil nofac. That is what brought you to the place you sought—a place which you knew existed through both your study and through your faith. This is the land where nephilim, or elves, as you call them, live," Enosh said.

"You knew this all along?" Fong asked amazed, looking more intently than ever at the precious stone in her hand. "Why didn't you tell me?"

"For a time it was just as well that no one knew the difference—especially you—for in order to be a part of the noble community of the nephilim, one must understand and practice that priceless and most noble of attributes. And prior to the battle, you had not yet done so," Enosh said.

"What attribute?" Fong asked as her eyes started to tear up again.

"Unconditional, sacrificial love," Enosh answered. "You entered this land selfishly, believing your own agenda to be more important than the well-being of the guest you brought with you. You sacrificed Eric's calling and then Candice's safety so you could do things your way. But since then you have changed—risking your own life in order to fulfill Eric's and save Candice's. You have learned to love, and that has gained you access to the world you seek," Enosh explained.

Fong's tears ceased and she stared in amazement at Enosh. Spellbound, she asked, "Did you just say I gained access to the world of the nephilim?"

"Indeed you have, for you diligently sought it. And now you have matched your diligence with obedience—the obedience of sacrificial love. I suspect you will be back here again, and probably soon," Enosh said with a twinkle and a grin.

Fong hugged him tight, overwhelmed with emotion. Then she hung the nofac around her neck and the two of them joined Thogwok, Lawth, Sean, Braulio, Candice, and Eric at the center of the festivities. Chief Barzuga motioned them to sit at the high table, which was barely visible beneath the array of delicacies. Then the chief called for everyone's attention. There was an instant hush.

"It is with great pleasure," he boomed loud enough for the hundreds hoisted far up in high branches to hear, "that we can honor those who came here to serve us, sacrificing themselves even to the point of near death, and consequently rescuing us from impending doom."

A cheer like the roar of a thunderous waterfall rose from the nephilim.

"I ask our other esteemed guests to please step forward at this time to pay tribute to our heroes," the chief directed as he stepped aside.

Sean and the others had no idea of whom the chief was speaking. In fact, there were so many large nephilim around the table that the kids had not even noticed any other guests. But as soon as the chief summoned them, one wise man after another emerged out from the crowd of giants. They positioned themselves in front of the huge table directly across from Enosh and Lawth.

One of them was Yarthuselah—the golden-haired, Grand Master Element Wielder. He whirled his staff several times in the air high over his head. A shower of sparks, followed by a cloud of vapor, sprayed forth from his staff and paused directly over the crowd. A portrait of Enosh emerged from the sparks and vapor and hung suspended in the air above the huge table for all to see.

"Accomplished Element Wielder Enosh, wielder of three elements," Yarthuselah proclaimed in his ever mellow and sagacious voice, "your leadership and your integrity have been reported and noted with esteem. Because of your success in the mission you led—uniting the air georb with its elementary essence—you no longer shall be known as *Accomplished* Element Wielder. We, in our authority as the Council of Wise Men and Noble Giants, confer upon you the title of *Master* Element Wielder."

The crowd of guests gave a cheer that to the kids sounded like a jet engine.

Yarthuselah bestowed Enosh with a colorful braided cord which he wrapped around his head, replacing the older, simpler one. Yarthuselah then whisked away the image of Enosh with a swish of his staff. He zapped the air with a beam of red light and immediately the area above the table was tattooed with an image of Lawth.

"And as for you, Apprentice Lawth," Yarthuselah said, turning to the real Lawth while a three-dimensional image of him shimmered in the air. "Your bravery and selfless sacrifice have been reported and noted with great admiration. Through your actions, you not only accomplished the mission, but you saved the lives of those entrusted to you. You have grown greatly in selflessness, and, consequently, you have grown greatly in your ability to wield the elements. In order to save others, you decided to wield selfless, sacrificial love. And when you tapped into that, you unleashed the greatest power there is! It is with great pleasure, therefore, that we no longer call you *Apprentice*, but rather we confer upon you the title of *Accomplished Element Wielder*, for now you are a true element wielder in your own right!"

Yarthuselah wrapped Lawth's head with a new braided headband—more colorful and elaborate than the one he had before—and all the nephilim cheered. It sounded like a rumbling, reverberating thunder clap. Enosh cheered even louder than the nephilim. Fong wondered whether that was due to a good teacher's pride in his student, sheer relief that the job was done, or perhaps a little of both.

The apparition of Lawth's head dissipated and Yarthuselah and the rest of the council of wise men stepped aside as the huge nephil, Chief Barzuga, smoothly slid forward and stood before Thogwok, his stature making Thogwok look unusually small.

"Thogwok," boomed the chief, "you have always been a loyal nephil and have served as a valiant warrior whenever called upon over the last few centuries."

Eric snuffled a laugh. Centuries! He couldn't get over how normal everyone else acted about Thogwok's age.

"In fact," the chief continued, "it was precisely because of your loyalty and bravery that you absorbed the injury many decades ago from which you still suffer. But never before in all your heroic battles have you faced such a dark and deadly enemy as this last one. You rescued captives and you saved lives—even at your own peril. And because you carried this through to the end, you saved our village and much of the Earth. For this, we, the village of Erflanthina, grant you the most esteemed award we have: the *Highest Hero Gemstone of Honor!*"

All the nephilim rose to their feet in a thunderous blast of cheering loud enough to make the kids plug their ears. The nephilim knew the significance of this award. Very rarely was it bestowed, (some of the younger nephilim had never even seen it before) and it was the highest honor any nephil in the village could receive.

Chief Barzuga draped the magnificent gem around Thogwok's neck. It was a richly colorful, radiant stone; larger than a georb and exceedingly valuable. It hung magnificently on a heavy gold chain.

"You have earned the highest award we have to offer, due to your protection of the Chosen One and for saving the village—your village—Erflanthina. However," the chief continued, altering his tone a little, "there is still one serious matter we have overlooked. Come with me."

The chief took Thogwok's arm and held it firmly as he walked him steadily over the shifting platform. Thogwok's sons followed close behind, ready to catch and steady their dad at a moment's notice. All the other village dwellers and their guests followed in a long stream of movement down the wobbly walkway and in the branches above.

There was a hushed buzzing among many nephilim, but Fong and the other teenagers could not make out what they were saying. Turning a corner, the chief pointed down and said, "Thogwok, behold your new home!"

Thogwok couldn't believe what he was seeing. Before him was a tree dwelling far grander in every imaginable way than his hut in the forest. At five stories tall, it was enormous, having rooms on the ground and rising four levels more. A clever elevator constructed with pulleys could get him quickly from one floor to the next. Ropes and railings and all manner of holds were fastened anywhere they might be needed. Running water flowed through a mini aqueduct system throughout the house, with waste water pouring out on the ground level where it irrigated a large garden that was poised and ready, with dirt freshly tilled, beckoning Thogwok to plant whatever and whenever he liked. From bottom to top, through and through, it was a house built especially for his sons and him.

"I have come to realize how improperly I have treated you, Thogwok," the chief confessed. "Is it right that you who saved your village must dwell outside your village? You are one of us and you always have a place with us, here with your children in your own house in your own village."

The crowd of nephilim and wise men roared their agreement. Thogwok tried to hold back tears as his two youngest sons gave him a tour of their new home.

When the crowd had gathered back at the banquet table, Chief Barzuga called for attention and honored each of the kids for their individual acts of selflessness and bravery. Special recognition was given to Eric, who arrived late but played a key role in liberating Candice. Candice was commended for surviving even though she was face-to-veil with Maboa. (She had never told anyone how she had distracted the rephaim from their plans for Braulio.) Fong was complimented for her stunning mind and how she had used her knowledge and her bold assertiveness to get Eric, rescue Candice, and help others. Braulio was lauded for his face-to-face battle with Maboa's dragon. The young nephilim boys asked to hear that story again. And Sean, of course, was considered the biggest hero of them all. Every nephil in the village listened closely as Lawth and Sean together explained in detail how Maboa almost got the georb but got sucked into an elemental storm instead. The nephilim loved it!

The celebration lasted deep into the night. Eating, storytelling, dancing, and some of the most amazing singing resounded beneath the revolving stars. As the first fingers of dawn crept over the horizon Enosh pulled the kids aside and said to them, "It's time, you know."

"Time for what?" Sean asked, having a great time limberly dancing around in a new pair of flexible nephilwear.

"It is time to change out of those clothes and go back to your place and time," Enosh said solemnly.

"It is?" Fong asked. "Why can't we stay longer?"

"Your task has been accomplished and you are free from your obligation," Enosh answered.

"It seems like I just got here," lamented Eric.

"You did just get here," Candice glumly pointed out.

"Isn't there something else we can do? Like isn't there another way we need to save the world?" Braulio asked in only partial sarcasm.

"Regrettably for all of us, your time here has expired," said Enosh.

He didn't need to announce to the village that they were to be on their way; nephilim could sense such things. The slightest change in mood gave them the only clue they needed, and all gave one, unified heartfelt 'goodbye'.

Serflina and Azmarpin led them to their bedrooms where their normal clothing hung from the rafters, having been taken from their now dirty travel sacks and cleaned. In a few minutes, the five were wearing their own clothes and long faces. Thogwok ambled up to where they all were gathered. Lawth was with him—following at a safe distance. Even *he* seemed a bit sad, though he tried to hide it. Thogwok just outright bawled, loudly and shamelessly.

"Fong, you have tapped into the secret of the nephilim," Enosh said barely loud enough to be heard over Thogwok's cries. "You have eagerly sought, and so you have found what you sought. Then, once there, you forsook your former way of selfishness for the more excellent way of love." Then he leaned in close to her and whispered, loud enough for only her to hear, "Always remember that is the reason why you have earned the right to both enter and return again to the land of the nephilim. With your nofac, you can return when the time is right."

Enosh, Thogwok, and Lawth escorted the five of them back to the portal where they said their goodbyes. Enosh gave a warm embrace to each of them—even to Braulio, who stiffly received one. Lawth stuck out a hand and gave a quick shake to everyone which was more akin to a grab and release. He still was not entirely sure how to do a handshake and not at all up for a hug. Thogwok kept uncontrollably sobbing. Wide streams streaked his huge cheeks. Fong, who was also teary-eyed—a state that until now had been very rare for her—tried to comfort him. She whispered in his ear what Enosh had told her about the nofac.

Thogwok's face immediately brightened. "Yuz bean yuz'll be mack?"

Fong gave a subtle shush sign, not sure whether such knowledge should be public yet. Thogwok got the hint and gave a watery wink. No one else seemed to catch what Thogwok meant except for Enosh, who gave Fong a knowing nod of approval.

"Are you ready?" Enosh asked the girls.

"Ready or not, I suppose it is time," Fong replied.

Eric nodded in agreement.

Candice looked around at everyone, now with more feeling than she had ever had for any of them before, and finally nodded also.

"Alright then, repeat the enchantment," Enosh said to Fong.

Fong unfurled the little leather wrapping with the parchment inside it. She took both Candice's and Eric's hands and recited the words. A tumultuous mini-whirlwind engulfed the three of them and in seconds they were gone.

Thogwok bawled even louder than before.

"And how about you two?" Enosh asked Sean and Braulio. "Are you ready?"

"Well, yeah, I guess so," Sean replied. "But neither of us have our georbs anymore."

"True, but it just so happens that Lawth and I know a little something about time travel," Enosh said, pulling a stone out of a pocket in his robe. Lawth did the same. It was the same stone he kept in his pocket and had used to locate Sean back at his college dorm.

"This is not something we use often," Enosh said to the boys, "but when necessary, some of us element wielders traverse time in order to take care of important matters. You first," he said, motioning to Lawth.

Lawth took hold of Braulio's sleeve and rubbed his stone vigorously between his thumb and index finger while reciting an enchantment in a language which the boys couldn't understand. In a moment, the two of them vanished—leaving only Enosh, Sean, and a completely wrecked Thogwok.

"Lawth and I will be back soon, my good giant," Enosh said to him comfortingly.

Then with one arm around Sean's shoulders, Enosh briskly rubbed his stone and recited the enchantment. He and Sean promptly left behind the wailings of the inconsolable Thogwok.

Fong, Eric, and Candice emerged from the cluster of trees where the girls first met Eskes Hosswee. Fong again apologized to both Candice and Eric—to Candice for endangering her life by taking her to a place she had no business going, and to Eric for being too selfish to include him when she knew she should have. Candice admitted she shouldn't have pressured Fong to bring her along.

"I just wanted to come along because Eskes Hosswee was so gorgeous. Kinda got myself into that mess and it was totally selfish." Candice scuffed one foot in the dirt. "I was an idiot."

"Me too," said Fong. She smiled wryly at Candice.

It was beginning to get dark. Candice noticed that the sun had moved a bit since she and Fong had last been there together. But weeks in Early Earth time appeared to be only an hour or so in their time and only just a few minutes since Fong and Eric met the officer. Eric figured he was probably nearby keeping an eye out for them. Emerging from the tree cover, they could see off in the distance the students in line for the dining hall—much the same as it had been when Fong found Eric. Candice spotted Rocky a ways off, catching a football that was hurled to him across the lawn from one of his friends. He cheered himself on for making such a great catch. And aware of a pack of girls watching, he did a showy victory dance.

"I'm hungry," said Candice, rolling her eyes at Rocky's showboating. "Mind if we sit together?"

"Sounds great," Eric replied. And looking at Fong he continued, "I can't think of anyone else I'd rather eat with."

"Remembuh speak English," Fong reminded them. "And good idea only share story wif dose who believe."

Eric and Candice agreed. And off to dinner they went.

Braulio and Lawth suddenly appeared in the same cave where roughly one hour earlier Braulio had abandoned Juan. Plunged into darkness, Braulio couldn't see anything. But the dank air and rocky floor betrayed where he was. He immediately called for Juan while his eyes adjusted to the darkness. There was no answer.

"Juan! Jua-a-a-an! Where are you?" Braulio yelled.

"Remember to speak your other language," Lawth said from the darkness.

"Oh, right," Braulio said. After a moment of mental gear-switching he belted out the same call in Spanish.

Silence.

Braulio now could see a thin trickle of light hinting the way to the entrance. Scrabbling over the uneven surface, Braulio stumbled his way out of the dark and closer to the light. He reached the cave's opening and shielded his eyes from the burning sun as he panned the rugged horizon of his Spanish homeland. Mountains, the Mediterranean, a curving coastline, and acres of land stretched out before him—but no Juan.

"Jua-a-a-an!" Braulio yelled as he tore down the rocky slope toward the place where they left their motorcycles. Braulio felt stupid. He knew that weeks had passed since he left Juan in the cave. Why would he still be here? But for some reason he yelled for him anyway. His thoughts on Juan, Braulio completely forgot about Lawth as he ran to find his friend. Approaching the top of the rockslide where he had left his motorcycle, Braulio noted that it was no longer there. Concerned, he wondered what may have happened to Juan and whether or not his motorcycle worked for him after he had taken that spill. This was the first time such a thought had occurred to him. In fact, with his focus on Juan's well-being, Braulio hadn't even considered yet how he would get himself home.

Still moving as fast as he could, Braulio angled sideways down the hazardous mountainside and came to an abrupt halt at the top of the rockslide. Looking down he smiled for the first time since arriving home. Juan was still there! He had just finished gingerly walking Braulio's motorcycle down the treacherous slope and was putting down the kickstand on level ground when he looked up and made eye contact. Never before had Braulio been so pleased to see his friend.

<hr />

"So I take it you know the way back from here," Enosh said with a blue-eyed, twinkly wink at Sean.

"Yeah, this is definitely that weird room under the library," Sean replied as his eyes adjusted to the dim lighting of the Archives and Ancient Manuscripts Room.

"Ah yes, but weird only if one does not take the time to get familiar with it. Perhaps you now have more reason than you had before to explore the writings of the ancient world," Enosh posited.

"Definitely! I had no idea stuff back then was so cool," Sean agreed as he widened his eyes in the dark room and took note of the many ancient books.

"Glad to hear it! Enjoy your studies, remember to resume speaking English now, and don't forget that Spanish you are studying either. I believe your door to the outside is right over there," Enosh said pointing.

Sean looked and now could see it in the darkness. It was the same door that Lawth had taken him through weeks ago, which Sean would soon learn was only hours ago in this world. Saddened by the thought of leaving as he stared at the door, Sean said, "Thanks a lot, Mr. Enosh Dude, you have really helped me a lot."

Sean turned around to give the elder a high five, but Enosh was gone.

———◆———

Braulio ran and skidded down the rockslide with the finesse of an alpine goat. Overcome with joy, he gave Juan a hug that might have been confused with a linebacker's tackle (Braulio was not a hugger and was about as adept at it as Thogwok was at handshakes).

Stabilizing himself and gasping for a breath, Juan broke free of Braulio's embrace and looked at him with suspicion. Braulio looked different. He had several scratches and bruises that Juan had not noticed on him earlier that day. And there was something about his skin— something that was hard for Juan to put words to. It had a healthier tone, almost a glow to it. Before Juan could ask what had happened, Braulio said something to him—something Juan had never heard him say before.

"What did you say?" Juan asked, making sure he got it right.

"I said, 'I am sorry, Juan,'" Braulio repeated. "I will tell you everything that happened. But first you need to meet Lawth. Hey, Lawth!" Braulio yelled turning around and scanning the mountainside. But Lawth was gone.

———◆———

Sean opened the door to his dorm room and the smell nearly knocked him over. "Whew!" He pinched his nose closed and in a plugged-nose sort of way said, "Dube, I neeb to clean bad!" Opening the window wide for some fresh air, he immediately started putting things in order. In a day or two the place would be like new. He would also start focusing on his classes immediately. The semester was only half over; if he worked hard he could catch up. Out of habit he flicked the switch on his stereo. Nothing happened. Then he remembered that Lawth did something weird to it on the day they met. Back then he was upset about a little thing like that, but a broken stereo didn't matter to Sean anymore. He smiled at the thought of Lawth and continued picking up the mess, contentedly whistling and making his own music as he cleaned. His world had just grown dramatically bigger and better. He figured no one in this present time would ever know what he had done, and he was okay with that. He now knew his life had meaning and purpose. That was what he needed. And he looked forward to the next adventure.

Printed in the United States
By Bookmasters